Other Publications by the Autl

MW00936593

- *The Media and Criminal Just.* (2011)
- *Introduction to American Policing: An Applied Approach*, Jones and Bartlett (2010)
- *Police Officer Stress: Sources and Solutions*, Prentice Hall (2008)
- *Community Corrections*, Prentice Hall (2006)
- *Community Policing in the 21st Century*, Allyn Bacon (2003)
- *Case Studies of Community Policing*, Allyn Bacon (2003)
- *Policing and Community Partnerships*, Prentice Hall (2003)
- *Case Studies of Community Policing*, Prentice Hall (2001)
- *Measuring Performance: A Guide to Evaluative Research*, (2001)
- *Perspective in Corrections*, Coursewise (2000)
- *Inside the Mind of the Serial Rapist*, Winfield (2000)

Chapters Provided by the Author for other Books

- "Sexual Offenders." *Prison Abolition: Unchaining Ourselves from U.S. Imperialism*, Kaltefleiter, Nagel, & Nocella (Eds.) (forth coming)
- "Police Stress." *Encyclopedia of Psychology and Law, 2nd ed.* Brian Cutler (Ed). (2007)
- "STING Tactics," *Encyclopedia of Police Science, 3rd Ed. Jack Greene (Ed).* Jack R. Greene (Ed). Routledge (2007)
- "The History of Prisons: Continental Europe and England." *The Encyclopedia of Criminology.* Routledge/Taylor & Francis (2005)
- "John Wayne Gacy: The Killer Clown. In Frankie Y. Bailey and Steven Chermak (Eds.). *Famous American Crimes and Trials.* NY: Praeger Publishing. (2005)
- "Police Officer Stress and Occupational Stressors." *Policing and Strategies.* Heith Copes (Ed), Prentice Hall (2005)
- "Civil Liabilities and Arrest Decisions," *Policing and the Law*, Jeffrey T. Walker (Ed) Prentice Hall (2002)
- "Education Programming for Offenders. In *Compendium of Corrections. Compendium 2000: On Effective Correctional Programming.* (p. 57-64). Provincial Government of Canada. Correctional Service of Canada (2001).
- "Justifiable Use of Deadly Force for Law Enforcement Officers Serving U.S. Department of Energy Sites." Wachenhut Industries. (1997).

DENNIS J. STEVENS, PhD

WICKED Women

A JOURNEY OF SUPER PREDATORS

iUniverse, Inc.
Bloomington

Wicked Women
A Journey of Super Predators

iUniverse books may be ordered through booksellers or by contacting:

iUniverse
1663 Liberty Drive
Bloomington, IN 47403
www.iuniverse.com
1-800-Authors (1-800-288-4677)

Because of the dynamic nature of the Internet, any Web addresses or links contained in this book may have changed since publication and may no longer be valid. The views expressed in this work are solely those of the author and do not necessarily reflect the views of the publisher, and the publisher hereby disclaims any responsibility for them.

ISBN: 978-1-4502-7404-3 (pbk)
ISBN: 978-1-4502-7405-0 (cloth)
ISBN: 978-1-4502-7406-7 (ebk)

Printed in the United States of America

iUniverse rev. date: 1/7/2011

Dedication

This work is dedicated to the victims who have suffered at the hands of super predators. It is also dedicated to the unknown victims who remain silent because of despondency, guilt, and shame. Those who have not heard your silence will never understand your misery, and justice is forever cheated. "Never be bullied into silence. Never allow yourself to be made a victim. Accept no one's definition of your life, but define yourself." —Harvey S. Firestone

Contents

CHAPTER 1
An Explanation of Crime and Predators

Battle not with monsters, lest ye become a monster, and if
you gaze into the abyss, the abyss gazes also into you.
—Friedrich Nietzsche

Introduction

Brutal attacks by a single predator, depicting barbaric torture and
children snatched from the comfort of their beds are sensationalized
at local theaters, on television, and in the news. "If it bleeds, it leads,"
a magazine editor told me early in my career. "It doesn't matter if it's
true or not," she added. We think in terms of a single awesome event
with lots of blood and gore and a single perpetrator. When we watch
the opening segments of our favorite crime drama on television, we see
a lot of blood, a naked female dangling from a chandelier or hidden
in sewer pipes deep below the bowels of the city. We assure ourselves
that our own intelligence, experience, and defense strategies will help
fight off attackers. We think the set of keys in our hand is enough to
win as we walk to our automobile in the shadow of a new moon. Our
sense of safety comes from believing we know what violators look
like and where they live, thanks to the false illusions provided by sex
offender registries. But massive attacks by super predators are rarely
reported. Super predator descriptions rarely conform to the traditional
or established stereotypes of their photographs, behavior, and cruelty.
This book describes the life stories of fifteen incredibly wicked predators

1

that were imprisoned and under my care and supervision for a short period of time. Because the twisted accounts of twelve female predators were rivaled by three males, I have included their stories, too. Neither predators nor their victims can be stereotyped as male or female - that's Hollywood. What isn't Hollywood is that most predators are rarely identified, apprehended, and convicted. If they are convicted, it is often for less an offense than expected. In this sophisticated, technologically advanced century, Joe—or in this case, Joanna—Bogyman can easily possess the technology and professionalism of a CIA operative, a Wall Street entrepreneur, or a Disney executive and yet remain a fairy tale, unless Nancy Grace attempts to boost her Neilson ratings with a flood of incompetent sorcerers' apprentices and a mouse named Mickey.

I spent several years among high-risk felons in some of the most heavily researched penitentiaries in America, while teaching at universities. At the core of *Wicked Women* are the essays and journals of prisoners I encountered in prison classrooms, group sessions, and counseling meetings, and their official records. Many of their ruthless accounts have never been made public, nor have these offenders been identified as the perpetrators of bizarre crimes. In their youth, not one of them had ever experienced abuse, poverty, or parental violence, other than the violence each of them administered to parents and grandparents, siblings and friends, teachers and neighbors. Each wicked predator possessed the incredible opportunities, privilege, and political power common to children of their families' socioeconomic class. Yet they rejected those amazing opportunities for a life of cruelty and destruction.

I lecture on the behavioral sciences (psychology, sociology, and human development) and criminal justice (police, courts, and corrections) at universities (currently the University of North Carolina–Charlotte and formerly at UMass Boston) and law academies such as the North Carolina Justice Academy. I lecture about predators who escaped detection and were subsequently released from custody or confinement. Often the most intellectual students, many of whom are in the justice profession, are horrified at the justice system's revolving door for dangerous violators. At times, the legal efforts of politically correct liberals result in the release of dangerous predators because of technical violations (think about O. J. Simpson). Yet at the same time, those liberals neglect to afford the opportunity of reform and recovery to nonviolent prisoners, who have little promise once incarcerated in America's violent penitentiaries.

I have published numerous textbooks adapted by various universities and law academies, and have written over ninety empirical studies about predatory dispositions, as well as about sophisticated techniques for lowering recidivism (future violence and crime) rates among nonviolent offenders. For instance, in studies among female prisoners, I found that women prisoners who completed university studies while incarcerated rarely return to a life of crime once released.[1] Unfortunately, state legislators eliminated those budgets for university studies. Yet, on the other hand, those same legislators worked hard to release wicked pedophiles from prison, because of the legislators' naïve misperceptions of dangerous predators.[2] For instance, then Governor Mitt Romney of the Commonwealth of Massachusetts approved the parole of a convicted pedophile who had hit the national limelight because of his place of employment—a day care establishment. The convicted pedophile had sexually assaulted numerous children, including children who were handicapped. He submitted numerous legal appeals to the courts, aided by Harvard-type supporters. Today, this pedophile freely roams the streets of Boston without concern of apprehension or supervision.

Through this sort of political dialogue, some of my books and studies were buried, along with the studies of my colleagues, which addressed both ends of the spectrum (predators and nonviolent offenders). This abyss of righteousness continues to reinforce the American liberal perspective that everyone should win a race and everyone is equal. The truth of the matter is that predators are winning, and none of those predators are equal to hard-working, law-abiding people who do the right thing for themselves, their families, and their country. At professional conferences, such as the Academy of Criminal Justice Sciences, American Society of Criminology, and American Corrections Association—of which I have been a member—presentations about professional and efficient enforcement and custody management have been attended by curious new scholars trying to find their own way. However, because recommendations that arise from these conferences and from studies don't fit what is on the television, those recommendations are often dismissed.[3]

For instance, similar to the above suggestion that education among prisoners can and does reduce recidivism rates among selected groups of offenders, other studies detail recommendations for nonviolent offenders. They have little hope once they are incarcerated in violent prisons. They conform to the violence level of prison, and when they're released, those nonviolent offenders engage in violent crime. Violence begets violence.[4] Prison is not always the answer for first-time violators, nor does prison serve the greater good. It does not, as an institution, go to the root of the problem, nor does it deter violent crime or predators, scholars argue.[5] But there's more! What is known about predators, aside from their cruelty and victimization, confirms Friedrich Nietzsche's advice: "Battle not with monsters, lest ye become a monster, and if you gaze into the abyss, the abyss gazes also into you." What monsters seek through their gazes or observations are clues about the vulnerability of individuals and the justice systems that protects those individuals. Attacking the organization that provides individual rights weakens or discredits the organization. One way to better understand this perspective is to consider how America's enemies such as predators and terrorists use the US Constitution against the very people it is designed to protect.

Mastering Their Craft

This work departs from the antiseptic world of popular media dramas, which fictionalize the apprehension and legal conviction of heinous violators in less than sixty minutes (minus commercials). Instead, this book offers a frightening glimpse of the cross-eyed creatures that lurk on a different plane of existence; who accept their wickedness through a mask of sanity, as they evolve into masters of human devastation with the aid of redundant criminal policy. The foundation of each account or vignette in the chapters ahead reveals that official policy, linked to popular media dramas, is flawed. Yes, the media's version of enforcement and criminal activity produces moral panic and a huge flow of income. But neither enforcement nor the media have a real impact upon the twisted, wired-wrong creatures who commit most of the heinous crimes. Clearly, enforcement and conviction policy linked to the identification, apprehension, and criminal conviction of wicked offenders is frightfully misguided, because the justice system is plagued with political-correctness issues and filmmaker versions of crime, which stifles America's defenses.

Publishers, too, especially academic publishers, hold either a right-wing (conservative) or left-wing (liberal) orientation about super predators. Consequently, I published this work without their aid, which offers me the extraordinary opportunity to present the outrageous thoughts and gruesome destruction of super predators without the political police manipulating those descriptions.

This work doesn't offer blame or boost personal safety. The preponderance of evidence offered is as varied as it is disturbing about the long and destructive journeys of super predators. Finally, because of confidentiality and constitutional concerns for victims, justice personnel, and offenders, actual names, dates, events, and places have been changed. For all practical purposes, you might say that the following fifteen vignettes are a work of fiction.

Chapter Flow

Chapter 1 includes an explanation of crime and an introduction of the wicked offenders. Chapters 2-16 contain the individual life stories, experiences, and criminal violations of each wicked offender. Chapter 17, although brief, offers tentative conclusions about super predators. Chapter 18 contains fictional short stories about fourteen of the offenders. One last thought before moving on. The chapters ahead are jammed with bizarre accounts of incredible human cruelty of every variety, so caution is advised.

Particulars of This Case Study

Wicked Women is focused on the journeys of super predators, from their early life experiences and criminal activities, through the time when they interacted with me in prison. Then, too, this work reveals the fascinating relationship between legal reasoning and societal values. The story of crime and punishment does not always end when an offender has been apprehended or convicted. The real mystery is when justice will be served, because the super predators featured in this book have been released from prison or will be released in the near future. That includes the police officer on death row, thanks in part to bleeding-heart liberals who think her trial was prejudicial from the start. My thoughts echo with the actions by the perpetrators who committed fraud, prostituted themselves and their families, sexually assaulted or butchered their own children, as well as brothers, sisters, parents, and strangers. In this regard, I had one advantage over other personnel and correctional service providers. At the time I gathered this evidence, I was not a "mandatory" reporter. Justice personnel are often required to reveal anything they hear or observe if a reasonable person would believe that a crime has been committed, a crime is in process, or a crime will be committed. Few inmates were concerned with what they said to me or wrote to me, furthering the uniqueness and the importance of this work. Mandatory reporting requirements have changed. By today's standards, to gather similar information of a similar nature is virtually impossible and could encourage litigation.

Definition of a Super Predator

John J. Dilulio, Jr. defines super predators as a cohort of offenders who developed through lifestyles of moral poverty, in homes where unconditional love was absent.[6] His definition has been discredited by uninformed academics, but his warnings are much more than crying wolf. Dilulio was an aide for President George W. Bush for eighteen months, until he was figuratively spanked in public for "baseless and groundless" commentary. That said, think of the "poor little rich girl" syndrome pervasive among Hollywood's bad girls, such as Paris Hilton, Lindsay Lohan, and Bijou Phillips. If you or I behaved like Hilton, Lindsay, or Bijou, a criminal sanction of ninety days in jail would become ninety months of hard time in a state penitentiary. What about Barbara Hutton, whose parents were Edna Woolworth (of the five-and-ten store chain) and Franklin Laws Hutton, cofounder of the E.F. Hutton brokerage house? She inherited millions, her seven marriages included one to Cary Grant, but she died with less than $3,500. Or Doris Duke, who was once referred to as the richest girl in the world, with an estate estimated at $1.2 billion dollars. Her father was James Buchanan Duke, whose multi-million-dollar endowment gave rise to Duke University. At fourteen she sued her mother; her only child was born prematurely and died within twenty-four hours; she killed her best friend in a freak car accident; and she legally adopted a thirty-five-year-old former Hare Krishna, whom she believed to be the reincarnation of her dead daughter. Like many children whose parents could give them the world, a young life without unconditional love and supervision can set decadence and corruption in motion. I can only guess at the origins of homes where moral poverty and unconditional love never existed. Perhaps in 4000 BCE the archetypal poor little rich girl was the motherless Sumerian child of a father too busy inventing the wheel to pay her much attention.

Dilulio's definition is consistent with the characteristics of the *Wicked Women* participants. His description, however, must be expanded to include the evidence provided by the participants in this work: super predators inflict unmerciful violence incessantly upon their parents, siblings, neighbors, and anyone else who crosses their paths, including their own children and spouses. Without a moral compass, individuals who are also prone to violence, or what can be called biologically wired-wrong, can easily accept their destruction of any living creature, regardless of the creature's age (such as six months old to ninety years of age), conscious state (such as functional, intoxicated, or mentally ill), or physical condition (asleep, recovering from surgery, or physically handicapped). Once criminally violent activities become second nature or an ingrained habit, there's no turning back.[7] No rehabilitation. No resolve. But some argue that because predators ability to adapt their appearance to their social environment, to blend in or camouflage themselves, they must have a moral compass of sorts. Yet this automatic change in appearance to blend in is explained by scholars—not predators—as similar to explaining why an octopus opens an empty jar of peanut butter.

Participant Selection

The participants in this work were chosen because their violent criminal careers can be traced and documented throughout their early childhood. They could have been identified as such if they had been less clever or poor, or if the system was better prepared and adequately funded. Yet none of these predators was ever officially exposed or prosecuted as an unrelenting predatoral monster. The strange thing you will discover as you page through each vignette, is that when they were in grade school, everyone around these predators knew they were corrupt. Equally important, their socioeconomic privileged family environments were decisive factors, and each was highly verbal and physically aggressive in prison programs: hands waving, palms tapping the tables or desk, eyes flitting, feet or legs in motion while seated, comments and quick responses to those seated next to them or others across the room. And they talked and wrote volumes about themselves.

Gangbangers, members of organized crime, foreign nationals suspected of terrorism, and celebrity-type criminals are not among the participants of this book, although I encountered convicted felons fitting those descriptions, such as John Wayne Gacy and Richard Speak at Stateville near Chicago; Gerald Amirault at Bay State in Massachusetts; Pamela Smart and Kathy Boudin at Bedford Hills in New York; Donald Gaskins at CCI; and Susan Smith at Leath in South Carolina.

All the *Wicked Women* participants wrote about their experiences in personal journals. The journals were a requirement for prison college courses like abnormal psychology or introduction to business; and a requirement to be a prison in-group participant. Participating in groups or taking college courses or vocational training can earn early release or parole for prisoners. Therefore, some prisoners worked hard in those activities. For instance, Annie (chapter 2) over a two-year period wrote two journals (approximately 125 single-spaced handwritten pages in total) about her experiences. Underworld Lilith wrote more, but Margo wrote less. Then, too, the participants were individuals whom I employed to do research, and some were trained to interview other prisoners, such as Val and Joey. Others were interviewed, such as Mary, Devin, and Wilma, who later became in-group participants or prison students.

My experiences are common among prison advocates, in-group leaders, and teachers. Additionally, all of the participants, without exception, were remarkable students. Their work efforts at their studies were excellent, their motivation to compete with one another was extraordinary, and the quality of their work (given the resources of prison programs) was superior when compared to a typical group of university students at the undergraduate or graduate level. (Sorry to say that; and yes, this finding is consistent with the academic literature.)

Gathering Reliable Information

Information about prisoners can be found in presentence investigation reports (PSI), classification records (treatment, program, and supervision requirements), and records of social service and health providers— i.e., visitor reports, mental health evaluations, medical, dental, and religious reports. For instance, visitors of prisoners must produce current driver's licenses and other forms of resident identification. Should spouses, children, parents, and friends reside in another state, additional identification is required and investigations are conducted. When family and friends visit, they often bring packages containing an assortment of items for the prisoner, in keeping with prison regulations: books, clothes, food, shoes; and in particular, candy bars, canned fish, deodorant soap, and instant coffee, which are "prison currency." They can be traded for other commodities and services because prisoners cannot carry money.

Presentence Investigation Report (PSI)

Prior to sentencing a guilty defendant in criminal proceedings, when confinement is an option, a PSI is provided to the judge to guide the sentencing process. PSIs are mandated in many states, regardless if the defendant accepted a guilty plea or after a jury or a judge's deliberation. The Federal Rules of Civil Procedure and Criminal Code provisions adapted in many jurisdictions require a PSI before sentencing, at least in felony cases. A PSI is just that—an investigation of the guilty defendant. It is a report about the defendant's character and background, and can include interviews and reports from victim(s), arresting officers, the defendant, and his or her family members and friends. Also, a PSI is part of the prisoner's file once he or she is imprisoned.

Intention and Throwbacks to Prehistoric Behavior

My intention is to provide perspectives consistent among behavioral science experts. Also, I want to engage your thoughts about creatures that exist on this planet who are throwbacks to prehistoric beings, linked to apes and chimpanzees because they engage in border raids, brutal beatings, cannibalism, homosexual and heterosexual rape, and warfare among rival territorial gangs. Gorilla males murder infants fathered by other males to free nursing mothers for breeding; orangutans resort to rape if their mating overtures are rejected. Rival gangs of chimpanzees wage bloody border wars (similar to the Arizona Alien Laws and practices) to protect their turf or to enlarge their harems. Mass killings, homicides, and assaults are documented consistently in both the Old and New Worlds. And the evolutionary big brother of all these creatures, mankind, has committed more crimes of violence against its own species, including genocide, war rape, and human trafficking. Finally, no form of social organization, mode of production, or environmental setting appears to have remained free from interpersonal violence for long. A distinctive difference between animals and human predators is that humans have evolved to singular heinous activities. That is, a human predator does not require or seek an audience, recognition, or a collaborator.

Consistent with accounts of previous generations of privileged nobility and high society, violent predators like Countess Elizabeth Báthory, Bucharest's Vera Renczi, New Orleans's Madame Delphine LaLaurie, and Dr. Linda Burfield Hazzard chose lifestyles that allowed them to seek and destroy human lives. The wicked participants in this work are similar to their earlier counterparts, in that all prospered in amenable social environments that provided the conditions for them to violate helpless victims. Their cloak of wealth and status disguised their wicked and vile behavior as *compassion*. That compassion was a sham, a masquerade. *Wicked Women* participants disguised themselves as caring human beings in their quest for human destruction, and each played her role with the talent of a Broadway star.

A Starting Point Linked to Criminological Theory

A worthy starting point of criminological theory is with Cesare Lombroso, an Italian prison physician, who in the late nineteenth century was regarded as the father of criminology.[8] The American study of crime and how to control it was advanced by one of America's earliest criminologists, Edwin Sutherland.[9] However, criminology has evolved in such a way, that everyone is an expert, especially the mass media. This produces dubious official policy and practices. For instance, sample descriptions of three predators described in this book:

- Annie, a young, white middle-class homemaker, killed her police officer husband with his service weapon as he slept. He had discovered that she was a serious player and financier of the rave club drug scene at distant universities, private clubs, and aboard pleasure crafts. One of her drug-trade partners and protector, a state trooper, was eventually apprehended. Annie lived two lives and had more than one residence, including a fabulous condo at the beach.
- Mickey is a bishop's daughter who returned a hero from the war in Afghanistan. She worked as a big city police officer and administered justice as an executioner, using her killer expertise as part of her vengeance kills. Her prey included her former husband; her sister and her sister's college roommate; her ex-husband's former lover, her father's former lover, and her second husband's lover. Today, after serving a brief prison sentence, Mickey sits at the head of her family's corporation. That corporation owns so much real estate from Boston to Belize, Donald Trump's empire looks like a third-world nation in comparison.
- Underworld Lilith, an attractive, well-educated woman, became the boss of the East Coast underworld, which operated sex clubs and influenced labor unions, after her father's mysterious death when she was twenty-six. Her human trafficking initiatives remain the benchmark of underworld operations throughout the Western world. Lilith was so dedicated to her mission, she turned her Cape Cod estate into a sex club and trained her young son in

the "art of prostitution." After serving a prison sentence, Lilith continues to operate those sex clubs.

Experts would *agree to disagree* about motive and dangerousness of the above offenders. Equally important, while the work of experts is meritorious and can add to the criminological baseline, their perspectives can misguide appropriate and legal practices to identify and apprehend predators. That is because no clear definition or policy is applicable to these predators, and that includes characteristics offered in the American Psychiatric Association's bible, the DSM-IV.[10]

Added to the mix is the idea that most of my justice and behavioral science colleagues are dealing with the politics of university tenure, political correctness, and mandatory demands to appease the entitled class of students who lack integrity, discipline, and the basic skills required of a university student. This is not to say that the students I have taught for over twenty years are dumb or stupid. Most held a high standard of personal accountability, which added to their success as positive contributors to society. Nonetheless, the dumbing down effort of many universities can result in rewarding failure as excellence. A halo can become a noose, and will set students up for failure, which results in a spike in both frequency and intensity of violent crime and victims. So many in our "me-centric" society feel entitled and many feel that the world owes them something for nothing. The "I'm special" attitude of a generation of students who insist that teachers inflate grades because of their attendance is commonplace. The gentleman's C grade, particularly if you attend an Ivy League school, blows an academic's mind, since it suggests that some institutions of higher learning are more concerned with Daddy's money than the offspring's intellectual achievements. Having a problem with an example? Consider Yale's finest, George W. Bush, and Harvard Law School star Mitt Romney. In the adult world, triumph of adulation over authority rang clear when Tiger Woods expressed, "I knew my actions were wrong, but I convinced myself that normal rules didn't apply. ... I felt I was entitled."

Then, too, local police investigators employed by thousands of departments across the country hold a different set of experiences than wannabe crime fighters (mass produced by inadequate college classrooms and law schools, with the aid of television), public expectations, and sensationalized mass media (i.e., motion pictures, popular television dramas, news reports, and books). News reports are inconsistent with official records. This thought is borne out by my earlier work, reporting that the media change real world expectations about crime and criminals by suggesting that every crime is detected or reported, every violator is found, and every criminal is convicted.[11]

One myth arising from the distorted realities induced by the media is that the American judicial process is flawless.[12] As a result, official misconduct is tolerated, wrongful convictions continue, and capital punishment allegedly serves a higher purpose. Then, too, those distortions mask the enormous forensic science backlog experienced by most laboratories, increasing the number of unsolved crimes. For instance, a study reveals that the huge backlog of criminal cases in homicide and rape investigations included approximately 52,000 homicide and 169,000 rape cases in 2003.[13] These unsolved cases include homicide and rape cases for which law enforcement has submitted a range of existing evidence for analysis to forensic labs. What you will learn from each vignette about the participants in this book is that fictional accounts promoted through the popular media serve the evolution of super predators, while providing a false sense of security for the public. The justice agencies are left to police a lawless population of predators, who hold more rights and have violated more victims than a thousand Ted Bundys.

Examples of the CSI Effect can be found among supposed experts who describe criminal behavior from case files, controlled interviews, and after-the-fact evaluations. (See former FBI expert John Douglas in *Mind Hunter*, and Stephen Michaud and Roy Hazelwood in *The Evil that Men Do*.) Those junior G-Man are under the impression that an interview with Ted Bundy produces truth! Most of us realize that violators lie about everything all of the time, especially when talking to the man—an enforcement officer. Other experts use the scholarly literature laden with theoretical misunderstandings.[14] These reckless experts pass along their well-written and promoted findings as cutting edge, such as Kim Davies's *The Murder Book* (2007), Lonnie H. Athens in *The Creation of Dangerous Violent Criminals* (1992), and Robert J. Meadows and Julie Kuehnel in *Evil Minds: Understanding and Responding to Violent Predators* (2004). Others describe the hardships of American female prisoners. They indulge in political agendas while neglecting to inform readers that their startling storylines were obtained from rough-shot interviews, similar to the federal-agents-turned-authors, who took refuge in "truths" supplied by convicted felons with little to lose. Examples of those are *Women Behind Bars: The Crisis of Women in the U.S. Prison System* by Silja J. A. Talvi (2007); Kathryn Watterson's *Women in Prison: Inside the Concrete Womb* (1996); and Barbara Owen's *In the Mix: Struggle and Survival in a Women's Prison* (1998). Additionally, other presumed experts acquired recommendations from *O: The Oprah Magazine,* such as Cristina Rathbone, author of *A World Apart* (2006). She sat in the visiting room of a Massachusetts prison to gather data, and produced a few hundred pages of (excellently written) revelations about the difficult life among incarcerated felons (which can hardly be disputed). For example, "women behind bars are startlingly unlike their more violent male counterparts. ... (largely convicted of) drug-related offenses, they are frequently mere accessories to their crimes: girlfriends, wives, or lovers of drug dealers" (p. 22). What these authors fail to mention are the sober realities of prison life for women. For example, in 1998, in state and federal facilities, 139 female (and 2,900 male) inmates dead while in custody, eighty-seven because of illness or natural causes, fourteen from AIDS, and thirteen from suicide.[15] It's likely that some of those deaths were the work of predators locked in with the garden-variety prisoners. Also, consider that in any given year, an estimated 145,000 prison rapes occur and few predators are ever punished for those crimes.[16] Even in prison, predators rule.

Predators are competent at manipulating an overcrowded and politicized justice system filled with soap-box crusaders, clueless academics, and bleeding-heart misfits, equipped with skills that are better at boosting their own insincerities than securing lethal misfits, who can boost a three-year-old child and your neighbor's soul without missing a beat.

Something Unsettling

As a consequence, many experts publish in the prominent press, obtain prestigious recommendations and financial grants, and win validation because of their benefactors. History is primarily written by the privileged, argues Professor Randall G. Shelden.[17] For instance, it is difficult to take a position counter to that of a Harvard psychologist, even if the psychologist is full of himself. It is easier to accept the messenger than the message. That said, this can lead to an assumption that the inefficiencies identified in many justice studies (such as the failure of police to clear the parks of the homeless, the inability of the prison system to rehabilitate, and probation and paroles failure to reduce recidivism rates) are closely linked to those writers' naïveté or lack of practical experience, rather than to a flaw in the criminal justice program, practice, or perspective. The truth of the matter is that recovery and rehabilitation programs, including sexual registries, have been in place for a long time without tangible evidence of success. So argues Norm Pattis, a Connecticut defense lawyer. Frankly, I think there is something unsettling about advice from popular writers—even if they work at Yale—fear-peddling entrepreneurs, and bleeding-heart liberals, who proclaim recovery and protection is a breath away for every chronic pedophile and every serial murderer.

Serial Murderers

No single model fits every serial murderer, but a serial murderer can be defined as someone who has killed three or more people over a period of more than thirty days, with a significant cooling-off period between the killings. Or you can watch my favorite TV drama, *Criminal Minds,* and learn all about it. But there were almost 600,000 reported homicides in the US from 1976 to 2005, and almost 14 percent were committed by strangers.[18] Also, a little over a third of homicide reports say that the relationship between victim and killer was undetermined.[19] Approximately 16,000 murders are reported each year. Six of every ten known murders result in an arrest, and an estimated 40 percent of known murders end in a conviction. (As a matter of concern, sexual assault convictions are estimated at 5 percent.) Then there's that nasty number of 2.4 million alleged natural deaths, including accidents reported each year. There are also ninety-one suicides a day across America. All of these statistics represent observable corpses. What about unobserved corpses? Disposing of a body or altering the circumstances of death so that it appears to be accidental can't be that difficult. Therefore, in a final analysis, any rationale about a killer's motive is at best ambiguous, particularly when we add the thought that theoretically, anybody could have hidden twenty bodies under John Wayne Gacy's house when he was alive, or a hundred bodies at the bottom of the wetlands after Hurricane Katrina.

Sexual Homicide: Catathymic and Compulsive Murderers

Serious limitations exist that characterize sexual homicide, because it is not defined by criminal statute in most jurisdictions. Researchers either ignore or are uninformed about the distinctions between *catathymic* and *compulsive* murders, as explained by Louis B. Schlesinger.[20]

There are clear distinctions among sexual murders. The murder itself can be sexually arousing; the murder is committed in order to cover up a sex crime; or it is a homicide that has some sexual component, but has an unclear motive.[21] In addition to definitional and crime-incidence complexities in research of sexual homicide, there are practical obstacles too:

- Sexual homicide is a rare event and difficult to detect.
- Sexual murderers are not identified as such either legally or institutionally (DOC).
- The background of a sexual murderer, which is important for understanding motivational dynamics, is often incomplete and inaccurate, because of various legal restriction as well as personal motives to lie, exaggerate, and distort.
- Most predators are convicted for lesser crimes (if apprehended at all) for a variety of reasons: lack of evidence, prosecutorial discretion, or just pure incompetence or laziness of the part of investigators or prosecutors.
- Mental health professionals have worked independently of other practitioners (e.g., criminal investigators) and possess a wealth of information about sexual homicide, but from a different perspective.

Both types of sexual murder have a basis in underlying sexual conflict. However, the nature of the sexual conflict differs.

- Catathymic homicides are typically single explosions triggered by some type of challenge to the individual's sense of sexual competence.
- Compulsive sexual homicides stem from a longstanding and developing urge to kill, which itself is eroticized.

Some argue that the motivational process during a catathymic crisis and a compulsive sexual murder are linked through a varied five stage process:

- A thinking disorder occurs in the mind of the offender.
- A plan is created to commit a violent criminal act.
- Internal emotional tension forces the commission of the criminal act.
- That leads to a superficial calmness, in which the need to commit the violent act is eliminated and normal activity can be conducted.
- The mind adjusts itself and understands that the thinking process that caused the criminal act was flawed, and the mind makes adjustments in order to prevent further criminal activity.

However, the serial killer never reaches the fifth stage, but returns to the second and operates in a cycle between stages two and four. One flaw in that thinking is that killers can and do kill for other reasons. During homicide investigations, investigators seek to learn why the victim was murdered, and who had the means, opportunity, and motive (MOM) to commit the murder. Since mankind has been on this planet, motives to kill have changed little.

Motives to Commit Violent Crime

Motivation to commit a violent crime can include boredom, cowardice, envy or jealously, greed, ignorance, lust, pride, rage, and revenge.[22] Then, too, violent crimes can be the result of cultural and patriotic perspectives (suicide bombers and the military). Additionally, there is little question that violent crime can be linked to accidents, drugs, gangs, and crimes of passion. Yet many of us have been envious and burning hot with rage, but we rejected violence as a solution. Bottom line, the trigger or motive among super predators to engage in criminally violent behavior is sorted into three different categories: pleasure seekers, controllers, and revengers. Each category is detailed below, but first there are three myths that require acknowledgement.

Three Myths

After lecturing university students for over two decades about crime and criminology, I have seen three myths frequently emerge:

- A belief reinforced by the popular media, which perpetuates the myth that crime can be eliminated. Emile Durkheim advised over one hundred years ago that crime is a natural social activity, "an integral part of all healthy societies."[23] The best we can do is to control crime. It will never stop.

- The media promotes the image that every crime scene will yield plentiful evidence that can be analyzed through foolproof forensic science techniques, and will be utilized toward a lawful conviction. Evidence reveals that justice accountability does not depend upon whether an individual committed a crime or not, but how the media portrays the individual in relationship to the crime.

- The illusion that every crime committed is known by the authorities and that every offender is apprehended and convicted of a crime, a result of the CSI Effect. Evidence shows that approximately less than two of every ten property crimes and a little more than four of ten crimes of violence reported in 2007 ended in an arrest.[24] You already know the statistics for the number of crimes never solved as shown above.

Meet the Participants

To protect victims, justice personnel, health providers, and offenders, all the information that follows should be looked upon as fictitious. I am no longer able to access the documents I used to develop this work. That said, when they were imprisoned, Annie, Brother Pious, Devin, Dory, Janelle, Joey, Brandeis, Margo, Mary, Mickey, Sweet Jenny Lee, Tammy, Underworld Lilith, Val, and Wilma averaged twenty-nine years of age, with a range from sixteen to forty-one. Devin and Sweet Jenny Lee were sixteen; Wilma was forty-two. Only Margo and Tammy had been previously arrested, Margo for drug possession and Tammy for DUI.

Education: Annie, Joey, Mary, Margo, Mickey, and Wilma graduated high school. Margo enrolled in college when she was twenty-three, but never completed her first semester. Devin, Sweet Jenny Lee, and Val never graduated high school. Devin and Sweet Jenny Lee were below the compulsorily school age when imprisoned, and were mandated to attend high school classes at the prison under the tutelage of certified state teachers. Dory attended two years of college, so had fourteen years of education; Tammy quit in her last year of college despite a 4.0 average. Brandeis, Brother Pious, and Underworld Lilith had bachelor's degrees and were honor graduates, and Janelle had a law degree. The average number of years of education among the fifteen participants was 13.3 years, which is higher than the average number among national inmate populations.

Number of Children and Martial Status: Annie, Brandeis, Dory, and Wilma have one child each; Mickey, Tammy, and Underworld Lilith have two children each. Val has three children, and Janelle and Joey have four children. Brother Pious, Devin, Margo, Mary, and Sweet Jenny Lee have no children.

Convictions and Sentences: The participants were convicted or accepted a guilty plea for crimes ranging from capital murder to criminal conspiracy to driving while intoxicated. All of the participants in *Wicked Women* attacked strangers, yet they also attacked family members, siblings and accomplices, their own children, lovers, and friends. Prison sentences ranged from execution (Mary), to life (Annie, though life in the state where she was convicted is twenty years), to two years (Sweet Jenny Lee). Regardless of their original sentence, all but two served less prison time than expected, and have been released or are about to be released at the writing of this work.

Plea Bargains: Seven of the participants accepted a guilty plea during their jury trial but prior to the jury's deliberation; six accepted a guilty plea prior to trial; and two were found guilty by a jury. Across America, nine in ten felony convictions are reached through guilty pleas. The relevance of judicially accepted guilty pleas is that a defendant loses his or her constitutional due process rights, but all investigations are halted—an error that incredibly favors a defendant.

Motivation or Triggers: Following are the three trigger categories of the participants: pleasure seekers, controllers, and revengers. These triggers are not mutually exclusive, and often participants can demonstrate components characterized by more than one category. In the final analysis, it is likely that a predator categorized in one category can act on the impulse of components in other categories.

Pleasure Seekers

Pleasure seekers (Annie, the rave drug dealer, chapter 2; Dory, the drifter, chapter 6; Joey, the day-care worker, chapter 8; Margo, the college student who was born a boy, chapter 9; Sweet Jenny Lee, the high school student, chapter 12; and Underworld Lilith, chapter 14) seek activity to relieve boredom and pursue behavioral patterns that victimizes others. Who they victimize doesn't matter: friends, strangers, relatives, spouses, even their own children. Their methods of victimization are eroticized, and thereby fulfill sexual or lustful objectives, yet sex is not a primary goal. At first, I was under the impression that the six pleasure seekers sought sexual encounters in order to engage in the sexual abuse of their victims, but unlike controllers, their encounters were not necessarily intended to end in their own sexual gratification. Should sex occur, and it often had, pleasure seekers considered it "gravy," as Dory wrote. Pleasure seekers are optimistic about the future and their ability to commit whatever crime is helpful for them to pursue their destiny—pleasure.

A common thread among pleasure seekers is that they are expert schemers or manipulators. They seek challenges in everything they encounter. So as you can imagine, they are excellent students and learn faster than any other group of students in the locked-down or the free world.

Close relationships for pleasure seekers are tedious, uninspiring, and routine. Each pleasure seeker had many lovers, and they sexually assault those lovers and many strangers, more than once, regardless of the stability of their love relationship. A partnership is only as good as the moment, and if a pleasure seeker has to choose between an intimate relationship and being alone, being alone wins. They're loners despite their many friends and lovers, who tend to serve a purpose. They use people. It could be said that pleasure seekers possess, or at least demonstrate, little patience to develop a close relationship with others, including their own children. Pleasure seekers are energetic, high-spirited, and animated.

Pleasure seekers make little distinction between violent and nonviolent behavior, yet typically prefer armed robbery, rape, extortion, and every variety of crime, as often as an opportunity arises to enhance their senses. Pleasure seekers choose victims they can shock through their attacks. Vulnerable victims don't represent a challenge. The pleasure seeker wants to hunt down a victim and manipulate him/her or the circumstance into vulnerability. This hunt for prey plays an important role in the pleasure seekers' self-centered quest to amuse themselves. The hunt justifies a deep gratification, and they speak about it the way a college student would talk about acing an exam. The rationale for criminal offenses is hedonistic behavior, which can be linked to new experiences, excitement, and fun.

Pleasure seekers mask their own behavior to appear non-threatening to others. Once confronted or attacked, they viciously respond. In this regard, their victims rarely have defensive wounds (for instance, lacerations to the forearms or other signs that they protected themselves) on their bodies, because pleasure seekers keep superb control over their victims by force or deception. For pleasure seekers, rehabilitation or recovery programs are useless. They might excel during a recovery program because they are hunting for new victims, and when the program ends, old behavior returns. Violence is their life's work.

Controllers

Controllers are comfortable in their social environments, but are often under attack by their own sense of personal inferiority widening their own feelings of insecurity and sudden doom. Their anxiety to maintain or regain comfort or balance is complicated by their own fatalistic idea that imminent danger is always present. Controllers include: Brother Pious, the orphanage worker, chapter 4; Devin, the high school student, chapter 5; Janelle, the federal special agent, chapter 7; Mary, the urban police officer, chapter 10; and Wilma, the prison warden, chapter 16. They are huge pessimists, the complete reverse of pleasure seekers. Doom is evident, and they individually represent tools that aid doom. For instance, Devin sees himself as a doom machine hunting zombies. Since everyone will die eventually, he figures, what's the commotion about "getting people there faster."

Through control and dominance, the controller blocks those nasty feelings of insecurity. Controllers appear to be unapproachable, or detached, arrogant, and lethargic, while in fact they struggle with inner conflicts of inferiority and insecurity. Cordial greetings and politeness to controllers is met with disdain and disgust. Consequently, their victims are beaten and tortured. Their victims, if discovered, have multiple defensive wounds and lacerations. The controllers' arrogance is a sham, a fraud.

Controllers have no compassion or feelings about their victims or authority. In prison, controllers are disciplined because of their lack of respect for authority; that is they are written up, restricted, and locked-down in segregation or isolation units more often than other prisoners.

Controllers are characterized by perfectionism, orderliness, workaholic tendencies, an inability to make commitments or to trust others, and their underlying fear that their personal flaws will be detected. Their greatest threat is individuals who can pierce their armor of arrogance and see the real "them." Therefore, controllers stay clear of social service providers, probation and parole officers, and others trained to detect frauds.

Controllers are cowards and terrified of their own vulnerabilities. They possess an urge to control challenges, causing others pain and stress in order to maintain their sense of balance and order. Controllers possess a high pain threshold, and that threshold increases as their criminal activities take new twists and turns. Yet meeting new challenges or dealing with those twists and turns, casts them into compulsive repetition of violence. They repeat the same pattern of violence again and again in an attempt to master their anxiety and to cope with the trauma of losing the battle.

Controllers rarely experience satisfaction, yet they continue to fight the same threat, with increasing severity and stubbornness. Consequently, violence, torture, sexual assault, murder, cannibalism, necrophilia, and other heinous offenses represent a progression of survival tools. The crime in and of itself holds little significance or meaning. Rather, the criminal act is a path to a good feeling (or balance) about themselves.

Like politicians, controllers employ spin strategies to provide an appearance of being non-threatening, but they do this for different reasons than pleasure seekers. This spin is meant to reduce a victim's defensive action. Props, such as weapons, are unnecessary because weapons imply a poor self-image. Nonetheless, a victim's submission must be swift and uncompromising. Victimizing a person more than once is preferred, and a perfect victim is a person who knows how to behave like a victim. Rehabilitation is implausible and impractical among controllers because after a controller has systematically violated twenty-five children, she won't hesitate to attack another child, especially if that child has already been victimized.

Revengers

One way to describe the trigger of four participants is revenge: Brandeis, the high school teacher, chapter 3; Mickey, the city cop, chapter 11; Tammy, the soccer mom, chapter 13; and Val, the gypsy, chapter 15. Their plan is retribution, but more than that, they believe they individually administer justice. Some might relate this perspective to the biblical perspective of *lex talionis*—the law of retaliation and revenge, also known as an eye for an eye or a corpse for a corpse.

As such, rage is a self-invited weapon to fulfill desires. Rage is used to describe the power behind behavior, and relates to an alleged "out of control" temper and blackouts. Alleged, because they employ their temper to carry out what they have already decided to do. Yes, the tempers are real, but turning those tempers off and on is another matter. Equally important, the revenger is easily victimized by others. That is, revengers believe—and sometimes it's true—that they have been violated by others. They pay back the person, or someone who looks like the person, who victimized them, or they pay back for violations (perceived or actual) to their community—Val paid back because she thought others disrespected her heritage—or their country, their favorite television performance, or their favorite teacher. In this regard, the justice administered by the revenger is rarely a single action or victimization; it is multiple actions and repeat victimizations. For instance, over many years, Val sexually victimized the same children and extorted funds from the same victims.

Consistent with the old approach of the culpable victim, as influenced by Sigmund Freud, revengers can unwittingly seek their own victimization as a means of abating their feelings of guilt and insecurity from sexual dysfunctions. They allow or orchestrate the opportunity for a violator to harm them, and then the revenger has cause to torture or murder those violators. The revengers I studied conveyed a need to rid the world of what they considered the immoral or the unworthy. They righteously represented the moral police. That is, they offered a higher order to validate violence.

Another important characteristic of revengers can be an obsession with either a codependent relationship with an alpha personality, or a dominant ideal that monopolizes thoughts and decisions. For Brandeis, it was Joanna; for Mickey, it was her bodyguard, Emma Tower, God, and country; for Tammy, it was the ideal of giving birth to Aaron and his death twenty-six days later; and for Val, it was her community of Irish Travelers. What it came down to was that, their individual happiness or pain depended upon persons or ideals outside themselves. Their needy mentality sought approval or an enabler that helped the revenger to justify actions, which included murder, sexual assault, and so on. Recovery or rehabilitation programs provide revengers with new information to justify their pursuit of death and torture. To this end, all violent actions can be justified by this offender.

Making Sense of Life Stories

Narratives provided by the participants about their previous experiences and their life stories can represent a pathway to a better understanding of them. The way individuals describe their lives as having significance, the language or jargon use in those descriptions, and the connections they make can reveal the world they see and in which they act. A life story is a self-construction of a person's reality—not necessarily the way it was, but how it's perceived. Most of us are memory selective. We select only part of our past experiences, and mold them to come out the way we want them to look. Life stories are essential for critical self-assessments, and often lead the way toward choices that closely align with an individual's goals and values. The life story format allows people to select key events over the course of their lives and to synthesize the learning. People can clarify their own priorities, values, identities, and relationships, and become aware of the long-term impact of key life events.

It is likely that predators highlight their most significant violations and disregard the numerous other violations. By describing significant experiences, violators can better understand the relevance of their own experiences, which pave the way for future violations. Their historical accounts are not for the benefits of a listener, but for themselves. It's a thinking out loud process that contains worthless clues, not necessarily to misguide a listener, but to aid in their own decision-making process. They see a light at the end of their descriptions, yet rarely articulate the intensity of that light. Only through a process of connecting all of those conversations, journal entries, and written projects with official reports, can the shape of a predator's intensity be recognized. Like a jigsaw puzzle, it all slides into a single picture; and in this case, it's a picture of a super predator engaged in a journey.

In part, some of those worthless clues and individual fantasies of the participants helped frame the fourteen short story portrayals or characterizations found in chapter 18. These stories can aid in understanding the participants, but are subjective, fictitious, and driven by the imagination of the author. Finally in this regards, in keeping with Paul Cromwell's observations found in the pages of *In Their Own Words: Criminals on Crime*, (5th edition) quality ethnographic (intensively studies a specific social group by observing the group in its natural setting and participant observation) is research centered on the ultimate criminological resource. Cromwell concludes that offenders' own account of their experiences can enormously aid in an understanding of the criminal mind.

CHAPTER 2
All about Annie

An Overview

Annie Louise Shepherd was raised with an older sister, Angela. Their mother was a high school math teacher in the city where the girls were raised, and their father was a veterinarian with a lucrative practice. His father, too, had been a successful veterinarian. The Shepherds moved twice in Annie's young life, once from Cleveland, where Annie and Angela were born, to the medium-sized southern metropolis where Annie's mother grew up. Annie was in third grade at the time. She graduated from the same high school her mother had graduated from and where her mother worked.

The Larsons, Annie's grandparents on her mother's side lived in the area. When Annie started sixth grade, the Shepherds moved to a large, comfortable property outside the city. The home was part of a beautiful horse ranch where Annie and Angela spent a good portion of their young lives, jumping thoroughbreds at competitive events, riding the endless trails, and having ranch parties. Annie's favorite mount was Spuddling, whose "bloodline goes back to Sir Gaylord, settles mares, is sixteen plus hands, athletic and a big mover, light on the bit, with a puppy dog personality," she wrote. For the trails, Annie's favorite was Dixie Blue, a gray mare, although Annie referred to this mare as simply Blue. She was a sweet girl and very quiet, even though she'd been bred from both successful racing and sport lines. Tanya, Annie's best friend and constant companion, rode the trails with her and also had a favorite mount, Renegade. The ranch contained three hundred acres of tall trees, a pond big enough to fish—although no one ever caught any fish—and winding horse trails that connected to the state park's horse trails, extending a Shepherd's ride by more than two hours.

In school, Annie was a member of her high school's ROTC, book club, and the Spanish club (she spoke Spanish fluently). A bright person, she was always on the honor roll, and a member of the student council, according to her high school yearbook.

A correctional officer described Annie's appearance as "the girl next door, until you get to know her." First impressions of Annie can be summed up by another officer's two words—"amiable and naive." Annie said that she must look naive, because she "lived a blur." She explained that "something inside me pushes me to do nasty shit to myself and other people. Can't explain it but it's like there's a big ole' parasite living in my belly. It would chomp on my insides if I didn't drink [alcohol] or do drugs. But I never felt anything when I was on Blue." When she described her early life experiences, she said in-group that her parents gave her everything she wanted and never laid a hand on her, although she wished they had. "My family," she wrote, "lived in a house whose people sit in darkness at the dinner table and dust was their conversations and clay was their food. I hated it—every creepy second of it."

Three weeks after graduating high school, Annie married Barry, a horse lover but not a rider. The newlyweds lived at the ranch with her parents. Tanya, who always slept in the guest room, continued to spend all her time with Annie, despite Barry's insistence that she go home. "But I am home," she answered him, Annie reported.

A year later, Annie gave birth to a son, Andrew, yet some of Annie's friends and her parents joked about the birth, saying that the baby's father was really Tanya. Annie made life difficult for Barry: always demanding, always dramatic, always giving little in return, and she mocked him and said things that disrespected him. For instance, she told him at one of her many ranch parties, "Why can't you make me feel special like my Tanya?" Everyone laughed, and both Tanya and Annie stuck out their tongues at Barry. One afternoon, he went to the food store and never returned. Even his parents never heard from him, but Annie said that he filed for a divorce. Once the divorce was final, she married Larry Jordan, a local police officer who was twenty-two years older than Annie and the father of one of her high school friends. Annie and Andrew moved into Larry's city home, and once typical marriage life set in after their Hawaiian honeymoon, Annie was again on the prowl or at the ranch riding with Tanya. Annie, Andrew, and Larry lived together for the next four years, until Annie murdered Larry with his own service weapon and was sent to prison. Records show that Annie was released in the fall of 2010.

Early Memories

Comments in Annie's prison journal implied she was a prankster before first grade. She would move her parents' and sister's clothes, toothbrushes, and shoes to other rooms, or sometimes hid those items in the dishwasher, oven, and clothes dryer. Annie thought it was amusing as her family searched around the house for their belongings. There were times when she hid her family's personal items in the garage, backyard, and garbage containers. She took items to her grandparents' house, and often stole things from their home and hid them in her house.

"During Christmas week," she wrote, "I took a couple of presents from under the [Christmas] tree with Angela's name on them and fired [burned] them up in the garage. That was incredible. Mom, Dad, and Angela tried to put out the fire after I started yelling 'fire fire' as loud as I could. They're yelling and screaming at each other about what to do. It was so cool. I was in my PJs watching the whole thing. I cried when it was over. When Mom asked about my tears, I said something like I didn't want Teddy [the stuffed bear she was holding] to catch fire."

Annie's earliest recollections about "creating a fuss" were when she was a first grader, but she wrote about those early incidents in the later months of her writing endeavors, rather than earlier. When asked about the delay in writing about her young life, she said that "it isn't important. A lot of stuff happened like that but I don't pay it no mind." Her sister whined about Annie's behavior in first grade for some time, and since Angela was bigger, Annie had to try a number of ways to stop her, but to no avail. Until, "there was a pot of boiling water on the stove and I tried to splash it on her but it was too heavy. I dropped it, jumped, and cried. I didn't cry because I hurt myself but because the pot was too heavy for me to splash her with the water. I said it was an accident. I knew next time to scoop a cupful of water from the pot. I filled a cup with hot water and chased Angela around the house. I hated a moving target. What worked was fire and she never messed with me after that. I waited till she was asleep and lit up her blankets. My parents knew it wasn't an accident, but they ignored my attacks on Angie. They searched my room for matches, but didn't find any. That meant it was open season on her."

Stealing Binges

In seventh grade, Annie and Tanya went on "stealing binges" to Walgreens, CVS, and Wal-Mart, among other retailers. The dynamic duo ripped off large quantities of expensive lotions, perfume, and cosmetics.. When Annie talked about stealing from stores, her light-colored eyes intensified and her voice heightened with glee. I got the impression that the thrill of stealing was a high that was rivaled only by competing at horse shows or riding the trails on Blue. Annie remarked, "Never little stores. There's no fun there since they don't have security cameras or security people. [Stealing from those big stores] was like kicking back with a handful of sweet dilaudid [a semi-synthetic drug derived from morphine] and soaking up sunlight. Life was so easy then."

Reading these accounts and listening to Annie's commentaries gave me the idea that when Annie was bored, she stirred things up. The payoff for her was relieving her boredom. Yet these early experiences also aided her in developing reliable excuses and justifications for her actions, particularly her criminal behavior.

The Blur

Annie was about sixteen when the "blur" started. That was also when she met Lorrie at church. Lorrie was fifteen years older than Annie, a single mom with two daughters. Lorrie was a small-time business woman who provided services to various criminals. Annie babysat for Lorrie, and Tanya often joined Annie. Annie explained to her parents that she babysat two or three times a week, and even overnight on occasion. Sometimes, Annie brought Lorrie's kids to the ranch and hoisted them aboard mares, and they went on glorious night rides. The little girls shared saddles with Annie and Tanya. There was some implication that Annie and Tanya compared their "private parts," as Annie wrote, with the girls. "It was exciting to see Tanya touch herself and one of the little girls at the same time. She would only do it when I told her too. I remember this one night when the colossal moon was ominously glowing. The moon's orangey light slid down on the trails and the trees and made them look really bizarre. It reminded me of a Halloween night. It was creepy out. I stopped Blue and turned her around in front of Tanya so that me and my little passenger could watch. I told Tanya to go ahead and mess with her rider. She lifted that girl into her arms, slid her little dress back, and played my rider's sister like a ukulele. We laughed and laughed. Tanya made faces and sang, too, in a funny little voice as she often had. She howled at the moon like a dog. The little slut [girl] was getting off too, big time. All of us smiled like two fools."

The girls did not understand that they were being sexually abused by Annie and Tanya. Annie explained that they were members of a secret club, and that they promised never to tell on each other. Annie manipulated the little girls into touching each other and laughing about it. It was their secret, and often, they grabbed each other's hands and sang something like "secret Blue friends forever." Apparently Annie's mount, at least in name, was part of the secret society and their rituals.

The Blur and High School

The "blur" was well-defined for Annie before her high school graduation. That was also the time when Annie and Tanya often used drugs, and Annie's insatiable appetite to be "chilled" and "thrilled by it all" was beyond her control. Annie and Tanya probably got hooked on cough medicine, dilaudid, and alcohol while in high school. With freedom from her parents ("who were trying to do the right thing and be my friend") and with Lorrie's encouragement, Annie and Tanya stole high-quality product that they sold for large financial gains. The three of them often got high together after Lorrie put the kids to bed. On Lorrie's instructions, the two girls stole cartons of cigarettes and over the counter drugs, especially sinus and cough medicines. Sometimes, the girls targeted delivery drivers. While one girl distracted the driver, usually with "sexy talk and little touches," the other girl helped herself to the boxes in the rear of the delivery vehicle. Sometimes Lorrie sent along a young man to help. They stole the same product from the small carrier vehicles: cough and sinus medication and cigarettes.

Lorrie treated Annie like a daughter, not only because her own daughters were totally devoted to Annie and listened to whatever she said, but because "there was a spark of interest on her part to touch my sweet ass which I shoved in her face when she forgot. Like I would drop something or showered at her house and asked for towels." Sometimes Annie brought the girls into the shower and washed them, a task Lorrie appreciated, but probably would have stopped had she suspected that Annie would slide their bodies over her own, making sure that their "little holes were clean." As for Tanya, Lorrie didn't care too much for her, and said that Tanya behaved like a "vegetable or a no-mind" (Annie wrote), depending on Lorrie's disposition. Lorrie described Tanya as having a dependent personality, which was reinforced by her excessive dependence on Annie. "You should find better friends," Lorrie told her one day. "Like you?" was Annie's question. "Yeah, because Tanya has difficulty in making decisions, and is totally helpless without your direction. She has no self-reliance."

Fact is, Annie wrote, "I could piss on her knee and tell her it was raining, and she believed me. But Lorrie didn't know how dependent Tanya was on me. She thought because she's older that's she smarter." The only time Tanya disobeyed Annie was when Annie told her to alter the timing of her period, because its arrival was too close to her own menstrual cycle. "Other than that, every organ in her body obeyed me or suffered the consequences, but it didn't take long for Lorrie to say, yes ma'am to me too."

Traveling

Annie and Tanya traveled over one hundred miles from their hometown in every direction—which included the ocean to the east and two state lines, north and south—in their crime spree. They became familiar with the surrounding communities, highways, and retailers over the next two years. Lorrie taught them tricks, such as using different vehicles, and wearing male clothing and sunglasses during the commission of their crimes. They kept their fingernails short and unpolished, refrained from makeup, and did not talk more than necessary or show their teeth. Lorrie also taught Annie that when things looked bad, "Snap a photo with your cell phone and play the recording previously placed on it that said in a black male's voice: 'Got your pic, dude. Try anything stupid and I'll find you and jack you up, got it?'" Lorrie never realized that she was grooming Annie to be her partner before the girl turned twenty.

It is possible that Lorrie fenced stolen items in order to feed her children and pay her mortgage. She was not a risk taker compared to her understudy, who would eventually dominate her, and turn out her children to control the cops and her criminal accomplices. Lorrie would buy stolen property and unload it to legal businesses and individuals through her home computer catalog. Some of the managers and owners of the stores Lorrie sent Annie and Tanya "worked" with Lorrie, and received a commission for their cooperation in the thefts.

Pushing Buttons

Annie possessed both the aggressiveness and the energy to do whatever she wanted as a criminal, and was never afraid to show it. She could function extremely well as a student but was better at jumping off a cliff with Sigmund Freud, and no one would be any wiser. High school personnel whose job it was to keep track of students fell under her influence or abuse, because Annie was promiscuous, knew how to dazzle and confuse others, and possessed an almost innate ability to manipulate people. She was an amazing schemer. When her parents thought she was sexually involved with a high school teacher, which she was, she aggressively tormented them with stories of rape and sexual pleasure, and flirted with her father, igniting her mother's rage. Annie knew which buttons to push. When her mother became her adversary, she also became subject to Annie's manipulation whenever she wanted to ground Annie. What really set Annie off was when her mother tried to keep Annie from riding Blue, but "of course she wouldn't stop me from riding competitively because that brought money to the ranch, the little bitch." Annie pitted her parents against each other and involved

Angela, who was away at college. Angela sided with her little sister and thought their parents were being mean to sweet Annie.

More than one teacher and educational psychologist resigned from their jobs while Annie was a high school student. It is likely that she intimidated her advisors and probably her teachers, and used whatever devices were available to her to get what she wanted. Annie possessed few personal boundaries, despite her naive Mona-Lisa appearance, and her dominant alpha-personality was masked by a charismatic and dramatic nature. "Wow," was an expression many correctional personnel and prisoners recited in private after watching Annie in action. She had mastered the technique of drinking you in with her eyes and holding you in state of suspended animation until she was done with you. But some of us saw Annie when she behaved like a desperate junkie, with large glassy eyes and thin pyramid-shaped brows that stayed put even when she frowned.

Raves, Club Drugs, and Murder

It's unclear when Annie started trafficking in drugs or when she became financially involved, but age twenty seems to be the time when she took control of Lorrie's life and her associates, got rid of her first husband, Barry, and neither Lorrie nor Tanya ever said no.

Annie became an intricate part of Lorrie's life, and it could be assumed that Annie, because of the way she operated, developed a sexual relationship with Lorrie. However, how she tells it, it was Tanya who actually delivered sexual satisfaction to Lorrie, while Annie and Lorrie's children watched television in another room. Nonetheless, it was clear that Annie wanted more than just Lorrie's attention, home, and criminal contacts. Annie demanded "Lorrie's being," and took it. Through Lorrie's contacts, Annie eventually met Lenz, a state trooper who patrolled the eastern section of the state near the beach. He was fascinated with Annie's charm and mesmerized by her age and her eyes. But it was Tanya who had a sexual relationship with him. To manipulate him into acceding to her list of demands, Annie set it up for one of Lorrie's underage daughters to meet him at a motel. Tanya delivered the child. Lenz became so frustrated with the young girl's inability to satisfy him, he begged Tanya to finish him off through oral sex. Tanya held the child with one hand as she accommodated Lenz. Annie emerged from the closet, snapped a photo with her cell phone, and sent it to her e-mail.

Apparently Lenz was going through a midlife crisis and Tanya made him feel invincible. Things worked out for Lenz and he got his wish—he was in love with Tanya. She made him feel like a king. Strings were linked to the relationship, and Lenz hooked up "his loving girlfriend" and her Annie, with a Jamaican drug trafficker whom he had stopped on the coast during a police sweep. Annie explained to Lenz that she and Tanya would purchase rave drugs. Months later, Annie clarified the relationship to Lenz: "We're going to sell some product on the coast to our college girlfriends and need you to protect our asses." There was some back and forth on the subject, but Lenz was out-manned in more ways than one; and he knew that Annie possessed the photo that could send him to prison. Further, he was in too deep with Tanya. Annie wrote, "I think he thought protecting our asses meant he would get our asses and our girlfriends' asses too. He was thinking with another part of his anatomy."

Annie became a serious rave-club drug trafficker and financier. She described raves as a "high energy, all-night dance party with real fast music with a hard beat and laser shows, don't forget the laser shows." Tanya and Annie's earnings, which were originally bankrolled by the money earned from theft and remortgaging Lorrie's home, helped Annie get started. Lorrie signed the papers for Annie's apartment in a college town, some sixty miles from where Annie lived with her son and husband; and another residence on the Atlantic shore near a yacht club. Often Annie's raves were on secluded beaches, aboard pleasure crafts, and in the mansions that towered above the towns and beaches.

"And yes, Lenz was blessed with so much young ass that the poor darlin' was suffocating on fresh ass. I saw to that. But he and his little friends [other law enforcement officers] had all the ass they wanted."

Annie's Dr. Jekyll and Mr. Hyde Lifestyles

In many respects, Annie lived a Dr. Jekyll and Ms. Hyde lifestyle. To those who knew the real Annie, she was deeply disturbed, generally high on illegal substances (but as a matter of trivia, Annie never used her own product, the club drugs), dangerous and sexual, but highly functional. It is hard to imagine what Annie did at home after she married the man she would murder. Her older sister, Angela (prison social service providers often meet family members, especially of prisoners who are in a program or treatment), described Annie as a homebody who hated to go out, even to the food store. Angela once remarked, "You'd think she was a robot *Stepford Wives* from the movies. Yep, when she was a young girl she did things, but once she found Jesus, she changed. I don't think she has a bad bone in her body."

Few individuals accepted Annie's dark side until well past her trial and conviction. Years later, some said that Annie was innocent of Larry Jordan's murder, and that she was framed by some mysterious bad guy who held a grudge against Larry. And those other infractions of the law, which included selling drugs and running a chop-shop, couldn't have happened. What many townsfolk and her family members revealed was that like most predatory criminals, Annie worked hard to fit in with her community while conducting another life.

Annie successfully led two lives: one as a homemaker and loving mother, a daughter, and a sister; and a second one as a ruthless drug trader who used sex, violence, and a quick wit to corner the club drug trade along a stretch of the interstate, from her home to where two universities were located, as well as several high-tech corporate giants. When Annie and Tanya went to work—she told everyone that she worked for an airport shuttle service, trying to help her husband make ends meet—she dropped her son at her parents' ranch or with Lorrie, changed cars, and drove the sixty miles to her apartment. There she dressed in her rave clothes and peddled drugs, wearing an endless little smile, her eyes saying she loved only you.

The vehicles Annie drove eventually wound up at the chop shop, which Annie and her chop-shop boyfriend operated. It was alleged he knew nothing of her husband, her drug trade, or Lenz. It was likely that Lenz knew that Annie's husband was a local police officer, and he might have thought this knowledge gave him some control over Annie. It didn't.

Because Larry Jordan was a local municipal patrol officer, one thought is that the chances officially or unofficially of crossing paths with any of Annie's suppliers, clients, or accomplices was slim. Also, Annie had several sets of identification, including driver's licenses and picture identifications from the universities where she sold drugs. Photographs of Annie dolled-up when she trafficked drugs look like another person, compared to the woman I saw in prison.

Annie's Partner and Accomplices

The heavy hitting story lines of tattooed, shoot-'em-up drug kingpins as portrayed in popular TV dramas are nothing like Annie and her rave-club drug trade. Her business depended on her expertise in reading and manipulating people; her financial support to fund rave events, which often were attended by hundreds of partygoers; and on her partner, Lenz who protected her, kept her ahead of local police raids, and his associates provided secrecy and muscle. Most often the local cops were under the impression that a few preppy kids were letting go at college parties, and that drugs were incidental. None of those officers were close enough to the action to realize the players or the extent of the activities. Some of Lenz's associates were obsessed with sex, and Annie arranged for college girls to "go down on the cops." Neither Lenz nor any of his associates realized that the drug business they protected was a high stakes enterprise producing extravagant lifestyles, as well as degradation and corruption of the worst sort. They never realized the major role they played in Annie's business, let alone the disgrace they brought to hard-working officers across the country.

Lenz was obsessed with Annie. On one occasion, he was so enraged with lust for Annie that he entered a rave party, something he never had done, and sought her out. In his patrol car, she refused to have intercourse with him, but offered oral sex as a compromise. She rapidly aroused him, but then stopped before the "happy ending," as she called it, forcing Lenz to finish the job himself. She laughed and snapped another photo of him with his penis in his hand as he sat in his trooper Crown Vic. "He never learned, the dumb cop," Annie said. As she walked back to the party, she said over her shoulder, "You will never enter my parties or my mouth again. After that, it was clear who was in charge." She said later, "I controlled those big bad cops with my little lips. They were such big babies and dogs, but then most men are—dogs. After that, I told the sweet officer what I expected of him and he performed well as a dog. He and Tanya were two dogs in a peapod."

This incident reinforces her predatory evolution, from dropping a pot of boiling water to scooping water from it, to using children and her best friend to exploit a state trooper and his associates, to murder and destruction. How many lives she afflicted is unknown, but considering all the players involved with her enterprises, the count is huge. Yet it is unlikely that many knew the incredible amount of corruption she visited upon everyone in her path.

Lenz was apprehended after Annie was prosecuted for murder, and is currently serving a life sentence in a state penitentiary. Lenz was married with three children prior to his arrest and conviction. He never revealed his drug suppliers or accomplices. Annie's case was eligible for the death penalty (because she killed a police officer), but since she produced sufficient evidence to indict Lenz, the capital punishment option was removed from her case. I spoke with one of the prosecutors for Annie's case, who said that if Anne's case continued at trial, it would have taken only one juror to think Annie was too cute and too young to commit cold blooded murder. During the trial, Anne accepted a guilty plea with the possibility of parole in 12 years. The prosecutor offered the plea because there would have been a complete investigation into police command, police officers, and business operators, which might have resulted in many prominent individuals dragged off to jail. Maybe the prosecutor wasn't ready for Anne's case and all of its implications, or maybe the jurisdiction didn't have the funds to conduct a massive investigation or to complete a trial of that magnitude.

Prison

What you already know about Annie is that at the time of her imprisonment, she was twenty-four years old, a high school graduate, twice married and with one child. She was convicted of first-degree murder through a plea bargain. She was forty-four years of age when released from prison. Annie had committed other crimes for which she was never prosecuted, primarily because no one knew she had committed those fouls act—or maybe they didn't want to know. Annie has a duel addiction to heroin and antidepressants (prescribed by prison health services), and was also an alcoholic prior to imprisonment. It is likely that Annie was addicted to cocaine when she arrived at the women's prison, but cocaine is not as available to prison populations. Annie was placed on suicide watch more than once. Although she often broke the rules, she was not written up because she talked her way out of disciplinary action. She learned which custody personnel wrote up prisoners and which ones don't. She has not been placed on restriction (off-limit areas in the prison visited by the general population), but has been put in segregation a few times (see Annie's Journal Account below). Her general health is good to fair. She sleeps and naps less than three hours in a twenty-four hour period. Indicators are that when she was a free woman, her sleep patterns were similar.

Drugs and Motivation

Because of Annie's appearance when first imprisoned, her intelligence, and her quick wit she was stereotyped as just another sassy teenager. She looked amazingly younger than her age and her behavior rarely betrayed her ruthless experiences. What was learned about Annie was that she remained thin and youthful when she abused drugs. Her clothes size was XS, or 0 or a 2. As she aged and continued to snort heroin, she maintained her sassy teenager appearance. When Annie abused drugs, her drive to accomplish merged with her lethal personal style creating an Annie who is dangerous at any age, yet drugs or more to the point the lack of drugs played a primary role in her trigger which is best characterized as a pleasure seeker. She sought excitement, which includes surprising or shocking her victims by first overwhelming them with charm and then viciously attacking them. However, when Annie abused drugs, she doesn't appear to be high nor does she first resort to violence; sex is her weapon of choice although she rarely receives satisfaction from sexual relationships, she wrote. While in prison, everyone recognized when Annie abused drugs because she became pathetically thin and took on the role of a sophisticated lady during interactions with inmates and custody personnel alike. Days before visitations with her family members she dolled up and snorted a few fatty lines of heroin. The important finding here is that Annie has always possessed the capability and the ambition to terrorize, exploit, and murder others but these traits are more persistent when she is *straight* (drug free).

39

Hidden within her is a person who, at times, re-enacts altercations she has had with others. She mentally verbalizes conversations between herself and others, over and over and over again. This give-and-take internal discussion I call emotional flooding. Annie's emotional flooding goes on for hours resulting in a lack of sleep. Often Annie sleeps less than three hours in a given twenty-four hour period.

When Annie is drug free, her salient patterns of behavior can be best characterized as *compulsive*. She possesses few personal boundaries and attempts to alleviate a psychological disadvantage or what I refer to as Annie's altered state of consciousness. When she is drug free she studies her social world with an intense obsession to over perform. To say that Annie is a high achiever when straight is not enough. She focuses on the process of her behavior rather than its morality. Annie decides what encounters are volatile, as opposed to the circumstance. She can interpret a peaceful exchange as volatile.

Obviously as you can imagine from the above descriptions, Annie is most volatile and lethal when abstaining from drugs (and probably alcohol). Incredible as it sounds, drug abuse seems to subdue her urges toward violence. During alcohol or drug withdrawal, when she demonstrates behavior that can be best characterized as dysfunctional and unstable. Her weight escalates, her patience vanishes, and she is highly volatile. One guess is that she murdered Officer Larry Jordan when she was abstaining from drugs.

Annie's Journal

I have paraphrased the following accounts that Annie wrote in her journal:

"Maxed-out" is a phrase linked to the completion of a maximum sentence. Some of us have an unusual maxed-out date: a body bag. Any person given a life sentence has a maximum sentence of death. One must die or be paroled or max-out by their own hand. It was time for me to max-out. My depression resulted from several weeks of being on a natural high, awaiting the outcome of my appeal on my sentence. Cold news. "Turned down," the notice said. How would I deal with this news? I'm a lifer. I first turned to God, but the anger inside me pushed him away from me. I could feel the tension in my neck and shoulders.

Something was wrong inside me. I talked to other inmates, but they all had the same response—"Deal with it, girl." If only I found one person to listen to me and help me with my troubles. The depression sank low in my stomach as if I swallowed a thousand pound anchor and was tearing at my insides. I cried every night. The pain wouldn't go away. Calling home wouldn't help. I refused to see any visitors too. I needed to escape. I was desperate. I couldn't pray, eat, or go to the bathroom. Cleaning everything became an obsession and everyone seemed to know how to light my fuse. I went to in-group but that was crazy. I sat on the floor listening to everyone's problems and they all sounded like me. I tried to talk to God, but the only one listening was the evil one. He scooped me up and took me away by giving me three traps. The first trap was my parents who now have custody of my son, Andrew. They threatened to kill me—they found someone inside the prison and they paid them to ice me. They refused to bring Andy to visit me because I was trash. I wasn't like the others who had HIV or mersa [an acronym for methicillin-resistant Staphylococcus aureus; a staph that causes open, oozing scores). My mom told the authorities that she knew I was dealing inside and the [prison's] first-response unit searched my bunk area several times. The drug thing bothered me because I'm an addict with a very strong addictive personality. I know that and so does everyone else.

The second trap picked up on the drugs. My tight muscles pushed my tension even further, and that sent me flying to the infirmary. The doctor prescribed Flexeril [a muscle relaxant closely related to tricyclic antidepressants]. Although my body was recovering, I wasn't. I used it for two days and then Benadryl three times a day and Naprosyn [which contains naproxen, a nonsteroidal anti-inflammatory drug] for thirty days. It only took one dose of Flexeril to kick in my addiction, which quickly consumed my thoughts and actions. I began to smile again. I knew my ray of sunshine was chemically induced, but everyone told me I looked good. My addiction loved those encouraging comments and Satan had another victory. I was his.

Sinking deeper into the pills and the love of the guards and inmates was a huge green light. I felt good. I began missing in-group and classes. Truth is, while my prescription called for a certain amount each day, I didn't need to take them all and at the end of seven days, I had four pills left. My weight fell and I was around 110 pounds and I felt good.

But my descent was swift, so I needed to stay up. For my own sake, and realizing the eventual outcome, I requested mental health treatment. The officer on duty gave me a referral sheet and tried to talk me out of completing the form. I went to my room and wondered about my next move. I sat down and stared at the form for what seemed like forever. I didn't know what to write. I wanted my head back—the tension and my headaches and the anchor in my stomach were unbearable. I don't even remember the last I went to the bathroom or if I even had my period last month or this month. I filled out the stupid form and got my answer in the morning through the guard—unless Annie is going to hurt herself, we can't see her right now. Once alone, I swallowed my pills for the day and the ones I saved and bite my wrists until there was blood everywhere. I was scared but I couldn't see my son, I had no one to talk to, and mental health, my only salvation, said no. I opened my eyes in the infirmary and was told that mental health would see me now, but I had to sign up and the first available appointment was in three days. My wrists were bandaged and I was strapped down to the bunk for the next day or two.

Finally, I got to go to mental health and begged them to see me. The girl made an appointment with me and I wiped the running tears from my face, thanking her. Now could I wait three hours? On my way to my dorm I had a confrontation with some of the girls from west wing, my mortal enemies. The next thing I knew I was in the captain's office explaining my case and my appointment with mental health. He called them, only to discover that I didn't have an appointment and that I was rude when I was there. It was the "hole" for me for three days, but it might as well have been a death penalty. Once released I flipped out, and searched for the girls I had the problem with and choked one of them unconscious until a guard pulled me off. I bite her too. That bought me another thirty days in the hole. Alone in that dark place without medication, my son, or a god, I went mad.

When Annie recovered she worked for the state tourist board inside the prison facility, four days a week, five hours a day. She answered telephone inquiries from people interested about visiting the state where she was imprisoned. Prisons attempt to provide employment and training opportunities for inmates. One day Annie mentioned to me that one-half of her wage of $7.50 an hour was deducted by the department of corrections to pay her keep.

Pregnancy

During Annie's fourth year in prison, she was raped and impregnated, but she couldn't identify her attacker. No one was ever charged with the violation. Some speculated that Annie wanted to become pregnant to help in her appeal of her case. After the appeal board denied her, she fell, causing the death of her six-month-old fetus.

As shown above, Annie is a highly vindictive person. During two different in-group sessions at the prison, another prisoner openly rejected Annie's thoughts about something. The prisoner never attended in-group again. I inquired about the missing prisoner, and a custody officer informed me that the inmate had been hospitalized due to a fall. Also, in prison Annie had a partner, a pretty, small woman with long stingy hair who continually showed signs of abuse—broken wrists, broken arms, bite marks on her chin, black eyes, and small bruises here and there. More than likely, Tanya, too, had been continually battered by Annie.

Some Observations

Newspaper reports show that a Jamaican gang was the primary drug distributor on the two campuses where Annie eventually ruled, but the leader was apprehended by a state police drug sting and sent to prison. The primary arresting officer was, yes, State Trooper Lenz. Two of the Jamaican's soldiers were discovered decomposing on the beach near Cape Fear, North Carolina. Some say it was Annie, Tanya, and Lenz who did it, but no one really knows for sure.

Then, too, a year before Annie was arrested for Larry Jordan's murder, Tanya became attached to Lenz. Annie probably realized that it was only a matter of time before Lenz would figure out how to control Tanya. A week after Tanya told Annie she might be in love with Lenz, Tanya died from a drug overdose. Experienced drug users aren't as likely as an inexperienced user to OD from a familiar product. It would not be a far stone's toss to suggest that Annie compelled Tanya to consume more drugs than her body could handle and those drugs were probably laced with something that led to Tanya's demise.

Then, too, there remains a serious question about Annie's first husband, Barry, who lived at the ranch with Annie. He was never seen by anyone, including his own parents, after his disappearance. No official files show that a divorce ever took place. Annie said Barry went to Las Vegas and faxed documents, which she signed and returned, never thinking of keeping a copy. Barry's parents are convinced that Annie and Tanya buried him somewhere on the horse trails. If Annie was never divorced from Barry, Larry Jordan's estate never belonged to her. That is a moot point, however, since Larry's parents froze his assets after her arrest. The state surrendered her son Andrew to the permanent care of her parents.

What of Annie's assets from her profitable business and real estate? She said she had none, but the way she bought people in prison suggests otherwise. Annie is a clever woman, and probably way ahead of any tax collector. But in looking at her recent prison photograph, she doesn't possess a youthful, sexy body anymore, and her brains are probably rotted out from drugs. That suggests that violence remains her single tool, along with her stashed cash—wherever it might be. Yes, I asked her, but she turned the tables on me and asked, "Why? I'm not enough for you, doc?" and gave me a coy look, as any charmer would. However, other prisoners and prison personnel suggested that Annie continued to run drugs after being imprisoned. It is possible that custody officers, prisoners, or social service personnel were helping her. Traders with that sort of expertise don't change spots once incarcerated. One drug dealer told me that he behaved in prison so that he would be reclassified and reassigned to a lesser security prison, which would open the door to a thousand new clients. Monthly, one of Annie's *alleged* cousins was her regular visitor. Prison documents show that he was a CPA from a large accounting firm from a distant municipality, suggesting that he flew to the prison to visit Annie. His vehicle was registered to a rental agency at the airport. When the two of them met, he did all of the talking in almost a whisper. Her only contribution was a yes or a no, judging by her facial features, and her eyes were always fixed either on him or any correctional personnel that came close to them.

As for her "happy endings"—"Twice with Tanya and both times by accident, bless the little slut's most blessed body part—her tongue."

CHAPTER 3
Brandeis the Sad High School Teacher

Introduction

Brandeis Pettet Anderson was twenty-eight years of age, with one son, when arrested. Through a plea bargain process, she was sentenced to seven years in a state penitentiary for unlawful possession of a controlled substance. Brandeis had mousy hair framing a pretty, friendly face that sparkled if you could catch her small smile. Most often she locked her eyes on the ground rather than at anyone, listening to the miniature voice in her head. She earned a bachelor's degree in education from an Ivy League school and graduated *summa cum laude*.

Valedictorian Address

In high school, Brandeis Anderson was the valedictorian of her graduating class and was fluent in French. Her valedictory to her classmates in the gymnasium on a rainy May afternoon included the customary thanks to parents for support and guidance, to teachers and advisers for integrity and knowledge, and to classmates who helped one another. She discussed current events and future ambitions of the graduating class, as they proceeded to occupations, the military, trade schools, and college. She left them with an Erma Bombeck quote, first in French: "*Il prend beaucoup de courage pour montrer vos rêves à quelqu'un d'autre.*" Translating, she said, "It takes a lot of courage to show your dreams to someone else." Brandeis added, "But Erma Bombeck also mentioned that dreams have only one owner at a time. That's why dreamers are lonely." She paused, glanced quickly at the 125 graduates seated on the gym floor, and then up at the audience in the bleachers. "Those of you who will dare to dream, be prepared to like yourself for what you are and what you will become."

Brandeis liked herself for what she had become – a valedictorian, a dreamer, and a single yet lonely being; yet she acknowledged that as far as she could remember there were "elements within my spirit that pulled, taunted, and insisted upon other compassionate outcomes that I couldn't figure out. It was a matrix of sorts of my design," she wrote in her prison journal. Through it all, Brandeis never grasped that she would become: a heroin addict, a child molester, and a convicted felon. On the plus side, Brandeis worked relentlessly hard and had an amazing intellectual aptitude. Therefore, it was "difficult to accept that I also held a propensity toward self-destruction and the exploitation of less fearless individuals than myself," she added.

French Teacher

Brandeis's parents were pleased with the quality performance of their only child, who rarely wanted for anything since birth. The only time they had any doubt about her was at her criminal conviction, but even then they rarely attended court. They continue to doubt the indictment and the rumors about their daughter. Yet it should be mentioned that her parents weren't particularly pleased that she wanted to become a French high school teacher, a goal she had proclaimed in middle school, first to her teachers, her classmates, and eventually to her parents, when they reviewed a presentation she had made in class about future occupation. Her parents, both from large families, were unable to have more children, and they tried desperately to devote their lives to Brandeis. Their careers, however, always took precedence over their family life.

Brandeis's Parents

Brandeis's mother—the Pettet side of the family—was a successful corporate real estate agent who traveled the globe, spoke three or four languages, including French. Occasionally Brandeis and her mother—whom she called *Maman*, French for mama—had conversations in French, much to her father's annoyance. Her mother also had a law degree from Stanford University. Her dad, also a graduate from a prominent law school, was a patent lawyer who worked for a large law firm headquartered in Washington DC. For the eight years prior to Brandeis's conviction, he headed a local office comprised of almost a hundred employees, including twenty attorneys. His office was a few miles from Brandeis's childhood home, yet despite that, he was an infrequent visitor to the family's old-world estate, surrounded by crystal blue pools and breathtaking gardens.

Holidays in the Catskills

Brandeis's holidays were spent at their summer home in the Catskills, and when she was younger, she often had friends join her. Her priorities changed once she entered middle school [seventh grade] in the private girl's school she attended. Brandeis now spent most of her time studying and little time with friends. Her parents encouraged her to reduce her social time to maintain her grades. Her self-imposed isolation from friends continued right up to graduation.

Home Alone

Most often, Brandeis was alone in the family estate with a nanny whom Brandeis didn't care for. When her father was there, dinners were often interrupted by phone calls. Maman would drop in, but was less likely to spend time with Brandeis. She would be in her office located in the small guesthouse just opposite the pool grotto, behind a waterfall. "Maman had no idea what my school uniform looked like," Brandeis wrote in her journal. "She didn't know that I liked Frosted Flakes and bananas for breakfast, thin-crust pizza with lots of cheese and a diet soda for lunch, and any kind of Chinese food with hard noodles for supper. Maman had no idea what my favorite colors are, what books I read, who I dated. Well, no one for some time, or when I had my period. But she demanded that I respect and love her, and of course I do." I can imagine that as she wrote those lines, her small chin would lock in place and she would stare at the words in disbelief. This writing process was a time of discovery for Brandeis, and often she crossed words out as if frustrated. Other times she drew pictures of birds and other flying things on the right hand side of the page. Always to the right, never to the left. It might not be important, but on any given page, there were more than five individual words and at least two sentences crossed out. One reason for my concern was that few of the other participants ever crossed out anything. Of all the journals and papers from prisoners I had seen, Brandeis' was the most unusual and the most complex.

University, Scholarships, and Joanna

Brandeis was offered full scholarships from various colleges and universities while in her junior year of high school. She was interested in two schools, and the one she liked the least was pushing for her to make a decision before entering her senior year. If she did decide, she would have that settled once and for all, and she could take high school courses that would prepare her for some of the college courses. She would also be able to transfer some high school credits for college credit hours if the college approved.

The colleges had their own reasons for pursuing girls like Brandeis. Her parents and the corporations that employed them represented excellent resources for endowments. It was a win-win situation for any university. They enrolled girls like Brandeis, and her parents' checkbook or guilt-money came with them.

During one campus visit, Brandeis's mother went with her for a tour of the campus. Brandeis thought it awesome that her mother took an interest and had actually made time to visit the campus with her. A private luncheon was planned by the recruiters, for Brandeis and her mother and for another candidate, a French girl named Joanna and her father. They were from Nice. The recruiters felt that the two candidates and their parents would connect. Joanna's father, a retired Air Force pilot for the French military, was the president of an international commercial air carrier. Brandeis, Joanna, and both of their parents engaged in a French conversation that the recruiters couldn't understand, and the deal was sealed.

During their conversation, Joanna mentioned the panoramic views of the sea and the hills from her bedroom. She added that sometimes if she looked hard enough, she could see the ornate ships of the Arab "oilty" in the Monaco harbor. Her father explained that he had found the property, a remarkable chateau, after leaving the military. The Batiments de France, the French historical society, agreed to assist financially in its renovation.

By the time lunch was over, Brandeis and Joanna agreed to sign letters of intention to enroll in the university. Their parents shook hands and seemed pleased with their daughters' decisions. Joanna's father turned to Brandeis and said, *"Venez s'il vous plaît nous visitent, mon cher. Nous avons beaucoup de chambres à coucher supplémentaires, mais personne avec la vue de Joanna."* (Please come visit us, my dear. We have many extra bedrooms, though none with Joanna's view.) Brandeis's mother whispered to Joanna's father, *"Oh, j'irai faire, mon homme doux."* (Oh, I shall, my sweet man.) And the foursome wandered off, pleased with the day and their new friends.

Shared Dorm Room

Brandeis and Joanna shared a dorm room and bathroom and a life of isolation from their parents. The room had but one closest. Joanna was about the same size as Brandeis [size 2], so the girls had "sharewear, with the exception of jeans," because Brandeis was taller. There were other positive things, Brandeis remembered. "We had similar grades, similar scholarships, interests in education, and Joanna was an only child, too, which meant we both understood what being a spoiled rotten kid was all about. She was cute, with longer dark hair than mine, but she had a prolonged smile and very bright eyes that sought a person out and made them feel important. She made others laugh even when they were strangers. I liked that girl the instant I saw her, but she had these mascaraed eyelashes, like spider legs. Once I got over those eyelashes, things were fine. I didn't find Joanna annoying."

Brandeis wrote, "I'm a clean freak and tidy person with my stuff and my bod. Little did I know when I met this girl that she knew nothing about hygiene, and I would have to teach the doucheless dirt bag how to keep herself clean. She turned out to be a slob. A slob who made others happy with her laughter, but nothing organized in her room, clothes everywhere, clean and dirty clothes in the same pile and shoes were stuffed in her dresser drawers." Brandeis said that Joanna learned how to be a slob from her father. "Isn't that just like men, slobs." Joanna's mother died when Joanna was born, and her father never remarried.

College Life

Brandeis and Jolo [Joanna's nickname] shared a dorm room their first two years in college. Jolo cleaned herself up at Brandeis's insistence and eventually removed her shoes from the dresser. Brandeis's rule was that Jolo could not sharewear any of her clothes until she had her act together. Brandeis said, "NGL [not going to lie], every so often, Jolo pulled flip-flops from her drawers with one hand and panties with the other." Jolo followed Brandeis's lead in those matters, but it was Jolo who was in control when the girls went to parties or were around other students. "Jolo was a dick magnet but preferred manthers [older men who preyed on younger women] who spend lots of cash on her and me."

Brandeis wrote that "Jolo the queen bitchhh" described Brandeis as a "low-functioning drunk," and that she was "so reserved and totaling passive" after two cans of beer. Little did Jolo know, Brandeis clarified, "How passive I really am. I go out of my way to avoid people. I don't know what's wrong with me. I bunch myself up and am afraid to get involved with people—well, boys!" For instance, when Brandeis went to church, she avoided others when the congregation greeted one another as a regular part of the weekly ceremony. "They're shaking hands and welcoming people around them, and I fell to my knees and pretended to pray so I wouldn't have to touch anyone. How lame is that?" When Brandeis was alone on campus, it was because she designed it that way. She said she felt uncomfortable around other students unless Jolo was present.

It was Jolo who eventually convinced Brandeis to dye her hair blond. Being blond made a decisive difference with boys, Brandeis found. "They loved me. What a difference! But pushing out my 'blond' when I talked to boys was a big-time challenge."

One time, a graduate assistant at the college named Tim offered the girls a sample of china-white [heroin]. They thought it was an exciting experience. Tim was fixated on having sex with both girls, but that never happened. At least, Brandeis doesn't think it ever happened, because of her "alpha male allergy."

The girls survived college in part because they each provided different skills. Brandeis wrote, "I was the brains and *mon chéri* Jolo, the brawn for the streets. When she met guys, it was like she had a brain-bleach or something. Strangely enough, our 'friends' started at the same time, but Jolo's lasted forty-eight hours longer. She was my bud for life." Brandeis drew a smiley face at the end of that sentence, and yes, the smiley face was on the right side of the paper.

One thing Brandeis learned in college was that she didn't care for the taste of beer or liquor, but wine—especially sweet white French wine—agreed with her taste buds. "My capacity wasn't too great. But at least when I was high, I didn't redline [avoid] everybody."

She went on, "Girls are catty and jealous of each other, but Jolo and I were able to keep focus without getting ourselves or each other into trouble, except for the drug thing and my conviction. Sometimes my little Jolo could be funny and loud, and sometimes totally disrespectful, but she never disrespected me or my family when—or should I say, if—they came to visit. My dad took us to great restaurants around town, and it was a great relief because I hated the food in the college cafeteria. Their food was jammed with carbs, carbs, and more carbs. Jolo's father came around, too, and treated us to great seafood, and sometimes delicious French desserts. But I really didn't eat any of them. Maybe a bite or two. Jolo said that her father was always telling her what to do, and she wanted to please him more than anybody in the world."

Off-Campus Apartment

In their third year of college, the girls moved into a spacious off-campus apartment. They recruited a third roommate, Gwen, and hired housekeepers to maintain the apartment and their clothes. Each girl had her own bathroom, bedroom, and closet. Gwen's small bedroom was off the kitchen and similar to Jolo's and Brandeis's rooms in that it had a little balcony. Gwen was shorter than her roommates, and as assertive as Joanna and almost as bright as Brandeis. She had short straight red hair and shining blue eyes, which apparently was common among her family members. Their pictures graced her cluttered bedroom walls, alongside posters of her favorite bands, Tortoise and Isotope 218. The girls battled over parking. Each owned a sporty vehicle, and fighting for parking places was an ongoing frustration. Jolo rented garage space and parked her vehicle most of the time. She got around using public transportation. Brandeis said it was "disgusting" to use "random public transportation." Gwen had little or no opinion on the topic. She usually remained neutral on any of Jolo and Brandeis's differences. Gwen understood food-chain rules and stayed in her own world, unless Brandeis or Jolo invited her to participate.

Most often the girls studied and read most of the time. Only twice in the first two years either Jolo or Brandeis brought a boy "home." Tim was invited to the apartment. He and the girls smoked grass in Brandeis's room, but then Gwen went to her own room. "Tim and I just lay there in my bed doing nothing. Jolo was behind me, breathing hard on my neck and holding me. Tim scooted closer and tried to kiss me, but I turned away. Then he lifted his head to kiss Jolo, who softly told Tim to get out. I said nothing. He was never invited back." Jolo said she would have jumped in with the two of them, but "I would have been there for you, not him. Can't envision a boy humping me when I only want to make you smile. That's like disloyalty."

Brandeis isn't sure when Jolo understood that betraying her in any way would "fire-up my juices. I totally had no clue where my little *chéri* got that idea about me," Brandeis wrote. "But she's right, you know. I would have torn her sweet clit if she messed up that time." The problem with Tim, Brandeis explained, was that he never tried to have sex with Brandeis. That was why she didn't want his kiss. Brandeis had brief encounters with other boys, and her opinion was that "I don't care if they say they like my hair, adore my body, or are trying to up their bragging rights. If they don't smooth talk me and aren't sensitive to my needs, they get nothing from me," she said at long last in-group. "I gave him what he deserved—nothing—and Jolo had my back. That's the way it's supposed to be," she said with a small laugh.

Note: the in-group leader didn't catch the humor, but the twenty-four women prisoners shared some snickers, quick small talk, fast body gestures, and wide grins.

Teachers and Drugs

Brandeis, Gwen, and Jolo were all in the educational department of the university, although their interests varied. Brandeis's interest was French; Jolo's was math; and Gwen, natural science with an emphasis on horticulture and biology. During their senior year, they each tutored other students and participated in the student teaching practicum at a local public school. On several occasions the girls smoked heroin from a glass bong. They sat around the small table in the kitchen of their apartment, the door locked and their cell phones turned off. It was, Brandeis said, "very homey, but without my cell it was like death until I caught the wave that floated me off." They talked the night away, or at least seemed to. Brandeis and her roommates felt safe using drugs, because they were not injecting them. They made a pact with one another that they never would inject dope into their veins. "The funny thing is that in college we never called it dope."

Holidays and Christmas in France

Their first year in college, Jolo discovered that Brandeis's parents were not going to be around for Thanksgiving or the Christmas holidays. She spoke to her father about it, and he again personally invited Brandeis to their home in Nice, France. For the next three years, Brandeis traveled with Jolo to the south of France for the Christmas holidays. Jolo also brought Brandeis home during other holidays, including spring break. The girls enjoyed the beaches, shopping, and road trips to exciting places. They quickly jumped into Nice's incredible nightlife at the amazing international hotels along the coast. Sometimes the girls partied in Monaco, and Jolo seemed to know everyone and everyone wanted to be seen with her. In the harbor, too, there were fabulous yachts of all descriptions belonging to oil tycoons, international celebrities, and royalty.

On one occasion, aboard a fantastic cruiser docked at Monaco Bay,

Brandeis ran into her mother, who had known Brandeis was visiting Jolo. They were excited to see each other. Brandeis, Jolo, and Brandeis's mother spent the remainder of the night together, celebrating, dancing, and talking. "It was one of my most treasured moments," Brandeis reported.

Jolo loved Brandeis's mother and always asked about her, but it was clear that the relationship between Jolo and her father was nothing similar to the relationship between Brandeis and her parents. During the evening, Jolo asked Brandeis' mother, "Please help me understand. This is the most time you've spent with my best friend, whom I love, in a long time. Never having a mother, I don't understand it. Why wouldn't you spend more time with her?"

"She was a difficult child. Demanding. Crying. Screaming. Never a moment of peace. Always even before she was born, fighting and demanding her own. I would give her anything but my soul. I stayed out of her way. Now that's she such a lovely young lady, maybe things can change between us," was her answer.

Brandeis overheard their conversation, and upon hearing her mother's response, her brutality surfaced. "I'm motherless like Athena. Too late," she screamed in English, and struck her mother down with one slap. That was the last time she saw her mother until she married Robert, although Brandeis wrote that she didn't want her mother at her wedding.

Robert, Her Future Husband

Brandeis met Robert [everyone called him Bobby] Jones at the university. He was a graduate assistant and knew Tim, but wasn't his friend. Brandeis was in her third year of college when she realized that most boys meant little of what they said, and really said anything to get what they wanted—bragging rights about how many girls they'd slept with. Yet she was okay with that, and in many ways, she enjoyed their lies and foolishness. "I knew that all they wanted was to get off, so why let them do it alone." Brandeis knew that she was "easy," and that was why she loved Jolo. Jolo kept her focused. Brandeis admitted that drugs helped her hide her inability to get along with others. She felt, however, that she was strong enough and smart enough to control heroin. The girls went to parties, sometimes all-night raves, but Brandeis "hated those things until I used, largely because I felt uncomfortable, almost insecure, around other people unless I was waved out on heroin or some other good shit." Brandeis usually sought college boys who would not challenge her intellectually. When they tried, they lost. Yet, the use of heroin started what Brandeis called "a voluntary experiment" that sent her into a mind-set that challenged her more than her studies. Even after graduating, especially once imprisoned, Brandeis's behavior was not necessarily under her control when she was using drugs. "That's why I needed *mon chéri* Jolo."

Nonetheless, Brandeis could count on one hand the times she and Robert touched each other. Robert appeared to be sensitive to her needs, and she felt he was worthy of her time. He never "told me to do this or that," and she admired that and he took his time when they were in each other's arms. He seemed content just holding her and gave off no signs that he wanted more. "Most guys are slobs about it. Always pushing, pulling, and demanding." Robert was a pretty bright guy, although hardly an intellectual match for her. He was more Jolo's speed, because of a shared interest in math. Robert was a quiet, tall boy from the country, and his father was an architect. *Time* had published an article about his architectural designs. Brandeis and Robert hung around from time to time, but her studies and Jolo came first.

Marriage

A year out of college, when Brandeis was twenty-two, Robert reappeared in her life. After several dates, she brought up the idea of marriage, suggesting he must not love her since he hadn't proposed. Robert followed her lead and asked. Their wedding was at a country club, and four hundred guests attended, many of whom Brandeis didn't know. Jolo was the maid of honor and Gwen was one of two bridesmaids. Robert's sister was the other bridesmaid. Many of the guests were colleagues of her parents, and a few were Jolo's friends [some of whom Brandeis had never met]. Some were fellow teachers from the high school where Brandeis taught French, some were college friends. Only four or five of the guests went to high school with Brandeis.

Their honeymoon was a fantastic summer in Switzerland, with

extended side trips to Paris and Brussels. They were also guests at Jolo's father's estate overlooking the sea in Nice. Brandeis, Jolo, and Robert spent time at the Promenade des Anglais, which is at the heart of this international seaside city. Brandeis adored the line of cafés situated directly on the beach, and all of its a bustling activity, including the cyclists, runners, walkers, and Rollerbladders. It was very exciting, Brandeis said, and she was ready to move to Nice and live out the rest of her days there. Of course, she also wrote, being with Jolo held many rewards, but Brandeis did not qualify or quantify those rewards. Nor did she draw any pictures or cross out any words in that section. Nonetheless, it was time finally to return to America, because in less than five months, Brandeis would give birth to her child, Leroy.

At birth, Leroy was diagnosed with Down Syndrome and needed to eat a special diet, which Brandeis happily prepared. Brandeis believed she was responsible for Leroy's condition, because "Down Syndrome usually stems from the mother of the child. I think it was payback for messing with drugs." But Brandies knew that nothing done before or during pregnancy can cause Down Syndrome. She mentioned that Down's occurs in all races, social classes, and in all countries throughout the world. It can happen to anyone.

A year after Leroy's birth, Robert's National Guard battalion was ordered to the Mideast. Nine months later, a half-filled casket returned. Robert was buried with military honors in his hometown, a few hundred miles from where Brandeis and Leroy lived, at the insistence of his mother.

Brandeis Vacations with Jolo in the Bahamas

Brandeis reported that she had taken a short vacation to the islands during her summer break from teaching high school. She visited her husband's grave and left her child with Robert's parents prior to her vacation with Jolo. Jolo had won an all-expense vacation for two: airline tickets, a hotel suite, meals, beverages [including alcohol], and excursions for four days at a tropical casino in the Bahamas. Jolo was single, and she asked Brandeis to join her a week before the flight's departure. Although they arrived separately at the island's airport, a shiny limousine transported each of them to the hotel casino on the beach.

"It was a fabulous experience. Our suite overlooked a crystal blue ocean skirted by pure white sand. It was paradise. Appetizers like sautéed balsamic seasoned shrimp and black pepper crab dumplings prepared at poolside, and piña coladas topped with delicious fruit served from a bar in the middle of the pool. The desserts like crème anglaise were to die for."

Tanned, fat, and tired, "we were dressing to go home, when Jolo handed me panties with a pad, after I asked if I could chip in to pay for anything. What's this, I asked." Jolo told her that cocaine was hidden in the pad and to act normal. Things would move along well. Customs personnel were part of the drug-trafficking scheme. Brandeis wasn't certain if Jolo was kidding her about the cocaine. She said that she tried to get out of it, but Jolo reassured her that all would be fine. When they both returned home, they would get $5,000 each. Jolo said that she was in debt and needed money to pay her credit cards. She cried about how life sucked, and that she was caught up in problems that wouldn't go away unless she had the money. She couldn't tell her father because he would be disappointed in her continued shopping sprees.

"S'il vous plaît m'aider, mon amour. Je suis désespéré." (Please help me, my love. I'm desperate). Brandeis couldn't refuse her in her time of need, and after all, she had had the time of her life in the Bahamas.

On the flight home, Brandeis "visited the bathroom twice to dump the drugs down the toilet, but thought twice about it" and about the consequences to Jolo. "Imagine, flushing thousands of dollars' worth of drugs, and Jolo's sweet head would be served on a platter. I couldn't do that to my friend, but I never thought I'd get caught. I swore then and there that I would never be taken in again, even by my BFF."

After Brandeis's jet set down, things went well through customs, and she climbed into a taxi. She wondered how Jolo's flight had gone, but was so nervous, she forgot to call her. Jolo had said someone would contact Brandeis, and gave her a cell phone that she should throw away after the telephone call. The call never came. State troopers stopped the taxi and arrested Brandeis.

Criminal Conviction of Brandeis Andersen Jones

The conviction that brought Brandeis to prison was unlawful possession of a controlled substance. In the jurisdiction where she was apprehended, 750 milligrams is considered trafficking. Brandeis had a little less than 100 grams (around 3.5 ounces), which carried a sentence of five to twenty years, with five years the minimum mandatory that had to be served. The judge's sentence after a review of her PSI and a discussion with Brandeis, her attorney, and the prosecuting attorney was seven years and no early release. She actually was released after thirty-six months, but was re-confined months late because of drug possession.

The court believed that Brandeis was not drug trafficking, or at least that the prosecution had not produced evidence beyond a reasonable doubt that she had. However, in the jurisdiction in which Brandeis was prosecuted, the amount of drugs she transported dictated otherwise. Therefore, intent to distribute illegal substances and criminal conspiracy (an agreement or a kind of' partnership in criminal purposes, in which each member becomes the agent or partner of every other member) were used to leverage her plea of guilty.

There should have been many questions about Brandeis's activities, and one concern was that considering her occupation and academic achievements, how she could have been so naive as to accept around one hundred grams of drugs to transport to the US from her best friend, herself a teacher in France.

Presentence Investigation Report (PSI)

The investigators learned that Brandeis and Jolo had been guests at the resort in Bahamas. They learned Jolo boarded an Air Liberté flight from the Bahamas to Nice. Investigators were at a dead-end with Joanna, though. The French police suspected Joanna of being a drug mule (smuggler) yet because she was a French citizen they were reluctant to aid American law enforcement in an investigation of one of their own. State prosecutors decided to follow through with Brandeis, who was represented by a very experienced defense lawyer. The investigators were aware of her occupation, her husband's death, and her family's prominence in the community.

Transported to Prison

Brandeis remained handcuffed while the judge read her sentence—seven years to be served at the department of corrections. Brandeis had little clue what she would experience during the four-hour ride to the department of correction's intake center, and during her two weeks being processed at the reception center. But rarely would she have time to think about it. "I was so scared, I had no idea what would happen next."

Brandeis climbed into the oversized white van and was greeted by a hard-looking correctional officer, who shackled her ankles and chained her to the other offenders already sitting in the van. As Brandeis darted a look at the others, she realized that they were handcuffed, shackled to an iron loop set in the floor of the vehicle, and chained to one another. The driver and the guard in the passenger seat were separated from the inmates by a thick plastic shield that had several holes in it, apparently so they could listen to the prisoners. Another guard sat in the back of the van next to a toilet. No one said anything, and Brandeis's traveling companions looked deep in thought. The drive seemed to take forever, and the prisoners were without water or food. Later Brandeis would discover that most of the prisoners were thinking about having to leave their children, their homes, and their freedom. One prisoner asked if she could use the toilet, saying, "When ya gotta pee, ya gotta pee." The male guard in the back of the van unlocked her ankle restraint, and disconnected the chains that connected her to the other inmates. She raised her cuffed hands, but he said, "No." Because there was no curtain, everyone could watch her relieve herself, but only the guard kept his eyes on her. She easily raised her county-issued muumuu and sat down. When she returned from the toilet, the guard locked her ankles and reconnected her chains without saying a word. The sounds that lingered in the van were the spinning sounds of the tires rolling over a hot but mysterious highway. It was the middle of July, and the sun was especially bright. The van was air conditioned, but heavy perspiration still rolled down Brandeis's back.

She was prepared for the trip. She had done her homework and had secreted a few antidepressants in her pocket prior to being put in the van. Those sweet little capsules were in her mouth before she was turned over to the sheriff's department for the trip to the intake center.

She was very relaxed during the journey, thanks to her magic pills. She had also prepared two boxes filled with items she would need in prison, giving them to her parents to mail to her. Brandeis had checked the Department of Corrections' website for items that weren't considered contraband, made a few phone calls to get a better understanding of the regulations, and went on a buying spree. She bought, among other items, two sports bras (white, no lace, no underwire), sneakers, flip-flops, a denim sunflower dress, panties, peanut butter, canned fish, deodorant soap, shampoo, instant coffee, and lotion. She also purchased a small television set to be delivered a month after her arrival, and gave her folks $4,200.00 to be placed into her prison account at the rate of $50.00 a month, which was the prison limit. Prisoners were not allowed to have money, so she used those funds at the prison commissary.

Brandeis's Prison Intake Experience

The reception center, or intake process, was actually on the grounds of a male prison, but separated by a high fence and towers. The guards in those towers watched everything, even the dry wind, with hard, constantly moving eyes. Brandeis didn't count the number of women processed, but she thought thirteen or fourteen was a reasonable guess. They were told not to say a word unless asked a question by prison personnel. Brandeis wrote that two of the prisoners were black, and the rest were white except for one Spanish girl. Most of them were around her age, except two, who seemed to be around sixteen or seventeen years old. One of the prisoners was handicapped and very old, and required a metal walker to move around. If Brandeis guessed, she would have said that most of them looked like junkies, and two had deep-lined faces that Brandeis called an alcoholic's face. They were all fingerprinted and photographed.

One prisoner kept looking at Brandeis even after a guard told her to stop. She didn't stop looking until Brandeis said, "Baisez vous." (I kiss you.) The prisoner didn't understand Brandeis, but the guard yelled at the women to walk single file into a trailer that stood in front of the tall, forbidding prison. First, jewelry was collected, including wedding rings, and then they were ordered to remove their shoes and clasp their hands behind their backs. After their shoes were collected, they removed their socks, their muumuus, and their bras and underwear. All were told to line up between two rows of toilets and use the facilities, whether they needed to or not. The correctional officers and other prisoners observed them the entire time. If a prisoner wanted more than three sheets of toilet paper, she had to ask. When it was brought it to her, it was placed on the floor so she had to bend down to pick it up.

The prisoners took showers two at a time in lukewarm water. After drying, the ladies—that's what they were called—were told to hold out their hands, fingers spread to insure there was no contraband between them or under their nails. They were instructed to lift their breasts, comb through their hair with their fingers, rub their belly buttons, comb through their pubic hair, raise their arms, show the underneath of their feet, and separate each toe. Brandeis noticed that two of the prisoners had serious hair growing over large parts of their bodies, and one had a horrible scar, perhaps from an appendix operation that went bad. Two of the prisoners might have had breast implants, because their breasts were rigid.

The prisoners were instructed to face the wall, squat, and cough three times as an officer held a mirror under them, checking their vaginas for contraband. A female correctional officer wearing vinyl gloves conducted a full cavity search on two of the prisoners. Brandeis later learned they were probationers who had violated probation. Each prisoner's body was closely observed for scars, tattoos, and any other identifying marks, and the findings were entered into a computer.

After disinfectant was sprayed over every inch of their bodies (they were told to cover their eyes and keep their mouths shut), they were given pants that resembled scrubs without a drawstring and a top. They would not be issued undergarments until classification was completed (at-risk inmates had to be bare under their uniforms), white gym shoes (no socks until after classification), a bed roll (two sheets, two blankets, one pillowcase, one towel, one washcloth), and a small brown bag containing a tube of toothpaste, a toothbrush, Vaseline, roll-on deodorant, single-blade razors, and shampoo. The ladies walked single file from the trailer into the huge, cold building Brandeis had first seen upon her arrival. As they entered a room with rows of steel bunk beds, each inmate claimed a bed, broke out her bed roll, and fixed her bunk. During the night, although it was hard to tell which prisoners were crying and which calling on Jesus for help, many were also calling out names, presumably their partners' or children's names. In the middle of the night, the prisoner that had been staring at Brandeis caught her off guard and slapped her several times, drawing blood from her nose. She could have done more damage if another prisoner hadn't pulled them apart. Guards eventually intervened.

During the following two weeks, the prisoners were given a physical, including dental and eyes exams, and were tested for TB, HIV, and STDs. Brandeis's group was also given a psychological test: The Minnesota Multiphasic Personality Inventory test. Each of them was interviewed by a staff psychologist, and classification was determined over two days. Brandeis also completed an education test called the TABE (Test of Adult Basic Education) to measure her reading and math skills. Finally, the ladies were transported in a van from the reception center to the place they would call home for the duration of their sentence. The ride took a few hours, but it was hard to tell time, because no one had a watch and no one talked.

Brandeis's Addiction

What is known about Brandeis's youth, other than her intellectual capacity and her need to be alone, is that she had used Vicodin more than Dilaudid; and once imprisoned, heroin more than liquor. When she arrived at the women's prison, Brandeis had a dual addiction: her drug of choice was heroin, and she was also addicted to antidepressants. Antidepressants, such as Prozac and Zoloft, were new to the market at that time. Brandeis had to give up her old antidepressant prescriptions, and the DOC's mental health unit prescribed the new medications.

It would not be surprising if a psychologist advanced the idea that Brandeis had low self-esteem, little regard for herself (particularly since she was always on suicide watch), and that she was extremely passive when dealing with individuals in authority or the alpha-prisoners who dominated other prisoners. This thought could confirm what many correctional personnel thought about Brandeis at the time: she was an easy target. There is a *but*. "Screw her over, and it would be like feeding seven cobras and running out of food," said a correctional officer. Another added, "She gives the ladies prison-house recipes (on making alcohol) with one hand while her other hand tricks-out (deceives) their minds with the easy (suggesting her vulnerability) Brandeis' thing, but under all of it, she wants to be beaten and eaten so she can get her revenge." This latter thought suggests that Brandeis attempts to manipulate other prisoners and custody personnel toward antagonistic behavior in order to justify an attack upon them - it's all about validating her vicious aggression upon others.

Brandeis's Drug Supplier

What was learned about Brandeis after imprisonment was that she was, indeed, a drug addict and sexual predator prior to her incarceration. She provided heroin to her victims either through a water pipe, mixed it with marijuana, or they snorted it, which was called chasing the dragon. This was the method Brandies preferred.

She sexually assaulted young boys. Brandeis sought approval from others, including her victims. Her permissive nature allowed her to accept any directive. If she did something she later regretted, she would get even with the person who had given her the bad advice.

Brandeis also held a fear, a very powerful fear, of emotional dependence on her drug supplier. If she broke off the relationship with her supplier, she couldn't care for herself, she implied in her prison journal. Her view of what she had become told her to stop trying. Brandeis reported never experiencing poor quality product (drugs), which can lead to the theory that she was the recipient of high-quality substances. Her supplier had to be an individual well acquainted with Brandeis and someone who had excellent drug connections—Jolo. This would help explain why Brandeis attempted to traffic cocaine from the Bahamas to the US. She had probably done it in the past, more than once. If Jolo were her supplier, Brandeis would have held little ill will toward her. If Jolo did not have a hold over Brandeis, Brandeis would have engineered a way to harm Jolo, even after Brandeis's arrest and imprisonment. Two points became clear: Brandeis was vindictive as sin, and the emotional bonds between the women implied a sexual bond as well. The few known facts about Jolo suggest that if she were a participant in a sexual relationship with Brandeis, it was to keep Brandeis controlled and above all, happy. That is, Jolo understood the consequences of getting on the wrong side of Brandeis.

Other Crimes Committed by Brandeis

The crimes Brandeis implied she had committed, during conversations in-group, during class participation, and in her papers and journal, include contributing to the delinquency of a minor; lewd conduct; and sexual assault of minors, specifically several high school and middle school students. Brandeis never exhibited behavior that suggested depression or frustration because of her husband's death, or the loss of her freedom, or never seeing her child while imprisoned. Nonetheless, before discussing Brandeis's sexual assault crimes, you need to know what it means to contribute to the delinquency of a minor.

Contributing to the Delinquency of a Minor

One definition of contributing to the delinquency of a minor can be any action by an adult that allows or encourages illegal behavior by a person under the age of eighteen, or that places a child in situations which exposes him or her to illegal behavior. In Brandeis's case, she served both alcohol and heroin to minors. Still more egregious is sexual exploitation, which in her case includes sex assault.

Brandeis and Sexual Assault

By the time Brandeis arrived at prison, she had been a French teacher in a public high school for seven years. The school board was proud of her because she was an award-winning teacher: Best New Teacher of the Year, Best District Teacher, and Most Popular. She received national teaching awards too. Her future was indeed bright, and everyone wanted to know her. But prisons have a leveling effect, and in this upside-down world, Brandeis was considered a "no-mind." She quickly had to connect with an alpha-prisoner herself. Carla, the inmate who intervened when another prisoner slapped Brandeis at the reception center, was Brandeis's prison partner and part of the answer. When Carla was present during in-group, Brandeis said less than when Carla was not there, unless it had to do with her dead husband. One time, when Carla attended fresh out of her usual restriction or isolation for fighting, Brandeis explained that sexual relations with her husband had been unpleasant; that, in fact, sexual relationships throughout most of her life were unpleasant, until she arrived at prison. Carla caught the look from every inmate and smiled.

Brandeis continued, saying that boys "always told me what to do. They would yell at me that I wanna see this or that. Blah, blah, blah. I'm not their little sex machine. My real boys never told me what to do or how to do it." Younger aged school boys were little challenge in this respect when she was a teacher. An impression that seemed linked to Brandeis's thoughts was that she had sexual relationships with male high school and grade school students when she was an adult. Some of the indicators were in her writing: "I didn't see any harm by inviting a student home to tutor him in French if he really wanted to learn." Brandeis had tutored several boys at her office and in her home. She hired some of her students to babysit "so I could go shopping." Always boys, never girls. Two were her favorites, and she talked about those boys during in-group, although she never admitted that she had sex with them specifically. But the other prisoners rolled their eyes and made comments like, "You go, girl."

"On a scale of one to ten, how are little penises when not connected to giant pricks?" one prisoner asked in-group. "They beat the midnight wiggle [masturbation] by a hard-pressed mile," whispered Brandeis. She added, "Maybe an eight—but you send them home when it's over and they don't give you any crap about what I should do or what I shouldn't do. They're trainable. They appreciate everything, every moment."

Brandeis and Leroy. According to Brandeis's accounts during in-group programs, she would shower with her son Leroy, holding him tight "as the water would beat down on our bodies." Brandeis often rubbed Leroy over her body, including her breasts and private parts, sometimes for as long as an hour, or until the water turned cold. She used Leroy's body as one would a sponge between her legs. Sometimes Brandeis would experience an orgasm from this practice—a practice that continued until Brandeis dropped Leroy off at Leroy's grandparents' home and boarded a jet to the Bahamas. Experts refer to this practice as frotteurism—touching or rubbing against a non-consenting person. From her writings and comments, it appeared her sexual exploitation never went any further. One indicator of that is that Leroy was only around ten months old when Brandeis first brought him into the shower with her. Although pedophilia is a paraphilia that involves an abnormal interest in children, Brandeis was not sexually aroused by Leroy. He was a device she used to gain her sexual relief. Also, Brandeis didn't imply that she ever had any recurrent intense sexual urges or fantasies about Leroy. Still, she never considered his suffering or possible humiliation later in life, if her activities were made public.

Friends at First. Brandeis's attack on one child started out as friends at first. At three years of age, her son was in a martial arts class, just before and after his father was deployed to Mideast. Leroy was partnered with an older boy, Jason, who was around ten years old. Brandeis attended most of the practices, which were after school. On many occasions she had conversations with Jason's mother, a single parent. The boys seemed compatible, and a few times, Brandeis drove Jason home after practice because his mom had to work late. For the next year or so, until her arrest, she drove the boys to her home and sexually assaulted Jason. Most often Leroy fell asleep in another part of the house. From the information provided by Brandeis, she sexually assaulted Jason at least once a week for over a year. On some of those occasions, Leroy observed the encounter, which qualifies as reckless endangerment. Most often Brandeis performed oral sex on Jason, yet she never disrobed. Additionally, she implied that on more than one occasion, she forcibly inserted an object into Jason's rectum moments prior to his ejaculation. On a few occasions, a fourteen-year-old high school student, Edmond, witnessed the sexual assault of Jason. Edmond participated at her insistence. All accounts suggest that Brandeis never provided heroin to Jason, but Edmond was different. When she encouraged Edmond to perform orally on her victim, she rewarded him with drugs and "stroked his little penis."

Brandeis added another technique, which included using drugs, porn, and the weakness of the child against himself. Most often teenage boys want to be grown up—a man. Having sex with your high school teacher was one way to being a man and cool at the same time. Therefore, in some cases the child encourages the sexual act without realizing the dynamics of act. Once her boys were hers, she would hurt them on their bottom, making them believe they had pushed her over the edge. How many victims had Brandeis attacked? By her own count, "forty, if you count the twins." Yet many of her descriptions suggest that the forty boys were victimized more than once, and many of them participated in her victimization of other boys at her home. They would get a special treat if they brought her a "new boy. Boys are best. They're not emotional."

Being Wicked Is Good

Brandeis displayed a "needy" behavior, a passive acceptance of everyone's thoughts or suggestions, no matter the validity of those thoughts or suggestions. A caveat of this passivity is easy victimization by others, who target such individual for goods, services, and pleasure. To some extent, Brandeis was characterized by a passive-aggressive personality disorder description. This disorder was a long-term condition. She would appear to comply with the desires and needs of others, but actually passively resist them through a number of tactics, such as avoiding responsibility by claiming forgetfulness, being inefficient on purpose, procrastination, and resisting others' suggestions to enhance herself.

You might be interested to learn that despite this disorder's recognizable behavioral patterns and long-term consequences, the American Psychological Association (APA), in some profound moment of wisdom, no longer recognizes this condition as an official diagnosis, once again demonstrating its inability to aid the human behavior specialists who deal with actual patients as opposed to theoretical notions.

Finally, what came out during in-group journal writing exercises is that Brandeis recalled her disruptive behavior as a child, which had been blocked from her memory until prison. Going back to her mother's statement to Jolo that Brandeis had been a difficult child, she was right. Brandeis recalled that she had been verbally and physically aggressive and abusive to her parents, hired domestics, teachers, and friends. She concluded that she in part pushed her parents away through her behavior, but she struggled with her mother's decision to reject her and at least not try to discipline or control her. She was equally jealous that Jolo's father held such an important place in Jolo's life, and his disapproval of any of Jolo's behavior represented another round of struggles for Brandeis. More than likely what eluded Brandeis's understanding of Jolo was that the girl and her father were partners in drug trafficking to the US. A law enforcement connection suspected that every trip Jolo made home from college included money one way and drugs the other way. Brandeis was either blind, part of the plan, or she didn't care. What is doubtful is that Jolo would have approved of Brandeis's sexual attacks.

In prison, Brandeis became increasingly hostile, angry, and vindictive, but those emotions did not show themselves until action was required. Her response behavior was similar to a pot of water on the stove that boils over when you're not looking. Individuals with her disorders, despite their intellectual capacity (or socioeconomic standing in the community), develop a codependency relationship with an aggressive alpha personality: someone who understands the weakness and vulnerability of this victim. Equally important to the equation, that someone also has the manipulation skills and intent to dominate (and victimize) the victim. Jolo initially filled that role, and once Brandeis was imprisoned, Carla did. What it comes down to is Brandeis's happiness or pain depends on how this dominant person treats her. Brandeis could love Joseph Stalin and bear his children. She could get used to anything, including the Chernobyl disaster, if Stalin rose from his grave and said it was necessary. Then too, if Stalin explained that his rising from the dead was an imperative to fulfill some explicit mission to enhance the couple's children, and Brandeis challenged his intention, she could justify lethal violence upon him and then ask his corpse for forgiveness.

Brandeis seeks approval from those who take charge, such as prisoner leaders, group leaders, and prison personnel. When Brandeis feels low about herself, she's upside down. Her appetite for drugs and crime are fostered by her perceptions of good and wicked. Being wicked enhances goodness.

The short story in chapter 18 entitled *Voices* characterizes Brandeis Pettet Anderson's character and narratives.

CHAPTER 4
Brother Pious and Orphans of the Storm

Introduction

Alberic Pious, known as Brother Pious, is a Roman Catholic monk whose last job was at an American orphanage near Atlanta, Georgia. It goes without saying that he never married. This thirty-five-year-old has a bachelor's degree in biology, and a jury trial found him guilty on twelve counts of sexual assault of children over a three-year period. Yet twelve counts of sexual assault might translate to a good weekend for Pious, because his victims numbered in the hundreds. Nonetheless, Brother Pious received a twenty-year prison sentence, completed his sentence, and was released in 2010.

Alberic Pious was never identified as an offender in his own country of Germany, or any other country where he worked, except in America. Had he been arrested in those countries, it would have been for the crimes of murder, cannibalism, coprophilia, sexual assault of minors, and necrophilia. He had little experience with alcohol, drugs, or people his own age. He never dated a woman and never paid a prostitute. While imprisoned, he was never on suicide watch, and his health was excellent for the most part. It's a wonder he slept eight hours a night, because his massive feet hung over his prison bunk. It seems a bit peculiar that he ate a small amount of food and absolutely no junk food, despite the excessive load on his six foot five inch, making him look like Friar Tuck. As you might imagine, he has a remarkably round, almost hairless, pasty white face, with unfriendly, small eyes hidden by dropping eyelids, making it impossible to determine their color. His health report said they were gray. I imagined they were cold steel-gray. When he speaks, words slide over dry, thin lips, which seem not to move. His behavior can be described as generally compulsive and out-of-touch with the world. As for his personal style, it can be described as swift and violent. Alberic Pious's primary motive, or trigger, to commit crime is control, prompted by coprophilia (an obsession with and often sexual interest in feces and defecation), but I will spare you the particulars of his heinous acts linked to that behavior.

On first sight of this huge man, *unfriendly* might be a typical thought. And after he acknowledges you, you wouldn't want to be his friend. For one, he has little knowledge of the things most of us know about and ignore, such as voting for politicians and surgeon general warnings. He is ignorant about many things most Americans take for granted, like cell phones, debit cards, and twenty-four-hour fast food joints. Although it is easy to say that his lack of understanding is connected to his experiences, it is likely that he rarely ventured out of his immediate environment, whether he was working at an orphanage in Georgia, at refugee camps in former Soviet republics, or at a children's hospital in Egypt. He never watched television, never interacted with adults, but always had a condescending tone in his voice. While he was imprisoned, his visitors were volunteers representing the Holy Order of monks. They came four or five times a year, although he refused to see them. He refused to visit with Helga, his oldest sister, who is a nun with the Sisters of St. Joseph. Prison mailroom personnel told me that "Big Al" never received mail. The general prison population was unaware of Alberic Pious's sexual orientation (that is, he prefers males to females), but viewed him with disrespect because he was an "SO" (sex offender) and a foreigner. If the truth about his crimes and his desires had been known, he would have been beaten to death by the prisoners, or accidentally murdered by correctional personnel, or poisoned by health care providers. Brother Pious wrote that he was the anointed cherub, like Lucifer; and his crimes, linked to *"agresseur d'enfants,"* of hundreds of mentally handicapped children in the Egyptian city of Alexandria and helpless children in the civil-war-torn Balkans was an act designed to help them "deal with the savageness of reality."

Alberic Pious's Youth

Alberic was born to a prominent village official and his wife. They already had six children, and named the seventh child after a Christian abbot who helped found the Cistercian Order of monks in the Black Forest. The Pious family lived in Bad Herrenalb in the district of Calw, Germany. Bad Herrenalb is in the southwest corner of Germany, in the Black Forest, which borders France and Switzerland. The town grew around Herrenalb Abbey, a Cistercian monastery founded in 1148 and dissolved in the nineteenth century. The buildings and the order lived on, however, and was a daily reminder to Alberic and his family that Catholics had an eternal life. Most of the village population was Lutheran, yet a few families—such as the Pious family—worshiped in the Catholic Church. Alberic and the second youngest brother shared a bedroom facing the village, while his older brothers had their room. Two older sisters shared a bedroom that faced the distant mountains. Often all the children piled into the girls' room to see the mountains' snowy peaks in the spring. It was an amazing sight, and often they ran yelling into the boys' room to see the flowers in full bloom in the valley. Their fragrance was a captivating experience for the other children, but not Alberic. I can easily hear him say "Humbug," with a wave his giant hand toward the flowers.

Alberic's parents met during World War II. She lived in the big home above the German village; he was an officer in the French military. Their first child, a girl, was born a few months after they wed, and in rapid order, six more children were born. Eighteen months after Alberic's birth, another brother was stillborn. A couple of years later an older, sickly brother died, while four-year-old Alberic held the child and shook it into eternal silence. Also, two of Alberic's other siblings were born with serious mental illnesses, which impaired their functioning and confined both of them to wheelchairs.

The children played throughout the sixteen rooms of their home. Some rooms had pale parquet wooden flooring, while others had dark wood. In some rooms brick fireplaces darted from the wood-paneled walls, and were surrounded by large Tyrolean period furniture and comfortable dark leather armchairs. White French doors led to balconies, and intricate crown moldings decorated the ceilings. The home had stairs, ramps, and many cathedral ceilings, so that it resembled a monastery. Christian crosses in various sizes covered the walls, and small candles stood in the children's bedrooms "to burn away the evil spirits." The house, which Alberic's mother had inherited when her father died, was isolated on a ridge, peeking out at the village below.

Alberic's mother's substantial inheritance provided well for the family. Alberic wrote about sea cruises on the Baltic, holidays in Paris and Geneva, and worship at the Vatican. He wrote that because he had so many brothers and sisters that privacy was always an issue for him. His parents rarely showed him any attention or affection, because they were busy with his disabled siblings, and he often got the impression that they disliked him for some reason. Maybe because of his intellect, he speculated. Or maybe they ignored him because of all the accidents his mother experienced that were linked to young Alberic's awkward behavior.

"I was climbing into Helga's wheelchair at the top of the ramp and Maman was coming up from floor below. Helga forgot the brake and the chair slid into Maman." Alberic guessed he was three or four at that time. "But I didn't know that the Nazi whore was coming (up the ramp). She was a *femme méchante* (wicked woman)." Another accident occurred a few months after his older brother's funeral, when his mother shaved her legs in a locked bathroom. Alberic explained that respectable women in that day never shaved their legs. He shut off the electric power to the bathroom, screamed, and banged on the door, causing his mother to cut herself miserably. Alberic told his father that he had thought his dead brother was in the room, not his mother. He held considerable contempt for his mother for some unknown reason; and when confronted with his contempt, he simply brushed the question off with a fat waving finger. "Bosh, bosh," he said. I'm not sure what he meant, but it was clear he wasn't going to talk about it. When I asked how he knew what his mother was doing in the bathroom, he replied, "I am not a spy." Yet in subsequent conversations and journal entries, Alberic revealed that he knew a lot of what his mother did behind closed doors, and did not approve of any of it. Once he caught her smoking and informed his father at the dinner table, even saying where her cigarettes were hidden. It caused such an uproar that his father almost hit his mother, but the oldest child intervened. Everyone then turned to Alberic with a look of contempt, he recalled. "Bosh, bosh," he said about the incident, with a flip his fat hand.

Favorite Time of the Year

Alberic wrote about one of his favorite times of the year, the German Carnival, or Fasnet, as it is commonly called in the Black Forest. Fasnet occurs on the Monday before Ash Wednesday, during the Catholic holiday lending to Lent. He and his siblings—he never mentioned anything about friends, and based on what I saw in prison, he had none—wore masks and paraded the streets of Bad Herrenalb. Alberic wrote a great deal about Fasnet, and said that he would have liked the holiday to happen every day of the week. His one dislike of Fasnet was that most of the participants spoke German. He had to remind everyone that France had won the war against the *"Les barbares germaniques d'Allemagne"* (Teutonic barbarians from Germany). Fasnet was the one time when he could venture outside the circle of his siblings and interact with other children, but he really had little to say to them. A few times, the family attended the Stuttgart Spring Festival in Stuttgart, about fifty miles away. They traveled by rail, which was faster than driving small and winding back roads.

At twelve years of age, Alberic sexually experimented with his second oldest sister, Helga, who was nineteen or twenty years old. It is not clear if their experiment, which continued for a month or two, was consensual, but there was no mention of any repercussions. Also, Helga was one of the siblings diagnosed as seriously mentally ill. Alberic described her as heavyset, and their experiments did not include penetration, just touching, or so he wrote. But the touching led to *"les exclamations sexuelles dans elle"* (ejaculations while in her), suggesting that he didn't present the whole truth. The fact that Alberic was a habitual liar became clear his first day in-group, as he often contradicted himself. However, prior to prison in-group meetings, had he ever been in the company of adults—violent offenders, at that—who were not shy about their comments. In-group participation represented a new experience for Alberic, because his life work had involved dealing with children who never talked back; and church administrators who hide the truth about Alberic's sexual attacks on children.

Alberic was also intrigued with his "newfound feelings with his sister," so he also experimented with Stephen, a brother who was about fifteen months older than he. Stephen was the other sibling who was mentally ill, and was also confined to a wheelchair. Two of Alberic's siblings discovered Alberic playing with Stephen's penis one afternoon and smacked Alberic around. When their father arrived from work for lunch, he was told of the incident. It was decided that the Alberic and Stephen could never be alone. The two siblings who smacked Alberic once again pounded him after their father went back to work. It is doubtful that Stephen was a willing participant. Years later in prison, Alberic referred to Stephen and Helga as "*le repas sur les roués*" (meal on wheels).

Education. Alberic, like three of his siblings, attended comprehensive school in preparation for the university. This information suggests that Alberic and some of his siblings had good academic records and were intellectual enough to be guided toward a college education. In the American system, going to college is often a student's choice; but in the German system, while education is compulsory till age sixteen, students in the ninth and tenth grades are steered toward either vocational training or university training. Alberic was steered toward the university.

Father and Mother. His father spoke French and his mother spoke German, so all of their children spoke at least two languages. Alberic and his brother Sebastian also spoke English, and the both of them took classes that were taught in either English, French, or Swiss German. Later, Alberic easily learned Egyptian Arabic too. Knowing many languages was not necessarily a mark of intelligence as much as it was a mark of survival, or in Alberic's world—staying ahead of detection.

Alberic's favorite school subjects were biology and chemistry, and he had an interest in ancient Rome and the history of early French emperors. In particular, he read a lot about Charlemagne, favoring his father's heritage. "*Par l'épée et la croix*" (By the sword and the cross) was a comment Alberic said and wrote often, and that phrase "can be traced to Charlemagne." Alberic wanted little to do with his German heritage, including his mother. "She was a child-machine," he said, "and other than that, served little purpose under the sun."

Another point deserving attention is that Alberic wrote about his favorite pet, giant earthworms called *Lumbricus badensis*. Found only in the Black Forest region, they can grow two feet long. He often played with them for hours when he was a child. He said they helped him study too. One time he brought two of the creatures to bed, but his oldest brother forced him to take the earthworms outside. He ripped them into pieces and ate them.

When he was thirteen, Alberic, who was already tall and heavy for his age, cornered his eldest brother (who was probably around twenty) and anal raped him. He made Stephen watch from his wheelchair. Alberic remembers the day because, he said, it marked his independence. It was his oldest brother who had beat him up when he caught Alberic fondling Stephen, so Alberic was probably referring to independence in sexual matters. However, judging by other comments Alberic wrote, it appears he and Stephen continued to experiment sexually. Alberic wasn't about to give up any meal, particularly the two on wheels. "I would not tolerate Stephen's or Helga's lack of attention to my needs." Eventually, it came out in prison that Alberic often forced both Stephen and Helga to consume more of their medication than their recommended dosage, so that they became, in essence, complete vegetables, ripe for Alberic's picking.

Joining the Holy Order

Al—as he was called in prison—wouldn't get the chance to become a college student just yet, because his father insisted he apply to a catholic order of monks. Al did, and Stephen joined the order, too. A short time later, Al and Stephen were separated, and Al began the monastery's "step" program to become a monk—postulant, novitiate, temporary profession, and final vows. While completing his novitiate step, Al fulfilled one of his dreams and attended the University of Hohenheim at Stuttgart, Germany. Al would have preferred a French university, but took what he could get. He graduated at the top of his class with a degree in the natural sciences and a focus on biology. While at the university, Al tried to contact Stephen, but was unsuccessful. His two older brothers were officers in the German military. They had attended the Bundeswehr University in Munich. His older sister joined the convent and lived somewhere in Europe, while Helga continued to live at home, still confined to a wheelchair. No one knew where Stephen lived, or if he continued to live or not. Al would never see any of his brothers or sisters again.

Mentally Handicapped Units. After graduation, Al was assigned to a Catholic center in Alexandria, Egypt, for the mentally handicapped. With the help of a medical practitioner, a child lodged a complaint against Al, alleging that Al had beat the child after the child rejected his sexual advances. This was not the first complaint against Al. He was transferred within the week to a similar mental health unit in Cairo, where months later a young male disappeared. The boy had had one leg amputated and had been confined to a wheelchair. Years later, while imprisoned, Al solved the disappearance of the young boy.

The boy had been screaming in pain, and Al said he had needed to "sanctify the child." When he couldn't quiet the boy, he said he panicked—yet all observations and information suggest that Al never panicked. While in the process of hushing the child, he covered his mouth from behind; as a result, the struggling child defecated on the good brother. That experience moved him to a new level of satisfaction, a behavior that can be referred to coprophilia, as described by the Diagnostic and Statistical Manual of the American Psychiatric Association (DSM-IV-TR), and classified under 302.9 Paraphilia. Coprophilia suggests that sexual pleasure is derived from human feces. But it was more than feeling and smelling the human feces of young children for Al. He professed that because God had bestowed his divine favor on Al, he consumed the feces.

Back to the Continent. Brother Pious was transferred to France, where he refined his sexual techniques on male children through the Catholic ministry. He educated and counseled gypsy and refugee children fleeing from the civil wars in the Balkans and other former Soviet republics, such as Ukraine. Those children were referred to as "orphans of the storm" by many human health providers at the time. It should be noted that because of the urgency and frequency of fighting in Eastern Europe, it is difficult to estimate how many children fled, how many children were cared for, and how many children went missing under anyone's care, including the Catholic Church. In almost every catastrophic disaster or the vast emergency response activated to deal with that disaster, it is difficult to ascertain the exact number of victims or to assure the quality of the emergency response, as individuals who experienced such events as 9/11, Hurricane Katrina, and the Haitian earthquake of 2010 can attest. Testimonies from the Mississippi Gulf coast during Katrina reveal that copses can be disposed in numerous ways without detection.

Brother Pious was reassigned to an American orphanage somewhere between 1989 and 1991. He didn't want to leave Europe. "I was needed," he wrote.

Dynamics of Compulsive and Out-of-Touch

Compulsive criminals similar to Al Pious are guided by obsessions. Typically, a compulsive act is performed in an attempt to alleviate discomfort created by an obsession. Or, in Al's terms, a mission. I took that to mean, a vow. However, the most predictable perspective of Al is that he possessed few if any boundaries. For him, nothing was sacred—marriage, children, rules, laws, accepted behavior. Al learned not to press correctional personnel, who would easily write him up for a disciplinary action and move him into a segregation unit or into isolation. During his first two years of confinement, Al was placed in isolation at least once a month. Eventually, he learned that he was not in control of his environment, but isolation was a respite from the other prisoners, who prodded him into verbal disputes when they had little else to do. Unlike the other participants in this work, Al did not show his compulsion or his pent-up energy through body language. He guarded his feelings and was hard to read. That is probably one reason the other prisoners did not include him in their conversations, unless they were "mind screwing" him, which he most often rejected. He did not take their bait and remained detached from the other prisoners.

Correctional personnel were bigger threats to Al, because they were in control of time and place. That significantly annoyed him, which led to more disciplinary action for the slightest infraction of the rules. For instance, typically before Al arrived at the classroom, we would hear the hallway personnel directing him to, "walk faster," "walk slower," "turn left," "eyes up," "eyes down," and so on. Sometimes, we'd hear, "Come on, Big Al, move your feet." Many personnel maintained control by backing prisoners into corners, but Al was not vulnerable to their intimidation strategies. So correctional personnel pretended he had broken a rule and punished him by sending him to isolation. At least, that was the intent. But through it all, Big Al kept his cool and never fought back. Of course, it wouldn't have done him any good if he had.

One whisper I heard was that in the event of a riot, stay clear of Big Al, because the prisoners would kill him before they killed a guard. Prisoners and personnel were not aware of Al's crimes, but he was still hated because of his arrogance, his foreign citizenship, and his size. But also because sexual assaults in prison increased dramatically after Al arrived. His choice prisoners were youthful offenders who had no one to protect them. Young men arriving in prison are sexually assaulted by prisoners similar to Al within the first two weeks of their arrival, unless those young men pair up with a protector. However, most are too idealistic about life and death and survival to ask for help.

How can I be sure of Al's involvement in prison rape? When Al was in an isolation unit, fewer victims of violent rape were taken to the infirmary than when he roamed the cell blocks looking for prey. Al was a vicious rapist. He pulled hair and anything else protruding from the body of his victims, rammed deep, and thumbed eyeballs. No one would identify Al as the rapist, probably because it all happened so fast and from behind, and because they feared him. If it was Al who had attacked a prisoner, then the correctional officer assigned to keep tabs on the big man would also face charges. So inmates had two fear factors working against them. Similar to little children talking about the bogeyman, they were imprisoned with him, whoever he was; and there was nowhere to hide, nowhere to run.

Out-of-Touch. The true measure of Brother Pious is that he was "a picture perfect arrogant slob," one prisoner said—although not to Al's face. Al's world was composed of one person—him. He was the supreme ruler in his world, and he knew little and identified less with the rest of the world. Everyone was here for his use or his convenience, including children. The contribution of children was that they had needs, and he filled those needs "through prayer." Al told people he was the light bearer, but neglected to tag on the rest of the truth—"better known as Lucifer." And like Lucifer, Al was wired wrong.

One way to translate the above information is to say that predators similar to Al have few hurdles in finding vulnerable prey in America or anywhere else, including prison. It wasn't necessary for Al to work in a war zone among refuges, or at a mental ward in Alexandria. Any orphan in the storm would do as long as he drew breath. He used religion as his excuse, suggesting that he used "Lucifer's Hammer" to make children strong, so they could survive a tragic world, the tragic world he helped build. Be sure to read the short story in chapter 18 developed from some of Brother Pious's fantasies, entitled "Unknown Flavor."

CHAPTER 5
Devin the Vampire

Introduction

When you finish reading this chapter, you'll be out of breath. As Devin Palmer and his repugnant conduct come alive and play on your mind, you'll wonder how Mother Nature allowed Devin and those like him to exist in our incredibly technological advanced society. You might have wondered about that when you read the accounts of Annie, Brandeis, and Brother Pious. But as you attempt to minimize Devin's account and consider that sensationalism is the writer's incentive, the absurdity is that Devin has committed more frightening acts than those described. We'll never know all of the ghastly acts committed by the *Wicked Women* participants, particularly Devin.

No single event, experience, or circumstance leads to a predator's creation and feeds its evolution. Yet should Darwin be correct in his analysis of natural selection, how do primal instincts that are similar to a swarm of mindless insects remain among the human species? It is said that evil often triumphs, but never conquers. Yet at the end of the day, the participants in *Wicked Women* feel little shame about their decadence, unlike, for example, Lady Macbeth, whose conscience propelled her to take her own life in a quest for absolution. Devin and the other *Wicked Women* partners raged with lust to triumph over good. Their rage will continue long after these wicked creatures no longer exist in flesh and blood.

Devin Palmer provides a frightening glimpse of a miswired

creature that sees wickedness through delusional shades of sanity while unswerving narcissistic (self-centered) behavior triumphs over decency and compassion.

After Devin's arrest, because of the crimes he was charged with and his age (sixteen years old), he was tried in adult court, similar to some 12,000 juveniles each year. Devin accepted a plea agreement and was convicted on two counts of aggravated assault. A smart move on his part, because the case never went to trial; and once a guilty plea was accepted, all the criminal investigations ceased, with the exception of a presentence investigation report (PSI), detailed below.

A Description of Devin

Devin is a drip of boy, tipping the scales at one hundred and thirty pounds and standing about five foot six. When he stands still, people might guess he's nineteen or even twenty years old, but when he talks, he seems much younger than his frail frame suggests. Descriptions like "confused," "scrambled," and "disconnected" were mentioned by police officers who arrested Devin, and by jailers who supervised him before he was sentenced to prison. His ravings were those of a bewildered child who had lived through traumatic experiences, due to alcoholic parents and the death of his sister, which was blamed on Devin but who is a victim, the PSI report proclaimed (see below for details). "At first, I thought Devin was a girl. I was shocked to discover that she, I mean he, was a boy," said the arresting police officer.

However, after imprisonment, correctional personnel described Devin differently. Typically, Devin was thought to be an individual who smiled endlessly about anything, including devastating natural disasters. His voice chimes with a freshness that gives the impression of a bright and caring child. Devin was also described as an intent listener, with steady eyes, and he seemed unbothered by bright lights and loud sounds. Devin was confident and in control.

Before Sentencing

Devin's defense attorney articulated that Devin was angry and felt rejected, because his mother had married a much younger man than her first husband, Devin's father. This new stepdad was the father of two little children who took over the defendant's childhood home. Devin would go for weeks without hearing his mother's voice, Devin's defense lawyer argued, because she avoided him. Defense said that Devin was seen as a "disposable child, and that no parent really loved him and never really provided attention," especially as "the defendant grew to four years of age and lost some of a child's cuteness. Then both parents threw the child out like an old rag." However, the prosecutor said that what Devin felt as rejection was actually his parents attempting to regroup, because Devin had been on a conscious campaign to destroy them.

The defense lawyer countered that Devin tried to repress a deep love and dependence for the only person who had shown him love, his mother. But now she was deeply involved in her new life with her new husband and his children, after running off Devin's father, a wealthy real estate broker who moved back with his parents several blocks away. What was a child, deep in rejection and without anybody to guide him, to do? the defense attorney asked. So the child did it—he cried and begged a neglectful mother to spend some time with him. She did, but then she rejected Devin again. That time, the child cried like before, but he was alone with his four–year-old stepbrother and six-year-old stepsister. The three of them were on his natural father's sailboat, securely anchored at the boat club, while armed police officers directed Devin to get off the boat or they would shoot. Devin refused because he was in such deep agony, defense argued. And, the lawyer added, it was hotter than Hades that day, so of course all the children took their clothes off. That's what kids do.

Devin Palmer's Presentence Investigation Report (PSI)

Devin Palmer's PSI reported that neighbors believed Devin had attempted to kill both his father and stepfather. This accusation could not be substantiated through any evidence or during the interviews with Devin's father and stepfather. If it was true, it probably had more to do with Devin's medication than observable behavior, investigators decided. The PSI reported further that Devin set fire to the stepfather's dog by stuffing a cherry bomb in the animal's rectum. Devin also jammed the family cat into the dryer and turned it on.

Before Devin's stepfather married Devin's mother, Devin stole money, jewelry, liquor, clothes, and sport's equipment (such as golf clubs and tennis rackets) from his parents. In school, he was bullied by classmates, and a teacher accused him of stealing. He became the subject of a police-teacher meeting about drugs and pornography, but it was subsequently learned that Devin was a victim, not an aggressor (more details below).

Devin's behavior before the arrest was discounted because of the trauma of his parents' divorce and the death of his three-year-old sister, Emily. Investigators did not report that Devin had orchestrated the separation and eventual divorce of his parents, who were at wit's end because of Devin's uncontrollable behavior. Both of his parents relied on alcohol to cope, and that worsened Devin's dysfunctions, as they continually left Devin unsupervised. Devin's parents gave up on the child, Devin's defense attorney clarified. The parents had come to the conclusion that no matter how they reacted to Devin, nothing would alter his behavior or what they thought about their child.

Emily's Death

When Devin was seven, he tried to teach Emily how to swim by the pier where their grandparents' yacht was docked. Emily accidentally drowned. Devin blamed his parents for her death, and his parents and grandparents blamed him. They said Devin was angry over all the attention Emily received from her parents and grandparents, and that Devin had purposely tossed the child into the water, not helping her once she started to sink. To Devin's parents, Emily's death was the beginning of the nine years of victimization, worse than any of their son's earlier violent pranks. Devin called it "cold-hate, that's how they all treated me." Cold-hate was also what he called the vast amount of alienation and hostility displayed between his parents, and the vast amount of alienation and hostility displayed Devin's family, neighbors, and friends displayed toward Devin. Everyone blamed Devin for the death of little Emily.

Devin's Neighborhood

The Palmers lived near Devin's grandparents' estate in a seaside gated community, the PSI reported. Most of the magnificent estates have their own boat piers in front, and some have hangars to store their aircraft connected to a maze of little runways at the rear of their home. Their awesome gardens, containing literally hundreds of flowers and plants, were maintained by a small army of gardeners. Devin's parents owned a slick Piper Cherokee 6/300, and the grandparents had a Sea Ray 290 Sundancer, just right for jet skiing, sunbathing, and cruising the adjacent harbors and resorts. Devin's grandfather taught Devin early how to pilot the sport cruiser.

Devin's father and his mother met at high school and were married before they were twenty. After Devin's father graduated from a prominent law school, he and Devin's mother moved to within several blocks of the father's childhood home. The happy couple worked hard to enhance their lifestyle, and once Devin was born, they looked forward to more children, a fulfilling family life, and country club activities. Devin's mother was the oldest of four siblings, all of whom continued to live with her parents during Devin's youth. Most often, Devin's uncles and aunts partied aboard family yachts, in the country club's banquet facility, or while away at college.

Devin's dad traveled almost every day, and the mother did "important business" at the club and church, the Devin's PSI emphasized. Devin explained that with complete freedom, "I snuck into my uncle's vehicle and found pornographic magazines. Later, I snuck into his bedroom on the assumption he had more magazines. I was right."

School

Most of the kids in Devin's neighborhood attended the same nearby private elementary and high school. Devin recalled that in the second grade, several months after Emily's death, "I showed a porn photo to some classmates on the playground during recess. One of them ratted me out." When confronted by a teacher, Devin said that an older kid had given him the photo, and he showed it to the other kids because he didn't know what to do with it. The older kid, Devin said, also talked about drugs and "I think sex too." Devin told the teacher that, "I can't remember what the older kid looked like because he'd kick my butt or worse and I was afraid." Subsequently, parents, teachers, and police met at school to discuss the incident. The only thing that came out of the meeting was an occasional police patrol at school and a small disclosure that "an older unknown student tried to entice Devin Palmer into porn and drugs without success."

What the PSI didn't report, Devin clarified during an in-group session at prison years later. "Because I didn't fit the profile of a porn freak, nothing happened. I know how to look stupid." Once the police patrols stopped, Devin cornered the kid in school who told on him.. He made sure witnesses were present. He took the kid's lunch money, his sneakers, and his pants. Devin smacked the boy hard with a bloom stick from the janitor's closet, and then he told teachers that it was a matter of self-defense "from the bully who made up stories about me." They believed Devin, and when PSI investigators asked, that's what they wrote down.

Judge's Sentence

Once the judge reviewed Devin's PSI and the defense attorney's statements, she provided a criminal sanction of four years in a state prison with early release possibilities after two years. Devin could have been convicted for aggravated kidnapping and sexual assault of two children. The state sentencing guidelines would have called for ten years in prison for each offense, or twenty years total.

Behavior Not Reported in Devin's PSI: Early Behavior

The following details were never reported in Devin Palmer's PSI. He wrote in his prison journal that the servants in his home stored fresh bath towels and bed sheets in different closets throughout the house. Devin packed feces into layers of towels and sheets, and urinated on them in the months before Emily's death. When locks were used to secure the closet and bedroom doors, nine-year-old Devin used a crowbar to open those doors and continued his destruction of the family's linens. At ten years of age, "I sliced the tires of my mother's vehicle and smashed the windshield." At eleven, Devin placed numerous telephone calls to phone sex numbers, and set fires in the backyard for fun. "I threw human sh.. and dog sh.. into the pool." He sliced up small animals he found around the neighborhood, packaged parts of their bodies and their internal organs, and placed those packages into the refrigerator in the kitchen and the freezer located in meal preparation room. Each time Devin was disciplined, the destruction temporarily ceased. When it started again, it was worse. Servants kept quitting because Devin victimized them too.

When he was twelve, Devin attacked both sets of his grandparents, who then refused to spend holidays with his family. He hid animal packages in their refrigerators and freezers too. Devin's behavior pushed his own parents into bitter disputes with each other. The roots of their fights had to do with disciplining the young child. His mother wanted to enroll Devin in a boarding school, and his father wanted to use reason to solve the problem. The fights between Devin's parents grew harsher and harsher, finally ending in their marital separation. But it really didn't matter, Devin said, "because nothing changed."

Before the divorce was finalized, Devin's mother became romantically involved with a new man. Her boyfriend and his two children moved in with Devin and his mother before the marriage. This piece of information found its way into Devin's PSI and confirmed the trauma the child was *supposedly* experiencing. However, I suspect that Devin's stepfather was concerned with Devin's frequent attacks on the woman he loved, and that compelled him to move in before the wedding.

Devin's stepfather padlocked his children's bedroom doors and their adjoining bathrooms. He installed a new security alarm to detect moment throughout the house. Devin had mastered the old alarm, which was designed to go off when anyone broke in. This new system had a different purpose. Devin's grandparents installed new security systems as well. Then Devin was introduced to a therapist, who talked to Devin every morning before school. Devin's stepfather and mother were convinced that Devin was rehabilitated. They were unaware that Devin had new targets.

Devin the Babysitter

Devin babysat four-year-old Tabitha when he was in the eighth grade. Tabitha lived a few doors down the beach from Devin, and her mom needed someone to watch the child when she went on errands and attended charity events in the afternoons. Tabitha's dad worked for an international construction company and was frequently out of the country. Tabitha's family was new to the gated community where Devin lived, so consequently had little knowledge of the cold-hate their neighbors had showed Devin after his sister's death. Devin's parents accepted the babysitter job as an opportunity to get him out of the house, and as a sign of his rehabilitation.

Devin often wondered how much Tabitha liked to touch her private parts, and liked her eyes growing big when Devin touched her. Each time Devin babysat, he got braver. Tabitha seemed to like being touched everywhere, especially on her back. Sometimes Devin sat on own his own hands until they were totally numb, and then smoothed his index finger around the outside of Tabitha's little private parts and tried to push fingers inside her. Once, Devin saw blood dripping from inside her vagina. He tasted the droplets, and then put his fingertips in Tabitha's mouth, so she could taste her blood too. As he told this story during an Aggression Replacement Training Program in prison, Devin made every effort to convince me, the group leader, that he felt sorry for the pain he inflicted upon the little girl.

Liar was all I could think, but said nothing. I maintained a blank expression for the sake of the other participants, who no doubt also knew Devin was lying. The group prompted Devin to talk more about little girls, and they obviously enjoyed hearing those dreadful descriptions. Eventually, Devin revealed that he had "deep-touched into Emily's private parts too. That's why the little bitch had to go. She was stupid. She was going to tell."

One implication of Devin's admission was that Emily's drowning wasn't accidental. People are injured or die around super predators all the time, and very often those injuries and deaths are labeled accidental or linked to someone else's neglect. A study of the number of deaths and injuries that occur around an alleged predator would be quite revealing.

Several times Devin described how he ejaculated on Tabitha's buttock as he spanked her. He said that one time he made Tabitha "look like a stray cat with rabies who'd been hit by a car," because he had worked her little mouth so very hard with his penis. Another time he recalled wiping semen off her face when he heard her mother's vehicle entering the garage. He tickled Tabitha, forcing a wide smile on her pretty face, as her mother walked into the kitchen. Tabitha's mother kissed the child's cheek at the very spot where Devin had wiped his fluids. When asked how he felt about that experience, he grinned hugely. He continued to discuss the experience with the urgency of a new car salesman. Other group members encouraged his descriptions, and whenever he was accused of making up a story, he detailed his victimization so realistically, not a single offender in the group disbelieved him. "Yep, that's how it works," one group member commented in satisfaction of Devin's descriptions.

Other times, Devin and Tabitha played games like baker and doctor. He waited for an opportunity to teach her how to give him an ejaculation with her hands. He tried many ways and finally succeeded. He played with her mind too. He convinced Tabitha that she was a bad girl and he would tell her mother about what she had done. As expected, she cried and cried until he promised he would never tell. "Let's keep our secret," he said. Molesting the child was simple after that—no more games. During his exit interview from prison, he asked, "Do you think Tabitha ever remembers how good I taste?"

Pretending to Sleep

Devin pretended to be asleep on the sofa when he heard Tabitha's mother arrive at home after shopping. She was using the toilet when he attacked her. He was unsuccessful, because she was too strong for him. He cried, telling her that he thought of her as his mother, and that he didn't know why he'd behaved the way he had. She forgave him. Weeks later, while she and Tabitha were away, he broke into the house, filled the bathtub with water, waited for her to return, and submerged himself in the water, pretending to commit suicide. Her comforting hands saved him from his doom, and he talked about the kindness of her touch. A few times while at home in his bed, when he had concentrated on her rescue, he pricked his scrotum with a pin and masturbated, thinking of her facial expressions.

Several months later, he crawled through a window and attacked Tabitha's mom as she slept. Devin was not able to rape her or, as he said, "to be inside the whore." She was still more powerful than Devin and held him on the floor until the police arrived. Devin cried and wailed in pain. He said that the woman often forced him into oral sex and that this time he had refused. After an investigation, they charged Tabitha's mother with felony rape of a minor. Devin refused to testify, although his testimony wasn't necessary. The charges against her were eventually dropped.

Devin returned again to rape her while she slept. This time he tied a noose around her neck and shoved amphetamines down her throat. After he pushed a few straight pins through her nipples, he assaulted her with sex toys, because he wasn't able to maintain an erection. He tied her wrists to the bed and choked her until she agreed to provide oral sex. She was not aware that Tabitha was sitting in a chair watching. Devin was angry that she had betrayed him by calling the police in the past. Now, he wanted to call the police, and this time, he told her, he would testify. As his last act, he grabbed Tabitha and ripped off her pajama bottom. He put a dildo close to her private parts and said to Tabitha's mother, "If you report me, I'll be back." She was amazed that Tabitha had not screamed, but rather smiled at Devin and kissed his cheek. Before leaving, Tabitha yelled, "Don't leave me, Dev!" He stole several items from the house and threw them in the ocean on his way home. A few times, late in the night and evening particularly when he was stoned out of his mind, he returned to Tabitha's mother bedroom. She never fought him again.

High School

Many of Devin's elementary classmates enrolled at the same private high school. Many of the upper class students knew various members of Devin's family, who had also graduated from the same high school. Knowledge of the family members, in addition to Devin's reputation as a "crazy kid," meant that few people, including teachers, challenged his aggressive behavior. Realizing his advantage, he often went "trash bagging," which meant he took items from student lockers, gym lockers, teachers' cars, and offices. Devin was a crime wave all by himself. Most of what he took he dumped in the ocean, except for the laptops. Those he used to stalk others. One time, a student accused him of a theft. It was the same student who had ratted him out earlier, only this time, Devin said, "the bully had an accomplice who supported him, a high school teacher." Devin stalked the student, broke into his home, and stood on top of the boy as he slept in his bedroom.

"When the little creep opened his friggin' eyes, he saw me standing on him. I told him, next time I'll cut your friggin' dick off." Devin said grabbed the boy's neck and squeezed until the boy passed out. According to Devin's PSI, the boy recanted his story about Devin's theft. He said he had stolen the missing items and then blamed it on Devin. Poor Devin, a victim of foul play by a school bully and a teacher.

High school counselors labeled Devin "incorrigible," but because the label was part of Devin's school records, the counselors were unable to provide this information to PSI investigators. But the principal of the school gave the official assessment that Devin had an exceptionally high IQ. He was ranked in the top five percent of students nationally.

Experts say that exceptionally intelligent children differ qualitatively from other children, and tend to be socially isolated. Children similar to Devin remain a mystery to parents through their own manipulation and cunning. Yet experts can often miss the wetness of the ocean. They tend to view educational options for exceptional children as effective, because exceptional children like Devin are allegedly under-challenged and should take advanced classes in whatever subject they excel at. What those experts failed to recognize in Devin's case is that what he excelled at was a struggle box of his own choosing. He was the straw that stirred the ocean. That is, Devin is wired-wrong and enjoyed *festival* before he was arrested and still in high school.

Festival

One day while cruising on his grandfather's boat, seeking victims for *festival* (that's what Devin called his sexual attacks), he saw a young girl and a baby sitting on the shore under a large green umbrella. He remembered Tabitha's "stray cat look," and was so excited by that memory, he instantly docked and sought out the young girl and the baby. He maneuvered the girl into touching the baby's private parts. "I left her as she played with the baby. You should have seen this little Cosette. She had no idea what she was doing, but I had to get out of there."

Pornography

Devin explained that when he was seven years old, he came across pictures of naked women engaged in sexual acts (Note: it was around the time his sister drowned). He found magazines hidden in uncle's car parked at his grandparents' home. Devin thought that his uncle was about twenty at the time, and that his uncle was drunk a lot. Devin had few reservations about breaking into his uncle's bedroom to search for more magazines. He found cigarettes, pictures of his uncle having sex with his girlfriend, bottles of Jack Daniels whiskey, sex toys (including the large dildo he used to later attack Tabitha's mother), and tons of magazines. Devin took some of his loot and sneaked onto his grandparents' boat at the pier. He smoked the cigarettes, drank the Jack Daniels, but spit most of it out, and masturbated to the pictures of his uncle with his girlfriend. But first, "I'd lie on my arm until I lost feeling in it and played with myself, hard, while looking at my uncle and his girlfriend."

Seeking Porn

Devin explained that somewhere around thirteen years of age, while he was babysitting Tabitha but before he had sex with Tabitha's mother, he visited porn movie shops that charged a quarter for four minutes of movie clips in private booths. His uncle took him into the first porn movie shop, probably because Devin manipulated him into it. It is assumed that Devin had enough evidence on his uncle to bully him into doing whatever Devin wanted him to do. Devin had a lot of experience with manipulating and terrorizing others by that time. It's also likely that when Devin's uncle introduced him to the proprietor, the proprietor was not pleased with Devin's youth. Still the proprietor would have known better than to say no to Devin's uncle. Also, the proprietor probably never thought Devin would become a regular customer, even if he wished he would. Devin's presence would enhance his business. The proprietor was wrong on one count, but correct on the other count.

Devin eventually learned that if he touched himself at the porn shop while viewing video clips, his safety was assured. Men would ejaculate in private booths adjacent to his as they watched him. The observers also paid Devin's entrance fee and provided all the quarters he needed to view the clips. They gave him extra money when he left the curtains open to his booth. The walls in each booth were approximately six feet tall. The floors were tilted, and one seat was permanently centered in the stall, facing a screen. A small metal coin box stood on the right side of the stall. The stall was a little larger than a restroom stall. The smell of the bleach and ammonia used to clean the floors teaming with semen lingered in the air and could only be cut with a butcher knife. Porn shops of this variety are common in downtown areas and continue to operate nationwide.

By fifteen, Devin visited porn shops twice or more a week, but overall, he masturbated twice a day at a minimum, to a high of six times a day. When he was in school, he visited a toilet stall, pulled out a picture he had hidden in his pocket, and stroked his genitals until he ejaculated. Once it was over, he pitched the picture into the toilet and flushed. Devin never saved pictures, magazines, computer images, or movies. He learned never to save anything. They weighted him down, they were a liability, and saved items could lead to his detection. Devin remembered his uncle's stash—looked what happened to him.

Devin was always excited about pornography—soft pornography, retro pornography, raw pornography, and eventually fantasy pornography, which included forced oral sex and rape. The scenes that excited him at first were photographs of females engaged in oral and anal intercourse with two different males. Devin recalled that during the time when he was he babysitting Tabitha, he got excited about black gangbangers engaged in multiple sexual activities with a single blond female. The younger the better. Largely, Devin studied the face of the females. His focus was not on sexual penetration. "It's her facial features and the agony in her eyes that's the turn on," he reported. He tried bondage, fantasy bondage, and straight sex pornography, but returned to gangbangers because he was assured that the females "were in fear of their lives, because they were terrorized by those big black male sex organs."

The Eyes Have It

Painful facial expressions of both males and females who were sexually penetrated are the primary ingredient to Devin's erotic fantasy. He said that he saw those eyes in Tabitha's mother, too, and that's why he had to do rape her "It was her fault that I attacked her," He explained. From time to time, he reported that he cruised gay pornography in magazines and online, enjoying images of young boys who had breast implants and other cosmetic surgery, making them look female, except "a she-male with an erect penis." The most exciting photos and movies for Devin were she-males whose bodies were viciously attacked by an uncaring man or men, who would terrorize their victims with a large male organ. "It wasn't a male or female thing. I'm not gay. It's the facial expressions and the screaming and the fighting off of their attackers that gets to me." He mentioned that the position of their legs, the pain in their expressions, and the sweat on their bodies captured his attention and were the most relevant part of his search, but he always studied the eyes. If the attacked person's eyes contained even a glimmer of pleasure, "that was a turn off. What I care about is getting off, and it's all in the eyes. Tabitha's mother had those eyes. It was her crime of passion that jolted me to be with her."

Saved Things

Devin saved his thoughts, which contained his observations about pornography. Sometimes, he would dream about porn. When he awoke, the sights and sounds of whatever he had observed earlier dominated his thoughts. He slid two fingers over his bottom, passed his genitals, smelled those fingers, and ran his fingers over his tongue. As he reached an ejaculation in his own bed, he tasted his fluids and wiped his eyes with wet fingers. He said the wetness from his sperm on his eyelids made them heavy and he fell asleep, but not before he envisioned the facial expressions of the individuals who'd been assaulted in the porn video clips or photos.

Devin said that even as he conjured those facial images, he knew—given his physical equipment—he would never be able to bring a victim to the painful heights that gangbangers did. He had to bite victims hard on the neck to produce the same effect, whether he had penetrated him or her with his own flesh or a sex toy. Sometimes when he masturbated, he cut his arm and sucked the blood. Devin is a cutter. He would watch his face in a mirror when he cut himself. He finally decided he was a vampire. His goal was to reproduce the agonized facial expressions he had seen so many times.

Stalking

Devin's compulsion with masturbation was rivaled by his stalking activities. "Carrying a weapon made me a target for detention, special classes, and the cops. Carrying a laptop is another world totally. Everybody's lookin' for Teddy [Ted Bundy] and ganged-up goof balls. Nobody's lookin' for me, but I'm sure as hell lookin' for them."

Despite his age, Devin knew how to drive a car and pilot a boat. When he was fifteen, a typical routine for Devin was to ignore school and travel the countryside. He said he cruised the resort areas aboard his grandfather's boat, seeking, searching, and remembering. He talked to himself all the time. Expenses, such as gasoline, lunch, and dinner, were put on credit cards; or he used cash given him at the porn shop, or what he took from servants and his uncles or Tabitha's mother. His parents had four vehicles and were rarely home. His stepdad's kids were in day care. But he remained within the state where he lived, because in another state, his driver's license might be scrutinized and his out-of-state license plates might prompt law enforcement to inquire about his presence.

One sunny day, he drove through a seaside resort complex and spotted a young girl in a bikini. In her eyes. she possessed "the look of a great victim," Devin wrote. "She knew it, too, because she stared at me, waiting for me to ask her into the car, which I didn't do. I drove away. Parked at a busy gas station and walked back. She came out from one of the units. We hooked up and walked to the beach. We went to a totally deserted part and kissed. I felt her heat immediately hammering through her tight little body. When I bit her neck, I couldn't help myself, I had to look into her eyes. Yep, it was there—that look in her eyes that I so love. For the next few weeks I thought only about those eyes. I thought about those eyes widening from pain. When I touched myself, all I could see were those big blues shouting with pain. God, I popped just thinking about it. I cut myself and sucked the blood, but it didn't taste like her blood. I had to find another sweet thing like her, or her again."

Devin explored the countryside by day, often using different vehicles; and at night he explored websites: pornography sites, as well as Facebook, Bolt, and MySpace. He sought "the look. I'm a zombie tracker. The people I mess with will die eventually, so their little life on this planet belongs to me. How could I be arrested for any crime when everyone eventually dies? I was dealing with corpses. That's why I'm zombie tracker."

Pictures of pre-teens and teenagers on the Internet were easy to track, because "arrogant kids often think they're superior to everyone else and leave clues in their photos about their life, their school, or whatever. They say stupid stuff on websites, making my job big-time easy. These young things are cute but stupid. I can find everything about everybody just knowing a little something about them. Public records are easy to hack. Cops are stupid, too, because they think that they're smarter than everyone."

In chat rooms, Devin used different e-mail addresses, server names, and passwords. Several of them were random, and were confirmed by other e-mail providers, such as Gmail and Hotmail. He had more than one computer, and the ones he used for "zombie trolling" were laptops purchased with cash or ones he's stolen from stores, schools, and neighbors' homes. His Internet providers were other customers' providers in the community. He pirated their connections by hacking into their systems. A Holiday Inn was a few miles from his home, and often he connected to their Internet server. Devin knew enough about the Internet to delete his browser after every use, to wipe his hard drive with an electronic cleaner that made forty-eight passes, and at least weekly, he used ComboFix on his hard drive. He also frequently changed his e-mail addresses, profiles including photos, and computers.

Drug History

Devin's juvenile mental health records were not available to the investigators who developed his PSI, or to the Department of Corrections, because he was sentenced as an adult and the records were developed when he was a juvenile. However, when Devin entered the prison system, he was tested for drug use. He appeared to be addicted to cocaine—which would be replaced by heroin after imprisonment—and to inhalants, LSD, mescaline, and antidepressants. The antidepressants were prescribed by mental health providers in the free world, and then by the mental health unit in prison. He was probably fourteen when he started using drugs, and his suppliers consisted of the men at porn shops. Also, because Devin was a chronic thief, he stole drugs from various homes. Because the drugs were illegal, the owners weren't likely to report those break-ins. On a regular schedule, Devin burglarized the same homes time and again.

Devin's Classification and Housing

Devin's classification showed that he was at an at-risk security level. He was assigned to a maximum custody facility, and to a special wing within the prison that housed four other teenagers. Two were from Section 8 housing in a large metropolitan area, and one was from the fringes of an upwardly mobile county-club environment, similar to Devin's.

Devin and Suicide Watch and Restrictions

Devin was placed on suicide watch at least four times within the first ten months of his imprisonment. It became evident that he would harm himself when the opportunity arose, and isolation and medications were used to control him—or so authorities hoped. Devin was always restricted to many common areas of the prison, such as the gymnasium, cafeteria, library, classrooms, visiting areas, ballpark, bathrooms, showers, commissary, without an escort. The rationale of the prison was that Devin was a youthful offender. The reality was that Devin would disrupt other prisoner activities, promote violence between other prisoners, and perform in such a way as to irritate other prisoners. For example, while standing in the lunch line, Devin would fart and belch loudly. On one occasion, he bit himself hard enough that blood flowed from his fingers. He blamed it on the prisoner behind him in line, and then sucked the blood and allowed it to run down his chin.

This particular action was caught on a security camera. The behavioral scientists and correctional personnel reviewing the video were astounded that Devin had not been classified as a high-risk prisoner and transferred to the mental clinic facility across the state. For some reason, when DOC officials tried to transfer Devin to a mental unit, the request was denied. Apparently, his sentence was being appealed, and it looked as if he would be released. What custody personnel and prisoners alike knew about Devin was that he stalked their brains. Late at night, when they suddenly awoke because the liquor or the drugs they had consumed to help them sleep didn't work, there it was. Devin's face was there, in the dark of the room, smiling at them.

Tentative Conclusions

Comfort is a necessity for Devin, similar to the other controllers in this study. Yet controllers struggle between trying to feel comfortable and their feelings of inferiority. This produces both an insecurity and fatalistic thoughts that foretell imminent danger. Because controllers hold this pessimistic view about themselves, they often believe they are unloved, stupid, and doomed to live as a worm would below the earth. That regardless of the many times a worm wiggles or how loudly it screams, no one can see or hear it, even if it has changed. Therefore, the only plausible solution to their struggle to feel loved, intelligent, and superior is to control others, places, and circumstances. It doesn't matter how many times they twist and scream, or what violence they commit or upon whom, all acts reduce their sense of inferiority, and comfort is momentarily established.

Similar to many parents, Devin's parents blamed themselves for his wicked behavior, and were embarrassed to provide details when interviewed by investigators after his arrest. Behavioral experts say that parents of violent children often feel bewildered and helpless as their offspring reject their guidance and, eventually, become offenders. For decades, psychiatrists, psychologists, social workers, and educators have convinced parents and policymakers that parents hold the primary responsibility for shaping the destinies of their children.

One expert advises that the parents of a gun-toting uneducated thug on the streets of Washington DC and the parents of a crooked Georgetown business executive, feel equally responsible for their offsprings' behavior. Unpopular studies have shown that some youngsters and adults will harm others and engage in radical, violent behavior no matter what society they were raised in, or how hard their parents worked to provide a positive environment for them. Devin's parents fit the profile, and they committed suicide the week it was announced that Devin had been wrongfully convicted and would return home.

Wrongful Conviction

All total, Devin served twelve months of a four-year sentence for aggravated assault, but some correctional personnel thought Devin should have been strapped to Ole' Sparky and a million volts of electricity shot through his body. Devin was to leave the high-custody lockdown institution, where the state of Florida accommodates the worst of its youthful offenders. The do-gooders and bleeding-heart liberals who continue to slam the system that protects them, provided evidence that showed Devin had been wrongfully convicted. The entire justice process, from the wavier to adult court, to adult sentencing, to the plea suddenly became an issue for the high court, its liberal financers, and the press, whose members were never required to invite Devin to the dinner table with their spouses and children.

Looking up from the file as prisoner 24601 entered, I said, "Hi, take a seat," and dropped the file on the desk.

"Tell me about your earliest experiences—" I was going to end my question with the words, "at this institution," but Devin cut me off.

"You writing a book?"

"Sure."

"Confidential, just like during group?"

"Absolutely."

He nodded. "If you say anything, I'll hunt ya down, doc."

I smiled. "The hunt-down won't be your greatest performance, Devin. But I'll be careful."

"Let me explain. I was bitten by a wild pack animal in my fight to stay in my mother's womb. I held on to her filthy bowels during my descent, yet I spit on her tubes like a sailor pitched from a whorehouse in Amsterdam. She's a vile person who deserves no mercy, not even from a vampire. I bit the cord like a wild dog and sucked up her waste," he said on that pleasant Tuesday afternoon in early spring. "I made her a clean woman and then she carried that little bitch Emily in the same sack where I was formed and that pissed me off."

That was one of the few times I caught a glimmer of his soul, and it wasn't humanlike.

CHAPTER 6
Dory, an Angry Woman

Early Life

Dorothea Marquette Henderson was her given name. She was born three weeks early on October 8. Juan Peron, the president of Argentina, Jesse Jackson, and Matt Damon share that birthday, but it is also the day when, in 1871, Catherine O'Leary's cow tipped over a lantern and burned down the city of Chicago. Dorothea was named after the famous US photographer, Dorothea Lange, whose photos of the homeless during the Great Depression led to her employment by a federal agency to bring the plight of the poor to public attention. One of her most famous photographs is on display at the Library of Congress in Washington DC, entitled *Migrant Mother*.

The family hoped that Dorothea, the fifth and last of the Henderson children, would follow in the path of her namesake, a great humanitarian. Her father, a United States District Court judge for eleven years, was an important man among government officials and the wealthy who summered on Cape Cod. The judge and his wife had attended all the right schools, including Boston University Law School, and it was expected that Dorothea and her four brothers would also graduate from their parents' alma mater. Life pleasures are predictable among Boston's Irish royalty, and it was believed that none of the Hendersons would ever work in Manhattan or cheer for the Yankees. Yet whispers of decadence and shades of betrayal by nannies with British accents and Harvard therapists who owed little to the

Irish establishment were ignored by the Hendersons when it came to their baby daughter. Maybe if someone had listened, life would have been different for Dorothea. But it's doubtful there would have been any changes, because she was a hard-headed girl who hated music and loved drama, but only the drama she produced.

Dorothea was a sweet-looking child with long dark blond hair and brown eyes accented by brows that never seemed out of place, even when she was a child. Yet she had an angry expression on her face that would never go away. Her frame was shaped like a thousand other girls, but what eventually caught your eye were her elegant hands and long fingers, which were always polished in a French manicure. She never liked how she looked and never looked in a mirror, no matter her age. If she had, the anger in her face would have spoken about today's weariness and yesterday's sorrow. I suppose if I were a psychologist, I'd say she possessed little if any self-respect, and less respect for others. Dorothea was always bored, but with all the drama of many young girls, she never cared for herself. She was a fireball, and perhaps flames from the Chicago fire reached out and scorched her patience and ignited her ruthlessness the day she was born. But as she toddled the blue-blood streets of Boston, she seemed to quiver with an incredible "fire down below," as Bob Seger sang. She was always in heat!

Young Dorothea

Dorothea was a handful, hateful and unconcerned about events and others around her as a child and as an adult. One servant said that Dorothea was always high maintenance, draining her mother's breasts so aggressively that she left marks and bruises, and a few times, her mother pushed Dorothea away. Eventually, Mrs. Henderson stopped breastfeeding the child, and left her in the care of a nanny. Sigmund Freud might say that little Dorothea somehow experienced her mother's rejection, and somehow those actions manifested into Dorothea's violent behavior. Nonetheless, her nanny had high hopes of nurturing baby Dorothea, only to desperately plea to be allowed to return to her kitchen chores and allow someone else to tend to Dorothea's unreasonable demands. To clarify Dorothea's behavior, one of the reports implied that Dorothea hardly noticed anyone in a room and kept to herself, unless she wanted something to eat or something to play with. She didn't respond well to other children or their toys, and it seemed that right through grade school, Dorothea tended to notice only items worn by others, especially jewelry and shoes. Dorothea always demonstrated a short attention span, and flip-flopped from subject to subject, item to item, person to person, and shoe to shoe, without drawing a breath. No item, person, or event captured her attention for long; after that it was all downhill. Some of these behaviors were observable when Dorothea was imprisoned. When she wrote about herself, it was clear that she was excessively self-centered and rarely moved by the needs, requests, or directives of correctional personnel, prisoners, and visitors. It can be concluded from all the evidence available that during Dorothea's youth and adulthood, she and she alone was the focal point of her concern, a position sadly opposite that of her namesake.

During prison in-group sessions, Dorothea rarely acknowledged anyone, although she was aware of what was going on around her. She focused on the slightest hand gesture or movement of someone's legs. Sometimes, I thought she had actually counted the number of times someone's knees bounced back and forth. During a correctional social service meeting, my description of Dorothea, although hardly a clinical perspective, was that she was outrageously arrogant or bodacious (my favorite word) and self-centered or narcissistic and deadly. Blink, though, and it could be over. This thought suggests that when given the opportunity, Dorothea would never hesitate to utilize lethal force against anyone—relative, priest, partner, even her own child. Some might say that Dorothea was wired-wrong from birth. My critics would condemn that suggestion, and perhaps that's one reason super predators tend to be largely undetected in the first place.

Dorothea's mother admitted foretelling the future best described by Dorothea herself, as she wrote in her prison journal years later: "I'm usually on the prowl for an unsuspecting fool who thinks he can jack me up, and to his astonishment meets my little friend [a six inch razor sharp stiletto]. I'll slit his throat enough to hear him beg and then I'll laugh." Dorothea's obsession with knives was actually a fixation with hunting and hurting victims (in contrast to Annie, whose obsession was excitement). The more Dorothea hunted and harmed others, the better she felt about herself and the better she related to her circumstances. Violating others produced a serene, almost comforting effect on Dorothea.

Siblings and Parental Absence

As the youngest Henderson, Dorothea was spoiled rotten. John Henderson was about forty-two years old, his wife a year older than he, when Dorothea was born. Dorothea's four older brothers attended universities in New England, and one of them was a law clerk for his dad. When Dorothea legally changed her name to Dory, she was in the eighth grade and about to enter a private boarding school in Massachusetts, where one American president had sent his daughter. Dory's brothers had all moved from the family residence. Her parents were thinking about retirement, and they did little to constrain Dory's behavior. Actually, Dory's parents felt she was a boarder instead of a dependent, who was full of rage over every little thing, including the way her dad drank his coffee in the morning. Eventually, he stopped drinking coffee at their fashionable condo overlooking the Boston Commons, and walked the few blocks to the club downtown to enjoy his breakfast.

Dory's mother also found reasons to be away from the family home. However, both of Dorothea's parents spent more money on her and gave her more money than they had their four other children. Maybe it was guilt or a way to compensate for their absence. Whatever the reason, Dory had few limitations and less supervision until she attended boarding school. There, they had rules. But she finessed her way around those rules like all the other kids with similar backgrounds. For instance, she didn't care for the mattress in her dorm room and ordered a new mattress and bed frame, as had several other students. The beds were delivered and installed as if it were a routine matter. What is also known about Dory in high school is that she was a straight A student with a capacity for the natural sciences, especially chemistry. She was elected each of her four years in high school to represent her classmates as either class secretary, treasurer, or class president. Dory was accepted at Harvard, Brown, and Princeton, but decided to attend Boston University. She lived in a dormitory, "like a peasant," she said. Her dorm was eight blocks from her childhood home, and overlooked the Charles River and the Prudential Building.

Boston Night Life

The city of Boston boasts an estimated 250,000 college students enrolled at more than 30 colleges. Nightlife entrepreneurs take advantage of the opportunity and operate a couple thousand bars, dance clubs, restaurants with bars, and strip clubs in the city. Requiring identification from boys is a must, but hot girls like Dory are dragged off the street, rarely pay for a drink or a line of cocaine, and sit center stage as any trophy would. Bars operate well into the early morning hours, and being able to walk to your dorm room or ride public transportation there makes it easy as sin to get totally wasted. Especially when the Red Sox are playing at home. Their stadium is across the street from Boston University and within easy distance of fifteen universities, including Harvard, UMass Boston, and Suffolk University. Someone like Dory adores Bos'tune (as she called it), and there's never a hassle to get whatever when you're hot. Dory got it all, whenever.

Caught in a Trap

It's unknown if Dory fell into the trap while at high school or college, and couldn't or wouldn't get out of it. She chased a breathtaking rainbow that wouldn't let her catch her breath. What started as a voluntary cure against a dull world, and I am referring to cocaine, became a flood of decadence for Dory. She drowned in a storm of her own making, because she forgot or didn't care to remember that you can't beat your master with your master's tools. Dory always believed that she alone held the power. How arrogant of her to think that she could save her butt, for in the end, rainbows fade, no matter who's chasing them. When she was imprisoned, she said that the previous five years of her life were a haze, and bits and pieces popped into her head every so often. She recalled giving birth to a child, maybe more than one, but couldn't remember high school other than she had brought a new mattress.

Dory's Disappearance

Dory was in her second year at Boston University. It was a Tuesday when she didn't attend class, and the next day, one of her professors called the Henderson home. Her late model sports car was parked in the dorm's parking lot. All of her belongings were in her dorm room, including her backpack and pocketbook, which contained makeup, her American Express and Visa cards, university identification, and her driver's license. On Saturday the Hendersons filed a missing person's report with the police. The evidence and Judge Henderson's position suggested foul play. Posters with Dory's picture flooded the Boston area. Her classmates, professors, and friends were questioned. Weeks passed, and little was learned about her disappearance. Many tips suggested that a guy named Jamie Morrison, a chemistry graduate student at BU, might have knowledge about her disappearance. Morrison was unable to help the investigators, but provided information about her cocaine addiction. Until that time, the police had not turned up any indicators of her addiction. Morrison was arrested for possession of cocaine with the intent to distribute, and was eventually convicted of those crimes. But Dory Henderson's whereabouts remained a mystery. It was theorized that she had been abducted by a stranger who also had an interest in cocaine, but considering who her dad was, that angle was played down. The question in the bars and post office was "Have You Seen Dory?" Boston was in an uproar over her disappearance, bars started to check IDs, and universities took an active role in policing students. The Henderson family wouldn't learn about her whereabouts until she was convicted and imprisoned six years later.

An Explanation

When Dory was imprisoned, she explained that she had grown tired of her life on campus and in the bars, and had left town. Her prison journal explained that she went on a drug binge and left a party with a drug dealer she had recently met. She became aware of her new lifestyle several months later—sort of. She was casually walking down a busy street, when some guys in a sport utility vehicle started talking to her. They were looking for, Dory explained, "a date, which means s-e-x." She climbed into their vehicle, took on three males, and inhaled a rail of cocaine. She exited the vehicle and walked away with a hundred dollars, plus a pack of Marlboro cigarettes. A large black man approached her and asked her for the money. He was her protector, but the cops said he was her pimp. He slapped her hard, "Give it up, hoe," he bellowed. She tore into his eyes with a cold hard stare then ran, only to stop, turn back, and give him her earnings. "Here, sweetie," she said.

Dory's accounts suggested that she lived in Philadelphia. Her pimp and several members of his posse lived in a fortified home with all wood floors and a brick wall that wrapped all the way around the property. The windows had bars on them, and he drove a supersized sport utility vehicle. Most often they or others gang raped her, spread her thin in several different directions at once, filled every cavity she possessed, and called her filthy names. Her pimp pushed into her ear, when it wasn't filled with anything else, and said, "I owns you, hoe, and I knows you love it." And she did. "There was something eternal about it. It was me they labored hard over and so I was in control, not them. When all was said and done, I wrapped my arms around my big African man and smiled at him. He gently wiped the male fluids from my face."

When her body wasn't spread out, filled with male parts and kisses from other prostitutes owned by her man, and wet from a sea of sweat and sperm, she walked the streets looking for "dates." Her man watched her every move. There was no escape. She was told which vehicles to approach, where her date must park, how to know if her date was sick or carrying a weapon, and always told the client, "My man is very possessive. Don't piss him off." One time, her date tried to drive away with her. Two vehicles filled with her man's posse closed in on them. At an intersection and in the middle of day, the other men beat the man's face with a tire iron as he sat in the driver's seat. Dory escaped and jumped into her pimp's vehicle. The cops never showed and nothing ever came of it. More than likely, they were being paid off, because she never saw a cop anywhere, no matter who the posse beat up or where.

Another time, she remembered that a date drove her to his home in a suburban area outside of Philadelphia. She ran from his vehicle when he stopped, waiting for his garage door to open. A taxi just happened to be in the vicinity and took her back to her pimp. The taxi driver seemed to know who she was and who her man was. He drove her to 5th Street and Howard Street without question. Later, she pointed out the house to her man, he and his posse broke into the suburban home in the wee hours of the morning and beat the man, his wife, and their three children. She watched and took a few of own swings. "There I was in the middle of this black crowd, ripping up this white guy's family, and I rooted for my handsome African man so hard that I peed in my pants. I was so excited."

By that time in her life, Dory's five foot four inch frame tipped the scales at maybe ninety-eight pounds, her cheeks were sunken, and she had blurred vision. But worse, she realized that she could not be alone or straight. Yet the weather in Philadelphia was hard on her, and she couldn't get warm. The snow and ice had its own way on her thoughts, and she knew she looked much, much older, because the guys didn't stop as often as they had for a date. She asked her man to move her to a warmer climate. Finally, she realized she was experiencing something different in her body. She was three months pregnant. That was the jolt back to reality that moved her into action. She was twenty-one years old.

Bye-bye Philadelphia

One morning, as everyone slept, she pushed some of the posse members off her and went for the door, after grabbing some clothes she had placed near it. She jumped into her man's SUV, shoved the spare key into the ignition, and sped off. When the vehicle ran out of gas, she hustled a few travelers into paying for a full tank of gas, and eventually made her way to North Carolina. She parked at a highway rest stop. After sizing up several travelers, she spotted a local traveler who could be convinced to take her to his home. He was a slender, shy man with big nasty eyes that looked at every female regardless of her age, and he had outrageous eyebrows. When women flipped him off or rolled their eyes because of his stare, he looked down pretending to see nothing. What a fraud! "His name was Ralph and took me to his house where he raped me. I set the stage, but he was so slow in attacking me that I had to show him how it's done. Then I followed up with guilt on the little guy. He took care of me when he discovered I was ill and pregnant because of him. Life was a boring hell," she explained at length. "I missed my man and nothing Ralph could do made me a happy woman. But I also needed my rest. I convinced Ralph that he was responsible for my pregnancy, what a friggin' dummy. It wasn't fun because I needed cocaine and I dragged him to the local bars. I easily scored. When those cowboys in the bars started making over me, I explained to Ralph that after his crazy rape of my body, I couldn't control myself. He brought out the evil in me. I couldn't control it. He said he would watch me have sex with those cowboys. Through sex and his meager income, I was finally able to get high enough. But my appetite for more than one man had returned, and I was going through worse than hell trying just to breathe. Ralph and I stayed together until I went into labor. Ralph was shocked when my child was black. But look at me Ralph, I'm white. You must have black in your family. How could you do this to me? More guilt, and the little creep bought anything I said. If you just counted the months, he would have figured it out. Even God can't fix stupid."

Jockey Stops

When her son was about five months old, she left in Ralph's car. She took his credit cards, jewelry, and cash, and stopped at an ATM machine to get everything else he owned before hitting the interstate. Again, Dory hustled men for money to buy drugs at truck stops—known as jockey stop—along the interstates, which most often are busy twenty-four hours a day. Drivers of the huge 18-wheelers slept in their cabs and welcomed hookers, drugs, and gambling all night long. Every jockey stop along the interstate is a little Vegas, except for the smell. A blast from a deodorant bomb and no one knows the difference.

Jockey Hookers and CIA Operatives

After a time, there were few jockey hookers Dory didn't know, and fewer still who didn't know her and her son. Her son was her constant companion, even as she worked the jockeys in the big rigs parked at the all-night jockey stops. Most of the working girls knew each other at least by sight. In the diners little nods would go in the direction of a jockey who paid well, and eyes would roll toward the ceiling to indicate those who didn't. There were other motions. A girl tapping her shoulder signified a jockey that liked to slap girls around. A tap to the heart meant a jockey was easily swayed by a good story of hardship, resulting in extra tips. At many jockey stops across the nation, a small band of working girls covertly gathered information, stealthily engaged in criminal activities, and secretly passed information to one another with more efficiency than CIA operatives. Other information was readily available, such as what the jockey was hauling. In some instances, that information could be sold to hijackers who sought specific cargo. Dory sold information from time to time, but never to foreigners and never about weapons or things of that nature. Prized freight was specialized machinery, tools, and electrics, and Dory wrote in her prison journal that she earned an easy thousand dollars through one of her tips. After learning that a jockey was hauling freight someone she knew was looking for, she called that individual. She received the money at the next jockey stop in cash. Dory said that it was when she and son were in that diner, that a girl looked at her, tapped her heart, and then turned her look to Britt.

Jockey Stop Man

Dory met the man of her dreams one night in late August at the Saris Truck Plaza, a few miles from Bishopville, South Carolina. By that time her son was four years old, and she had been working the jockey stops for some time. Nonetheless, she described the man of her dreams as the cross-country truck driver of a Big Red, a bright red Kenworth loaded with 450 horsepower and lots of chrome, in and out. The Kenworth had a "palace" sleeper, with leather, mirrors, television, and a computer. Britt was a reefers hauler, and his trailer was chromed too. The unit was equipped with an air conditioner in the front of the trailer. Largely, Britt hauled food products that required refrigeration. His unit had the capacity to keep products frozen, and he made plenty of money. He also moved cocaine in those freezers. Frozen dope cannot be detected by drug-sniffing dogs or seen by somber weight station attendants. Britt never transferred large quantities, never enough to change the drug trade or make the competition jealous. But there was always enough for him and his new girlfriend, Dory.

"He was tall, slender, and southern, with large hands, a warm heart, and he knew how to keep a girl happy," Dory wrote. "But I ain't a fool. He had bucks and pure-ass drugs, too, and that set him apart from the other jockeys. Most jockeys had money, don't get me wrong, but they had old ladies, and she got the lion's share of his cash and his drugs. My Britt was different. The only hitch the jockey had was a kid, a six-year-old girl who lived with him on the truck. Because she couldn't talk, he took her everywhere he went. Said he didn't trust anyone to take care of her. His wife died giving birth."

While Britt and Dory were being intimate in the rig's palace, Britt's daughter and Dory's son sat in the front seat of Big Red. The four became happy travelers together. Dory even added thick gold brackets to her already jewelry-clad arm. She called her left arm her trademark, because people remembered all of her jewelry was on her right arm. She was a southpaw, the only arm she used when she worked. Otherwise everyone could hear the jingle jangle of her jewelry.

Sometimes when Britt was driving the big rig, Dory would stretch her body out across Big Red's passenger seat. Lying on her tummy, she would dry-hump the leather seat to keep his focus on her. With the kids in the palace, she would satisfy Britt with mouth and hand. When the "moment" arrived for Britt, he pulled the horn-lever, which bellowed out a train horn sound that caught motorists by surprise. Most of the drivers hit their brakes, and red brake lights glittered the highway. The two of them would laugh while Dory zipped his pants and reached for the children. She was never concerned if she wiped Britt's semen off, because "God created all the fluids in the world, and to deny children from tasting God's fluids might be a crime. I'd pull my son down from the palace and kiss him on the lips, and if I was really happy, the girl too." Dory made a similar comment about cocaine. "How could anything coming out of God's earth be bad?" Britt asked her if she wanted to give her son a hit of cocaine, because that way both children could enjoy the world. She said no at first, yet eventually had little choice. "Everybody deserves to be happy."

Living High on the Hog

About six months passed, but Dory isn't sure of the time frame, because she was busy entertaining jockeys and high. She enjoyed those experiences probably far more than Britt understood, and more than an observer could expect. Life was good, Dory explained. She had a man, drugs, shelter, dined at restaurants, and when Britt slept in the palace with the kids at jockey stops, Dory worked the jockeys for sex and drugs. But it was more than sex and drugs. It was that she was the center of attention. She liked that very much, and mentioned that that was something she never experienced as a child in Boston. With Britt, she had her son to show off in the diners, suggesting that she was respectable person with a child; but late at night, she didn't have her son, so, her thinking went, she could service more jockeys than ever. Dory entertained around ten to twenty jockeys a night, every night, since Britt was "addicted to the boulevard." According to Dory, customers paid for her services in cash. She had few expenses other than condoms, and she said she "lived pretty high off the hog." When she had entertained on the streets in Philadelphia, her expenses had amounted to payoffs to the cops and pimps. Her income as a street-date amounted to zero because her "man" kept all her money, and she had no say whose vehicle to entertain in. Now, she worked the boulevard, which was pretty big time for Dory, in comparison to those streets in Philly. These guys had more money, more drugs, and a whole lot of action. She had stabbed more than one guy, and robbed anyone that gave her a chance. She controlled her dates, and during the entertainment portion of the date, she assessed their vulnerabilities and their assets, including jewelry, cash, and items in the vehicle. However, there were two experiences that were significant in Dory's life on the road, and the second one completely changed her life.

A Significant Experience

Big Red was parked at the Flying J Truck Stop near Pecos, Texas on I20. Similar to most jockey stops where Britt parked, there were two hundred parking spots. The place was packed, so Dory knew she would entertain as many as twenty jockeys for thirty minutes each and earn about $50 a throw. She was very often excited about new johns and new circumstances. Sometimes, a jockey would have his partner participate; sometimes the partner was a woman. Dory found that exciting, too, if the other woman knew what to do. But usually women talked too much, where men just got into the moment and performed without a lot of conversation. She liked her occupation. Her income would be more than a $1,000 a night. Depending on "generous guys who wanna play Donald Trump, I might double that, get all the drugs I needed for the next day or two, and anything I could steal. This one time I leaped from an International 9400I rig and had plans to jump into a big Mack, when something caught my eye in the rig next to me. The driver lowered his tinted window and said, 'Hey, Dory, it's me, Festus. Come on, girl.'

"I'll be damned. He knew my name, and he looked familiar, but I couldn't remember a jockey until I unzipped his pants."

She jumped in. He caught her by the neck and took away her knife. "

"The last thing I remember is looking into his eyes as he raped me with a baseball bat and threw me into the dead of night, somewhere along the boulevard. He took my money and my jewelry, which was really sad, but my pussy hurt like a sonuvabitch. I remembered his eyes as I was walking back to the jockey stop. I had robbed him at a Louisiana stop, but couldn't tell ya which one."

Once back, she climbed into Big Red three hours ahead of her routine schedule. She climbed in just as Britt and the children awoke, or so she thought. She told them the story about how she had been raped and robbed when she walked to the diner to use the bathroom. She carefully left off the part about knowing or robbing the guy. But something surfaced on their faces that told her something was wrong. Did they know she was a hooker? They couldn't, she thought, because every night when they slept, she worked the stops "as solid as a Sunday morning preacher. Then it struck me that Britt had a lover."

At a stop, she purchased a knife to replace her old one. She was angry, and angry women are capable of anything. The hooker at the jockey stop who had tapped her heart and looked at Britt was right about him, and Dory was very pleased that Britt was her new man. Britt was outraged by her rape story, took pity on her, and in the coming weeks, bought her expensive and finely crafted bracelets and rings to replace the ones that were stolen. Now, she charged more for her dates and stole more than she had before. But Dory continued to ask herself if Britt had a girlfriend. As Dory explained her thinking to me, my only conclusion was that if the fire in her eyes said anything, it was that this woman was not a woman to cross, or even look like crossing. In her eyes were those old flames from the burning city of Chicago.

Changes

A couple of months after Dory's rape, another experience occurred that would change everything. She decided to work only part of the night, and returned to Britt earlier than usual to see if he was "being true to me." I was hesitant to use her words, because Dory was not your ordinary garden-variety prostitute. She had more twisted stories to tell than Edgar Allen Poe.

Big Red was parked at the Flying J Truck Stop in Kenly, North Carolina off I95. Dory had her own remote button to open Big Red and did so. Finally, Dory saw Britt's lover. She "was right, but very sorry wrong. Britt was 'in' his daughter and his hands were on my son." He froze when he saw her. Maybe her wild accusing eyes said it all, or maybe it was the knife in her hand. She sliced his throat without hesitation. Blood gushed in every direction, including her face. The little girl's eyes widened, and Dory pushed the blade into her small chest, saying "Die, you fifty whore." Her son clung to her without so much as a tear. She pushed Britt's body to the floor and pitched his daughter on top of him. Dory reached down and touched the girl's vagina, and then brought her moistened fingers to her lips and to the lips of her son.

After wiping blood from the windows and her face and hands, she covered herself and her son with a blanket, and the two of them fell asleep in Big Red's palace. She put together the pieces and realized that Britt's daughter wasn't his daughter at all. She had sort of known that for some time, but didn't want to admit it. Dory decided that the little girl must be someone Britt had abducted. Because she was mute and young, she couldn't tell on him. She never had the opportunity. No wonder he didn't care that "I entertained the jockeys all night." In the morning, Dory took Britt's cash and valuables, including the cocaine in the freezer. She and her son had breakfast at the diner, ordered some take-out, and used the bathrooms. She hooked up with a rig jockey who was heading south. Once they were at full throttle on the boulevard, they heard an explosion from the jockey stop behind them. Dory had set a fire bomb in Big Red.

Dory and her son bailed about a hundred miles down the interstate, where they took up residency for the next few months under a bridge.

The Arrest

Five years after Dory left Philadelphia, six years after she'd disappeared from Boston, the state police in South Carolina received a call from a motorist at a rest stop. The caller said that he and his passenger had been attacked by a "crazy old woman with a knife" and they were bleeding. When officers arrived at the scene, they learned that the attacker was a derelict appearing female accompanied by a child. The officers helped load the victims into an emergency medical vehicle. The college boys described their attacker as a "mountain person who was like mindless, a random person that needed a bath." According to the report, their attacker offered "a good time" to the boys for money, and when they said they wouldn't touch her "if she was the last freak on earth with a box," she attacked them both, but they were able to push her away. "I think she was totally wasted," one of them told the troopers.

This was not the first report law enforcement had received of a "mountain lady" who bothered travelers at rest stops along the highway. Local sheriff deputies had had a person who fit the description of the mountain lady in custody a few weeks earlier, but they released her when the travelers who complained would not return to the area to sign a complaint. This time things would be different, because the boys had called one of their dads, who was now traveling to the hospital where both boys were taken.

The troopers made a sweep of the rest area. They assumed that the perpetrator was on foot with a child. The exits along the interstate were checked by other officers, and a police helicopter scanned the rural, wooded countryside for anyone walking with a child. Hours went by without success, and the search was called off. When the troopers returned to duty the next day, they talked to the sheriff's deputy who had apprehended the mountain lady weeks before. He said she had been seen at one of the bridges on the interstate by a sheriff patrol, but she probably had left the area. The troopers followed the lead and visited the bridge the deputy had described. Much to the troopers' amazement, they found her. She and her son were tightly wedged at the base, where the ground rises up to the bridge.

Once she and the boy were up and standing, the troopers noticed that the woman had several missing teeth. On both faces, the cheeks were sunken and they had dark spots under their eyes, but one of the boy's eyes wouldn't open at all. Fluid ran from their noses onto scaled lips. A foul stench emanated from the both of them. The boy appeared to be three or four years old and malnourished. He was actually five. The troopers had experienced much on the highways, but had never seen a child who was addicted to cocaine. The officers also noticed tiny creatures in the woman's and boy's thin hair. Both of them were such a mess that the troopers refused to put them into their cruiser and called paramedics for assistance. During jail processing, the woman had no identification, nor would she provide any information about herself. She was "totally stoned," the report said. She was incoherent, and the only thing the boy said was the name Britt. The officers estimated Jane Doe's age at forty-five to forty-eight. In fact, she was pregnant and twenty-six years old.

A complaint was signed by the victims against Jane Doe, and she was represented by a public defender. Her son was placed with foster care when Dory was jailed, because she could not raise bail, had no friends or relatives whom she could call, and was by all accounts a homeless alcoholic, cocaine addict, and street walker.

Guilty Plea

Dory accepted a guilty plea for two counts of aggravated assault. She was sentenced to seven years, and would have to serve five years before being eligible for early release. Her son became a permanent ward of the state. While in prison, Dory became addicted to antidepressants prescribed by the mental health unit, but most of the time her behavior was that of a high-functioning person. Sometimes Dory was restricted to specific areas of the prison, a result of her pregnancy and her detoxification. She was seldom on segregation or in an isolated unit, other than when she was housed in the pregnancy unit. Needless to say, her health was poor, and she rarely slept. Dory looked like a junkie and a hardened street hooker. But there was something else about her, besides hints that she was well-educated. When she talked, most everyone stared, because her appearance was so at odds with her voice, which was laced with a Boston accent, and she spoke with confidence, like a college professor. If you close your eyes and just listened to her voice, you would draw a different picture of her. But that could be a deadly decision, because this person has less compassion than Michael Vick in a kennel on Saturday night.

Prison

When Dory gave birth in prison, her child was a crack baby, born five weeks early. The child's gender was not known, and Dory was not permitted to touch the child. It is believed the baby died a few days after birth. Dory was placed on suicide watch in an isolated unit for three months, not because she demonstrated any guilt or sorrow about the child, but because of policy. Gossip from correctional personnel was that her son was addicted to cocaine, in poor health, and that Dory had rented him out for sexual pleasures to support her drug habit. It wasn't that Dory was a bad mother. She just needed her medicine—cocaine. Her thinking ran this way: "If I used crack instead of powder [cocaine], the impurities would be harmful to my body and my unborn child. So I used the best coke I could beg, borrow, or steal." When this information became known, Dory was immediately placed in protective custody, because the other prisoners would have killed her. They would kill anyone who disrespected children. Criminals have their own code of right and wrong, and of justice. Dory was attacked a few times, but, said a correctional officer, "she is a dirty fighter and goes for the eyes while she bites the shit out of anything near her teeth, what there are of them.".

An Interview with Dory

"It is hard to remember any of my past medical history, and answering questions has been terribly difficult for me. Or at least I think so. I remember coming into the [prison] system, even though I was cranked up. Then some fool who looked like he was twelve asked about German measles, my tonsils, and about STDs. Then he asked me the date of my last period. I was really bewildered, because I don't remember the answer and I wouldn't tell that kid anything so personal. I think my inability to recognize the appropriate answers for any of the medical questions is associated with my heavy medication and frustration at the time. Probably just as well. I appreciate everyone has their little program, but they really don't need to burden me with it. I want to move on, and I think my memory is functioning better each day. I'm pleased with myself if I can remember to keep myself clean, ya know, down there and to eat, and to try to sleep. But the image of me when I was living in the rig and then living under the bridge before my arrest rolls through my head like a dirty freight train in the middle of the night, going nowhere. I wonder if I'll shake the feeling, but I am not feeling guilty because I did it.

"A lot the women here wear some kind of medal on their shoulders as a victim of some circumstance. They feel guilt for being a broken woman, a beaten woman, a junkie, or a whore. Confessions I heard from the others at my first AA meeting drove me crazy. It was disturbing to hear the horrendous tales of their desperation and addictive lives. I think most of those stories are dredged up in a game of brag, to accommodate the meeting's success, and to add a shine to their medals. These confessions seem particularly poignant when told by the young and attractive ones. Then there's the one who carried guilt for having been on a week-long binge after her son was killed in a car wreck. How the hell, she asked, could she live with that? It was her fault that she hadn't had the brakes of the car repaired, and that's why she killed the auto mechanic in a drunken rage after she gave him head.

"Some AA members make a correlation between their flimsy victimization and their crimes. That's my problem. I was never anyone's victim, no one I knew died, I was never denied love, food, or comfort. My parents never quarreled, except when I harassed the shit out of them and I would laugh at them and hassle them more. I tried to carry on fragile shoulders some kind of guilt for my past crimes when I first got here, but I couldn't find room for guilt, because I'm not sorry for being me. When I'm released, I will be me again until I'm six feet under."

Question: "What can you tell me about your pregnancies?"

Answer: "I suffered with a bit of morning sickness for the first three months, but after that I felt marvelous and couldn't believe how energetic I was! This last pregnancy came as a surprise, because when I was arrested, I was already pregnant but didn't know it. I thought my body was just messed up because of the arrest and jail and such. I discovered my condition when the jail doctor examined me."

Question: "With your first pregnancy, how did you alter your lifestyle as a consequence of it?"

Answer: "The only thing I did was vitamins. The guy who knocked me up was far away in Philadelphia, but I'm not sure who he was. I gave birth through a caesarean at thirty-nine weeks. Before the child was a year old I was traveling, and I stopped at a free clinic in Savannah, Georgia. They wanted to keep my baby because I wasn't a good mother, they said. After giving birth, I never wanted to go through that again, but I wanted my baby. I remember the pain of it all. There was this medical assistant who took an interest in me in Savannah, and with his help, I skipped out with my baby and then dumped the guy and borrowed his car. This last time, because I was in jail, they wouldn't entertain an abortion. Something about regulations. I had such a terrible time of it. I tried everything to get rid of it. I fell, I punched myself. I tried to grab it. They drugged me. I slept a lot, but even in my sleep I was crawling through a furnace on my hands and knees, and my toes swelled with pain. No matter what I did, I was uncomfortable. I thought that maybe if I ended it, I'd have a brief moment of relief. It was worth it. I tried but failed at that too."

Question: "Suppose you met a person whom you feel in love with. Would that make a difference?"

Answer: "Then I won't have to hunt for them. But I'd still cut 'em bad and rob 'em blind after having my fun. You applying for the job, doc?"

Question: "No, I'm good. But would you tell me what you mean by fun?"

She did, yet you already know her answer. And I'll never forget her voice.

CHAPTER 7
Janelle the Mortgage Fraud Queen

Early Life Experiences

Glen Gregg, Janelle's father, always said he was "Scottish by birth, American by law, and a Highlander by the grace of God." Janelle was born the third child of a prosperous New England family. The family was rich in heritage and loyal to their religious faith. The Greggs were Mormons, and similar to most Latter-Day Saint families, they honored the Law of Tithing. The Greggs made enormous contributions to the church and to Glen Gregg's alma mater, Harvard University. Both the church and the college showed their appreciation to Greggs in their local newspapers, named a room after Gregg (the Gregg Room), and a building after the Greggs (that's right, Gregg Building). The extravagance of it all actually embarrassed the servants employed by the Greggs, who believed they were underpaid, especially when tending to little Miss Janelle.

Except during the summers, when the Gregg children attended athletic camps or went to the family's Caribbean island home (near St. Thomas), Janelle and her older brothers, Jamey and Keith, led most of the religious programs at church in their hometown of Portland, Maine.

The Gregg children were involved in sports. Both boys played first string basketball and football through high school, track at college; and Janelle played softball and was a band member, although she really couldn't play well. Softball won her respect in high school and a scholarship to Brown University in Providence, Rhode Island. The world looked bright for her, but suddenly in her second year at Brown, she weighed over 220 pounds, and even at a height of five ten, some would say she was fat. Then, too, it was common knowledge that Janelle couldn't keep her hands to herself at college, or when she was younger. There were several disciplinary reports about her fighting and slapping players in the locker room and on the field. Her father's influence made those college reports disappear, as he had done at Portland High, but the Brown's softball coach was unmoved by Gregg's prestige. He benched Janelle for the season. Her benching added to her frustration, and she became more aggressive during practice and in the classroom. She disrespected the coaches, too, treating them like servants, and that attitude landed her in hot water. She wasn't in Portland any longer, and few would put up with such aggressive behavior.

College Grades and Sports

Eventually, Janelle lost her softball scholarship. She wrote that it was "fine that sports were ending, because it got harder to run around the field and I was spending less time at practice. I had to enroll in a course that met in the late afternoon a couple times a week to keep myself lined up for graduation, and that's when softball practice was scheduled." Janelle's grade point average declined from 3.7 in her sophomore year to 2.4 in her junior year. More than likely, her grades were inflated in her earlier years, because her softball skills were sharp and her potential was promising. As she got heavier, she was surpassed by younger players who had excellent skills and equal promise, and were not aggressive with players and professors. The coaches probably took the pressure off Janelle's professors to provide her with high grades. Janelle also would have been encountering more senior faculty as she focused on her major (business). Those professors more secured in their position and could stand up to the coaches, unlike untenured instructors who taught introductory courses to freshmen and sophomores. When Janelle ran down another player on the field during practice, resulting in a permanent injury to that player, it was clear that her softball days were over. Her family paid her tuition and living expenses the last two years of college without hesitation. It can be assumed that by paying for her apartment, they bought themselves two years of peace.

Janelle rented a comfortable apartment off campus, furnished it, and bought a car that was envied by many. She lived alone and preferred life that way. During the summer of her junior year, she stayed in Providence and took a summer course. She was obviously a loner, and friendships were as unusual for her in college as they had been when she was young. For instance, she was invited to only one sleepover in fifth grade, and had few friends over to her family home, including softball players. Instead, she read everything she could get her hands. She loved romantic fiction, and always carried a different Harlequin book in her backpack. Sometimes she switched to mystery fiction, and liked Michael Connelly and Agatha Christie; but her favorite book of all time is *The Winds of Change ... and Other Stories* by Isaac Asimov. Apparently this book, with its dog-eared corners has some importance to her, because even in her prison cell, it sat on her bunk.

Consistent Behavior at College

During Janelle's undergraduate career, other than reading fiction, three things were consistent. First, she acquired over three hundred parking tickets at Brown University, and when her car was towed, her father paid the towing charges. These parking tickets, along with other outrageous behavior, suggest she ignored or just didn't care about authority. Second, Janelle maintained her loner lifestyle. She dated a few boys, but the relationships always soured and never lasted. She had difficulty talking with anybody, including students, professors, and university advisers. In her classrooms, she never participated in academic or informal discussions, even when she liked the professor. There was one professor she admired, but the others "wasted my time." Most often, she felt comfortable talking to university staff in the academic departments and in the dining halls, but other than that, this girl was mute—"unless," she wrote, "I was pissed off."

Third, Janelle was a bully. She responded quickly to anybody who annoyed her. She had a wild temper, which she turned on and off as it pleased her. But there were also times when she didn't care how recklessly she behaved toward others. For example, "While driving to

Portland from Brown, this guy cut me off on the interstate. I wasn't going to take crap from anyone, especially a man, and I wanted to help the little obnoxious bastard discover the error of his ways. I followed him for several miles, honking and driving close to his car. I scared him. He drove off the highway to a fast food restaurant, parked, and jumped out of his car with a crow bar. I stopped my car about an inch from him and jumped out and whaled on him. Made sure the obnoxious fool swung first, because a lot of people were watching. When the cops came, I told them that he bailed from his vehicle to assault me. He had a crow bar in his hands. I was defending myself and wasn't sure what to do. I was in fear of my life. He wanted to kidnap me and do strange things to me. People standing around supported my story." Road rage for Janelle was a made-to-order opportunity to attack others. It was a way to justify her violent behavior, a technique she had known well since grade school. It is unknown how many other incidents similar to this one occurred, but she wrote others stories of her efforts to "administer justice."

Seaside Resort and Law School

Janelle graduated from Brown, and neither her brothers nor her parents attended her graduation. She had not expected them to attend, and she didn't invite them. That summer she checked into a seaside resort near Newport, Rhode Island, and remained a guest until she departed for law school in Cambridge, Massachusetts. She had selected an apartment near campus with the aid of a rental service in Boston, had movers pack and unpack all of her belongings and furniture, and visited her new apartment overlooking the Charles River once. She spent the night and then returned to Newport until late August, when her first semester started at Harvard Law School.

She spent her summer reading fiction; sitting by the pool; shopping in Manhattan, Providence, and Boston; attending the music and art festivals; and going to a few Broadway plays in Manhattan. Twice she went to Broadway with a new acquaintance she had met at the resort, and once with her favorite professor from Brown. All three times, they traveled by train from Providence to Manhattan and taxied to the theaters.

It isn't hard to understand how she managed or afforded her lifestyle during the summer or later because of the enormous trust fund which kicked in when she turned twenty-one years of age. What is a puzzle is that Janelle was not an A or even a B student. So how was she accepted to Harvard Law School? Her GPA was not high, and the Law School Admission Test requires a strong ability in solving problems with logic. Janelle was weak at that. Her family must have had a hand in her law school admission. Both her father and one of her brothers were Harvard alumni, and family financial contributions had continued to be impressive. The Gregg family name was blocked in heavy black ink on Harvard's gift giver's list. Janelle's name appeared in smaller print under both of her brothers' names. The first time she saw her name there, she decided she would never change her last name, even if she married. She had kept that promise.

Looking for Employment

Janelle was a law student during uneventful boom years of the 1990s when interest in the legal profession flagged as college graduates were attracted by tales of instant dot com millionaires. Some, like her brother Keith, sought opportunities in other businesses, rather than law. Janelle's other brother was a junior partner in one of those big firms. His life was stable, yet many graduates, particularly graduates from mediocre law schools, were simply reviewing documents for organizations at $15 to $20 an hour. Janelle wasn't willing to do that work as an intern or once she graduated, "because I was educated for bigger things than that." The stories she provided suggest that no law firms offered her a position. Once recruiters got over the Harvard Hump and family name, it was clear that Janelle, although a nice person from a powerful family, was in the end simply Ham Jam, one of her nicknames acquired at Brown. It was also clear that her family, including her father, did not sponsor or endorse her among his colleagues or benefactors.

Most Harvard law students intern in law firms or the prosecutor's office, clerk for judges, or work with high-profile interest groups, such as charities or political parties. For example, Hillary Rodham, while in law school at Yale, worked in DC on Senator Walter Mondale's subcommittee on migrant workers. In the summer of 1972, she worked on the campaign of Democratic presidential nominee, George McGovern. It was there that Hillary met a southern man named Bill Clinton, but that's another story.

Janelle continued to seek employment after graduation, but another lingering problem was that she couldn't pass the bar examination. She also hadn't interned anywhere prior to graduation, and couldn't find an opportunity to clerk for a judge after graduation.

Janelle asked her brothers for help, but to no prevail. But just because she was fat, couldn't pass the bar, and neither her father nor any other family member would put in the good word for her, weren't the only reasons she couldn't find a job.

Janelle was interviewed ninety times and sent out more than three hundred copies of her resume after graduating from Harvard Law School. Through it all, Janelle blamed her failure to pass the bar exam three times on the pressure of those interviews and her first husband's immoral behavior. "I tried to do the right thing, but just knowing Neal was screwing other women, clouded my thoughts. He just didn't want to maintain his marriage vows." You'll find there is more to her story once you visit her presentence investigation report, but for right now her excuses seem plausible.

First Marriage

Janelle met Neal while at Harvard. He was also a law student, but he graduated a year before her. She called him the "second man" in her life, but she married him. After a Las Vegas wedding, and a year before Janelle graduated law school, he moved into her apartment. Eventually they purchased a brownstone in the Beacon Hill section of Boston with additional funds supplied by her father. A year out of law school, Janelle was still unemployed. She assumed her private life was stable, other than her unemployment, when she happened to discover Neal's red sports car parked at a motel as she was returning from a job interview about twenty miles outside of Boston.

Janelle parked her car across the busy street from the motel. She watched his vehicle for an hour or so, and nothing happened. She tried to get his room number from the motel's front desk clerk, but without success. He finally appeared an hour later, walking toward her car with one of their mutual friends from Harvard.

"I was just going to talk," Janelle wrote in her prison journal. "Until he called me a fat pig. What could I do? I beat the crap out of him and slapped the shit out of his slut. When the cops arrived, I told them my story, and one said he couldn't blame me. It's about justification. The cops told Neal to stay checked into the motel for the night and think about your life. They told me to go home and collect my thoughts."

The divorce was stressful, because Neal taunted Janelle "about everything. He called me names like fatso, ugly duckling, and you're not a woman, you're a pig. I look at you and go limp. That's why I had to find somebody. I have needs. It's your fault I had to find another woman." During the divorce proceedings, evidence emerged about Janelle's previous physical assaults on Neal, which had resulted in several emergency room visits. In those days, mandatory arrest policies were only on the horizon, and if cops made an arrest during a domestic dispute, the man would have been arrested every time, not the woman, regardless of the evidence. Janelle's family hushed up her aggressiveness. Neal agreed to keep quiet about the assaults, in return for possession of the couple's newly acquired brownstone. Janelle said she hated to lose her brownstone, but she needed to get out of her marriage. She said she was ashamed of herself, especially her weight, but blamed it on her circumstance. One *circumstance* that surfaced was the time Neal returned from the emergency room filled with pain relievers. Janelle took the day to beat him, all day long. Finally in the late afternoon, the police were called by a neighbor. Upon entering the brownstone, officers found Neal at the bottom of the stairs, covered in blood. Janelle said he had fallen down the stairs while she was out. She was glad she had returned, otherwise "who knows how badly my husband could have been hurt." When the officers questioned the blood on her clothes, she said it was because she tried to help Neal stand. She wanted to drive him to the hospital. The officer wrote in his report that he thought it strange that her hands were not bloody, but no arrest was conducted. The police record of the call was buried.

Many years later, after the police officer had retired and died, his spouse was paging through his old notebooks and reports. The arrest and indictment of an FBI special agent was front-page material in the newspapers and on television that week. The officer's wife e-mailed her discovery to a newspaper reporter. The reporter wrote a follow-up article about Janelle Gregg, which included the officer's consultation with her at that Beacon Hill brownstone years earlier. The DA's investigator conducting the presentence investigation saw the newspaper article and contacted the officer's spouse.

Janelle's response to that follow-up article once in prison was: "Sure I gave him a skull thump, but wore gloves lined with sand to kick his ass. He sinfully flirted with one of the nurses when I picked him up from the emergency room that morning. He had it coming."

Finding a Federal Job

Janelle explained that at one point, "between my weight, divorce, and the loss of my brownstone, I started hitting the bars and lost track of the world for a few months. No one would hire me. I was brought up to endure to the end and to remain free from coffee, tobacco, and liquor. Getting drunk every day wasn't the right thing to do. You know, the Lord loveth the revenge, and I wasn't right. I had to stop. One of my old professors gave me a lead to a federal job, and gave me a reference. I applied, and nine months later became a fed."

Janelle explained that she had several interviews with different people, but only two of them were special agents for the FBI. The others were employed by a private agency to screen potential employees. That might explain why many of Janelle's negative experiences were overlooked. Those included: physical aggression and physical abuse with her parents, and serious domestic violence issues with her first husband; low GPA at Brown and Harvard; and failure to pass the bar exams three times. Added to the list are the obvious facts that Janelle never held a job, is indiscreet and unpredictable, and demonstrates little respect for authority. Nonetheless, she became a candidate for a federal position, which seems hard to justify.

Training, Marriage, and Responsibilities

The FBI's website reports that special agent trainees begin their career at the FBI Academy in Quantico, Virginia, for twenty-one weeks of intensive training. During their time at the academy, trainees live on campus and participate in a broad range of training activities. Classroom hours are spent studying a variety of academic and investigative subjects. The FBI Academy curriculum includes intensive training in physical fitness, defensive tactics, practical application exercises, and the use of firearms. Physical fitness tests are administered, and those who fail are placed in a remedial program. Special Agent trainees are paid as GS-10, step one on the Law Enforcement Officers' salary table. Upon graduation, trainees are sworn in as FBI special agents. Newly appointed special agents are assigned to one of the FBI's fifty-six field offices based on needs.

Janelle was assigned to the FBI's Atlanta, Georgia, office, and attended additional training at the Federal Law Enforcement Training Center in Glynco, Georgia, for eight weeks. While working at the Atlanta office, she was drawn to the behind-the-scenes work of analyzing reams of information and looking for patterns and clues.

Janelle's division was primarily responsible for white-collar crime, and her specialty was bank frauds and mortgage frauds. She was one of the special agents that preliminarily investigated a multimillion-dollar mortgage fraud scheme orchestrated by Chalana C. McFarland. This racketeer was an Atlanta attorney who worked primarily on real estates. Forbes.com reported that the forty-one-year-old McFarland was the "queen of mortgage fraud." The government said McFarland orchestrated a scheme to inflate property values using real-estate-flipping deals and straw buyers, leaving lenders with $20 million of defaulted loans. Special Agent Gregg from the FBI's Atlanta office was one of three special agents who interrogated McFarland and her crew. McFarland was eventually convicted on 169 counts of an indictment, and sentenced to 30 years in federal prison. Once she was imprisoned, Special Agent Gregg continued to interview McFarland to develop cases against other members of her crew, for the purpose of dismantling the McFarland empire.

McFarland was the leader and organizer of an extensive mortgage fraud scheme, from 1999 through late 2002, involving over a hundred properties in the Atlanta area. While acting as agent for title insurance companies and the closing attorney for various lenders, McFarland generated false HUD-1 settlement statements that certified that she had received down payments and disbursed loan proceeds. In fact, her receipts and disbursements were not accurately reflected on the settlement statements. McFarland paid her co-conspirator $10,000 for each stolen identity. The primary appraiser who inflated property values got over $400,000. She paid others from her escrow account without reflecting such payments on the settlement statements, while failing to collect the required borrower down payments listed on the statements.

Janelle spent four years at the Atlanta office, where she met (during one of her investigations) handsome but mentally challenged twenty-two-year-old Teddy McIntyre from Stone Mountain, Georgia. He had two children from an earlier marriage. He and Janelle married, and they had one child before she was transferred to the Boston office. A year later, Janelle gave birth to another child. She returned to work four weeks later with the understanding that Teddy was the primary care provider for their children. He took care of the children while Janelle worked. Also, by all accounts, she was rarely home, and home was a brownstone down the block from Neal, her first husband. Both brownstones were a stone's throw from Boston Commons.

Conviction

Janelle Gregg was indicted and convicted by a state jurisdiction (as opposed to a federal jurisdiction) for criminal conspiracy; and through a plea bargain (and without trial) received a ten-year sentence. There was some speculation that the reason Gregg was charged and tried on the state level instead of the federal was because the feds didn't want to air their dirty laundry in public. Another rumor suggested there wasn't enough evidence to indict her federally, but there was enough evidence for a local indictment.

Conspiracy cases are defined as cases in which two or more persons agree and plan to commit a crime or to perpetrate an illegal act. For example, if two people make a plan to steal all the milk from a convenience store (illegal) to donate to a local orphanage (legal), the pair would be guilty of conspiracy. Conspiracy crimes can include conspiracy to engage in criminal activity, such as money laundering, conspiracy to violate federal laws, or conspiracy to manufacture drugs or weapons. The federal maximum penalty for conspiracy is a five-year sentence, while local sentencing can go to ten years. Also, in state court it is not necessary for the prosecutor to prove that all of the people named in the indictment were members of the scheme. In Janelle Gregg's case, there were many co-conspirators, and many of them were high up in the state and federal government hierarchies.

The mortgage fraud scheme linked to Janelle Gregg involved 133 properties and 21 financial institutions. Among the twelve conspirators charged and convicted were Janelle Gregg, Cornelius Robertson (a real estate attorney), Tammy Whittenhour (a Boston city inspector), and Megan Moore (a computer hacker and computer wiz who worked for the US Department of Housing and Urban Development), and Keith Richards (a known racketeer in the Boston underworld whose street name was the Cisco Kid). Richards testified against Gregg and the others.

Here's How it Worked. The defendants (Gregg, Robertson, Whittenhour, and Moore) purchased private and public properties— such as land leased to uptown parking lots, boat ferries on Boston Bay, and slum apartments—at one price. They immediately sold those properties to a straw-buyer (somebody who purchases property for another person in order to conceal the identity of the real purchaser) at a higher price. The straw-buyer stopped paying the loans, and rented out the properties, even after they went into default. Also, Janelle Gregg and her accomplishes conned 425 homeowners in the Commonwealth of Massachusetts with a debt-elimination promise. The homeowners ended up losing their houses, and the fraud schemers duped banks, savings and loans institutions, and credit unions into thinking they were lending against free and clear properties. It was a sweet plan that worked for seven years. Federal investigation efforts always came up blank (thanks to Gregg), state investigations were directed by the FBI (Gregg again); city inspections were delayed or redirected (thanks to Whittenhour); and other groups or individuals attempting to jump in were muscled into silence (thanks to the Cisco Kid, whose gang had its own agenda). One rumor was that Gregg used Robertson, Whittenhour, Moore, and Richards primarily because they were targeted by an FBI sting, which Gregg had headed when she first arrived in Boston. Those individuals testified that they were under the impression that after the sting, they were part of an ongoing federal investigation, as opposed to benefiting from a mortgage fraud scheme. They denied any wrongdoing and said they were directed by Gregg's subordinates. Several federal agents, all of them men, noted that they had substantial evidence that something was wrong in the mortgage and real estate industry in Boston, but they were politically challenged because of their gender in bringing charges against their female superior, Janelle Gregg. They looked the other way to keep their jobs.

Presentence Investigation Report (PSI)

Janelle's presentence investigative report (PSI), was conducted by competent district attorney's personnel, may help better explain Janelle's activities prior to her arrest. For instance, her parents remained distant from their daughter from high school through her graduation from Harvard Law, because both of them had been victims of her abuse. The undertones from some of the unimpressed congregational members of the Mormon church, who wanted to remain anonymous, told an investigator that on various occasions they had witnessed Janelle strike the younger brother and her mother. On one occasion, while waiting in the family car, Janelle apparently plugged in the car's lighter and burned her father's forearm. In addition, when Janelle was a participant in church functions, "she seemed to be a source of conflict and egged other kids on. Then she'd hit one." The investigator also heard verbal claims (as opposed to official school records) of Janelle's aggression in high school during softball practice, and unnecessary physical contact of other players on both teams during games. Although none of these claims could be substantiated, they were mentioned in the report, supporting a pattern of physical aggression "throughout much of the defendant's youth." Motives for her family's detachment to her became clear. The quality of the accounts wasn't in question, and because of the quantity of them, a pattern emerged, suggesting that those accounts represented "only the tip of the iceberg," as one investigator wrote.

Prison

When Janelle Glenda Gregg arrived at prison, she was thirty-nine, a little older than most of the other new admissions to the prison system. She was also better educated. Although her occupation was missing from the paperwork, eventually it was learned that she had been an FBI special agent for fifteen years. In her prison cell, a picture of a white bulldog named Spats was on her cell wall, with a paw print presumably belonging to Spats. At the end of her cell bunk, one of Isaac Asimov's books always rested. She was a "renter"—that is, she had been convicted in one state and was housed in another state's prison system, as were three other participants in this study (Margo, Mickey, and Wilma). For Janelle, the transfer to another state was part of her plea bargain agreement. It was reasoned that Janelle wasn't safe in Massachusetts, because she had been involved in numerous prisoner convictions, some of them wrongful convictions.

Janelle's prison life was similar to her free life: no visitors, few personal phone calls, and little mail. One explanation could be that her ex-husbands were ashamed of her. Her mail was re-addressed with a Massachusetts zip code and her telephone calls were identified with a Massachusetts area code, suggesting that her location was guarded.

While imprisoned, Janelle was placed on suicide watch during the first thirty days of her arrival, and again a few months later. Sometimes she was given prisoner restrictions into certain areas of the prison, because she failed to follow custody personnel directives, but custody personnel rarely put her into segregation or isolation units. Janelle is a rule-follower for the most part. Almost ritualistic, one custody officer explained, "but only when the rules matched her personal understanding of the rule."

Janelle was described as an authoritarian personality. She had an agenda, and she expected correctional personnel and prisoners to accept her ideas—until she was cornered. For instance, Janelle decided that she was not going to write anything in-group about herself, because "I have rights and zookeepers aren't entitled to mess with my head." Once she learned that if she didn't write, she couldn't attend in-group meetings, and her residence would be changed to a higher-security section of the facility, she wrote volumes.

Janelle had lower back pain, which was treated with spinal manipulation; and had a droopy eye, the result of a vehicle accident while pursuing a suspect, she said. However, both injuries are more consistent with individuals involved in fist fights. While in prison, Janelle wore thick eyeglasses and used a lot of eye drops, prescribed by a prison optometrist, who said Janelle would be blind in a few years. Prior to her incarceration, Janelle was a social drinker who preferred straight

Jack Daniels . She smoked a "joint or two," which she said was part of her job. Janelle also had aliases, which included Jam Murphy and Jam A. Richey. Her PSI and Department of Correction's paperwork showed that other aliases included Jen Meyers, Jen Allocco, Jennifer J. Allocco, Elaine Barstow, Jennifer Connelly, and Jam J. Barstow. She preferred to be called Jam. But prisoners and jailers who disliked her, which were most of them, called her Ham Jam, Deadhead Jam, or Jumbo.

Neal's *20/20* Interview

A year after her conviction, her first husband Neal was interviewed on a television show similar to *20/20,* because of his marriage to a convicted FBI special agent. He revealed that she was abusive. After their marriage, she imposed her rules upon him. If he didn't conform, she beat him. Even if he did conform, she sometimes threw a fit. He told about the time she told him to prepare two boiled eggs for her. "You boiled the wrong one, Neal," she screamed, and threw the plate at him.

Other deviant behavior came out through Neal's interview, including Janelle's physical abuse of her parents, her brothers, and most everyone (probably criminal suspects) she encountered on the job. Janelle had slapped her mother when she was in sixth grade, Neal said. Her brother attempted to defend their mother; Janelle punched him in the gut. The family members' many secrets will probably remain hidden, but indicators are that her family maintained a distance from Janelle out of fear of her.

During the interview, one commenter said she had no knowledge of where Janelle was serving her sentence. She implied it was at a local state facility or that the feds had housed her at the Federal Correctional Institution in Danbury, Connecticut. Her second ex-husband refused to go public when the show tried to interview him. It could have been because of their children. The interviewer closed the program by saying, "Money can't buy safety from your own children, no matter how much of it you have. I feel sorry for her parents, who have endured their daughter's aggressive behavior. What can be done about it?"

What Made Gregg Dangerous?

Janelle Gregg's salient behavior can be best described as swift, a person who took immediate action, or reaction, to others and circumstance. She was raw, direct, and to the point with her evaluations of persons, places, and things. She is also described as violent, a person who wouldn't hesitate to use force, but more force than necessary to resolve a problem or neutralize an individual. Cruelty and vulgarity are common patterns of her behavior. Yet these explanations are inadequate until some of the obvious issues are addressed. Janelle Gregg was highly trained, represented and directed federal legal authority. Her motivation to commit crime was a need for control. When in pursuit of a person of interest or on a mission, she could not be distracted from her pursuit. The problem was that that "person of interest" was always defined by Janelle. She decided who was bad and who was good, and what to do about it. She was a vigilante with federal authority. "Shoot first, ask questions later," was her motto. She would build the rationale for her actions, or redefine the details of the case to fit, so that the shooting, beating, false imprisonment, or the continued use of an informant was justified. How could a person with a low-skill level to reason things out create a mortgage fraud scheme of this magnitude? Some suggest that Janelle Gregg wasn't the kingpin, but more likely Chalana C. McFarland was, despite her imprisonment at Hazelton Federal Prison in Bruceton Mills, West Virginia (with a release date of April 4, 2031). McFarland was the brains behind Janelle's mortgage fraud scheme. Then, too, it was revealed that Janelle's young and mentally challenged husband was from the hometown as McFarland had family. She even had a stepbrother around Teddy's age, whom, by all accounts, McFarland adored.

Janelle Compartmentalized

Janelle compartmentalizes events, people, and circumstances. Everything has a place, a compartment, and each compartment is different from other compartments. Someone's single act represents his or her entire conduct. There are no mitigating circumstances, no mistakes, no screwups. Similar to the other controllers in this case study, Janelle's find little comfort in Einstein's thought that "Not everything that counts can be counted, and not everything that can be counted counts." For Janelle to engage another person, she first dehumanizes him. That person isn't a human being, a father or a mother or someone's child. "It" is a villain of some type, and needs to be dealt with as Janelle sees fit.

Many psychologists suggest that people like Janelle compartmentalize their thinking to avoid discomfort (i.e., cognitive dissonance) and situations that take them out of their comfort zone. Discomfort for controllers translates to someone else dominating their interactions and experiences. One way for a control freak to regain control is through violence. "Stand up to some bozo and he'll listen to you," explained Janelle. Most of us understand uncomfortable feelings, such as guilt, shame, or inadequacy, and we might attempt to resolve those feelings through activities like education and cooperation. For Janelle, what appears to be a control freak and an authoritarian is her salvation and the measurement of her strength. Her vague history shows that she was a bully in school, and used bullying or taunting techniques to maintain control, which often meant using her hands. Later in life, as a law enforcement officer employed by the federal government, she had license to ride herd over a vast number of people without worrying about the consequences—until she hooked up with criminals who were more resourceful than she. Her chances of taking control from them meant she had to submit to their code and rules of conduct. If McFarland was Janelle's underworld boss, that must have been uncomfortable experience for Janelle. McFarland had a superior track record, and Janelle's job was to make sure that McFarland would never be paroled. In the final analysis, Janelle and McFarland worked together by recognizing each other's strengths and their fuses.

Other Crimes

There were five official complaints against Janelle as a corrupt federal agent over a four-year period. None of the complaints were substantiated. One of the complaints alleged that Janelle had visited a female prisoner in the federal correctional institute in Danbury, Connecticut, and beat the prisoner, putting her in the hospital with severe injuries. Years later it was discovered that that particular prisoner had been a cell mate of an FBI informant, who later committed suicide. Another complaint alleged that Janelle questioned an elderly couple at their home, which resulted in a beating so fierce, the seventy-one-year-old woman remained in a coma for a year, and then died. A third complaint was filed by the Boston police department, alleging that a forensic lab employee had attempted to stop Janelle from removing evidence from the crime lab without permission. Special Agent Gregg savagely pistol-whipped the female clerk and her assistant.

Attempted murder and probably murder was part of Janelle's behavior, but police couldn't find the bodies or link Janelle to the disappearance of several local investigators. What was believed was that Janelle participated in the kidnapping and murder of three Massachusetts investigators. One was a private investigator hired by a business rival; and one was a state trooper who came very close to identifying Janelle and her mortgage fraud organization. Another state trooper investigator quit her job and moved from Quincy, Massachusetts to Manchester, New Hampshire, after her teenage son was killed in a suspicious car accident.

One of Gregg's FBI subordinates was a highly decorated Vietnam War military pilot and a lieutenant colonel in the Massachusetts National Guard. He and another special agent socialized with Boston mobsters, including James "Whitey" Bulger, leader of the Winter Hill Gang, and New York City's Tony "The Ant" Spilotro (who was portrayed in the movie, *Casino*). A female prisoner at Danbury, Connecticut, provided additional information on the murders committed by Gregg and her two henchmen, but she committed suicide just days prior to her grand jury testimony to indict Gregg's subordinates.

Further investigations into Janelle Gregg's activities revealed that her second husband and his relatives, many of whom were related to McFarland, were named on the deeds of forty-one properties in Boston. Jobs, bank accounts, employment verification, were validated through Janelle's influence. Individuals who resisted Janelle's bank fraud scheme were gone—just gone. These include two people who worked at a Section 8 housing agency, one who worked at the largest bank in Boston, and one state investigator. All indicators suggest that Gregg was involved in a gross obstruction of justice when the Commonwealth of Massachusetts investigated mortgage fraud. State police investigators were continually misdirected by federal agents through the directions of Gregg, the federal agent in charge. The newspapers gave Janelle the title of Mortgage Fraud Queen, which put stars in Ham Jam's eyes.

CHAPTER 8
Joey and Yummy the Crown

Introduction

Joey was thirty-five years old when he was arrested and convicted on fourteen counts of child molestation. He and his wife had four children and were married for twelve years. He pled guilty during the process of the trial, and his sentence is consistent with the sentencing guidelines for this crime: fifteen years, with early release pending Department of Correction approval. Joey was a high school graduate and worked at Little Tots, a day care facility owned by his mother-in-law, Bridgette Johnson.

Prior to prison, Joey occasionally used marijuana and heroin. His motivator toward crime, which includes the sexual assault of children, some of whom were physically disabled, can be best described as a pleasure-seeker. His health was excellent, and he generally slept eight hours or more a day while a guest of the state. Sometimes Joey was put on suicide watch, but he was never restricted in the prison facility. He was put in protective custody because of his conviction, which irritated many prisoners. Joey was paroled at the end of eleven years with the aid of the governor's office, which had little confidence in the process that had convicted him, despite public outrage. Joey was reviewed for civil commitment (to remain confined, but assigned to strict psychological programs), but he was not considered at-risk for recidivism (which doesn't sound right to correctional personnel or this author). Joey was released, and is the only offender in this book who is registered as a sex offender.

Joey's Early Life

Joseph Albert Cole was born July 14, and weighed seven pounds, four ounces. Medical records show that his mother labored less than four hours during his birth. This summer baby had three older sisters and two older brothers. A year later Joey would have a younger sister. Within the family, the girls resembled their father more than their mother, while the boys had their mother's high forehead and cheek bones, with small brown eyes and thick brown hair. Joey's high school picture shows long hair with bangs and a small wise-guy grin on his smooth face. Of interest, approximately eighteen years after his high school graduation, his prison admission picture showed a tired and bald man with drooping eyes and long, straight sideburns framing a deeply lined face. His picture suggests that Joey lived a hard life prior to his imprisonment, but nothing could be further from than truth. He lived a comfortable existence, and did pretty much anything his little heart desired.

Ralph Cole, Joey's dad, was a veteran of the Korean War, and returned to his hometown in Montana after receiving his honorable discharge. He lived at home with his parents, borrowed money from the bank, and with his brother developed a lumber business in the mountains. It became a financial powerhouse later in the game, rather than early. Ralph Cole hired Elizabeth "Lezzy" Albert, a new lawyer in town. At first he was hesitate to hire her as legal counsel, because she was a woman. At that time, women were entering law school in small numbers and had yet to prove their great potential. He was hesitant also because she was "a valley girl," from the other side of the frosted peaks that faced Cole's hometown. Lezzy represented Ralph Cole's business during some hard times. Both of these aggressive go-getters liked each other's style, fell in love, got married—to no one's surprise—and bought an abandoned ranch. With some effort they rebuilt it, adding several new structures and horses. Eventually the humble ranch turned into a horsemanship school and a guest ranch for families. All of their seven children worked the ranch, along with many hired hands. The ranch was so popular that when running for office, the governor of Montana spent a few nights there with his family and election staff.

All the Albert-Cole children learned how to manage horses, respect human beings, and how to pray to Jesus. Equality among the sexes was emphasized, and Joey's mother made decisions along with his father about the lives of their children and the ranch. From all accounts, Lezzy Albert Cole was a very bright person, and she spent time with each of her children and time with her husband. Locals described their marriage as perfect and loving. Joey learned that he had better respect females, or his mother "would come down on me like a ton of bricks," Joey wrote. Joey always had some reservations about "an equal thing," because he was not moved one way or another by events, situations, or emotions. Still, he learned how to use those things against others to get what he wanted.

Joey wrote about a filly that ran off one night during a heavy rain storm, only to be found tangled in barbed wire fence. The young horse eventually died from her injuries. Joey's brothers and sisters and many of the hired hands were grief stricken. Some cried and demonstrated behavior that Joey thought was playacting. Being younger than most of them, he kept his feelings to himself. He looked into his thoughts, trying to find sorrow or sympathy for the yearling. He was relieved that he felt little if anything about the tragic death of the filly. When he asked his mother about his feelings, she told him to "look into your heart for some pity for the pain the horse suffered." Joey felt nothing. As he grew older, he accepted his lack of empathy as a positive characteristic. Few experiences would bring him distress. He wrote that he continued to react differently from his siblings and the ranch hands, and he usually preferred to work and live alone. What he knew was that he watched the filly run off, and probably could have prevented the young horse's demise. But it made no difference to him. "I asked myself, what's in for me if I stop the yearling from running during a storm, and when I didn't have an answer, I said what the hell, let her go."

Most of Joey's siblings remained at the ranch after their high school graduation. Some of them went away to college, but returned to the rambling ranch for family, pleasure, and their future. Joey, however, enrolled in an East Coast college, and then dropped out at the end of the first semester. He enjoyed city life, but said he was ashamed of his conduct. That sounded more like an excuse not to return to Montana, some 1,800 miles from where he now lived. It is doubtful Joey had the capacity to be ashamed of his behavior. He took a job, despite money sent by his mother to help him with an apartment security deposit and a few months' rent. She wanted Joey to think over his decision and then return to Montana. She didn't realize that Joey's father had also sent money and had signed the lease for the apartment, because Joey was not yet twenty-one years of age. "The manager of the apartment building didn't want to chance anything," Joey wrote in his prison journal. "My pops was good to me, but if he knew me better, he would've kicked my ass."

With all the cash coming from Montana, Joey didn't require an income, but a great job "dropped out of the sky." A local police department's mounted division needed someone to tend their horses. Joey knew a great deal about horses, and the department was grateful to find someone with his experience. Joey was glad to have a job that really wasn't work. By the time he was twenty-three, he was the manager of the police stable and had met a young woman. Well, he had met many young women, but there was one in particular, twenty-two-year-old Jeanie Johnson, who easily could have been a contestant on the television reality series, *The Biggest Loser*. They decided to marry after living together for a few months. The girl's father was a police officer in the mounted division, and he liked Joey and his skill with horses.

Before they married, Joey and Jeanie traveled to Montana to meet his family. His mother noticed that he treated Jeanie with disrespect, and spoke to him about that. He explained that Jeanie had a flippant personality, and the only way to deal with her was to be direct. Months later, Joey called his parents to tell them that he and Jeanie had married in a civil ceremony and that she was going to give birth in a few months. Over the next five years, they had three more children, and Joey never returned to Montana. Jeanie Johnson performed in ways Joey had never expected. She wanted to be his girl, his wife, and the mother of his children, despite his demands and expectations, which included luring girls to their home for Joey's pleasure. When she ever so slightly suggested that maybe they could have a threesome, he said, "Don't be silly, we're married, and I cracked her one."

Jeanie's Story

Jeanie, an only child, was raised by a submissive alcoholic mother, but was forced by her authoritarian father, a sergeant in the mounted police patrol, to be a tough boy. She liked being a girl, and didn't care if she was cute and frilly instead of rough and masculine. In high school, the boys don't mess with her because her dad was a cop, and the girls found her to be understanding and easy to talk to Jeanie's father held an almost fanatical obsession that girls are victimized by males all the time. Therefore, Jeanie should become like him, which meant she should show absolute obedience to his authority, as opposed to expressing any individual freedom. Joey felt that the father—whom he referred to as the Sarge—was a little contradictory, in that he dominated Jeanie and her mother too much. This domination, Joey reasoned, that was one of the reasons Jeanie's mom, Bridgette, was an alcoholic. Or at least that was the story Joey offered about Jeanie and her mother.

Joey said the Sarge's viewpoint was similar to many of the other city cops', whom he knew through his job at the stable. "Women, especially wives and daughters, and horses are property," Joey said with a snicker. "Through these cops I learned a lot about women." A few times, Joey explained that the Sarge made it clear that "the job of the man in his family is control. It's on you, boy, to make the decisions and remain in control." Joey saw this perspective as an opportunity to behave as he thought a man should behave. Sarge "almost paid me to treat his daughter like crap, and I did, and her mother was so blitzed most of the time that she had no idea what was happening." Joey implied that this domination provided him access to both women. Joey had a difficult time comprehending that another human being could be so dedicated, trusting, and dutiful to another's needs, without his asking or plotting and planning. When it came to Jeanie's mother, he had to plot and plan, but eventually he got his way with her, after her husband met with an unfortunate accident.

Purchase of Little Tots Day Care

Jeanie's dad was thrown from his horse into the path of a truck. The accident left him paralyzed and unable to communicate for a few months. He eventually died from those injuries. An investigation of the incident found the girth on his horse's saddle was loose. Joey said that he prepared the horse for Sarge, and everything was in order when the officer left the stable.

A few years after Sarge's death, Bridgette purchased a day care center with her husband's insurance money. Joey had been urging her to buy the day care for a while. The business had been in operation for ten years prior to Bridgette's purchase of it. The owners wanted to retire, and their part-time maintenance man—Joey—said he could help them find a buyer. He introduced Bridgette to them, and she eventually made an offer to buy the business.

Bridgette said she always wanted to attend to children's basic needs, organize activities for them, and stimulate their physical, emotional, intellectual, and social growth. She wanted to help kids explore their talents. For Joey, the opportunities were endless, because now rather than being a part-time worker, he more or less had a free hand in running the business . A business full of children from ages of three to seven, some of whom were developmentally challenged. Both Jeanie and Joey played major roles in the daily operations of Little Tots Day Care Center.

Jeanie nurtured and cared for the children, including her own children, at the center. Joey continued as the maintenance man, supervised "time-outs," and, of course, advised Bridgette on what to do about everything. He resigned from the stable and spent his days at Little Tots. Joey would develop compelling stories for Bridgette that usually left her drinking more than she had before Joey sat down with her. "I talked BJ [Joey called Bridgette by her initials] into drinking it up . She had easy buttons. She didn't wanna get old, and to be young meant getting high and giving me what I wanted—quick sex. Bt it was always sloppy because she was a pig and smelled."

Incidents Leading to an Investigation

Three-year-old Judy Eberly arrived home from day care with scratches on her thighs. The following morning, Judy's mother inquired at the day care about the scratches. Bridgette said she had no idea how Judy got them. "Maybe a rash or something, sweetie," she said to Mrs. Eberly.

The incident was forgotten, until one afternoon when Judy's mom was picking up her daughter and spoke to another mother. The mother mentioned that the strangest thing had happened to her daughter Becky—scratches on her thighs.

The two mothers were curious about the scratches and quizzed Bridgette, who was unable to convince them that the day care was safe. Both withdrew their children from the center. The mothers made arrangements to enroll their children at another day care the following day. When they arrived at the new day care center with their daughter, another mother was there. She explained that she had heard about the scratches on their children. Her child, Randy, also had several scratches and bruises on his legs. She talked with Bridgette, too, and had withdrawn her son from Little Tots. One of the day care workers overheard the conversation between the three mothers and suggested that they contact the Department of Social Services and file a complaint. Within twenty-four hours, the three mothers were talking to a social worker from DSS.

The Investigation

An investigation of seventy-five children who attended the day care was conducted over a two-month period. It was concluded that several children had experienced scratches, bruises, and lacerations on their bodies. DSS notified law enforcement of their findings, and the police initiated a criminal investigation. Investigators distributed to parents a list of behavioral symptoms associated with sexual abuse, which included evidence of physical trauma to the genitals or mouth, genital or rectal bleeding, sexually transmitted disease, unusual and offensive odors, and complaints of pain or discomfort in the genital areas. Also, behavior like recent bed-wetting, defecating in their clothes, and children who suddenly were afraid to be left alone could be indicators of sexual assault. Because the investigators distributed the list before they made any arrests, Joey's lawyers argued that the police had tainted the minds of the parents with suggestions of sexual abuse, and his trial couldn't be a fair trial.

The investigators developed a case against three members of the day care and arrested each of them. A preponderance of evidence consistent with unnatural and lascivious acts with children was linked to Joey Cole, Jeanie Cole, and Bridgette Johnson. Joey was indicted on fourteen counts of child molestation.

Time-Out Room

What came out during the investigation was that the day care had a time-out room concealed on the second floor of the facility. It was reached by a small staircase on the outside of the building. The room was practically invisible from the street and the other three sides of the day care structure. The room's view was of a brick wall of a warehouse. The soundproofed time-out room was equipped with toys and a television set, where Joey allegedly engaged in Satan worship and terrorized children by forcing them to watch the mutilation of birds on a video. (The video was never found by the police.

How It Worked

Joey supervised the children's time-out. He wore a clown's outfit and told the children his name was Yummy. Jeanie testified against her husband and confessed her role in sending children to time-out. Joey would tell her which children needed to be disciplined, and Jeanie would take the child to the time-out room. She would retrieve the child thirty or forty minutes later, or when Joey pushed a button that illuminated a small green light that faced the outside playground. Jeanie said that if she thought anything strange was going on in the time-out room, she would have never sent her own children to that room. The evidence showed that Joey molested his own children in that room too. At one point while in-group, he said, "When you're having sex, who looks at a face? When I get going, I'm TNT, man. I'm dynamite. I'm a power-load," he sang as his favorite rock group, AC/DC, might.

Felony Convictions of Joey's Accomplices

For her participation in Joey's molestation case, and because she testified against Joey, Jeanie received a five-year sentence and was released on parole at the end of three years. She was not sentenced as a sex offender. Later, she recanted her testimony and confession, saying that she was under duress by police investigators and had been advised by her attorney that the five years was a good deal.. "They're going to convict Joey," she claimed her lawyer told her, "and you'll get equal prison time as a sexual offender." Some of the other day-care personnel testified against all three: Joey Cole, Jeanie Cole, and Bridgette Johnson. Bridgette went to trial and was found guilty of sixteen counts of reckless endangerment of a child, sixteen counts of custodial child abuse, and possession of a controlled substance (Vicodin). She was also charged with neglect of a vulnerable child (one of Joey's victims was developmentally disabled), but the jury found her not guilty on that charge. Bridgette was sentenced to ten years. Little Tots was permanently closed, and the state voided Bridgette Johnson's child-care license for life. Civil suits took the remainder of the insurance money from Bridgette's husband, their family home, and all of her assets. Other civil suits took the assets of Joey and Jeanie Cole. Their children were placed in the custody of social services, and evidence revealed that each of the children had been sexually abused from an early age. Both Bridgette Johnson and Jeanie were imprisoned in the same prison. Bridgette died a year later, officially of depression. Some say it was suicide, others say it was a broken heart.

Other Crimes

It should come as no surprise that Joey Cole had committed sexual assault on children, yet none of the children's testimony nor the medical examinations characterized the crime of sexual assault. In the jurisdiction where Joey was arrested and convicted, molestation consists of the crime of sexual acts with children up to the age of sixteen. (Legislation has changed the definition of molestation to sexual assault with the aid of the Adam Walsh Child Safety Act.) In this case, the prosecutor had significant evidence, which included touching and fondling of the private parts of fourteen children and exposure of Joey's genitalia to them. Only ten of the most believable children testified at Joey's trial, but investigators reported that forty-two other children over a three-year period had been molested in a similar fashion by the defendant. Of the children medically examined, none displayed indicators that characterized or were consistent with sexual penetration. The prosecutor said there were children who had been sexually assaulted, including penetration, but either the child or their parents were afraid to come forward, for fear the children would be labeled as sexual assault victims.

During trial, Joey accepted a guilty plea for the lesser crime of child molestation, as opposed to any of the other crimes. Those would have demanded a life sentence and, at the time and in some states, the death penalty. Nonetheless, it might appear strange that a grown man who fondled children and had few sexual boundaries—as evidenced by his manipulation of individuals, including his wife and mother-in-law—didn't harm defenseless children. Other crimes could have come out had Joey not accepted the guilty plea. Some of those crimes would have included aggravated kidnapping and sexual assault of minor children, attempted murder, extortion (of the parents of the victims), unnatural and lascivious acts, sodomy of children under seven years of age. There is another explanation that might prove helpful in understanding how Joey avoided a life sentence.

Victim Compensation Programs

California's Victim Compensation Program (VCP) was created in 1965 to lessen the financial impact of crime on qualifying victims. This program has paid nearly $1.8 billion to victims since its inception. In 2008, victims received more than $81 million. By law, VCP is the payer of last resort for eligible out-of-pocket losses resulting from crimes. New York accepted almost 14,000 claims for victim compensation in 2008 and paid out $28,000,000, of which $18,000 went to victims of personal injury as a result of a criminal action. Michigan reports three victim service programs providing over $20 million in services for over 250,000 citizens each year. And some states, such as Illinois, report that a victim of domestic violence or sexual assault is eligible to receive compensation of up to $27,000. Official statistics about how much has been paid out and to whom (other than a child) are not available. In the case of Joey Albert Cole, Little Tots had a $500,000 per-year-per-child insurance policy, which covered molested children. However, the insurance proceeds and funds from victim services provided, by one account, ten families with an estimated $16 million over their lifetimes. This could produce the best of two worlds: the person indicted of sexual assault accepts a guilty plea that produces a lesser charge, and the accusers walk away rich. Penetration is not necessarily the primary criteria for those victim services, but penetration changes the social label for those children. Some might say that that sounds like the Michael Jackson case, but with Jackson there was no conviction. For more details on a state by state case, see the Office of Victim Compensation at the federal website at: http://www.ojp.usdoj.gov/ovc/help/ voca_links. htm.

Joey the Jailhouse Lawyer

Joey became a jailhouse lawyer and assisted other prisoners in their legal appeal cases. A young man named William, whom Joey met in-group, asked him for help with his case. Joey wrote a fictitious short story that described an individual similar to William. Like William, the jury found the fictitious young man guilty of breaking and entering, aggravated sexual assault, and attempted murder. Joey said that the fictitious young man could not have waited at the entrance of a condominium complex, selected an elderly woman who walked every day at four, gained entry to her condo while she walked, and once she arrived home, tortured her for two days. All of this story is with William's case.

In Joey's short story, during the torture session, the victim pleaded with her attacker not to rape her. The attacker had no intention to commit that foul act, Joey wrote. But the old lady insisted time and again that the young man not rape her. He was so taken by her insistence that "Satan himself came down, begged him to do it, and loaded his love stick." Joey's final statement was that an honorable Christian boy like the young man he was aiding with a legal appeal would never have committed the heinous crime of rape, unless prompted by the devil himself. "Christ was tempted by the devil and walked away, but my client is not Christ and caved in to Satan's demands." Joey went on to say that the prosecutor had made up a story about William, and added "an alleged attempt to drown the elderly woman in her shower after raping her. None of it is true.

Joey's short story also consisted of thirteen explicit pages about the sexual assault that allegedly never happened between his client and the old lady. The details were dramatic and vivid. Additionally, there were several pages of dialogue between the fictitious character and the alleged victim. All of these pages totally amazed William, and he wondered why Joey wrote so much. You might ask if Joey's fabricated account was presented to the judge who oversaw William's appeal? Yes. Did William accept Joey's version of the crime? Absolutely not. William said he didn't know what to do about Joey's story. "I didn't break into anybody's home. I didn't try to kill anybody in the shower, and I didn't rape anybody. I mean, how stupid is that?" William said in-group. At the next in-group meeting, William looked like he had walked into a stone wall. Someone had beat him up, and he wouldn't lift his fixed stare from the floor. When I asked him a question, Joey answered, not William. "He's got nothing to say, Doc." It is curious that Joey also incorporated several pages in William's story/legal defense of a teenager sexual assaulting children. After reading through those accounts, I was certain Joey was talking about himself, because he mentioned a ranch, horses, and the majestic mountains of the west. This is a good lead into Joey's fantasy world of "The Shower" in chapter 18.

CHAPTER 9
Margo and Praise the Lord

Introduction

This chapter describes the twins Morris and Madelyn Clinton, and the Clinton family. It reveals some of Morris's experiences as a child, and his experiences as he transformed from a male to a female named Margo. It talks a little bit about gender reassignment therapy, surgery, and the life after a sex change. The chapter provides you with a view of the twins' high school experiences, Margo's life on the beach, and describes her first and second criminal convictions. The chapter provides descriptions of Margo's flight to prison, and her experiences during prison intake. It also describes Margo's arson activities. In the end, you'll be overloaded with images of scorn and savagery. In chapter 18 there is a short portrayal entitled "À la Carte: Fantasizing about Pregnancy."

Family Network

The twins were delivered by caesarean, because one of them was lying in an awkward position in the womb. Morris Clinton was five pounds twelve ounces, arrived first, and grew up to be right-handed. His sister Madelyn Clinton was five pounds two ounces, arrived thirty seconds later, and grew up left-handed. Morris and Madelyn were born into a family of already four children. The twins were the youngest members of the family, and their arrival on August 30 was both premature (by about forty-five days) and thirteen years after the last set of twins (both girls), who were already in eighth grade.

When their mom took the twins to the supermarket, to church, and on daily walks, she carefully tucked them in their twin stroller. Their golden curls and deep blue eyes seemed to move in unison, motivating passersby to stop, smile, and say something like, "Are those little girls cute or what?" They were dressed alike, their hairstyle was alike, and they'd coo at passersby alike. Their mom found it engaging that Morris and Madelyn looked like girls, but not just any girls. They were adorable little girls who captured the hearts of others, especially strangers. Retrieving them from day care, summer camps, dance lessons, and later from kindergarten, she would make a fuss, closing her eyes and asking, "Where are my cute little girls?" She'd open her eyes and volunteers and teachers would jovially offer the twins. "Here they are. And praise the Lord for these little beauties."

Years later, the mother felt responsible for Morris's gender decision (although studies show that her sort of playfulness does not lead to gender identity disorder (GID) or gender dysphoria). She would expressed her thoughts only to her own mother, known to the twins as Grandma Jones. That was not all she felt guilty about. The twins were small-boned with little features, and they were ill often because their immune systems were weak. Poor heath would be with them until the day each of them died. If a cold virus visited a few kids in town, the twins caught it. Ear infection—absolutely. Their mother had an open prescription at the local pharmacy for antibiotics. But they were so incredibly cute together! For Morris and Madelyn's mother, they were trophies, but trophies she or their father might dust off from time to time. The truth of the matter was that no one could have prepared these parents for the surprise birth of their adorable twins.

By the time Morris and Madelyn reached fourth grade, they were the only children residing in the Clinton home, except during the holidays, a few weeks during the summer, and occasional visits. The first set of twins were at different universities. The only son had graduated from college, joined the military, and was deployed somewhere overseas. Their oldest and prettiest sister, Bess, had graduated from medical school and was working in a hospital in Portland, Oregon. Bess lived with a woman whom she called her best friend forever. On a few occasions, Bess and her BFF flew the three hours to the Clinton home for a visit. Both of them took great delight with the twins, and played along with the children's routine.

Morris and Madelyn's mom was the primary provider for them, but that meant walks and pick-ups. The rest of the time, the "girls" were with care providers and housekeepers. Their father, an executive with an international computer company, traveled 80 to 90 percent of the time, and Margo has little recollection of him ever being alone with the twins. Despite his travels, he enjoyed the family home, their summer beach house, and was an attentive husband and parent when he was around. Morris was the father's favorite, or that is what Margo thought. But when asked if she could remember how often he hugged her, she said, "None—ever. I would have remembered that."

Their paternal grandparents lived on a ranch about fifty miles from where Bess practiced medicine. Although the grandmother's health was failing, she smoked all the time, much to her husband's dislike. Her smoking was the cause of heated arguments, that usually ended with Grandma saying she'd stop smoking. But then she'd be caught smoking again. The twin's maternal grandfather died when the twins were in third grade, but Grandma Jones was in good health. She lived in an exquisite beach house in an upscale community a few blocks from the Clinton's beach house, which was just as exquisite and about a four-hour drive from the Clinton family residence. It was all back roads, and therefore it was never an enjoyable ride to the beach.

Grandma Jones liked living alone, but every so often visited her daughter, staying for what seemed like many weeks, especially when the twins were in grade school. Madelyn enjoyed Grandma Jones's visits, because Madelyn was her favorite. This gave her an opportunity to stick her tongue out at Morris and say, "Ha, ha, Grandma Jones likes me best." Madelyn required a lot of attention. She was often depressed and was seeing a therapist, who prescribed antidepressant medication. Morris, on the other hand, was happy, and spent many hours talking and playing with Madelyn.

Various aunts and uncles and their families lived both near and far, and the twins and their mother often visited them. The most fun was with Uncle Bill, their father's brother, who lived at the beach near Grandma Jones. He, too, had twin children, although they were older than Morris and Madelyn. The holidays were family events that were attended by everyone, including their father, and the gatherings often continued well into the night with card games, board games, and lots of conversation. They were all very close—at least until the twins were eight or nine and Morris made his intentions crystal clear. Madelyn seemed to support those intentions without hesitation.

Morris and Margo

Morris was intrigued by the "secret lives" of little girls and with female life in general. He often talked about the fun girls had—the makeup, hairdos, impractical clothes, crazy shoes. What was not to be intrigued about? Morris wasn't sure if he absolutely loved everything girls did because he was actually a girl; or if it was because he and Madelyn were so strongly that being female comforted him. Things were difficult for Madelyn, because she was very self-absorbed. What Margo revealed in her journals was that Morris never had an interest in what boys did. In preschool he wanted to be Cinderella, and went through a phase when he was obsessed with the Disney princesses. His father said Morris was cute, and every so often told his wife that Morris would grow out of wanting to be a girl. "Not to push," were his words. In first and second grade, Morris continued to dress like his sister, and when asked his name by teachers, he said that he was Madelyn. Sometimes, Madelyn would say she was Morris. Morris began to use the name Margo, not as an attempt to being cute, but because when he heard that name, it sounded right.

Margo noted that she and Grandma Jones had long discussions about Morris's dreams about being a girl, and Grandma Jones seemed to approve, Morris didn't know that Grandma Jones had serious mental issues of own. She really wasn't responding to Morris, but to some ancient spirits of sorts. But based on his grandmother's encouragement, which Madelyn shared, Morris pursued his dream.

Busted

When the twins were in third grade, their mother came into their room unexpectedly to find Madelyn and two of her girlfriends playing tea party, Margo wrote in her prison journal. They were all dressed up in high heels, makeup, bows in their hair, and fancy dresses. "Where's Morris?" she asked. The girls stared at the floor. She asked again, and Madelyn pointed to the closest. As she opened the closest door, the girls scurried out of the room. Morris could hear their heels clicking on the wooden floor as their laughter faded from the room just before his mother's big eyes stared down at him. Her son was wearing a flowered dress, white lace tights and white shoes, a ruffled half slip, and white lace gloves. He was made up with lipstick, mascara, and eye shadow.

She said nothing, but dragged the boy from the closest and began to undress him. As she did so, she cried. When she removed the gloves, she saw that his nails had been polished; and as she unzipped the dress, she saw the lace camisole and white bloomers over the tights. She continued to repeat, "It's all my fault. Oh my God, what have I done?" Her final shock was when she pushed the bloomers down and realized that Morris wore his sister's panties under the tights. Tears filled her eyes, but she pulled Morris into the bathroom and scrubbed his face with a washcloth. Morris told his mother he hated everything about being a boy and would chop off his private if she didn't do something about it. That week was difficult for Morris, who now refused to have anything to do with Morris the male, and insisted that his mother call him Margo. "Come on, Mom, praise the lord, right?" She kept Morris home from school the following day, awaiting his father's imminent return from a business trip. who was out of town. When she told her husband what had happened, he again said it was a phase Morris was going through. "Let's just go along with it." The mother's guilt was so overpowering, she accepted her husband's decision and said little about it, ever. But when she went to church, she sang more loudly than before. And for some reason when she sang the word "praise," she emphasized it more than any other word.

"If you're having problems with it," Margo wrote in her prison journal, "it's PTL [praise the Lord] and it's a southern thing.".

Gender Identity Reassignment

By the time Morris and Madelyn were ready for high school, they had been enrolled and expelled from five different elementary and middle schools. Each school took official action against the Clinton twins, because of Morris's refusal to answer to the name of Morris, his refusal to use the boy's restroom, and the general difficulty and commotion the twins caused, especially when Morris and Madelyn dressed alike. Madelyn often played along, saying she was Morris when her brother used the girl's restroom. Finally, Morris's father decided that Morris wouldn't grow out of it and sought ways to resolve the situation. When he was thirteen, Morris saw several different therapists. Each was less skillful than the last, Margo wrote. The last therapist knew something about "Ms. Margo. Finally!"

The first therapist attempted to convince Morris that something was terribly wrong with his choices, and that no one in their right mind would want to be a girl. The second therapist wanted to put him on male hormones to enhance his masculinity, and the third one attempted to show Margo that in three or four years she would be sorry for making a sad mistake.

The forth therapist talked about the gender identity struggles that Margo was actually having. At first she suggested that most boys and girls with gender identity disorders (GID) outgrew their wish to change their gender. The therapist said that understanding of GID was still in its early development stages, and there were many things she didn't know. But after a few more appointments, she presented a diagnosis of GID to Morris's parents, along with a recommendation that he begin taking hormones prior to surgery. Morris was told that if the surgery—which involved removing his penis and testes—failed, he could never go back to being a male. Also, surgery would later change the genitalia and other sex characteristics that Morris possessed. The therapist added that Morris was psychologically stable and would be a good candidate for puberty-blocking medication, which started a month after family conversations. The therapist clarified that now was a good time to start medication, and that during the summer before his sophomore year in high school, they could perform surgery. Also, it was recommended to legally change Morris's name for school and official documents. The entire time, no one in Morris family questioned or challenged his decision to proceed with the medication therapy and the reassignment surgery. His parents never asked Morris a single question about his desire or his decisions.

Compared with the technological and medical advancements available in 2010, there were few if any child and adolescent gender identity clinics available. What all four therapists overlooked was that Margo thought of herself as a female almost since birth, or at least what she remembers about her early childhood. She now required to alter her body to conform to her understanding of herself. Margo enjoyed being a female. She successfully completed gender reassignment therapy, and had physically become a female by the time she graduated high school. Yet the therapists also overlooked that Margo was a successful female predator, as you will soon discover.

High School

Things would become tense if the twins ran into classmates from elementary or middle school, but that rarely happened, particularly because none of their old classmates had enrolled in the same out-of-state high school. With the influence of their father's parents, the twins gained admission to a private school near their grandparents' home in Oregon. When they enrolled the twins, their parents provided a legal name change and records that showed the girls were named Margo Morris Clinton and Madelyn Catherine Clinton. Margo and Madelyn were roommates. Neither school administrators nor their classmates were aware that during the twins' first year at school, Margo had male hormones and parts. Surgery was planned during the summer between their first and second years in high school, and in the meantime, Margo took puberty-blocking medication. Gym was scheduled as their last class of the day, and students were not required to change clothes or shower in the locker rooms. The pressure was on Margo, with Madelyn's help, to behave as a female (although, in fact, Margo was very feminine in comparison to Madelyn). Remaining hair free was another problem. Also, Margo had to sleep, or at least awake, in a room alone or with Madelyn. Otherwise, there were telling physical reactions that would be difficult for a girl to explain. However, in this regard, Margo disliked male parts so much, it was unlikely she could be intimate with a boy at that time. Margo and Madelyn talked about this topic several times, and it usually ended with Madelyn holding Margo close and saying, "Don't worry. I'll always be here for you."

The twins were so close (and often continued to dress alike) that when they had dates, they double-dated. For instance, during the school's homecoming dance, both Margo and Madelyn had dates, and the couples went into town for late night snacks. Their boys had a difficult time telling the twins apart. Double dates were interesting topics of discussions for the twins, and, of course, for those few who knew the truth.

One experience Margo shared was when she and Madelyn were in their junior year of high school. They were both attracted to the same boy, and the three of them went on a bike ride one Saturday afternoon in the spring. Margo stopped her bike and asked the boy to help her with her pedals. As he reached to adjust her pedals, Margo kissed him. Madelyn leaped off her bike and screamed, "You sneaky little slut!" Madelyn rarely reacted to Margo in that fashion, and that's what was so strange about that experience, Margo wrote. "It took weeks before Madelyn had anything nice to say to me, and I had to promise not to kiss that boy again. I explained I didn't 'want him want him.' I was curious about a kiss. But I personally thought the idea of being a slut was fascinating. I never thought of myself as a little slut. When Madelyn and I playacted, I had her call me that—slut."

During the holidays when the twins came home, they stayed at the house or went to the beach house.

Summertime and Beyond

The twins kept to themselves most of the time. The beach house was their sanctuary during each summer. Sometimes family members would visit the beach and stay a few nights. The twins spent a lot of time visiting Grandma Jones too.

Margo elected not to go on to college after high school, and busied herself at the family beach house. She spent time taking care of Grandma Jones, who passed on a few months short of Margo's twentieth birthday. With her grandmother gone, Margo had few excuses to stay at the beach, other than Uncle Bill. His children had gone to college, married, and moved away. For the longest time, Uncle Bill and Aunt Saddie thought Margo was Madelyn and Margo never corrected them. Things were better that way. Margo had a job at a local convenience store and lived comfortably at the beach house. Most of the people at the beach only knew her as Margo, and that suited her fine.

Sex Life and Tattoos

Margo moved permanently to the family's fantastic beach house with its gorgeous indoor-outdoor pool and gardens without her parents' say-so or input. She rarely heard from them before her move. But after moving from her family residence, Margo only heard from her parents through their assistants who called about maintenance work schedules at the beach home.

Margo worked during the day and visited the local hot spots at night, danced with men or women, but she never brought anyone home. Once when she made out in a guy's car, she was excited by the kisses and the touches. She felt warm, although she also knew she was a little drunk (her preferred state of mind, Margo said). She wouldn't allow him to penetrate her vagina, but he successfully piloted his penis into her mouth. She gagged, tried to spit it out, but that excited him more, and he continued to force himself upon her. She didn't have the physical strength or the mental will to push him away. She was curious how it would play out, but decided then and there never to place herself in such a passive position. She cried at her own helplessness. Her arms were behind her back, pressing into the seat, and he held her head still with his powerful hands as his shaft jammed her again and again. He froze for a heartbeat, and Margo understood why as hot salty fluid flooded her throat, and she felt useful. Triumphant laughter slipped from him. Margo laughed too, joining in on his good fortune. But she was more grateful to be in control of her arms and her body again. He said something like, "You're not very good at this," to which she answered, "I haven't done it before." It took so little to make boys happy, she wrote. Later that evening, she wondered if Morris's penis would have been as large. "I walked into a hornet's nest to rid my skin of male things, and now I'm swallowing one," she wrote. A week later she had a rose tattoo engraved on her right forearm, signifying her love for her sister. Another week, another tattoo—an eagle on her right shoulder. Finally, she had a rosary with ten red beads tattooed around her shoulder.

Margo explained that she had intercourse, despite her commitment not to have sex with boys. They had to wear condoms, because their fluid had no place to go inside her, except out. It was easier to be drunk than sober during sex, because of her fears. Her greatest fear was to be pinned down and unable to move. She would never let that happen again, so she took the offensive. She imaged during sex what her eagle tattoo was doing, and if the big bird saw the guy inside her body, and if he noticed the rosary on her shoulder. Margo's other fear was that some boy would try too hard and rip her insides, so she became a fast lover and helped him to ejaculate as quickly as possible. She wrote that she was not happy about intercourse, although it made her happy that her body was useful to more than just her. "Sex can't be immoral because animals do it all the time," she wrote.

Convenience Store Work

Working in a convenience store, Margo learned who the locals were and who the tourists were. That meant she usually knew which houses were occupied and which ones weren't. Often, she broke into empty houses along the beach and stole items that she liked, such as mirrors, canned food, and small household appliances. Large items, such as televisions and computers, she didn't bother with. She broke in to satisfy her curiosity about a home, to see the furniture. Sometimes she slept and bathed there, and sometimes, if there were clothes in the closets or dressers, she would try them on after she smelled them all over.

Theft, Liquor, and Shoplifters

Margo drank all the time. She was able to get beer and liquor from the convenience store for free, since she often worked alone or with only one other clerk. Over a five-year period, she was never caught or suspected of theft. One way she avoided detection was not to ring up a customer's purchase for a single item, such as a six pack of beer. Other times she overcharged customers, particularly tourists, by a few dollars for a single item. She took out the difference between the real price and what charged the customer with such items as beer and vodka, and maybe some cash. She drank half a bottle of vodka every three working days, along with two or four beers (her counts always had to be even numbers). She'd pour vodka into four or six cola cans (half cola, half vodka), and on many occasions drank in front of the owner without ever raising his suspicion that she was doing anything wrong.

Additionally, catching a shoplifter at the convenience store became a new source of crime for Margo. She took shoplifters into the back room. On a few occasions, the shoplifters were so frightened that they had been caught, they did whatever Margo told them do. She would have them empty their pockets and handbags and carefully examined the contents of their wallets and pocketbooks. She kept some of their identification and told the thieves "never come back. I know where you live." Sometimes later, she would apply for a credit card using a shoplifter's identification and use a beach house address that she knew would be unoccupied for some time. She kept the shoplifters' money and jewelry. Most often, shoplifters were young runaways, or down-on-their-luck drunks. Rarely would locals steal from a local store.

Beach, Madelyn, and First Arrest

Margo's parents and family members had little use for the beach house after Grandma Jones's death. No one ever visited her other than Madelyn. They spoke or text each other almost every day of their existence. Margo and Madelyn discussed their sex experiences and compared notes. Madelyn visited Margo on many occasions and sometimes brought college friends adding to the festivities at the local dance clubs. Before going out to dance, the girls did some heroin and had a few mixed drinks. At the club, many patrons were curious about the two of them, but Margo's tattoos took some of the mystery out of who was who. She often tried to cover her tattoos.

The connection between the twins was as strong as always. At the beach, Margo and Madelyn developed their heroin addiction, and often they shared Madelyn's antidepressants. State narcotic officers arrested Margo for drug possession twice at the beach. Her first arrest happened when Grandma Jones died, and the police declined to charge her. The second time, Margo and Madelyn were semi-naked on the beach and "stoned out of their minds." Madelyn was released, because Margo said that she had nothing to do with the heroin and was on antidepressants. Margo showed the officers Madelyn's prescription bottles. Margo was charged and convicted. The sad thing is that Margo had enrolled as a freshman at a community college near the beach, and was looking forward to her first semester in a psychology class. She was twenty-three years old. Madelyn, who had a bachelor's degree in sociology and was working toward a master's degree, had encouraged her sister to enroll in college.

Margo's First Conviction

At the time Margo was first convicted for drug possession, she served six months of a three-year sentence in protective custody in a male prison, and filed suit to obtain her gender medication. Her litigation was not resolved, but she was released early for good behavior, mainly because the state was unsure about the situation.

Margo's Lawsuit against DOC

Once released, Margo brought suit against the state prison system, alleging that she had been handcuffed to her bunk and repeatedly raped and sodomized by three correctional officers for two days. Her suit stated that rumors spread about her, based on her civil suit linked to obtain her gender drugs, and she became fair game for anybody wanting to victimize her. When the guards learned that Margo had been born a male, they "wanted to see for" themselves. Upon discovering she had a vagina, they raped her, and two of the officers anally assaulted her "to be sure." When Margo was asked what "to be sure" meant, she said that she had no explanation other than, "Well, they're men and who knows what men think."

The lawsuit was dropped for lack of evidence, other than Margo's medical report describing her bruised and battered body, and the lacerations on her thighs, vagina, breasts, and anus. There was no sperm found on or in her body. Margo explained that the guards used condoms and latex gloves. Correctional staff reported that Margo had harmed herself, and that she was always a "suicide and psycho case." During the civil suit process, which took several months, two events happened that would impact Margo's life. First, Madelyn and Margo went to the theater to see a new movie—*Boys Don't Cry*, staring Margo's favorite actress, Hilary Swank. The movie was inspired by the real life story of Teena Brandon, who was a popular new high school student in a small town. Teena switched her name around and changed her appearance and behavior, and became Brandon Teena. Brandon hangs out with the guys, drinks, cusses, and bumper surfs. He charms a young woman, who says she never met a more sensitive and considerate young man as Brandon. Teena never tells his girlfriend that he is really a she. When the girl's two male friends make the discovery of Teena's real gender, they rape and killed her. In real life, the killers also killed two witnesses.

Margo's Second Arrest and Conviction

The movie *Boys Don't Cry* made such an impact on Margo and Madelyn, they sought more information about it. They also sought out heroin, got high for a week or maybe longer, had sex, and were eventually arrested at the beach house. A neighbor had called the police, reporting loud, continuous music, flames seen in different rooms of the eighteen-room house, and crashes coming from all over the beach home.

During the trial, the magistrate decided that Margo had not only violated the terms of her good-time release, but this second drug conviction was actually her third conviction. Therefore, she was a habitual criminal. In the jurisdiction where Margo was convicted, the sentencing guidelines mandate a life sentence for a habitual criminal.

Also, the judge reviewed Margo's PSI, earlier civil suits based on gender segregation, and the accusations against male correctional officers. The decision of the court was to ship Margo to a jurisdiction that recognized transgender rights. Gender would no longer be an issue. or at least Margo would not be in a position to litigate against the state that convicted her.

Margo is Exported

When Margo arrived at the prison where she would complete her life sentence, she was twenty-five years old and a college student. She didn't have children, nor had she been married. Her records identified her as "Margo Morris Clinton, female with restrictions." In prison talk, "with restrictions" could mean anything from pregnancy, HIV/AIDS, or mental health problems. But being a male instead of a female was not that common an occurrence, so few correctional personnel who reviewed those records would have realized that Margo had been born a male. It was not a point of concern, as long as Margo had all the female parts and none of the male parts. As part of the agreement to take Margo, the prison system agreed to supply the prescribed antiandrogens to Margo. The truth of the matter was that Margo no longer physically required antiandrogens, but she accepted the concession.

Flight to Intake Center

"Without so much as a blink of an eye, the judge said, life without parole for you, young lady. I almost passed out. I couldn't believe it! Here I was, a twenty-five-year-old woman who decided to go back to college to better myself, and the only way I would leave prison is in a pine box. My hands were already in restraints and I was dressed in a brown jump suit from the county jail. My hair was godawful and dirty and my sneakers didn't fit right, but I was pulled from the court into a vehicle, chained and locked, driven to the airport, onto the tarmac, and up metal stairs into a small, official-looking aircraft, and then whisked out of state. Thank God they had cut my hair, or I would have. And my eyelashes too. I felt so dirty."

Margo remembers one of her fears was that if the aircraft crashed, she was chained to the seat and there'd be no escape. She also recalled that the plane wasn't used for prisoner transport, but rather for officials of some sorts. Her chains were wrapped around and under the seat. On board other than the crew, there were four beefy officers. Two wore uniforms she had seen before, and the other two wore uniforms from the state she would call home for a long time. When an attendant brought refreshments to the officers, she made eye contact with Margo. Margo figured she was wondering why Margo warranted so much attention. "Maybe the little darlin' thought I was a mass murderer or something," Margo wrote.

"I knew I smelled like somebody's septic tank. I hadn't been able to wash during the trial, which ended when I accepted a guilty plea. I'm glad I had an odor. That was one way to get back at the guards, who never got to close to me. One mounty [sheriff deputy] who lawed me up [made the arrest] visited me twice before the flight and brought wipes and asked how I was doing. I think he liked me."

When the pilot notified the guards that the aircraft would be landing in fifteen minutes, the female guard stood up and unchained Margo, over the some objections of the new jailhouse guards. She said, "The child's still our property." She and the other guard walked Margo to the toilet. The lady guard held the door open and said, "Okay, hon, you go ahead and do what you have to do, 'cause once we land, the ride to jail is an hour or so." Margo nodded, dropped her bottoms, and sat down. The guard handed her a tissue for the tears running from her eyes. "You'll be fine. Keep yourself together, girl," the guard said.

Ground Transportation to Intake Center

Once the aircraft landed, two officers escorted Margo into a vehicle waiting on the tarmac. Margo recalled catching the stares of passengers behind the large windows of the small terminal. Some held children up to look out at the spectacle of a single woman prisoner, chained with angle irons that made her walk funny, and her armed escort. The new guards were less tolerant than those from her home state, and they were very animated now that they were on their home soil. They pushed Margo into the vehicle's backseat and hooked her up to the metal eyes on both sides of her. Clear Plexiglas separated her from the driver. Before the door was shut, one home state guard asked if she was okay, and added, "Just relax, honey."

"I heard the door lock mechanism connecting. That was it! The driver glanced back at me and said, 'Yeah, just relax, honey.' That's when I started to cry." The home guards got back into the plane, and the other two guards jumped into a vehicle that followed Margo's. "I was frightened out of my wits."

Margo's driver wore a black uniform with a yellow patch below the shoulder. His uniform was similar to the all the guards in the new state system. Later she learned that these escorts were part of a first response team, similar to critical-incident police teams. It would be these officers who raided prison cells late at night in search of contraband. In the months ahead, Margo would again see both guards. One time, the bigger of the two grabbed her between her legs. "Guess you don't have a dick," he said, and smelled his hand. "Hmm. Nice. Maybe next time we'll get to know each other."

Margo's driver spoke gently to her, and she enjoyed hearing a pleasant voice. He said, "Listen, honey, let me give you some advice. You gotta learn to protect yourself, because you're a pretty thing and there's some butch babes in this place where you're going that will tear you up. Careful in the showers and changing clothes in front of them. You'll be able to recognize them when ya see them. Margo wrote that she couldn't believe this man was going on and on about what she should do about those little bull dykes. He went on to say, "If you're not careful, you'll become one of their victims. So buddy up with a guard and do your own time." He asked about her prison sentence and glanced at her paperwork. "Holy crap!" he exclaimed. "Life! What did a pretty thing like you do to deserve that, honey? Oh, I know. Three strikes, right? Says here you're a habitual offender. Gotta tell ya, honey, that sucks."

For the better part of an hour, the driver continued his warnings but in a way, Margo said, he made her feel better. He made her feel like a girl. "I liked that. I kept saying to him, okay, yeah, that makes sense. Then I'd cry a little bit and catch myself. But I couldn't help but think that this was all a mistake. A dream that turned bad and hard, just like the one God played on me, making me a girl in a body with boy's weapon. For sure, I thought, I'd be out of prison in a few weeks. Some new assistant prosecutor would jump in and safe the day with evidence that I, Margo Clinton, should not spend the rest of her life in prison. I mean, oh my God, I'm only twenty-five years old.

"As I looked out the darkened windows of the van I saw it. The prison walls jumped into view; the state prison for women. The walls were high and dirty, and the few windows I saw were crusted with … I don't know, some kind of grime. Metal gates slid open, and the driver drove the van into the prison's belly. The title of a book I read long ago, *In the Belly of the Beast*, was about prisons. I never thought when I read that book that I would become a resident of a prison, and a female resident at that.

"From nowhere, many other people in different colored jumpsuits appeared from vans and buses that were already inside the yard. 'Okay, honey,' the driver said as he turned to me. 'You do everything I told you and stay safe in here. I'll ask one of my friends to keep an eye on you.' The van door opened, and a female guard unlocked my hands and yelled, 'Come on, sweetie, get your lazy ass out of that vehicle.'"

As she spoke, Margo remembered that her breath had a punch that she would come to call guard's breath. They smelled like each other regardless if they were male or female guards. "How strange," Margo wrote.

Intake Center and Substance Abuse

When Margo arrived at the intake center, correctional counselors learned that Margo was an alcoholic and would have to go through detox. The prison center had facilities, policy, and personnel to aid in various recovery processes before transporting a prisoner to a permanent facility. Male and female prisoners were detained at that prison center for various reasons, including detoxification. Some remained for physical treatment and mental health evaluations. Surgeries and other medical treatments were conducted at a local hospital. Some prisoners were held at the center because they were under investigation for unresolved situations; and others awaited the arrival of dentists or other specialty personnel. Margo was temporarily accepted by the correctional system pending examinations and evaluations. Otherwise, she would be returned to her state of residence, and it had no gender legislation. If she was returned, she would serve her life sentence in protective custody in a male prison. Needless to say, Margo was on her best behavior and answered all the questions asked, such as when was her last period and how was her flow. She was provided with prescribed antiandrogens and hormones to prevent masculinization. The prescriptions were not identified as gender drugs. When asked, Margo would say they were prescribed for her high blood pressure and heart condition.

Margo also knew that she really didn't require the gender drugs, but she liked the opportunity to talk to the medical personnel. It was something to do, and she knew that she could sell the gender drugs once inside prison. It had been ten years since her gender reassignment therapy, nine years since her penis and testicles were removed, and seven years since reconstructive surgery had provided the finishing touches on her vagina and the rest of her female body. The Department of Corrections did not want to expose itself to any lawsuits linked to Margo, and consequently provided more care and medication than necessary. But in truth, DOC, as well as everyone else, knew little about GID, how it worked, and how it could be handled under state sex discrimination laws.

Margo's GID and Salient Behavior Characteristics

Typical of most successful boy-girl GID, Margo had female parts, such as a vagina, and a female voice, which she developed with the help of gender drugs and a speech therapist that her parents paid for. Of course, menstruation and impregnation were not possible, because there was no uterus or no ovaries. Orgasm was possible, because there was erogenous sensation, and the mental component was also intact.

The term autogynephilia describes males who have "love of oneself as a woman." Based on what Margo wrote about herself, one way to interpret her perspective is that she loved herself as a woman and thought about her life as a female long before her body parts were altered.

What has been learned about Margo while she was in prison is that she was generally a drug abuser, most likely heroin, but was low functioning, similar to Brandeis. Other heroin addicts, such as Annie and Dory, were high functioning. Also, Margo used antidepressants. Her health was always an issue, and sometimes she was restricted to areas within the prison for failure to follow directives of correctional officers or some other disciplinary infraction. Because she's a schemer, she was rarely placed in segregation, but was frequently put on suicide watch. Margo is highly aggressive and quick with her responses.

Margo and Arson

Margo's obsession with arson was never suspected prior to her imprisonment. It was during in-group sessions that the truth came out, particularly when Margo was high. She described arson this way: "What I love about it is that it can destroy and I can create it. It is intellectual and primitive at the same time. It resists control. A tiny single flame can change moods and creates its own shadow and its own colors." In her journal when she wrote about loneliness, she added, "There is a place I used to be able to go when I felt lonely. At my place, I could do anything I wanted, and be anyone I wanted to be. Part of that place is when I cranked up my Zippo. I'm a god and a devil at the same time."

During an in-group meeting, she said, "Fire is a way of getting back at people you can't do anything else to. They're either too big or too brave." After some urging from her prison partner (Margo's partner was an aggressive alpha-type person), she eventually added, "Or so I'm told." The two convicts exchanged glances, and Margo sat down with a small but widening grin.

Margo followed the lead of her allegedly dominant mate, Cathy, who in prison substituted in some ways for Madelyn. This behavior is consistent with Margo's need for dominance over others, while allowing that individual to think he or she is in control. This manipulation is part of the pattern of behavior among schemers, as evidenced by Annie and the other pleasure-seekers in this work.

In this regards, it is likely that Margo reigned over Madelyn prior to imprisonment, and victimized Madelyn physically and emotionally. Fire was one of her weapons. Cathy was a streetwise gangbanger whose aggressiveness and colossal hands would make a gladiator blink. It is doubtful that she knew who Margo truly was, but she knew Margo's wrath could produce a fireball that even a gladiator wouldn't miss, but it would happen when the gladiator wasn't watching. However, Margo did not require the reorganization from others, a similar observation of all pleasure-seekers, for her destruction of property or people.

Memories of Torching

Other experiences Margo recalled were linked to the kids in middle school, who largely disliked studious kids like the twins, and often avoided to two of them. Margo was tired of never fitting in with others. She didn't play sports, and she wouldn't give up the two things she treasured most—school studies and her sister. She had a lot of time on her hands and few if any friends, other than Madelyn. But the twins liked to read. A lot. In grammar school, Morris read everything he got his hands on. He spent many hours at the public library and the school library. An article that caught his eye and impressed him for many years inspired him to experiment. The article, by Morley Safer, was about the Vietnam War, specifically US Marines burning the village of Cam

Ne with the aid of Zippo lighters. This article changed the perspective of the war, with its suggestion that American combat troops were setting fire to hamlets throughout Southeast Asia. One impression Safer left with his audience, including Morris, was of senseless and wanton destruction of ancestral homes, and the American military's disregard for human life. Safer implied that the Zippo raids were typical of many such actions that took place throughout the war. Margo mentioned Safer's article three times in-group over a four-month period. Margo said that she was so taken with the image of a military unit setting everything afire, she tried it for herself.

First, she needed to purchase a Zippo lighter, but was unsuccessful. She—although she was Morris at this time, for clarity's sake, I will refer to her as Margo—told the clerk that it was for her father, but that didn't work. Next, she asked Madelyn to distract the clerk by asking questions, and that didn't work. Finally, with Madelyn's help, she stole a lighter. It took her some time to understand that the Zippo required lighter fluid, but that was easily solved. Finally, a new Zippo was ready to go, and the twins admired the flame, the way it drifted in and out in different shades and colors.

Margo also stole a few BIC lighters as backup, but they didn't produce the unique sound of a Zippo lighter as its top is flipped back. At the park, she tried burning park benches and trees. She stared at the flame for long periods of time. Eventually, the flame by itself had promise, and she started to mess around with aerosol cans. She got the idea when she used a shot of hairspray to hold down some hairs on her head. She lit her lighter and pushed the button of the can. The flame actually shot off, and suddenly her loneliness faded. By eighth grade, although she had burned her thumb several times, singed her eyebrows once, and received a gash on her arm from flying shrapnel caused by an exploding aerosol can, her curiosity continued, and she experimented in various projects. Madelyn attempted to stop her, but Margo was, as she said, "hell-bent on fires."

Margo said that she never set fire to large things, but liked tossing something burning into an outside garbage can to see how long it took for the contents to catch fire. She would continue to walk past the garbage can, because she didn't want to be found as the person who started the fire; and above everything else, she didn't want to lose her Zippo lighter.

When people see smoke, even from garbage cans, they call 911, and Margo knew better than to be on the scene of a fire more than once. Sometimes she would position herself on a cross street where she knew the fire trucks would pass her. She would walk or ride her bike toward the fire station after starting a fire as opposed to away from it. This action contradicts most of the studies on fire starters, but heck, so do much of the contents of this book. Madelyn was upset with Margo's fire games. For instance, in seventh grade while awaiting the school bus in terribly cold weather, she lit a fire. It was blazing when the bus arrived. Because she admitted starting the fire, the school wanted to ban Margo from the bus. She broke down and cried and retold the story, saying that she felt guilty for the fire not because she started it, but because she dared a boy to do it. She had never seen the boy before, she said, "and I think he was going to hurt me and Madelyn you know where."

Madelyn never said anything to their parents about her sibling's desire to torch everything, particularly in the eighth grade, when the then Morris told Madelyn that he would burn her alive in her bed if she didn't help Morris become a girl.

Margo wrote about one incident that might be typical of her response mechanism. "When I was in high school, one of my teachers asked me to her office and later to her home, where she attempted to confuse me about who I was. Little did she know that Madelyn stood outside her door and comforted me afterwards. I left in a hurry, and the following day she again called me to her office and said she was sorry if she offended me. I said you're good. But it was a problem. I'm not a lesbian. She made me feel like a little girl without a brain and that just isn't fair."

The inside of the high school teacher's car was torched, several fires were lit in her garbage can, and mail in her home mail box was often burned. Margo made no attempt for recognition of any of her criminal activities. She understood the consequences of acknowledging her crimes.

Margo talked about fire and expressed the idea that because she could create it, it could destroy her. "Controlling a flame is risky if you don't know the rules. It is interesting that people need it and fear it at the same time. Messing with the flame is just a minor way of flirting with death."

How Many Torchings?

How many torchings had Margo started that ended in destruction? That's a difficult question to answer, it apparently was a device that Margo used from time to time. For example, she described how she torched one boy's penis using her Zippo and an aerosol. She put out the "burn" with beer when his pubic hairs began to burn too. She also torched another boy's penis—she guessed he was twelve—whom she met on the deserted beach during the off-season. She wanted to practice oral sex, but became so disgusted with her attempts that they smoked a joint instead, and "I lit him up." Incidentally, these are only two arson crimes Margo admitted committing. She was pleased with herself and her behavior toward both boys, because she used an alias, Brandy. I interpreted this to me that she believed that because she used an alias, she couldn't be identified. Hmm!

Also, Margo never admitted details, but it was obvious she was experienced at starting fires. But she also mentioned that the car belonging to the young man who had forced her to have oral sex with him was "firebombed and burned down to the ground in the early hours of the morning." Then there was the all-night convenience store where she worked, her uncle Bill's home, his car, Aunt Saddie's car, a shed in their backyard, and an all-night diner.

A check with the sheriff's department and the local police in a nearby village showed a spike in incidents of random fires during the five years Margo lived at the beach. Several house pets were killed, and property was damaged, including automobiles and summer homes that were not occupied during the off-season. Several vehicles near the club Margo frequented were torched. Random fires occurred more often off-season than in-season, which was different from other counties on the beach. One assumption that can be made was that during the summer season, Madelyn stayed at the beach house with Margo. When Madelyn returned to school after holiday visits and school breaks, random fires began again.

Observations

Tentatively, during in-group encounters and in Margo's journals, curious inconsistencies surfaced. The impression I am left with is that Margo lied about Madelyn. There was no Madelyn Clinton on the visitor's list, nor had a Madelyn ever attempted to visit Margo. But there was a Melvin Clinton. I suspect that Morris used arson to hide his homosexual feelings, but he also lied about his twin's sex. The twins were both boys at birth. When investigators conducted the presentence investigation, they were under the impression that the woman they interviewed was Madelyn, when indeed it was Margo. Additionally, when Margo revealed that she had been busted by her mother when she broke up Madelyn's tea party, in fact Melvin was there with two of his friends, but they were boys. They were not dressed in girl clothes, although Morris was, and it is likely that he was entertaining the three boys in some way or another. I can only speculate what Morris was doing, because Margo never revealed her twin's existence as a male.

CHAPTER 10
Mary and Stone-Hard Feelings

Introduction

This chapter will cut deep into your confidence level about police officers. The descriptions of Officer Mary Bayuga's corruption on the stone-hard streets of New Orleans reveal that a clear and present danger exists in the Big Easy. Yet, if you can admit that most cops are dedicated and work hard to help others through moments of misery, apprehend bad guys, and stand between us and anarchy, then feel free to finish reading.

Mary's affluent family continues to manipulate the outcomes of local and statewide elections and federal judge appointments. Frankly, they influence everyone in Terrebonne Parish, Louisiana, and everything of importance, including the BP oil spill in the Gulf of Mexico. This chapter describes Mary Bayuga's early childhood experiences, and reveals the conclusions reached by a private psychologist and a police psychological evaluation prior to her law enforcement employment. The chapter winds through police corruption, armed robbery, drug trafficking, sexual assault, and murder at the hands of an officer with stone-hard feelings, which matched the attitudes of people she served at the French Quarter, the Garden District, and on the west shore of the Mississippi River in the New Orleans neighborhood known as Algiers.

With all of our superior technology, media coverage, and federal oversight, some might wonder how a young police officer can commit numerous heinous crimes and get away with it. It might be sufficient to say that in the Big Easy, anything is easy. Yet if you're reluctant to believe Bayuga's accounts and how easy the Big Easy can be, let's consider the real story about a fifteen-year-old nicknamed Caveman. It was April 14, 2003, at 10:30 in the morning, when a high school football player named Jonathan (Caveman) Williams sat in his physical education class along with fifty other kids. Without warning, two men with automatic weapons strolled into the gym, located Caveman and blasted him, blowing off half his face and pockmarking the floor tiles underneath his body. Several others were injured by stray bullets. Police said the attack was payback for the murder of another high school student the previous week. No one would provide a description of the gunmen. Should you believe that Caveman's murder was an isolated incident, it is common knowledge in the Big Easy that an arrested criminal ends up back on the street before the end of the day. In 2004, Keisha Robinson, twenty-nine, was gunned down in broad daylight in front of her house, shortly after she testified before a grand jury investigating her younger brother's killing. Police can't be sure why she was attacked, because the cops never arrested anyone for her murder. But her murder, like Caveman's, is considered a revenge killing. Two months before Robinson was gunned down, Ryan Smith, a key witness in another murder case, was shot down outside his workplace. *Bienvenue à la Nouvelle-Orléans.*

Mary's Birth

Mary Zenaid Bayuga was born into the richest family in the small village of Chauvin, Louisiana, situated in Terrebonne Parish, about fifty miles southeast of New Orleans. Zenaid is her mama's surname, and her family members are fishermen. On her father's side, most of the men in the parish work on the shrimp boats and the shark boats, or aboard the offshore supply vessels trolling the Gulf of Mexico. The boats are owned or managed by her daddy's clan, but Mary had little interest in boats. From the early age of seven, she wanted to be a police officer in New Orleans. She was enthusiastic about police dramas on television, and little else caught her fancy—other than liquor, gambling, and violence. Five older brothers and three older sisters each knew there was a place in the Terrebonne Parish business for them, and they referred to the future as would a mystic reciting eloquent scripture. All of Mary's brothers and sisters graduated from either Louisiana State University or the University of Southern Mississippi. Two graduated from the Massachusetts Maritime Academy as officers, and trained aboard the training ship USTS *Kennedy* at Buzzards Bay, Massachusetts. Mary graduated from the New Orleans Police Department Academy, but should have been under the care of a psychiatrist or even the Department of Corrections long before she reached the academy.

Mary Wasn't Blessed

Most members of the Bayuga clan knew that Mary wasn't blessed with the Bayuga intellect, and consequently no one expected much from the runt of the litter. But townspeople and a few of her home-school tutors thought that despite her size and her uncongenial attitude toward everybody she encountered, she possessed intense survival instinct. It was never expected that little Mary was, in essence, a deadly predator-in-training, who would not sit on the company's executive board, but on the state's death row, awaiting execution. Because she was so wicked, some would call her Bloody Mary in the years ahead.

Mary has light black skin with almost a deep golden gloss. Her bloodlines include African, Filipino, and French, and some folks who know something about Louisiana history describe Mary as Creole. The Bayuga heritage is linked to *Les Gens de Couleur Libres* (The Free People of Color). As for Mary, she was always a petite child. As an adult she still only wore a size two, but her legs were long, measuring almost thirty-two inches. Her amazing black eyes possessed a sort of power that wouldn't let anyone look away from her stare. Truth is, once you gazed into those eyes, they seemed to sparkle with brown sugar and persuaded a "yes" from those who said "no."

Because Mary was the youngest child in an enormous family, and because she lacked parental and caretaker supervision and care, she got away with awful behavior. She had few fears of her parents, because they were always jetting off to Rio or New York City or wherever. The Bayuga elders owned an island off the Georgia coast, and spent a great deal of time there as well. And Mary had no interference from caretakers, who were more concerned for their jobs and their peace than about Mary.

She never cried or stamped her feet for attention; her eyes did it for her. She was careful about her expressions, which were rarely seen. Some say she had stone-cold feelings about things, and they were right. She never revealed what she was feeling, except when she watched the cops in action on television.

Young Mary was antagonized by her big brothers from time to time. They tried their best to rattle her, but she was stone-cold and stood perfectly still as she stared them down. They would hold her stare until she released them. Her sisters played jokes on her, but Mary was steadfast. Her sisters were careful not to look into her eyes; girls are usually smarter than boys. Humor was a stranger to Mary, or any joyful emotions. None of her brothers or sisters wanted to be alone with Mary, because Mary wouldn't hesitate to spit, poke eyes, pull hair, or stab them with her little pocket knife. She was small but quick and went for the jugular, and her attacks were often conclusive, despite her size. From the time Mary nursed from a bottle, given to her by a child care-provider, she had little use for others. When those around her became annoyed or nervous, Mary believed she was winning, and winning meant she was in control. She felt good about being in control and little else. She vividly recalled many of her early experiences, or she was a proficient liar. Yet it was more likely that her accounts were a reflection of both: a person who possessed a remarkable memory, and a person who was also an incredible liar. Mary's realities were fortified by the power held by Bayuga clan, which oozed from the gulf shores through the wetlands to the Louisiana schools, as revealed in the following experiences.

School Experiences

When Mary Bayuga attended Terrebonne Parish public schools, she instigated altercations that continue to be a source of frustration among retiring teachers and staff. Juvenile records aren't public record, but it's hard to stop teachers from talking about students, especially students who excel academically or otherwise. Mary was an "otherwise." For instance, during morning student recess at the red brick building known as Upper Little Caillou Elementary, one teacher's attention was jolted by several children shouting trash and pushing and shoving on the playground. Jane Baldwin knew who the instigator was before she intervened, and this time she asked Mary, who was in the third grade, why she was so mean. The reply was something like, "Mind your own beeswax." Mary punched a fourth grade boy and kicked another between the legs before walking away. "Just a minute, little miss," the teacher called.. "Shut it, ya ole mudbug," Mary shot back, and hit another student. Hours later, Mary's mother arrived at the school and said that she was sorry that she couldn't arrive earlier—family business. Mary was disciplined, but the principal warned Mrs. Baldwin not to bring the incident up again, or she'd face disciplinary action by the school board. The principal of the school knew he had to defend the Bayugas' honor, despite Mary's mischievous behavior. In the wetlands of Louisiana, righteousness can be found every Sunday morning at the local church. That is, if you hadn't practiced voodoo Saturday night.

Another incident that typically described Mary's behavior occurred when she was in the seventh grade at Oaklawn Junior High in Houma, Louisiana. This incident never died in the minds of some teachers, and continues to monopolize conversations at crawdaddy festivals and the state fair near Houma. Mary had clashes at school because she had, according to the principal, "a strong mind of her own." Neither Mary's mother nor her father was available for meetings with the principal, but that was nothing new to the public school teachers in the parish.

The principal at Oaklawn Junior High carefully conveyed his thoughts to Mary's caregiver that Mary was unhappy at Oakland. He wanted her parents to consider other educational avenues to make Mary happy. "Because many students are jealous of Mary, they cause problems for her," he said, and provided a cautiously worded example to make his point. Mary had been "compelled" to use physical contact against another student, when the student whispered a derogatory remark about Mary's outfit. Mary told the teacher, who stepped into the dispute and had little choice but to reprimand the other girl. Another incident at Oaklawn concerned physical education and Mr. Julian, the instructor. Mary felt she wasn't required to participate in the PE program. Mr. Julian felt otherwise, and told her so in no uncertain terms. Mary thought Mr. Julian's behavior was disrespectful. He made an inappropriate gesture that Mary interpreted as an attack. She pushed him. The inexperienced teacher yelled at her, and Mary ran toward the main corridor of the school. Claiming that she acted in her own defense, and with entirely understandable fears, she broke the glass that held a fire extinguisher, and without hesitation emptied its contents on the instructor. The principal assured the Bayuga family that he had disciplined Mr. Julian. The local newspaper featured the incident. It identified Mr. Julian but not the student, although it alluded to a powerful fishermen family. Mary claimed years later in her prison journal that she had been involved in the episode and that she didn't know what happened. She "snapped and went for a fire extinguisher to stop the nasty man who was going to hurt me."

Another incident at Oakland was about a metal object in Mary's pocketbook. She wouldn't give it up when it set off the metal detector as she walked from the cafeteria to class. The cafeteria was equipped with a scanning device, because students often forgot to leave their eating utensils behind. The metal object? Her little pocket knife, which Mary said she required in the event she was again attacked by a "nasty teacher." All of these incidents took place during the first few weeks of Mary's first year at Oaklawn. The principal conveyed to Mary's caregiver that several teachers were available to homeschool Mary. He would help to coordinate their efforts with the Bayuga staff.

Mary withdrew from the public school. The remainder of her education was provided at the Bayuga home in Chauvin. However, those school years were not without incident, including one young teacher who filed an assault charge against her. Many other homeschool teachers should have filed complaints, but accepted their fate and left Mary to her own self-destruction. One teacher summed up Mary's behavior this way: "Ever engage someone on a self-destructive mission? Their life is loaded with conflict. If they aren't fighting with someone, they feel rejected and still turn ugly. That's Mary Bayuga, and there isn't anything anyone can about it, thanks to her family's reputation and her parents' indifference toward her. Her siblings turned out all right. They had each other. Fix that and still something is indecent about the girl. I can't put my finger on it."

Here's the teacher's story. She had brought her toy terrier pup to the Bayuga residence at Mary's insistence. Mary had seen pictures of the pup and wanted to meet him. While the teacher was busy with completing some forms for the school district, Mary and the puppy played. To the teacher's horror, Mary superglued the puppy's mouth closed. When the teacher started crying, some of the Bayuga staff escorted her and her puppy to the door. The teacher said that was the first time she ever saw Mary smile, and it was a smile from ear to ear. The teacher never returned to the Bayuga estate, and some said that the teacher and Mary were intimate with each other. Mary never denied it.

Judging by the above revelations about Mary, few individuals challenged, corrected, or denied Mary Bayuga anything, including her self-destructive path. That is consistent with Mary in her teenage years, and the evidence mounts that what is indecent about Mary is that she was wired-wrong from the get-go.

Teenage Experiences

Mary always observed the fishermen when they joked about killing sharks aboard their fishing vessels on the gulf. They stood behind a shark and stabbed it repeatedly below the head, severing its spinal cord and paralyzing it. She took a fancy to one of young men, who showed her how to kill sharks. She convinced her caregivers, which didn't take much, that she could sail with a fishing crew. One morning when Mary was fifteen, she headed for a family shark boat. Everyone suspected that Mary had little interest in experimenting with any of the fishermen, because she had already demonstrated a sexual prowess toward females among servants, teachers, and caregivers. "Boys with their stupid little penises bore me," she wrote in her prison journal. Why Mary despised males, or to be more accurate, their stupid penises, is unclear. Nonetheless, that morning began as any hot humid July day would, with the night air dissipating into crystallized layers of brightness, which hung like meadows of heavy moisture above the tallest deciduous tree. The sun busied itself and sizzled every red leaf on those trees. Two things were inevitable: the red leaves high on the trees would turn yellow, and Mary had a plan to destroy something or someone.

Yet heat or no heat, the gulf waters remained impervious to the weather, with their own way of surviving the Atlantic crosswinds. That morning, the Bayuga shark boat with its crew of six entered a dead zone.

Mary became entangled in a set of circumstances that left one crew member lost at sea and another with severe lacerations from the boat's rigging lines. She and the remaining crew members were rescued by a US Coast Guard helicopter. The helicopter crew as well as other vessels, both Coast Guard and private, searched with no success for the missing crew member. Nobody was talking about the incident, including Mary, but the missing fisherman was the man who had shown Mary how to kill sharks.

Rescuers were confused by Mary's nonchalant attitude and demeanor. One report suggested she was in shock. A military physician examined Mary and reported that she was physically sound. The physician strongly recommended that she be examined by a psychologist. He tested her blood alcohol count after he smelled liquor on her breath. The report showed that she had consumed alcohol. Later, Mary said she had been confused and dazed by the incident, and had accepted a few drinks to relax her.

Frankly, being dazed and confused is an unlikely scenario for Mary. Whenever Mary appeared spontaneous or nervous before, during, and after an event, her behavior was an act. She was always in control and left little to chance. Even as a child, when situations arose among her siblings, classmates, and authority figures, Mary thought long and hard about what outcome she preferred, and then made every effort to move in the situation in that direction. For example, as Mr. Julian chased her as she ran from the gym, Mary had already planned to run to the fire extinguisher, break the glass, grab it, and blast him. And that is exactly what she did. What plans she had for the fishing crew were never known, but it is certain that Mary had a plan in place long before she boarded the vessel and long before the crew member went missing.

Another point worth mentioning relates to her hatred of males, her destructive pursuits, and her predatory mentality. If she had been physically stronger and more experienced, there is a strong likelihood that not one crew member would have been lost at sea, but all of them would have met their ends. One observation is that Mary was practicing, playing out her nasty plans, that would eventually come to fruition. That is, she was teaching herself through trial and error how to injure or murder another human being and get away with it.

Psychological Examination

Mary's caregivers accepted Mary's explanation that she didn't drink much, but still invited a psychologist to the house. They felt Mary required professional assistance, but they had thought that for a long time. Now the opportunity arose to get her help, and a young, pretty woman had recently been state certified as a psychologist. The psychologist knew Mary's parents, and was the daughter of a fisherman who worked for the Bayugas. Over five months, Mary sat with the psychologist twice a week, and often they were left alone in the library at the estate. "Let nature take its course," the caregivers hoped. However, no one read the psychologist's assessment reports until those reports eventually surfaced years later. If anyone had read them, they would have been seen that Mary was described as an individual characterizing a substance or alcohol-induced psychotic disorder, which had its roots in an earlier age, probably around twelve; and at the time of her evaluation, was at the beginning stages of delusions. Mary's personality was also consistent with a person who lacked empathy and was unwilling to recognize or identify with the feelings and needs of others. She had a sense of entitlement, and was often envious of others and believed that others were strongly envious of her. She was preoccupied with fantasies of unlimited success and power, and those fantasies were intensified when she was intoxicated. That is, Mary Bayuga's personality was consistent with the characteristics present in an alcoholic and a narcissist personality, as described in the DSM-IV-TR. Additionally, Mary characterized persistent and recurrent maladaptive gambling behavior. She was preoccupied with gambling, needed to gamble with increasing amounts of money, was restless and irritable when attempting to cut back, and totally relied on others to provide her cash. The psychologist suggested immediate treatment, and sent a registered letter stating her findings. She also telephoned the Bayuga home several times. Her warnings were buried in a sea of privilege. In response, and at Mary's suggestion, the Bayuga family regarded the psychologist as a new person trying to make a name for herself at the expense of Mary. Her telephone calls and letters went unanswered, her business license in Terrebonne Parish was cancelled, and her loan on a townhouse was called in, leading to foreclosure. Needless to say, the well-intended psychologist was railroaded out of the parish.

Mary, of course, acted as if she didn't own the secrets the psychologist uncovered, when in fact she was both the creator and actor of them. Everything worked together for Mary. Drinking, gambling, and violence were part of her everyday existence, and by the time she was fifteen years old, a homeschooled child from an affluent family, she was left unsupervised, which provided the means and opportunity for her aggressive and destructive lifestyle.

The Rest of the Story

What occurred aboard that shark boat remained a mystery for some time. No one would say anything derogatory about a Bayuga family member. The law of the parish was that no one betrays a Bayuga. It wasn't just that the Bayugas controlled jobs, but everyone's father worked for a Bayuga, and everybody's family lived in a Bayuga mortgaged home. Add to that, most of the community drove vehicles financed through the Bayuga Credit Union, which probably mortgaged their souls too.

"Ya don't betray God and expect heaven," said an intoxicated fisherman to a Parish deputy, who had stopped him for reckless driving. Once in lockup, the crew member finally broke the silence about the shark-boat incident. He told the deputy, "I'm going to tell you what happened out there with Mary Bayuga in the gulf, 'cause I can't take it. It's eatin' me, man. But you can't say I told ya, or my family will pay."

The deputy understood. His family lived in a home mortgaged through the Bayuga Credit Union, and he owed his job to the company store.

The fisherman said that Mary demanded that the captain sail into the dead zone. She wanted to see it. He refused. She said that as owner of the boat, she had say-so. The captain explained, "Cher, there ain't nothing to see. T'at zone is hypoxic [less than 2 ppm dissolved oxygen] water at the mouth of t'at [Mississippi] river." He probably explained that the zones between the inner and mid-continental shelf in the north gulf ran from the Mississippi River delta and extended westward to the upper Texas coast. "I don't wanna see Texas," she yelled.

"And by God," the drunk fisherman said "this *piti* thing reached up and decked him. We were surprised. She reached up to deck him again, and he pushed her so hard, he sent her flying into the water.

We tried to fish her out, but she kept swimmin' away, till the captain gave in. He'll sail to the zone. When we dragged 'er from the water she goes, I'll bet ya a month's pay we don't leave the dead zone with six of ya. That was it. We got caught in a mess. Some of us wanted to dump the *madivinez* [lesbian or slut] overboard again, after, I say, we should have sex with her first, then dump her. Use her pussy as chum . We fought each other, cuz one said she wanted to spiritually cleanse us. Hoodoo voodoo! A fire broke out, and I do believe that little fairy set it with her voodoo spell. Got to be, and the rigging was jarred, and shit was everywhere. She was right. There were only five of us when we was rescued. She demanded her money from each of us."

One assumption is that the fire onboard the vessel automatically released a distress signal to the Coast Guard—standard operating procedure for many of the vessels in the Bayuga fleet. The other assumption is that voodoo practices by the Bayuga family were commonplace and one means to their power, but Mary never confirmed nor denied voodoo as part of her life experiences.

Application to the New Orleans Police Department

At almost twenty-one years of age, Mary attempted to fulfill her lifelong dream of becoming a patrol officer for the city of New Orleans. Powerful recommendations from a Louisiana state senator, a Washington DC Louisiana senator, and the chief judge of the Eastern US District Court accompanied Mary's application. Turning Mary down for employment wasn't an option, despite the complications with her application linked to a juvenile record and concerns found in her psychological evaluation, conducted by a New Orleans police psychologist. Also, little was known, or at least acknowledged, during the hiring process that Mary had been undergoing electroshock therapy since she was fifteen years old. Some say it was linked to voodoo, but there is no evidence that electric shock is part of voodoo. Nonetheless, Mary claimed that it was for depression, which she never really experienced; and this information didn't come out until her trial a few years later. "But it [the electric shock] is amazingly helpful," she reported. And when she was incarcerated, she said that she had to "do maintenance every six weeks" or she "would die."

Nonetheless, Mary's earlier evaluation, conducted by the young Terrebonne Parish psychologist, was never considered along with Mary's application, even though its existence was common knowledge among many high-ranking police officials, the press, and virtually everybody in Terrebonne Parish, including the alligators in the wetlands.

Of greater importance, Mary scored far below average in the productive police officer categories. The police psychological report noted that her responses "characterized the behavior of a prejudicial and deceitful individual who also held a disrespectful perspective toward authority." In Mary's job interview with a newly appointed police superintendent, she clarified her sexual orientation, her hesitance in accepting directives and orders from supervisors, and her insecurity with authority. "I've always done what I want," she wrote in her prison journal. "The superintendent who interviewed me was fired after my arrest, and the chief was also replaced by some fool from DC [the Metropolitan Police Department, Washington DC]. I AM a very important person! When you use the letters in my name it comes out that I am an ARMY of one."

Academy Training

During Mary's police tactical training, it was obvious that she was no stranger to weapons or danger. "She squeezed the trigger of her service weapon without so much as a blink," her training officer said. He added that Mary Bayuga was a natural on the shooting range, and that he was glad she was one of the good guys. From a technical perspective, "She is big-time fearless, never seen anything like it. In hand-to-hand, she uses a defensive technique that lands her whole body on the back of her opponent." In retrospect, that is the position of shark killers. That said, even her training officer felt something was "dead wrong. We don't usually get trainees who have psychological issues, but in the shooting, driving, and fighting field, she's as competitive as I've ever seen. I've reported my concerns about her issues to no prevail. She ain't public safety material."

Street Training

Officer-in-training Mary Bayuga was assigned to District 4, referred to as Algiers, a crime-ridden piece of New Orleans across the river from the business district and the French Quarter. Her street training officer, Officer Javon Green, was a former 1st Calvary Division veteran, who saw combat during two tours in Vietnam, or at least he said so. He would have been terminated from the police department for false documentation, but apparently Mary had other ideas for his future, once she checked on him through her powerful connections provided by her daddy's name.

Special Task Force

Officer Mary Z. Bayuga was assigned to the dangerous Special Task Force of the New Orleans PD, consisting of seventy-five of the "most courageous police officers in the city." In a ninety-day police sweep, the unit conducted over 800 arrests of gangbangers in New Orleans, including members of MS-13, the Dooney Boys, and 3 'n' G, gangs all associated with poor neighborhoods in the city. New Orleans was a city divided by gangs. Some have said the New Orleans Police Department is the largest organized gang in the city, and then there's all the rest.

Several officers involved in the gang arrests received commendations for their part in the police sweeps. There were only three females, Mary and two others. The other women were in the Louisiana National Guard, but it was known that Mary was feared more, even by some veteran police officers. As one local newspaper reported, Officer "Bloody Mary" Bayuga drew blood when she conducted an arrest. Even the gangbangers called her Bloody Mary.

Bloody Mary and the Crescent City Connection Bridge Incident

Officer Bayuga first came to the attention of the newspapers when she responded to a call about a shooting at LB Landry Avenue and De Armas Street, near the base of the Crescent City Connection Bridge. Without awaiting police backup, she exited her police cruiser and approached a vehicle sitting in the middle of the road, its headlights on and its motor running. Since it was three a.m., few vehicles passed the scene. Visibility was clear, and the night air was crisp. Looking through the opened side window, Officer Bayuga saw two men—later identified as Reed Adams, twenty-one, and Rainey Stamwood, twenty-four—both suffering from several bullet wounds. Their blood was spattered all over the inside windshield. A third man, twenty-year-old Dioplous Fathorn, was in the backseat of the vehicle. His window was also down. He allegedly fired at Bayuga. Officer Bayuga, the report read, was forced to return fire. She fired from a distance of approximately six feet from the dark blue sport utility vehicle. Both Adams and Stamwood were pronounced dead at the scene. Fathorn eventually recovered. Assisting Officer Bayuga was her old street training officer, Officer Javon M. Green, who confirmed her report. Fathorn fired twice at her as she approached the vehicle, and she returned fire in her effort to "reduce imminent danger."

Mary Testifies

A year later, Mary would testify that Javon approached the SUV, grabbed her service weapon, and fired twice at the backseat passenger. Drawing his backup weapon, which was strapped to his ankle, he fired it twice toward the river, wiped it clean with a cloth, and tossed it into the backseat with Fathorn. Green, if alive, would have said that that was exactly what Bayuga had done. Investigators learned later that the three men were engaged in cocaine distribution in Algiers. One of their protectors was Officer Javon Green, who, the investigators reported, had several officers on his payroll, none of whom were Officer Bayuga. But the truth of the matter was that Mary was expanding her own drug business, and wanted Green and his soldiers out of the way.

Green Gunned Down

While Green was driving with his girlfriend to a football game at the Superdome a week later, he was killed by a passenger in another vehicle. Miraculously, his girlfriend escaped unharmed. No one would identify the other vehicle or its occupants. No one would break the Big Easy code.

Months later, Officer Bayuga arrested of Lamar Torrance, then twenty, for Green's murder. Torrance had been arrested nine times since his eighteenth birthday. He was also arrested for murdering a woman in Central City, a neighborhood between the Superdome and the Garden District. Torrance had a history of violence: as a juvenile, he was arrested more than a dozen times. When he was sixteen, he was charged with killing a thirty-two-year-old drug pusher in a housing project. A grand jury indicted Harris as an adult on first-degree murder charges, but the court considered his mental competency, and then the prosecutor dropped the charges after a key witness's testimony was deemed inadmissible. Torrance was freed. For the next two years, he cycled in and out of jail. Equally important, Torrance was not indicted on the murder of Greene because of his mental capacity, and he was gunned down by an unknown person as he sat at an outside café a week later.

Dioplous Fathorn and Mary Bayuga's Friendship

Officer Bayuga visited Dioplous Fathorn, the third man in the backseat of the SUV, while he was in the hospital. During one of those visits, she met Dioplous's mother and his tall and slinky eighteen-year-old sister, DeShawna. Dioplous, DeShawna, and Officer Bayuga became friends after Dioplous's recovery. Mary described her first impression of DeShawna as "some bitter, black, flip-flop wearing, twisted little braids popping through an ear-to-ear braid, Cheetos eater, who had an odor that could stop a Mack truck and was an ex-baby mama of a young black guy accused of a crime." Dioplous was facing a trial on drug charges and the unlawful use of a weapon related to the Adams and Stamwood case. The drug charges were dropped for lack of evidence, but at Officer Bayuga's urging he accepted a guilty plea on the gun charge. He received a year's probation. The court allowed Officer Bayuga, at her request, to help supervise Dioplous during his probation.

Mary Bayuga lived in the 1500 block of Southlawn Boulevard, Section 8 housing. Police officers receive free rent if they reside in problem parts of the city. Although Officer Bayuga was not necessarily pleased with being a resident of Section-8 housing, she accepted the apartment and encouraged Dioplous and his sister to move in. This way she could keep better surveillance on both of them.

Fancy Apartment and Coastal Drugs

Officer Bayuga had another apartment, an elegant condominium overlooking the Mississippi River and near the intersection of Bordeaux and Tchoupitoulas Streets in the swank Uptown section of New Orleans. During the day, she rode her bicycle through Audubon Park, several blocks away, and often rode through the Loyola and Tulane campuses, which bordered the park. When she really wanted a workout, she rode up St. Charles Avenue, under the interstate, to the French Quarter, and back on Market Street through the Garden District.

DeShawna and Dioplous were her constant companions. DeShawna often slept at either of Mary's apartments, sometimes with Mary present and sometimes not. Her brother was never invited to the Uptown apartment and DeShawna never asked. No doubt she enjoyed her late-model silver Porsche Carrera which suddenly appeared at Mary's Uptown apartment. The car was registered to DeShawna's parents in Biloxi, Mississippi.

Slender and tall, DeShawna made weekly trips for Mary, her lover and boss, to the coast village of Grand Isle, Louisiana, some 110 miles from New Orleans. Sometimes she added seventy miles to the trip and jumped over to Chauvin, Mary's hometown. Usually for those weekly trips to fetch drugs from a few of the boats that belonged to the Bayuga family, DeShawna drove Mary's Chevy Blazer. That is not to say that the Bayuga family was involved in Mary's drug business, but a few of the captains were in Mary's pocket. They followed orders and accepted her money. Often a tiny girl with long hair and huge breasts, Aanical Steel, joined DeShawna on those trips. Aanical had been Officer Javon Green's girlfriend, but because of Mary's persuasive tactics and her "abhorrence of anybody with a dick," she turned Aanical to a different sexual orientation. Aanical was already a junkie, thanks to Green, so no need to convert her to a chemical dependency. When DeShawna and Aanical picked up the drugs from the captains, part of the captains' reward was a juicy moment or two with Aanical. When she was unable to provide the captains with an ejaculation, DeShawna's lips granted the favor in less than a minute.

Mary worked the graveyard shift, eleven to seven in the morning, in District 4, and had three nights off. During those nights off, the threesome often went to Tipitinas, one of New Orleans's hot spots in Uptown, within walking distance from Mary's apartment. They would sing, dance, and drink all night long, and then stumble back to Mary's apartment overlooking the Mississippi. Mary and "her entourage," she called them, were night creatures in everything they did. Mary was the only straight one. She didn't do narcotics, she only trafficked in them.

Packlike Mentality

Mary, DeShawna, and Aanical played often at the Café Lafitte in Exile in the Quarter. It's the oldest gay bar in the city and maintains a dedicated clientele, even at this writing. Many of the customers were involved in packlike relationships, where the alpha wolf—in this case, Mary—protected the other members of her pack. That would be DeShawna and Aanical. Mary had a reputation that rivaled Dirty Harry's. When an unsuspecting local or tourist didn't know what Bloody Mary was capable of, the bouncers (who usually received a hundred bucks each from Mary) at the Café and Tipitinas would advise them accordingly. "Size don't count in the Big Easy," they'd say. "That's Bloody Mary and there's no way you're going to do the tango with her and win."

Because Mary had a reputation and spread a lot of money at the clubs, few would interrupt the trio. But if any of the three ladies called out a "hey" to anyone, it was advisable to respond in a pleasing way. Many of the bouncers along Bourbon Street knew Bloody Mary too, and many nodded to the trio as they passed. The three women were a familiar sight to many of the entertainers too. The Neville Brothers often played at Tipitinas, and Aaron Neville in particular often sat with the girls between sets. Little doubt that all of the attention DeShawna and Aanical received kept them in line too. It wasn't that Mary was just a cop in the Big Easy. She was a predator, and the girls were probably aware of Mary's stone-cold ability to kill.

On one occasion, after a night of dancing and drinking, the trio were making their way through the raw morning darkness from Tipitinas to Mary's apartment. Some young men followed them from the club. Mary recognized one of them as the white boy who had attempted to dance with Aanical, but had been shot down by both Aanical and Mary. He tried a few more times, and a bouncer finally pointed a hard finger in his face. Apparently he understood what that meant and left them alone. Now he and a friend followed the women, shouting something about lesbians. They ran up to the trio and confronted Aanical.

"Come on, girl, I'll show you a good time," the taller one said. They wanted Aanical to accompany them to their hotel.

"The girl said no," Mary said, and push one of the young men as he reached for Aanical.

A police car approached, its blue strobe lights flashing. The young men froze, but Mary waved the police car off, suggesting there was no problem. Turning back to the men, she suggested they join her and her friends at her apartment.

The two men, although somewhat incoherent and drunk, were ready for anything, especially the prospects of a night with three women. While walking toward the apartment, Mary suggested they go back to their hotel and check out first. They walked to the secured parking area where Mary's SUV was parked. One man sat between DeShawna and Aanical in the backseat, while the other jumped up front with Mary. She pulled on the young man's neck with one hand and his penis with the other. "Kiss me," she said. When he came up for air, she told Aanical to go down on the other young man. "And what do you want me to do?" DeShawna asked. "Kill him," Mary probably replied.

Months later, two unidentified bodies surfaced on the Louisiana wetlands, between Golden Meadow and Leeville, along the highway that continues on to Grand Isle. Apparently, the gators and other critters in those swaps weren't interested in the young boys' flesh, but the authorities were not able to identify the remains. The hands had been cut off both corpses, and they both had been emasculated. The stab wounds at the base of their necks indicate they could have been alive but paralyzed while they were tortured. Several years later, the bodies remained unidentified, along with many other corpses found in those desolate Louisiana wetlands. The authorities never connected Mary, DeShawna, and Aanical with the murder of those young men.

Armed Robbery

There was more to the trio's action than dancing and messing with tourists in the Big Easy. They engaged in armed robbery and aggravated sexual assault. During an early morning robbery at a dance club in New Orleans's District 1, the three masked bandits wore orange jumpsuits similar to ones worn by Orleans Parish prisoners. Witnesses said that it appeared the robbers were "stoned" teenagers, except for one of them, who was very calm and knew how to punch and crack a jaw without hesitation. Another threesome in orange jumpsuits and with similar behavior robbed another club just as it was closing, and took everyone's jewelry, wallets, and cash.

This holdup started when a masked person in an orange jumpsuit pulled an intoxicated female patron onto the stage, just as the Cajun band finished their musical set. The audience and the bouncers of the club thought they were watching part of the entertainment. Because the masked person stripped off the woman's clothes, the bouncers shut and locked the doors so that outsiders, including the police, wouldn't interfere in the fun and games. The masked stranger slapped the girl a few times, and the audience went crazy with howls and laughter. "Do it again!" they screamed in excitement. The aggressor remained fully clothed, but strapped a dildo between his/her legs. The yelling, hollowing, and clapping continued as the young woman begged and cried, and then was brutally penetrated by the dildo. The blood streaming from her vagina should have told the crowd that this wasn't playacting.

When the attacked girl's boyfriend finally intervened, he was faced with a .44 caliber revolver, and he dropped to his knees on the stage. The bloody dildo was jammed down his throat, and the crowd wasn't sure now. Some stopped laughing, and looks of shock and dismay replaced grins. But no one interfered. Suddenly, two other masked patrons in orange jumpsuits emerged in the smoke-filled room, weapons in hand.

"This here's a hold-up," the aggressor on stage yelled, and pistol-whipped the young man who had tried to save his sweetheart. The audience sobered in a heartbeat and handed over their cash and jewelry.

District 1 experienced four similar armed robberies and beatings over a twelve-month period. The newspapers referred to the trio as the Club Bandits. Mary took credit for those crimes once imprisoned. Whether DeShawna or Aanical were willing participators or not will never be known, but the savage beatings were always conducted by Bloody Mary.

Mary's Partner

In District 4, Officer Mary Bayuga was eventually assigned a permanent patrol partner, Officer William J. Townsend. He was a tall, handsome young man, twenty-four years old. He graduated from Tulane University with a major in sociology, and ended a relationship with his fiancée before joining the police. He didn't seem to mind that his training officer was younger and less educated than he, but her reputation was often the topic of controversy, particularly by the newspapers and neighborhood thugs. In a way, she was like a rock star, and he considered her a friend.

On some occasions, DeShawna rode with Bayuga and Townsend in their police vehicle. Mary explained that DeShawna was an undercover DEA officer, and that he was not to discuss her presence with other officers or their superiors until all the corruption within the department was worked out. The police officials who knew of DeShawna's federal employment wouldn't inquire about her, and those who didn't, would. Her advice to Townsend was conveyed as a joke and sounded like, "I'm your partner and if you screw me, you goin' to be belly-floating in the wetlands." Little did Townsend realize that Mary wasn't joking. She made him a promise that she would eventually keep.

The more Townsend saw while partnered with Bayuga, the more he suspected that something was wrong. They stopped several drug traffickers and released them even when drugs were found in their possession. Other black men were arrested almost randomly, based on a piss test they never took, though Mary said she'd gotten the results from the district attorney's office. When testifying to federal investigators who were investigating Mary, Townsend said that a few times she told a suspect that she had "walked down to Congo Square, called upon the spirit of Marie Laveaux, threw chicken bones on the ground, and the evidence for their arrest came floating to the surface. That was her probable cause."

Armed Robbery and Murder

The afternoon that Officer Townsend offered the above statement to federal investigators and identified a picture of a young woman as DeShawna, Officer Bayuga and he were on patrol in District 4. An emergency robbery call at a convenience store was dispatched via Mary's cell phone. "Roger that," Mary said, and gave Townsend the address. She hit the lights, and told him not to use the siren. A few minutes later they arrived at the scene of the crime and rolled onto the parking apron in front the store. Through the front windows, the officers saw the clerk's hands in the air, a masked robber dressed in an orange jumpsuit in front of the clerk, and another person—probably a customer—to the right of the robber. The clerk's area was elevated a foot or so off the ground, so that he was looking down at the robber and the customer. Officer Bayuga hit the police radio button to talk to dispatch. She gave their location and said that officer need assistance at an armed robbery. "Looks like the Club Bandits," she said.

Townsend and Bayuga entered the store through the front door, and Townsend made his way slowly to the counter with his hands in the air to distract the robber. Bayuga slid down an aisle to come up on the robber from the opposite direction, the store's walk-in cooler at her back. Once she was in position, Townsend ordered the robber to put his weapon on the floor. As the robber placed the weapon on the floor, Bayuga shot Townsend twice in the chest with a .44 caliber. As the robber turned toward her, Bayuga shot the robber with her service weapon.

Officer Bayuga then shot and killed both the clerk and the customer with the .44 caliber. She holstered her service weapon and placed the .44 caliber in the robber's hand. Mary would take credit for stopping one of the Club Bandits, and would always add that "it was tragic that a fellow officer had to die." The robber was later identified as Aanical Steel. Further investigation showed that Townsend had some of Aanical

Steel's clothing and other property in his apartment. Eventually, the evidence reported that Townsend and Steel were linked in a love affair gone sour. But the clothing was probably a plant by Mary or DeShawna; and Aanical didn't realize that the planned robbery was a setup for Mary to murder both her and Townsend. The customer and the clerk were "collateral damage," Mary wrote in prison. "I don't know their names. Is that tragic?"

Witness to Murder

What Mary never considered was a new employee had entered the walk-in cooler earlier to fill the empty Coke dispenser minutes before Aanical Steel arrived. She stayed silent and motionless in the cooler as she witnessed everything that happened. It took several months for the witness to gain the courage to testify against Officer Mary Bayuga, who continued to work as a patrol officer in District 4. Now, investigators felt that they could bring Bayuga to justice. Once a grand jury indictment was obtained, authorities attempted to apprehend her and DeShawna Fathorn, who was included in the indictment. The thinking was that DeShawna would turn state's evidence and save herself by betraying Bayuga. DeShawna's statement was that "Mary is a vulgar whore hound. Always in heat and on the prowl for drugs to sell, men to punish, and pussy. She's worse than any guy I've ever known." When parish deputies arrived at the jail to escort DeShawna to court to testify, someone stood behind her and repeatedly stabbed her in the back of the neck, severing her spinal cord. She died a week later, although the court allowed her statements to be read at Bayuga's trial.

As the witness from the walk-in cooler was transported to court in an unmarked police vehicle, another vehicle approached it in an intersection, and several shots were fired. The vehicle fled the scene. But the witness was unharmed and went to court, despite the failed attempt on her life. She identified Mary Bayuga as the shooter at the convenience store, who shot and killed Officer Townsend, the clerk, a customer, and the robber identified as Aanical Steel.

Eventually, Mary Bayuga was convicted of capital murder for the killing of her partner. But as the legal appeals continue twelve years after her conviction, it is more likely that Mary will be released rather than be executed. The state of Louisiana cannot find any other corpses to prosecute Mary Bayuga. Their remains may be in the wetlands. Hurricane Katrina helped float many bodies, but there were so many corpses, who knows how many will be identified.

The only warmth Mary ever experienced was the heat from her weapons. But somewhere during her prison experience, somewhere in time, Mary thought about her feelings and envisioned herself as a college student working as a part-time model for a clothing retailer in a cold northern city. Her thoughts as an almost normal young woman are captured in "Mary: If She Only Had a Heart" in chapter 18.

CHAPTER 11
Mickey the Bishop's Daughter

Introduction

This chapter describes the childhood of Mickey Stone and Ella, her little sister. Both were homeschooled, until the younger sister got away from Mickey's dominating, controlling, and abusive behavior. Mickey traveled and played in Europe's fashionable casinos and dance clubs to fulfill her amazing but bizarre objectives. Returning to America, Mickey's lavish wedding to her childhood sweetheart Tom Aiken was held in an international Boston hotel of considerable fame whose bricks are owned by her family (and leased to the hotel enterprise). Her father was the Episcopal bishop of a New England archdiocese. At the invitation of prominent people, Mickey joined the police department and the US Marine Corp Reserves. As a returning warrior from Afghanistan, she was promoted in the police department and continued to perform as an exemplary public servant. All the while she engaged in criminally violent behavior, including stalking, sexual assault, and murder. Mickey was eventually convicted of second degree murder and served twenty-four months of a ten-year sentence. Following are the accounts of her *vengeance kills*. Chapter 18 contains a story entitled "Free Again," whereby Mickey tries to represent a compassionate woman, despite her cold-blooded, predatory lifestyle. Welcome to Mickey's world.

Mickey's Parents

Michele "Mickey" Stone was born on Christmas Day. Ella, her sister, was born four years later. After reading this chapter, you'll probably come to the conclusion that Mickey fits the mode of her birth sign, Capricorn. She's confident, strong-willed, and calm, yet also ambitious, disciplined, and patient. She's humorous in a way, and reserved. But similar to most Capricorns, she is persistent, doing what it takes to accomplish a mission. And Capricorns can be vindictive creatures of the night.

The Stone girls, Mickey and Ella, were products of a wealthy Boston family that enjoyed winters in Palm Beach and Belize. They spent their summers at the Berkshires. The Stone family owns land and buildings, which includes two of the 229 skyscrapers in downtown Boston. One was constructed in 1975 and the other was built ten years later. The latter, at Copley Place, is leased by an international hotel chain. At the time of this writing, Mickey Stone is one of three Stone family members who holds a majority of the voting rights of the corporation that owns those properties, as well as fashionable apartment buildings in Manhattan, Boston, and DC, and other properties around the world, including Belize.

Mickey's parents provided their children with an exemplary environment, along with every amenity of a wealthy and powerful family. But along with those upscale amenities, Mickey and Ella rarely were comforted by their parents, because all of their needs were provided by servants. It can be said that a lack of parental supervision can enhance or enable a criminally violent aptitude, but I'm no shrink. Perhaps, Mickey's miswired brain is Mother Nature's way of evening things up among the rich and famous similar to the cursed Kennedy, Getty and Onassis families. Payback is hell, and that's one way to understand Mickey's trigger toward criminally violent behavior. Mickey Stone believes in payback—an eye for an eye, and a corpse for a corpse. Equally important, Mickey believes that it is her responsibly, as destined by some almighty, that she administer justice to us. If she could justify murder in her head, she murdered, regardless if it were a friendly dog, a cat, or a chubby little man like, well, me.

Early Stone Life

Mickey's childhood experiences were typical of many American heiresses. Her affiliations were linked to the country clubs, with few real her friendships other than boys she met at the club such as Tom Aiken. Other than servants and teachers, she never knew anyone who could be described as middle class, until she started working in her early twenties as a cop. Her debutante status matches many of the other heiresses across the country, and many of the wired-wrong individuals in this book.

Homeschooled

Mickey was homeschooled through high school by live-in help who provided nanny services, cooking, and education to both Mickey and Ella. Although Mickey received a quality education, she either didn't care about academics or had few incentives to excel in an academic environment. She did excel in her own world of crime, corruption, and destruction.

Mickey Stone has the round, white face of a naive child, and blond hair that runs in several directions at once. Some of those hairs touch her very freckled skin accented by the smooth pearl earrings she always wore, even as a child. She said her pearl earrings glowed, and that made her denim-blue eyes sparkle. But once Mickey was imprisoned, her eyes rarely shinned because she couldn't wear her pearls. She confirmed that her best weight was at least twenty pounds on the moon—that is, 120 pounds on earth—when she was pregnant. Her wit is usually consistent with the characteristics of the *Legally Blond Syndrome* but her affects upon others had less to do with the humorous accomplishments of Reese Witherspoon and more to do with the severity of an unexpected tornado.

Any interference into the daily routine of her life by family pets, teachers, and servants, or anything that annoyed her was shot down—sometimes literally. She said that anything competing with her "life flow was snuffed. Like I never listened to music when I drove or worked out, because those sounds interrupted my thoughts and my silence. I love my privacy. But I have to be nice to at least six people, because I need pallbearers. F*** the rest."

On the other hand, Ella Stone was highly competitive and motivated, and prettier than Mickey. She had the manner and appearance of a wealthy and intelligent child, and was an active, friendly girl. Being younger, Ella was doted over by visitors, family, and other homeschooled children and their teachers. Families who had their children homeschooled united for garden parties, birthday parties, and the holidays. Specialist teachers, such as those trained in calculus, psychology, and history, were often shared among the families, and almost became family members.

Martial Arts

Mickey began martial arts lessons when she was seven and Ella went to dance. Eventually, Mickey's Japanese trainer narrowed down her training to Okinawan karate. She had learned all the anatomy and physiology linked to pressure points, had a working knowledge of weapons, and owned her set of nunchucks. By age eleven, Mickey was a Nidan (brown belt with two stripes). Mickey competed in many competitive events throughout New England. She did well for herself and had learned to bow gracefully. Of course, her karate ability was one of her assets, making her invincible to unsuspecting targets. Often individuals underestimated her tactical skills based on her stringy blond hair and endless freckles only to discover that they were painfully misled by her physical characteristics.

Mickey now had help with her decisions from her martial arts training to fulfill her obsessions with vodka and her compulsive gambling adventures, or what Mickey referred to as Mickey's World. Mickey is self-absorbed to this day, and continues to display innocuous behavior influenced by the mental roller coaster she rides. Similar to Annie and Underground Lilith, Mickey is toxic when sober, although her motivation to harm individuals stems from revenge as opposed to a seeker of pleasure. "I'm sort of a god, you know," she said to me in-group one afternoon. "I champion the weak and smash the wicked." Acknowledging her experiences, there was little I could say other than, "Yes, ma'am, I know."

Dana Hall

The sisters were inseparable until Ella lobbied her parents to enroll her at Dana Hall School in Wellesley, Massachusetts, for her last four years of school. She didn't want to stay at home and continue homeschooling. Dana Hall is a private and expensive boarding school for girls. Many of Ella's homeschooled and country-club friends had also enrolled. Ella's incentive to leave home had less to do with academics and more to do with getting away from Mickey's incessant domination, and the humiliation she suffered as a result of that domination. For instance, Mickey wrote that her sister was obnoxious and uncontrollable, so it was up to Mickey to "keep Ella grounded. I hate violence but occasionally I would squeeze her little neck tight and she'd calm down."

When the girls were at the family's Berkshire home, Ella received the news that she had been accepted at Dana Hall. Mickey went crazy. "I was betrayed by my little sis and lifelong friend. I wasn't sure what I was going to do from that point on because I had graduated (from high school). I was thinking about studying art in Paris or music in Vienna. I was so lost without my baby sister. She never noticed my sorrow till it was too late." Ella's aspirations, first for Dana Hall and then Wellesley College or Vassar, aggravated Mickey so much that her use of alcohol and gambling increased and in a sense Mickey's World thrived.

Domination and Control

While at Dana Hall, Ella took her roommate, Jennifer McAllen, into her confidence and explained how Mickey controlled her life. Ella said that the turning point was a month or so after arriving at Dana Hall. She never really understood how much control Mickey held over her. Ella loved Mickey—or Miss M, as she called her—but she resented her control. One issue that annoyed Ella was connected to sex. Ella wanted to have fun with boys. Instead, Miss M explored her private parts, which made Ella feel strange and weird. Usually, Miss M would do those strange things after she drank a lot of vodka and after Miss M had sort-of a sexual encounter with Tom Aiken or any other boys she gathered from the country club. As a young child, Ella never really understood what Mickey was doing or why. Often Mickey would not touch her for weeks, and Ella shadowed Mickey's every move, right into the bathroom if necessary. The only way to win Miss M's approval was "to pull her hands on me, down there. Miss M would smile, and I pretended to feel better." When Ella was twelve years old, she wanted to know more about boys. But every time a boy got close, like at the country club, "Miss M popped him one. Nobody messed with Baby, Miss M would say. Unfortunately, Miss M saw *Dirty Dancing* and treated me like I was Baby and she was Johnny."

Another memory from her youth was when Ella danced with one of Mickey's so-called enemies at a country-club event. Ella tried her best to stand up to her sister, because Mickey threatened the boy with an "evil eye" and he ran. He was not the first boy Mickey had chased off, and most of the kids that the girls knew understood that Mickey offered few warning signals and no threats. She would just attack. Behind those freckles lay an amazing brawler, like a viper who smiled as she bit her clueless targets. The boy Ella danced saw Mickey's fangs and didn't wait for her coil.

Looking for comfort and understanding from Jennifer, Ella detailed Mickey's World to her. Since she was fourteen, Mickey drank anything liquid that contained any quantity of alcohol, including cough medicine, allergy remedies, and then she'd down Dramamine. She was no stranger to hard liquor either, like vodka and whiskey. As for gambling, she used cash from begging, borrowing, or stealing from her parents, servants, and teachers. The way Ella described Mickey's gambling behavior is consistent with the compulsive gambler as outlined in the DSM-IV-TR.

In Jennifer, Ella had found a friend who wasn't out to dominate her. The new relationship was a godsend, because for once she didn't have to win a person's approval for a smile. But this new freedom also took its toll on Ella. Four times she attempted to drown herself in the dorm's bathtub. Each time she was saved by Jennifer. Ella had trouble explaining her actions, saying only, "I'm so confused by Miss M's rejection of me. I'm really a piece of dirt." When Ella's self-respect was at an all-time low, Mickey's "flipping out" at her on her cell phone was too much for the girl.

You see, Ella had come to the desperate conclusion that there was no way she could stop her sister's hold on her. She tried to set limits on Mickey's participation at Dana Hall by removing Mickey's name from the registrar's list of approved persons who could talk to her teachers and learn about her class progress. But Mickey had built a strong rapport with several educators and students, and she communicated daily with them. Mickey knew everything that happened in and out of class. Ella tried to make a case with her parents to limit Mickey's discussions, but Ella's parents were hardly moved by her request. They were never around, nor did they understand the full scope of Mickey's control over her.

The only two methods that seemed to make Ella feel comfortable about herself was talking to Jennifer and maintaining a detailed diary. That diary became available to me after a sequence of tragedies befell both Ella and Jennifer. Actually, an e-mail with an attachment of eighty-five single-spaced pages was inadvertently addressed to me.

Nonetheless, Ella faced another annoying and rough road when Mickey went to Europe. She called Ella several times a day. Ella explained how she got through her day feeling better about herself for her decisions to talk to Jennifer and write a diary, but her sister would have none of it. She would be in Paris, Vienna, Palma De Mallorca, screaming on the phone at Ella, until Ella would break down in tears. "I don't know why I kept answering the phone, but yeah, I did. I'm so like lame," Ella wrote. She loved Miss M and appreciated everything she had done for her, but Ella needed to make her own decisions. She wanted to have a good relationship with her sister, but conversations with her escalated to complete frustration. It was almost better to accept Mickey's behavior than battle her, because in the end what Ella wanted was approval and love. Mickey had educated Ella in the fine art of dependence, and Ella had learned her lessons well. She also felt that eventually Jennifer would become tired of her incessant ravings about Miss M and leave her. Ella had indeed been well-schooled by Mickey, who had worked hard on Ella's insecurities and her lack of self-confidence. She even played on Ella's fear that she would lose Jennifer as a friend. She would tell Ella that when she confided in Jennifer, Jennifer would turn around and make fun of Ella with Cindy, Jennifer's childhood friend and, Mickey would emphasize, her *real* girlfriend.

Mickey's European Adventure

While Ella moved into her dorm at Dana Hall, Mickey jetted to Paris a few weeks before her nineteenth birthday. She didn't study art. Mickey didn't study anything other than the locations of unique dance clubs, retail shops, and casinos that catered to young rich girls like her. Of course, her marathon phone calls to her sister took precedence over everything else. Mickey had little contact with the few friends she had, and none of her family members wanted to talk to her.

In Paris, Mickey and her bodyguards occupied the presidential suite at the posh Meurice Hotel, with its Louis XVI decor. Her father's bodyguards accompanied Mickey everywhere she ventured. And venture she did: the Champs-Elysees, the Faubourg Saint-Honoré shopping area, and many other attractions, including the Louvre. Yet her escorts made her uneasy, especially when she visited dance clubs. Mickey wrote in her prison journal, "Had Father hired them to protect me or to protect the Parisians?"

Emma Tower, one of Mickey's bodyguards, is a short-haired woman and an obvious bodybuilder, who had served four years as a commissioned officer in the US Marine Corps after graduating from United State Naval Academy at Annapolis, Maryland. She was recruited by Blackwater (which has since changed its name to Xe Services). The international security company subcontracts security to celebrities, powerful families, and the American government. As Mickey visited her favorite places, Emma and her dark-suited partner shadowed her every move. Knowing that Mickey loved her privacy, I can imagine her escorts annoyed her big time.

Favorite Places in Paris

One of Mickey's favorite dance clubs was the Club Batofar, which sits on a red lighthouse boat moored on the Seine River. When she danced, with or without a partner, she practiced her karate moves. Although she couldn't remember the name of another favorite drinking and dancing club, it was on rue du Faubourg St-Antoine, she wrote. What she adored most was Latin music because it kept her body busy with motion. Some of her moves on the dance floor attracted onlookers, and when guys would jump in with her, she pushed them away. Good-looking ladies received a different response. She sometimes wore dresses that revealed her long legs. Other times she wore dark pants outfits with a large silver belt and soft comfortable boots. Her little sweet kisses and provocative touches to the breasts of her partners made up for the lack of visible skin. Paris Hilton could learn something from Mickey Stone about dirty dancing.

After the clubs and an early snack, it was a rush to her favorite casino, Barrière d'Enghien-les-Bains, on the outskirts of Paris. There are about forty games tables and 280 slot machines at this fancy casino, and Mickey tried them all. Her skill at baccarat, blackjack, and roulette rewarded her handsomely, but kept her escorts busy.

Mickey's favorite retailer was the Galeries Lafayette in the heart of Paris's Opera district, a retailer that claims to carry 80,000 different labels of merchandise on its six floors. Most often, after Mickey was buzzed after a day or two of drinking, dancing, and gambling, she cruised the Galeries Lafayette, among other stores. She spent money according to her casino winnings, and she would spend all of it, whether she had won five bucks or five thousand bucks. When she lost, particularly at blackjack, her favorite game, her penance was a total withdrawal from shopping. Mickey's World now included shopping.

Mickey never brought a man to her hotel. However, when she woke up one midday, which was her usual practice, Mickey thought she was alone. As she prepared to satisfy herself, she realized Emma Tower was in the bedroom. Mickey's knees were already up, lotion in her left hand, Magic Wand vibrator in her right hand, when she saw Emma sitting in a chair. She watched as Mickey pleasured herself, her hands at her sides, and a lack of an expression on her face. Both Emma and Mickey knew the rules, even if the rules were never articulated.

Before Mickey grabbed on to her "oh my gods," Emma almost smiled but never said a word, then or ever, about the incident other than to me. Mickey was neither intrigued nor upset that Emma watched. Ella her little sister had watched many times but that was okay because Ella was family. Mickey didn't care that Emma wasn't family. As she tumbled through the air, powered by her intense accomplishment, she stretched her lips just a little and stole a glance at Emma. Mickey sniffed as though she could smell Emma and fell back asleep in the comfort of her bed. Little doubt that Emma Tower was blown off the edge by her observations, but she was a professional who dealt hard with edges.

Another Birthday

Another year older and centuries wiser, Mickey left Paris and checked into the Bauer Il Palazzo in Venice, overlooking the Grand Canal. The phone calls to Ella continued, and Mickey's World had enormously escalated. Satisfying herself while Emma Tower protected her from intruders became routine.

Mickey was never sober and always minutes away from a blackjack table. Finding a casino with a dance floor was her usual objective, and if it was near a wonderful retail establishment, she was in heaven. But eventually Mickey grew discontented with Venice, especially its nightlife. "That wasn't me," she wrote. "I hate nightclubs. I just like to drink and dance. … The obnoxious paparazzi made me famous after a kidnapping attempt, foiled by my sweet Emma, who, of course, was mesmerized by every ounce of my freckled flesh. You know, I should have given her a tumble, but then I'd have to kill her," she said with a laugh during a prison group session, one bright afternoon. The other prisoners laughed, too, and one said, "Don't tell me, girl, that you didn't wanna taste that delicious pussy of that jarhead."

After the abduction attempt, although down deep Mickey loved it because it gave her something different to do, she telephoned Tom Aiken and said, "Please come to Venice and save me." He arrived a few weeks later and helped Mickey pack all of her new clothes and accessories, as Emma and her partner watched from a distance. *Anything you want, baby,* Emma thought. *Nobody puts Baby in a corner,* she recited silently, the words she had heard Mickey express several times to Ella. Emma Tower worried that Mickey suspected Emma had been involved in the abduction attempt, and Emma Tower would take the rest of her life to prove her loyalty to the woman she loved.

Tom Aiken and Mickey Stone in Palma de Mallorca

The happy couple spent several amazing months at a rented villa on a Balearic Island near the city of Palma de Mallorca. Emma Tower and her partner were there doing their job. From the villa's huge bay windows, Tom and Mickey had a breathtaking view of a cathedral, a gorgeous blue Mediterranean Sea, and a magical sunrise that would light up their thoughts for years to come. They were on the southwest tip of the island and could sometimes see Tarragona, Spain, across the sea. Tom had few experiences compared to Mickey's World, and according to Emma Tower, Tom didn't know what he was getting into. He wanted to run, but if he did, Mickey or Emma would track him down. He wanted to hide, but Mickey would find his hiding place and tear him apart, or Emma Tower would. Tom learned what Ella had learned—dependence.

The Wedding

When Tom and Mickey returned to the United States, the happy couple's wedding was in large bold print in every society publication across the nation. The print was larger when Tommy Jr. arrived a few months after the fabulous million-dollar wedding, which had included Mickey's favorite performer, Madonna, and a new artist on the horizon at that time, Celine Dion. Six hundred and thirty-eight guests attended the wedding. Some came from as far as the UK and the Continent. A few city mayors, two state governors, and a representative from the Vatican attended the event. Ella was the maid of honor, and Tom's sister was in the wedding party. Ella's roommate, Jennifer McAllen, was also in the wedding party. Jennifer made the mistake of attempting to befriend Mickey when the two of them were suddenly alone during the wedding rehearsal. While Emma Tower stood guard, Jennifer and Mickey drank. When Jennifer was intoxicated, she spilled her guts to the pregnant bride-to-be. Later, Emma reported, "Mickey exploded thinking about the new information she had learned from Jennifer. All I could do was look into her eyes and hold her down as she twisted and turned under me till she fell asleep."

Routine

Eventually the Aikens settled into a charmed lifestyle. Mickey played mommy to both Tommy Jr. and Tommy while he finished college. He got a degree in education and became a public school teacher. The Aikens moved into Mickey's parents' estate, because her father, the

Bishop, had left Alisha, Mickey's mother for his boyfriend. Mickey's son took center stage in Alisha Stone's life, at least for a while, and Emma had a new assignment with the Bishop and his lover, who was a professor at Harvard.

When Tom started his first teaching job at a suburban high school, Mickey was unsure what to do with herself. She hired a nanny and explored a career, the bars, and offshore casinos. She hadn't practiced karate since before Europe, and felt a void. She tried to find her old instructor without success. She was successful in finding a new instructor, recommended by Emma. The instructor was a city police officer who knew Mickey from competitive karate events. Mickey rented an entire gymnasium near her home for three hours during the day. It took several weeks for her to feel competent about her skills, and she was reassured of her progress by her talented trainer. The trainer told Emma a few weeks later that Mickey had made quick strides, and he had complimented her, patting her on the back and saying, "Good girl."

"I felt at risk," he told Emma, "and never would I commit that error again."

"I know," was Emma's response.

High-Tea Society

Mickey had high tea with her mother and several society women, including the wife of commissioner of police. "Why don't you become a police person, sweetie?" the commissioner's wife said, and handed over her husband's business card. Mickey discussed the possibilities of a police job with Tom, after she spoke to her karate instructor and Emma, of course. All thought Mickey should try it out. "It might be fun," Emma told her. Some discussions and inquiries were made, her application was processed, references of the highest order were hand delivered, and Michele Stone (she never took Aiken's last name) entered the police academy. She was sworn in as a municipal police officer eight months later. She was twenty-two years of age.

New Home

The Aiken-Stone family moved into a new home after Mickey's father passed on. Apparently the move from his country estate took its toll on the Bishop, and he died soon after. Tom taught school and Mickey patrolled the streets of the city. Alisha Stone closed her estate and moved in with her daughter and Tom to tend to her grandson, pushing Emma and her partner from a job. Mickey assured Tom that her mother would live with them for only a short time, and that she would return home after she "recovered from the death of my father and his foolish lifestyle."

The Aiken-Stone home was a modest yet new home in a high-end, decent neighborhood in the city, because the police department insisted that all police officers live within city limits. Mickey had another child—and then she signed up with the Marines.

US Marine Corp Reserves

After she'd served with the police for several months, Mickey's training officer convinced her to enlist in the US Marine Corps Reserves. It could help a law enforcement officer's promotion, he told her, despite a lack of college credentials. It would add to her presence as a hard-ass cop, and it would fortify her barroom fight experience. Her mother could easily care for the Aiken children, Tom suggested. Mickey's karate instructor, who had become her friend, said it "would be a perfect opportunity to enhance your imagine as an police officer. With your karate skills, the military should be a piece of cake." Emma Tower added, "I will miss you, my darling, but it is the best thing to do for your career. Stay safe."

Mickey, along with a few other police officers from her department, enlisted in the US Marine Corps Reserves. Her high scores on the General Technical, Special and Officer Programs allowed Mickey to complete the Law Enforcement Military Police Course at the United States Army Military Police School. She also successfully completed the Alternate Training Instructional Program of Marine Force Reserves, and received a favorable endorsement by an MP Inspector-Instructor.

While at boot camp on Parris Island, she fell hard for the Marine chant, "Highly motivated, truly dedicated, rompin', stompin', bloodthirsty, kill-crazy United States Marine Corps recruits." On the other hand, Mickey was not a thunderous killer, but a killer who preferred stealth strategies. No booyah for her or Sunday parades, simply "get 'er done." Even in mock combat zones, because of her size, agility, fearlessness, and training, she slipped in and out of insurgent dwellings, leaving firestorms behind her and permitting ground troops a better opportunity to secure the area.

Deployment

Neither Mickey Stone, the young officers who had enlisted with her, nor the police administration, anticipated their immediate deployment to Afghanistan, where Stone served valiantly for six months. Records support her claim that through her efforts, four of her colleagues were saved from serious injuries. Because of Mickey's meritorious achievement, she was awarded a bronze star.

Mickey's War Experiences

Years later when Mickey Stone was imprisoned, she talked about her experiences in Afghanistan, and revealed that she and her unit were plagued with sexual assault cases. American military men preyed upon military females, both Americans and NATO allies. The victims were from all military ranks, and the indigenous population was targeted too. One protective measure preached by Mickey was to "sleep with a blade in your hand," and while on duty "lock and load, screw orders shoot bastards." Much to Mickey's surprise, there were three sexual assault attempts made against her while in full combat uniform. She defended herself, fatally shooting one of her attackers and killing another in hand-to-hand combat. No charges were brought against Mickey; the killings were self-defense.

Another matter Mickey talked about, first in bits and pieces, and later, loud and clear, was her thoughts and experiences of the war. Her unit was deployed to the Korengal Outpost, known simply as KOP, which was high in the mountains in Afghanistan. Most of the fighting was some distance away, so she never ever got to see or had to deal with the effects of all that firepower. Often members from her unit would patrol the riverbed below and the flanks of the Abas Ghar ridge. The Marines at KOP were great at dropping mortars on the enemy, and sometimes Observation Post 3 participated in a brief campaign if the patrol units were pinned down. One time Mickey was pinned down by insurgent gunfire, and some in her unit thought they'd be killed. Mickey never thought about death. What she thought about was that if she was killed, it would end that hard sensation in her belly that she wanted more, way more than to be a victim. She became paranoid, not only because of her job, but because she was a woman in a place where there was no hot water, no cold food, insects everywhere, and the smell of decomposing meat driving into her nostrils with each breath. Death, she would explain to Emma in the years ahead when they would get drunk together and fool around, would bring peace to Mickey Stone. She knew then that death was a good thing for her, she would tell Emma.

In her prison journal, Mickey wrote, "Killing the enemy wasn't killing the bad guy, but not getting killed by the person a Marine just killed. The applause in your gut comes from knowing that that someone else will never kill again. Fighting another human being is easy. Combat is the game that the US had asked Marines to play and we were very good it."

Mickey Stone referred to the game of killing in combat as "democide" because her unit, similar to all combat units in the Mideast, were ordered to publicly and intentionally kill domestics. She used an analogy: "If I imprisoned several youngsters in my factory, forced them to do exhausting work throughout the day and night, forget food, clothing, and care, but watched them gradually die a little each day without helping any of them, then their inevitable death is not only my fault, but my practical intention. It's murder. Genocide comes in many forms, but this form is public murder and that's what's going on in the Mideast."

There were rules of engagement. "Just don't get caught, sort of like being a cop," Mickey said. "Do the right thing and eliminate the opponent. Then say the right thing to make your kill fit the rules or redefine your story." One of Mickey's positions on this matter was that warriors, from the ancient world to the modern world, were always given the same task—kill and justify your kill. While some members of Mickey's units were worried about ever being satisfied with *normal* again, Mickey was eager to experiment with her new skills on American streets. "I don't want to be bored," she would tell Emma months later. "Be careful what you wish for, my sweet," was Emma's answer.

A Warrior Returns from Afghanistan

Mickey returned home to her family and job. The police department bestowed prestigious honors on her, including a promotion to sergeant after an invitation to take the sergeant's civil service examination. She was twenty-five years old, with two children, a dedicated husband—or so she thought—a new home, and held the rank of sergeant in a big city police department. She was also a socialite who made the gossip pages every so often. A few caricatures of Mickey were printed in the local papers, with symbols of both the police and US Marine Corps on a frail-looking woman with crazy blond hair and pearl earrings. But now the bond that held Emma and Mickey together was greater, and they frequently high-fived each other and repeated the US Marine Corps motto, Semper fi.

A month or so after Mickey's return, she noticed that Tom's office hours had changed at school, and he arrived home later and later. Mickey decided to investigate her husband's activities, especially since their sexual relationship changed. "Hell, it didn't change, it stopped," she wrote. "That was really okay by me. I hate sex and he was bored with me hating it. I tried." But Tom was no longer the loving young man she knew. Much to her surprise, she learned that Tom was at school, but something bothered her about his schedule. She hired a private detective. In short order, he showed her photographs of her husband with another woman, a high school teacher named Molly Estes. Mickey recognized Molly as Tom's sister's best friend. Tom had always said that he was nice to her because of his little sister. "Nice to her, my sweet ass!" Mickey said. She went home, and she and Tom got into a serious fight. Tom knew better than to physically confront her, and he begged Mickey to forgive him. During the verbal battle, Alisha intruded, the children cried, and the police department called asking Mickey for information about a stop she had made earlier that day.

After the fight, Tom made a point of arriving home before Mickey, yet the two of them rarely talked to each other. Almost a year later,

Mickey arrived home much earlier than usual and found her husband and her mother having sex in her bed. She threw both of them from her home. They moved in together at the Stone estate. Mickey and Tom divorced, and a few months later, Tom and Alisha married.

Mickey married another police officer, Chris Wyatt. They had a daughter—Brittney Channel Wyatt—but Mickey threw Chris out before Brittney's birth. He was sexually involved with another woman, Janelle Hale, who worked in police dispatch.

About ten years later, Officer Mickey Stone (she never took Chris's last name) responded to a domestic violence call. She was the first responder, and upon arriving at the residence, it was clear that her former husband, Tom Aiken, had murdered his spouse, Mickey's mother, who had been confined to a wheelchair. Mickey went into a rage and, after restraining Tom, beat him to death, a crime that would eventually bring her to prison.

A Patrol Officer's Job

As a patrol officer for fifteen years, Mickey's responsibilities included 911 domestic violence calls, traffic accident investigations, and juvenile detail, such as shoplifters. She also represented the department in public safety initiatives at three area high schools. Mickey probably investigated hundreds of highway fatalities in her career, conducted domestic violence arrests, and negotiated with the parents of kids who stole cosmetics and candy bars from Walgreens and Wal-Mart. Often in her later years, Mickey rode alone and rarely requested police backup. She was often the first responder to many incidents and traffic fatalities, which included her first response to the Aikins' domestic violence call ... and the highway fatality that took the life of Barry Goldberg and his mother.

Murder Conviction and Prison

When Michele Stone arrived at prison, she was a sort of pretty thirty-seven year old, had worked as a police officer for a large city in New England for fifteen years, and had three children. After her murder conviction, she was dishonorably discharged from the US military. Needless to say, she was bitter about that. During the criminal law process, she accepted a plea bargain rather than chance a trial for second degree murder. Her sentence was ten years, and she was transferred to another state jurisdiction to serve her time. She was a "renter" in a another state's correctional system similar to Janelle, Margo, and Wilma. Mickey Stone would serve only twenty-four months of her sentence.

When Mickey arrived at prison she was an alcoholic. She hadn't used illegal substances, except for trying marijuana when she was in the military. Also, Mickey doesn't have tear glands, and uses eye drops constantly, which were prescribed by prison health services.

She was placed on suicide watch twice after arriving at prison. She was frequently restricted and housed in segregation or an isolation unit for her behavior. Her health was excellent, and she generally slept eight hours or more a day. Her general behavior is consistent with descriptions of an aggressive authoritarian who was slow with her responses to others, and she was categorized as lethal. That meant she would not hesitate to take a human life or inflict painful torture. Her primary motivator toward crime can best be described as that of a revenger. That is, she has a vindictive personality and a long memory. Mickey remembered people who had acted unjustly toward her, and she would think about it for days, months, even years. As she prepared herself for her revenge, she would evaluate the person and explore the opportunities, stalk the person, and then, in the name of justice, either destroy something the alleged offender owned, torture him or her, then murder him or her.

Mickey's Aliases and Tattoos

Michele's friends call her Mickey, although some refer to her as Maryl and others call her Mary. Mickey often used the aliases of Elizabeth Stone, Maryl Sweeney, and Mary McNally. She had driver's licenses, social security cards, and other documents with those names, complete with different addresses. Mickey has two tattoos: one on her upper back of an eagle globe and anchor, typically worn by many US Marines, with the words Semper Fi at the top of the globe, and the words US Marines was printed under the globe. Reports note she also has a tattoo on her lower back, at the top of her buttock, which reads I Own You Bitch.

Crimes Known, Never Apprehended

Mickey Stone committed crimes that never came to the *official* attention of the police, and include aggravated assault, conspiracy to commit murder, failure to perform as a police officer, grand theft auto, identity theft, murder, reckless endangerment, sexual assault of a minor, sexual assault, and stalking. I emphasize official because many of her crimes were known unofficially by other law enforcement personnel, and it is more likely that some of her crimes were "respected" as opposed to being despised by other officers. One police investigator who knew Mickey Stone said, "At least she has the guts to do the right thing, like with Tom Aiken. That prick would have gotten off. That's more than I can say about a lot of cops around the country." The concern is that few really knew the extent of Mickey's crimes, including her several revenge killings. Before moving on, it is safe to say that Mickey killed more individuals than those noted here, but these are the cases she referred to in her prison journal and during conversations. Additionally, similar to all the chapters in *Wicked Women*, research through newspapers, websites, and interviews produced some of the accounts presented throughout this chapter.

Vengeance is Mine

Mickey Stone believed in a corpse for a corpse, believed that she was ordained from above as the planet's primary provider of justice and punishment. The movie *Kill Bill: Volume 2* (2004), which features Umea Thurman, exemplified the old saying, Revenge is a dish best served cold. Mickey Stone even physically resembles Thurman. Along with noting that resemblance, several correctional officers reported that there was a smell about Mickey that was always present. It was hard to describe, except it smelled like a kitten. A calico kitten at that. Some people just have a scent about them, and Mickey Stone had her smell that would never go away—the smell of murder. Hard to tell if she had that smell growing up, since there are very few persons still around to say. Maybe I should purchase a lot of kitty litter in case Mickey Stone gets pissed off with me.

Vengeance Kill 1: Ella Stone

Mickey wrote that she "was glad Ella was gone. She's a bitch who should have vanished when I was in Europe. She was a little slut and she doesn't have a vagina and she couldn't fly. But it was her roommate, Jennifer McAllen, who killed the little whore. McAllen had a dog odor to her that drove me crazy."

Although there is reason to believe that Ella was not Mickey's first vengeance kill, what is relevant is that Ella was her first victim whom she tormented for years. Finally, when she came to believe that Ella had betrayed and disrespected her she while was in Dana Hall, Mickey wrote that "I don't think she shared my mother's womb with me. She's evil." Mickey felt that Ella was the product of a relationship her father had had with a member of his church. "Ella deserved to die," Mickey stated. Ella disappeared during her third year at Dana Hall. Despite all of Jennifer's insistence, Mickey was never considered a person-of-interest by the police. Also, Tom Aiken provided a solid alibi for her.

What was known about Ella's disappearance was that she received a call on her cell and took a taxi to the railroad station in town. That was the last time Ella Stone was seen. The taxi driver dropped her off and didn't look back to see if she entered the railway station or not. It was a typically busy day at 5 p.m., with commuters going in every direction. It was suspected that Ella entered a vehicle instead of the station, and her body was never found.

"Did I abduct her? Hell no. Did I have reason to do it, hell yeah," said Mickey. "But I had no justification to kill her, she was my little sis."

I took that to mean that Mickey Stone had killed her little sister after she justified the murder to herself. Ella had betrayed her by enrolling at Dana Hall, and she disrespected her to another female—Jennifer McAllen. During the police investigation, Jennifer had plenty to say about Mickey. Ella had told her everything, she said, about Mickey's World. However, none of Mickey's World could be substantiated, nor was there evidence available supporting Jennifer's claims that Ella's sister was a drunk and a gambler. European sources and Emma Tower swore that when Mickey Stone was in Europe, she shopped, prayed at famous cathedrals, and did a lot of soul-searching prior to her marriage to Tom Aiken. She was hardly a sinner, but more like a saint.

Vengeance Kill 2: Jennifer McAllen

"Come here, you little bitch," Mickey commanded, a firm palm at the back of her Jennifer's neck pulling her forward while two fingertips smoothed her G-spot. "How sweet is this?" asked Mickey. "I could have snuffed out her little dyke existence, watched her eyes drown in pain, and given her the most amazing ride to the stars, all at the same time. Stupid little butch-boy. She was probably going down on my little sister, and my intention was to scare her out of her panties. The last time I saw Jennifer McAllen was at the Boston hotel two days before my wedding."

Six months after Ella disappeared, Jennifer was supposed to meet friends at a ski lodge, but never showed. Her remains were found inside a stolen automobile in an ocean waterway near Portsmouth, New Hampshire. The state medical examiner said the victim's throat had been slit by someone who showed no mercy, semen from an unidentified male was discovered in her fallopian types, genital damage suggested that the victim was sexually assaulted, and she was infected with HIV. Her remains tested positive for cocaine. She was wearing Ella Stone's undergarments, which were identified by Ella's name embroidered on the clothing. In death, Jennifer was made to look like a junkie who had lied about Mickey Stone. She was sexually obsessed with Ella Stone and probably killed her in a jealous rage, the new thinking went.

It is suspected that Emma Tower helped Mickey abduct, transport, and kill Jennifer McAllen. It would have taken more than one person to accomplish this task, especially after the vehicle was sent into the water. Another car and driver would be needed for the getaway. However, Mickey rarely worked with a partner. It is possible that both Emma and Mickey sexually assaulted Jennifer at the Boston hotel, before Mickey's wedding. We know that Emma was in the hotel shadowing Mickey, she and Mickey were never sexually active at that time, yet a strong likelihood exists that Emma and Mickey assaulted the college girl together at the hotel. Later, when Mickey decided to kill her, Emma was already compromised and had to go along with Mickey's objectives. This thinking is consistent with Mickey's behavior. Where would Mickey have obtained semen? With her temperament, anywhere.

Vengeance Kill 3: Molly Estes

Mickey tracked down, stalked, tortured, and killed Molly Estes, Tom Aiken's lover when Mickey was in Afghanistan. By chance, five years or so after Tom and Mickey's mother married, Mickey was at a mall purchasing some clothes, when she recognized another shopper, Molly Estes. She nonchalantly followed Molly to the parking lot and copied her vehicle license plate. Once in her own vehicle, she called the DMV for identification. Address in hand, she cruised by the house where Molly Estes, now married to a man named Donovan, lived. The following day while on patrol, she requested a DMV photo of Molly Donovan.

Because Molly lived in another jurisdiction, Mickey drove her own vehicle into the community. Stopping at local stores, churches, and the school where the Donovan child was enrolled, she asked questions about Molly without providing her own identity as a police officer. "Not one person challenged me" she said, as she went about her investigation. That was one reason she wrote about it as much as she did. Mickey was "shocked that people, responsible people, some even in sensitive jobs, gave up so much information about an active and well-liked family in their community. And never did I say I was the police. I looked right into their eyes and asked the right questions. I wore a wig and changed my eye coloring. Made sure no one saw my vehicle too." Within a few months, Mickey owned a cargo ship full of information about the Donovans, especially Molly.

She observed Molly from a distance, too, and those closest to her. Mickey took photographs of the happily married woman, her husband, and her children. If Molly had been observant, she would have realized she was being stalked, or she might have realized that she kept seeing the same woman no matter where she went.

Mickey became obsessed with Molly Donovan. She conducted repeated calls to her cell phone, her work phone, and her home phone. She used different voices and sometimes she had different people talk on the phone for her. She used cell phones she confiscated from drunks, drug pushers, and wife batterers. Molly changed her cell phone number and her house phone number numerous times, but Mickey obtained those numbers and continued to harass her. Molly had no idea who or why she was being harassed. "That was the beauty of it all," wrote Mickey.

Molly also wondered about the flowers and candy sent by "a lover" and someone who wrote, "I still care." Molly's husband also wondered about those gifts, and the hang-up telephone calls, e-mails, and photographs of Molly at work, Molly at the store, and Molly at the gym smiling at random people. Tension in the Donovan home escalated when pornographic gifts arrived at the house and at the school where Molly taught.

The Donovans reported the harassment to the police. Molly was shocked when the investigators asked her about Tom Aiken and the other men and women she had allegedly been associated and intimate with. She admitted dating Aiken, long ago, but had no knowledge who the other people were. A few names she recognized as local teachers and retail store managers, but told the detectives that she had never been personal with any of them. She probably said, "There must be a mistake of some kind."

The detectives responded that mistakes do happen, but the issue was that some of the individuals mentioned had purchased pornographic items, rented rooms in trashy motels, and paid for male escort services for Molly Donovan. As the detectives inquired more into Molly's activities, her husband took notice of the extent of the evidence. The couple quarreled often, and Mr. Donovan became a person-of-interest in his wife's stalking. But when he was admitted to a hospital's emergency care unit as a result of Molly's explosive reaction to him during one of their fights, police turned their attention to Molly. There is little question that the Donovans were experiencing a tense relationship with each other as a result of the stalking and the investigation, but the evidence suggested that Molly lived on a fast track and was experiencing the results of that lifestyle.

As the investigation widened, Molly was suspended from her job, and then fired. The church congregation dismissed her as a Sunday school leader, and the Donovan children experienced ridicule at school among friends and classmates alike. As the stalking investigation came to a halt, officers said little could be done, because Molly could not identify any suspect, nor had any attempt been made to harm her. Mr. Donovan went camping with a friend for four days. When he returned, Molly, their children, and their vehicle were missing. He waited a day or two before filing a missing person report. He thought Molly had gone to a friend's home to think things through. When officers arrived at the house, Mr. Donovan told them that the home didn't look burglarized. There was no evidence of a forced entry.

The corpses of Molly Donovan and her child were found in the trunk of Molly's vehicle two weeks later, parked at the airport. The medical examiner determined that the murder of the victims was caused by a single and precise knife wound to their hearts by a ten-inch blade. The murder weapon was lodged deep in Molly's vagina, with only the handle protruding from between her legs. The last two fingers on her left hand and her thumb on her right hand, the large right toe, the tip of one breast, and her right calf muscle, were severed from her body. Also the victim's clitoris had been severed and jammed into the mouth of her dead son. His tongue was pushed back and superglued to the roof of his mouth, preventing the swallowing of his mother's sex glands. A plastic water bottle was superglued to his teeth and lips, which prevented him from closing his mouth. The boy's severed penis and scrotum were found in his mother's mouth, and her teeth were superglued shut. The action taken by the aggressor is consistent with someone who was enraged with hate and focused on sexual issues. There were no other bruises or marks on the bodies of the victims, other than blood. The child was blindfolded; Molly's eyes had been glued shut. The victims were naked and wrapped in blankets that came from the Donovan home. One blanket came from the master bedroom and one from the bedroom of the child. Each victim's ankles were duct-taped, and their hands were duct-taped behind their backs. However, the vehicle was not the crime scene. The bodies of the victims had been wiped clean with something other than the blankets they were wrapped in. Even the blankets were somewhat free of blood suggesting they were used days after the victims were murdered. Inside the automobile, no trace evidence or fingerprints from anyone other than the Donovans were found. A parking ticket on the dashboard was time stamped two days prior to the vehicle being discovered by police. The medical examiner estimated the time of death of the victims was approximately seven days before the vehicle was driven into the airport parking lot. The child died approximately six hours earlier than his mother.

The best suspect for the murder was Mr. Donovan. His motive was jealously and rage produced from learning about his spouse's lifestyle. The question investigators asked was, how could a stranger have obtained the blankets used in the murder? Mr. Donovan had access to the home and there were no signs of forced entry. Mr. Donovan never mentioned to police that blankets were missing. A search warrant obtained to search the Donovan home for blood and other indicators showed that the home was indeed the scene of the crime. In the child's bathroom, there was evidence that blood could have been spattered on floor and walls, but the entire area had been carefully washed with bleach. Why would the child's bathroom have been washed with bleach? Mr. Donovan hired an attorney and offered no comment.

"Another theory of the crime," Donovan's attorney suggested, "is that the stalker, whom the police were unable identify or apprehend, entered the home, brutally murdered Mrs. Donovan and the Donovan's youngest son and cleaned up the murder scene after removing their bodies while Mr. Donovan was camping with the Donovan's oldest son." But the bleach-washed bathroom suggested that the bathroom was the scene of the crime. Bleach consistent with the bathroom was found on Mr. Donovan's bedsheets. The prosecutor won an indictment against Mr. Donovan, and eventually Donovan was found guilty of first degree murder and sentenced to life in prison.

Mickey clarified years later in her prison journal, "I wanted to make Molly's life miserable, so I planted a little of this [probably false reports] and a little of that [probably false evidence] in her police file and life. Nothing came back to me as expected. I have no idea what happened to her or her poor child. But the little cheap ass whore had it coming and her last days on this planet she tasted a real prick and not the one that belonged to me."

Vengeance Kill 4: Barry Goldberg

Mickey knew Barry Goldberg, her father's lover, from a distance. They never had a conversation. Her notes in her prison journal do not specifically say when she decided to stalk or kill him, but she does mention his name after she threw Chris Wyatt, her second husband, out of her home and a few years after her father died. (Her father supposedly died of natural causes, but that raises another question and fits Mickey Stone's vengeance murder scenarios.) The fact that Chris Wyatt had an affair might have triggered Mickey to go after Goldberg, as she made a connection between Goldberg and her father cheating on her mother.

Goldberg was an associate professor of biology. He was younger than her father, and slender. He resided in the gay community of Cambridge, Massachusetts and often was arrogant about his sexual orientation, his occupation, and his sexual conquest with the Bishop.

Mickey had kept mental notes about Goldberg, she said. While she was pregnant with Brittney, Mickey wrote that she established a surveillance process that helped her discover a great deal about Goldberg. She visited the campus but kept her distance from him. When she put her plan into action, Goldberg experienced incidents like flat tires, empty gas tanks in his old Volkswagen, and mail and textbooks missing. Someone hacked into his computer, sending pornographic e-mails from him to his contacts. He was bombarded with instant messages, invitations to chat rooms, and links to erotic gay websites. He discovered that someone had posted his name, pictures of him—and some of them were naked—and invitations to sexual encounters at Craigslist, Backpage, and Yahoo. One ad included three photographs, one of Goldberg's face, and two of men's bodies from the chest to the knees, both displaying a huge and erect penis. The ad read:

Horny Men: First time customers free. We're building our client list. How would you like to be massaged by two very hot studs? Jason is 25 years old 6' tall and 190 lbs. Barry is 28 years old and stands 5'11" at 185 lbs. Dominican. Low rates. So book us today to fulfill every fantasy in your head. We accept Cash and Major Credit Cards. Don't miss out. Bi, Married, and First Timers welcome. Any race, any time. We travel and are very experienced.

This ad was e-mailed to Goldberg's colleagues in every academic department at the university. It was also e-mailed to Goldberg's student lists. Two days later Barry Goldberg disappeared from his apartment. This happened while Mickey was on maternity leave from the police department. No one would have considered a woman in her third trimester of pregnancy to engage in any kind of abduction, yet while in prison, all of Mickey's descriptions about the case, both orally and in writing, matched newspaper accounts of those events.

Months went by without discovery of Goldberg. Mickey probably took him to her home and kept him there, gagged and secured. The day after Goldberg disappeared, she went into labor and gave birth to Brittney. While the newborn suckled her mother's breast, Mickey slashed Goldberg's face, tortured him, and kept him alive for a month.

"The little fag had no clue what was happening around him. There I was chewing on his little wiener one day. I asked him if that's how my father did it? He cried. He had whatever happened to him coming... Joke joke," Mickey wrote. She never admitted killing Barry Goldberg, and claimed the above incident happened long before Goldberg was missing.

Mickey returned to active police duty after the birth of her daughter. She had hired a full-time nanny to tend to her children. Goldberg's body was discovered in the backseat of a vehicle that had crashed into an 18-wheeler on the interstate. There were two other people in the vehicle—the driver, who was a student at Harvard; and Goldberg's mother. The medical examiner reported that the driver of the vehicle died in the crash. He also determined that Mrs. Goldberg had died twenty-four hours before the crash. A single gunshot wound into her heart was the cause of death. The ME also determined that Barry Goldberg died at least twenty-four hours before the crash. Asphyxiation was the cause of death. A plastic bag from Wal-Mart was tied around his neck. Blood found on the bag was that of his mother's. He had been emasculated. He was wearing a pair of black cowboy chaps and a T-shirt, both covered with his blood. Inscribed on his shirt was the phrase It's Raining Men, Alleluia. His penis could not be found. But in the vehicle was a crumpled sheet of paper that had the Horny Men ad on it, an array of male sex tools, such as stud rings, a large black butt plug, and male enhancement tablets and gel. The ME also reported semen from two different males on Goldberg's face.

Barry Goldberg and his mother had shared an apartment, but Barry also had his own apartment, which he shared at one time with the Bishop. The police investigation was closed a month later. The local newspaper reported that Barry Goldberg's death had resulted from a love triangle that produced a violent disagreement among the victim and several unknown sexual partners. His mother and the driver of the vehicle were determined to be collateral damage of that disagreement.

Vengeance Kill 5: Janelle Hale and Her Mother

Mickey met a hard-drinking woman named Janelle Hale, the police dispatcher who was sexually involved with Mickey's second husband, Chris Wyatt. Janelle knew Mickey because she was a cop in the same jurisdiction where she used to work. Once it got out that she and Chris were involved, she lost her job and Chris at the same time. Mickey emphasized that she came upon Janelle simply by chance in her efforts to find a new place to unwind. "Because we shared a man means we have something in common, besides vodka," Hale told Mickey with a laugh. Janelle took the upper hand during their barroom activities over the next few months. She completely dominated Mickey, or so Janelle thought. When Janelle got into fights at the bars, Mickey would step in to help her. Now they shared vodka, fights, Chris, and the nights.

Early one night, while Mickey accompanied Janelle home to change clothes, Janelle introduced Mickey to her mother. The old lady lived with Janelle, and spoke with Mickey for some time while Janelle took care of business. Mickey remembers that as they were leaving, Janelle's mom took Janelle aside and gave her some advice: "Watch out with this one or she'll friggin' kill you. Stir her up the wrong way or do the wrong things and you're screwed. Don't ever think of playing up on her, she'll friggin' kill you." The old lady turned to Mickey and added, "Ain't that right, honey? Take good care of my daughter." Mickey wrote that she was "totally in love with people who are direct without all the crap. Maybe the old lady saw the heat in my eyes when I looked at her daughter. Old people can be pretty smart."

When Officer Mickey Stone was responding to fatal accident on the highway, the Hale home was caught in a firestorm produced from a gas leak that took the lives of both occupants, Janelle Hale and her mother, Norma Hale.

Some Observations

It is evident that Mickey rarely spent time with her children. Don't be too harsh on her. For wealthy Americans, tending to children is not an important social value, compared to the middle class who are under the impression that must spend every waking moment with their kids. Another observation is that the vengeance kills described above are only the tip of the iceberg for Mickey Stone. She killed Tom Aiken, yes, but had Tom killed his wife, Mickey's mother, or was that Mickey too? She could justify killing her mother, and for that matter, she could justify killing her father. After all was said and done, she was a guest of the state for twenty-four months. Once she was released, it is an easy conclusion that many individuals are, as usual, obligated to Mickey. It is also likely that the murder of Officer Wyatt, who was killed in a gunfight during a traffic stop on the same highways patrolled by his former wife, had to do with her ideas of retaliation. No one was ever apprehended for his death, and no one ever will be. What we don't know is how many other people were murdered by Mickey Stone. We do know that today, Mickey sits at the head of a wealthy corporation that owns so much real estate, including high rises from Boston to Belize, that Donald Trump's empire looks like a third world nation in comparison. Should you harbor doubts of a lack of consequences among powerful family members for improprieties, which includes murder, talk to the relatives of Mary Jo Kopechne, the young woman found dead at Chappaquiddick Island. She was a passenger in Ted Kennedy's car.

CHAPTER 12
Sweet Jenny Lee

Introduction

This chapter provides a description of Jenny Lee's early life, including her strong relationship with her grandparents who lived in Manhattan. It offers a look at Jenny Lee's four "dark moments" in her life and describes the crimes she committed. It also describes how her mother posted her bond, yet Jenny Lee stole her car, credit cards, and other items and ran away. She was apprehended by police officers, whom she attacked with a piece of broken mirror at a McDonald's. While awaiting trial, Jenny Lee was interviewed by an intake advocate, and eventually pled guilty to a lesser offense. This chapter reports on her presentence investigation and other crimes that she was never charged for; and characterizes this young lady's compulsive pleasure-seeker experiences.

Early Life

Jenny Lee, a slim and pretty sixteen-year-old about to enter her last year of high school was remanded to juvenile detention while awaiting the outcome of a waiver petition to adult court. Jenny Lee and her younger brother were raised in a small, affluent community filled with towering homes, creating a resort montage, while quiet foreign vehicles coasting up and down the smooth jet black streets. Wealthy people lived in the next neighborhood nestled along the coast. Her father, a tall, handsome man, was a commercial pilot for an air carrier. His flights and layovers took him, and sometimes Jenny Lee, to London, Naples, and Stockholm. Jenny Lee could recognize a number of international airports from the air, yet that was the only time she actually spent with her dad. At school, Jenny Lee was often the topic of conversations because of her excursions to faraway countries, yet many of her classmates asked specific questions, suggesting that they had visited those cities as well. Jenny Lee had developed two or three class projects in middle school about her trips, which earned her the nickname Frequent Hirer, which also alluded to her flirtatious manner. The local newspaper wrote a short story about one of those projects, and included Jenny Lee's picture standing next to her dad, wearing his pilot's uniform and a huge smile.

Jenny Lee's mother was often out of the house and attending charitable events, Jenny Lee and her little brother, who looked more like a giant cantaloupe than just a fat kid, had several nannies who followed the children around as if they were magnets. On occasion, when Nanny wasn't present, "Or fell off her magic wagon," as Jenny Lee wrote, it became Jenny Lee's task to watch over her baby brother, much to her displeasure. Because of her disgust in watching him, she would torment him and "mess with his private parts for laughs." But most often, Jenny Lee did as she pleased and was rarely under anyone's thumb. Sometimes she informed her nanny that she was going to the library or on an errand for her father. She always had some credible story leaving her orange-fleshed brother and supervision behind, especially in middle school when she was big enough to flirt with boys.

Jenny Lee was not a shy girl, but she wasn't outwardly aggressive either. She was just one of those people who suddenly appeared and disappeared. Sometimes she met new friends, but mostly she spent time with older acquaintances, who she thought were "very, very cool, but I knew how to slip and slide," Jenny Lee wrote. When asked what she meant by slip and slide, she said, "I've always known how to play people, even older people like you, Doc." Jenny Lee described her behavior as consistent with that of a schemer, a player, or manipulator since she was very young. A repetitive discovery about the participants in this book that I characterize as pleasure-seekers (Annie, Joey, Lilith, and Margo) is that they can easily detail incidents about their life, even as young as ages two to five. Jenny Lee remembered tricking others because she was generally bored with everything, or couldn't remain focused unless something exciting was happening.

Jenny Lee had an athletic frame and participated in competitive soccer, until one of her dark moments. She maintained her competitive spirit, although she was quiet and reserved. During the summers, she hung out with friends at the mall and at McDonalds on the beach, where she would tan, eat French fries drenched in ketchup, and play in the sand. She went to a few baseball games in the city, and took flights with her dad. The rest of the summer was spent at summer camp with girls she had known since daycare and kindergarten. Most of her friends annoyed her to no end, and "I'd weed 'em up [get them excited] to have some fun. Like I would smack one of them or hide their favorite clothes." She hated camp because of the restrictions upon what she considered her personal time and upon "my personal space." What she disliked most was being placed with a partner or in a group during sports events or playtime.

Her bedroom at home was always organized and too clean to be a young girl's room. She had every amenity known (such as, her own connecting bathroom, cell phone, computer, television, and tons of clothes). Her father said he would buy her a car when she got her driver's license. Since her birthday was in November, she could take driver's education in her third year of school. She often spent weekend nights at other girls' homes, and sometimes had the gang at her house, too. Her family's pool was an outside pool, and she took a little heat for that, because her friends had combination pools—half enclosed and half outside. During the winter months, they could swim in the enclosed end of the pool, but no one ever went into the water unless thrown in.

She was at the age of sexual recognition, but really didn't care if boys found her attractive or not. In one sense, she was a typical teenage girl, because she wanted to look pretty and she wanted males to be attracted to her. She continually checked her face in mirrors and judged other people's assessment of her, to make sure she looked good and that there was nothing wrong with her. She thought her hair was one of her better features. Jenny Lee knew she was pretty, but she didn't go overboard with letting other people know she knew. The only problem was that Jenny Lee was wired wrong, and after you had given her your approval about her looks, she could easily hurt you and think little about it.

Manhattan Grandparents

Jenny Lee's grandparents lived in Manhattan, high above Central Park, and Jenny Lee adored the park, the restaurants, and the young men who stared at her. Sometimes, she would stare back. Her heart was set on attending a private girls high school, but her parents suggested she try the public high school that was close to home. During her freshman year, she talked to her adviser and friends about Brown University, New York University, and MIT, and with good reason. Her grades and test scores were excellent, especially in physical science. Her mother had graduated from Brown, her father from MIT, and her grandfather was on the board of the New York University. Jenny Lee was fascinated with Greenwich Village in Manhattan, because of its ambiance. Even at an early age, she walked her grandparent's dog in the park for hours, and sometimes would walk to the Village, just to watch the tourists. She wrote in her prison journal that she thought her grandparents loved her more than her own mother, because they "denied me nothing, especially my freedom, even when I was in grade school." But everything would change. What also was revealed in Jenny Lee's journal and in conversations is that although physically comfortable, she had little supervision and even less emotional attachment to family and friends. This discovery is similar among all the participants in this book.

Dark Moments

Sweet Jenny Lee experienced some dark moments in her life. Her worst dark moments included:
- Sixth grade, when Olivia, her BFF, stole her boyfriend, made out with him, and then dropped him like a rock. Olivia and Jenny Lee fought it out in Olivia's bedroom when Olivia's mom went to the supermarket. Jenny Lee won. Police were called because, as Jenny Lee wrote, "I tore the little bitch up, then stomped her little sister's ass too. Then I trashed her room and tossed her television

through the window." Nothing came of the incident. But judging from what Jenny Lee wrote, she also pitched a hammer at the boyfriend's face. His parents wanted the police to intervene, but they refused, saying it was an accident. Olivia and Jenny Lee were never friends again, although every chance she got, Jenny Lee took the time to bring some discomfort to Olivia, by ridiculing her at school, revealing personal and confidential things about Olivia that the girl had shared with Jenny Lee, and pitting other girls against her. None of the students supported Olivia's claims that Jenny Lee had an ongoing campaign to isolate, harm, and stifle Olivia. But Jenny Lee was also responsible for Olivia's broken arm, the lacerations on her forehead, and other damages. For instance, she was behind Olivia on the school staircase, when her foot pushed Olivia down them. The lacerations to Olivia's forehead were the result of Jenny Lee attacking her with a hairbrush, and the contents of her school locker was doused with honey. If Olivia complained, the attacks worsened. While in prison, Jenny Lee wrote that she knew "Olivia would keep her little slut mouth shut. She wanted to be abused by somebody and I helped her."

- Jenny Lee had just turned fourteen in her first year of high school. It was a week or two before the Christmas holiday. She contracted a mild case of bacterial meningitis, which left her profoundly deaf in both ears. She recovered quickly from the illness with treatment, but the damaged ears were another matter. She remained deaf for life. At first her disability overwhelmed her, but with therapy, she learned to adapt to her new world. Olivia told her that being deaf was God's way of paying her back for her wickedness. Jenny Lee never accepted the guilt from Olivia. In fact, while in prison, she admitted that she never really felt any pain, or any joy for that matter, for any of her behavior. Dark moments were experiences that seemed to impact her life, but none of it was from her hand, she wrote.

- In part because of her meningitis experience, her parents arranged for her to see a clinical psychologist. He determined that she was manifesting depression. Jenny Lee protested. She wrote that she was never depressed. Her parents, who took little interest in her activities, would have no idea whether she was happy or sad. "Things just don't bother me," she wrote. "Never did. My parents if they were ever around would flip out over the dumbest of things. Like one time I think I was about nine or ten and went to the food store with my nanny and brother. I was talking to this stranger and Nanny told my mother, who flipped out like a crazy bitch and screamed at me. It was so like wicked annoying. I can handle strangers. I just can't handle people who think they can tell me what to do like that crazy bitch mother of mine who's never around to know who I talk to and who I don't."

- Jenny Lee was later diagnosed with attention deficit hyperactivity disorder (ADHD). At first lithium, and then Ritalin, were prescribed. Her protests were heard, but she soon accepted her fate and the incompetence of her mother, the doctors, and the world in general.

Jenny Lee wrote that because she was deaf and had been diagnosed with ADHD, everyone, including parents, treated her differently. "It wasn't a bad difference but a guilt-difference." She had more designer clothes, exquisite jewelry, and more gift cards for manicures and pedicures, McDonalds, and Starbucks than ever before. She hated jewelry and gave it away to girlfriends or even just random girls at school. Her parents never asked if she went to church, and didn't look into her room at night. She often spent her nights at girlfriend's houses, and several times slept in other rooms in her own house. She had been alone before, but now, she was also isolated. "It could be a good thing," she wrote, "because less was expected of me. I could do what I wanted big-time, like screw with people at the mall." When asked what she meant, she added, "You know, asking them for shit like drugs. Sometimes I traded my earrings and sometimes a blow job for something to smoke or whatever."

Prior to the ADHD diagnosis, she babysat, but after the diagnosis, she wasn't called anymore. "Parents didn't trust me with their kids anymore. It was like I had AIDS or something." What was curious was that she mentioned that teachers worked with her to help her finish her first year in high school, but things changed in the second year. The same teachers who had helped her stopped helping her, and none of the teachers asked for homework or any assignments. She had a weekly appointment with the high school counselor. Her sophomore year was a "joke. I did *nada*." The school administrators attempted to put her into a special educational classroom during her junior year, but without success. When the administrators kept the pressure up by isolating Jenny Lee, such as no gym and a special lunch room, her parents backed down. She lost faith in her counselor, who said she wouldn't help her. At the end of her junior year and at her insistence, her parents withdrew her from public school and enrolled her in the private girls school Jenny Lee had wanted to go. She asked her dad for the car he promised, but because she had not taken driver's education in high school, no car. "Take driver's ed and we'll see," he told her "He lied to me," Jenny Lee wrote. "He said he was going to get me a car. But at least he talked to me."

The Crime

During the summer before her senior year, Sweet Jenny Lee was arrested. She was sixteen years of age. The crime that landed her in prison was holding hostage, for two days, an eighteen-year–old girl with low functioning skills, and her two children, four-year-old Tommy and two-year-old Katie. She held them in an abandoned, boarded-up mansion scheduled for repairs. She cut Katie's arm several times with a serrated hunting knife, and threatened to cut Tommy's penis if Stacy, their mother, attempted an escape or tried to harm her. Sweet Jenny Lee held the boy's penis in her hand for hours at a time, just in case.

Her boyfriend, seventeen-year-old Shane, finally led police to the old mansion, where he and Jenny Lee had smoked weed and made out He told police that he thought she slept in the mansion on occasion.

Sweet Jenny Lee surrendered to police and explained that she had needed time to think. "That's why I did it. Stacy and her kids looked so happy. It's not fair," she said. The officer reported that Jenny Lee seemed confused. She couldn't remember her home phone number. Her eyes were narrowed, she was nauseated and had the shakes. She appeared to be very tired, especially after she was handcuffed. The reports suggested Jenny Lee was going through drug withdrawal, although the officer did not specifically use those terms.

Bond Posted and Run Away

After Jenny Lee's arrest, her mother, Alice, posted a $2,500 bond, and Jenny Lee was released to Alice's custody. Once home, Sweet Jenny Lee turned sweeter. She stole her mother's credit cards and charged around $5,000 on those cards in less than thirty days. When Alice confronted Jenny Lee, Jenny Lee said "she completely flipped out like a crazy lady. It's not like the money is hers in the first place. It's my dad's money. She's always been a latchkey wife. When the bitch fell asleep that night, I took her money, jewelry, car, kitchen utensils, switched her meds with mine, and disappeared. She is so totally clueless."

A few days later, police arrived at a McDonalds on the southern side of town on another matter. When one of the officers recognized Jenny Lee, she ran to the lady's room. The officers pursued her. Entering the room, they heard a crash. Jenny Lee had broken the mirror with the garbage container, and now stood in front of them with a chuck of the broken mirror in her hand, which was wrapped with toilet paper. While her blood flowed to the ground, Jenny Lee charged the officers. As they tried to subdue her, she spat on them, bit the face of one officer and drew blood, and used excessive foul language. After her hand was treated at the hospital, the officers processed her at the police station. She claimed to their superior that both officers "touched her down there."

A subsequent investigation proved her allegations were false. She was remanded to a detention facility to await the outcome of the petition, because of her juvenile status. She was charged with aggravated assault. Resisting arrest, assaulting police officers, grand larceny, and auto theft were considered, but dropped once Jenny Lee's ADHD, medication therapy, and deafness were considered. Also, her mother wouldn't testify against her, and claimed that she gave her the car (even though Jenny Lee didn't have a drivers' license).

Intake Advocate's Interview

When Sweet Jenny Lee was first remanded to custody to await adjudication, she was interviewed by an intake-advocate. The interview was recorded, and portions follow:

Jenny Lee: "Let me tell you about me. I'm no slut. I'm just me and some people think I'm as sweet as pie. It started when Alice … Oh, that's my mother. My dad didn't move out yet, but I watched Alice and her boyfriend go primitive. Gross! While they were doing it in the kitchen, I called the police on the bitch. He was a lame freak that thought he was hot. Not. He really is a perv-fag who had 'piss-haps' and never put the friggin' seat down. He watched me all the time. I split a couple of times just to show the perv-fag that I'm smarter than the both of them. They would never get it. When I saw my dad, I showed him a picture I took with my cell phone of Alice and her dickless lover-boy. Dad hit the roof and they fought. They put me into the public school and the place put me into a special ed class with retards, you know? I cut class and looked for good hangs in the teachers' parking lot. I smoked, too, sometimes weed if I could get it. I hate school now. Most kids don't know about the dudes and wannabes on the streets. If I was like them, I'd be out there more. When I was on the street [Note: this would have been around the time Jenny Lee was fifteen years old] even after my mother was out of my life for those few months, it wasn't always sweet. One time, this dude's chick beat me up so bad, you know, I woke up in a friggin' hospital. I left when no one was watching. Got stoned with some guy who cried about his little brother. Don't know what that shit was about, but he held me down and his friggin' friends who were like ten years old did me. On the street, the cops busted me cause I was fallin' down and when I couldn't see their lips [to understand what they were saying], they got pissed and thought I was trailer park trash or something. After the docs fixed me up, my mother came and got me because dad was on a flight like somewhere. I think the judge thinks I'm bad, but you know, I had a sup [juvenile supervisor] to talk over my problems, and I don't get into any fights, but I'm not going to school and I am not giving up cigarettes or weed or guys."

Intake-Advocate's Conclusion: "There is the sense," the intake-advocate wrote, "that Jenny Lee causes a lot of trouble for others, not because she's deviant but because she feels safer when supervised by community corrections personnel than when she is alone on the streets. Her youth was spent with parents who were excellent care-providers, except when it came to love and validation. Jenny Lee possesses little street experience in defending herself and is often victimized. This perspective is consistent with criminal justice professionals who advocate that correctional supervision can provide safety and order in the lives of some teenagers reported."

The Guilty Plea

After a psychological assessment, the examiner reported that Jenny Lee was mentally stable and competent to stand trial. Jenny Lee accepted a guilty plea during the trial process, prior to jury deliberation. The evidence was mounting, and her defense lawyer, one of the more expensive attorneys in town, suggested an alternative: a guilty plea with a two-year prison sentence, which included time Jenny Lee had already served in the juvenile detention center. Her mother approved of the alternative. There are indicators that Alice used the guilty plea to ensure that Jenny Lee was out of her home. While Jenny Lee was detained, Alice learned that Jenny Lee had sexually attacked her younger brother. But Alice did not share that information with anyone other than Sweet Jenny Lee. "You behave or we'll see what the state will do to you."

Alice's boyfriend had moved in with Alice. Jenny Lee voiced a strong disapproval with Alice when she and Jenny Lee's aunt Glenda (Alice's older sister) visited her at the detention facility. Jenny Lee yelled that she would "kill him first chance I get," and attacked her mother in the visiting room. She grabbed her mother's hair, tossed her to the floor, and jumped on her chest. A custody officer grabbed Jenny Lee, and as she was carried from the room, she screamed at her mother, "You bitch, you bitch, you evil rotten whore bitch."

Needless to say, that behavior sealed Sweet Jenny Lee's fate. Once the judge accepted the guilty plea, a pre-investigation sentence report was ordered.

Presentence Investigation Report

The PSI reported that Jenny Lee had been under the care of a psychologist and that she had been prescribed Ritalin for her ADHD. If Jenny Lee was sentenced to jail or prison, it was recommended that her medication be continued and the state should ensure that she took her meds. The report went on to speculate that it was likely that Jenny Lee had not always taken her medication, as evidenced by her drastic behavior. The report said that although Jenny Lee had been on oral contraceptives because of polycystic ovary syndrome (PCOS), largely irregular menstrual periods, cramps, and acne, since she was fourteen, it was not the obligation of the jurisdiction to provide this medication. Upon approval of a state physician, the jurisdiction would make the drug available, if her father's health care covered the prescription.

Jenny Lee's attack on the police officers at McDonalds and her attack on her mother in the visiting room were detailed in the report. Jenny Lee's other crimes were not part of the PSI. It was also opined that Jenny Lee's deafness was more the result of her continual "drama" and suggested that she might only be hard of hearing "when the subject wants to be deaf." Jenny Lee "played [her deafness] up for attention. This should not preclude any confinement consideration," was stated in her PSI.

Prison Sentence

Sweet Jenny Lee accepted a guilty plea for three counts of aggravated assault. Had she been found guilty by the jury and the judge had followed the state's sentencing guidelines for the charges against her—felonious assault with deadly weapon with intent to kill or inflict serious injury, abduction of children, kidnapping, and trespassing—Jenny Lee could have been sentenced to a minimum of twenty years, if the sentences were consecutive as opposed to concurrent. Jenny Lee was just barely seventeen when she arrived at the only maximum security penitentiary for women in the state of her conviction.

Other Crimes

Of course, you already know about Sweet Jenny Lee's other crimes of resisting arrest and assaulting police officers. However, Jenny Lee also attempted to murder her mother more than once in the two years prior to her arrest. She beat up her younger brother in addition to having oral sex with him on several occasions, drank excessively and used drugs. (She stole her father's beer and whiskey, and her mother's prescriptions and marijuana). Also, her mother did not report the $5,000 Jenny Lee charged on her credit cards, but she did report the theft of her vehicle for insurance reasons. Jenny Lee had developed drug addictions—heroin and LSD, mescaline, mushrooms, and antidepressants, as well as Ritalin. Her parents never knew about her addictions.

Oddly enough, heroin was not the drug of choice among the youths in the community where Jenny Lee lived. Her boyfriend Shane was interviewed, but he never provided the detectives with enough information to follow through with a drug investigation. Once during in-group at prison, Jenny Lee said something to the effect that her first experience with drugs was heroin, and she connected that experience to Central Park and Greenwich Village in Manhattan. This thought is contradictory and inconsistent with the "experts" who maintain that marijuana is the first step to a hard addiction. However, prison research reveals that whatever drug an addict starts with, they continue with that drug. That is, if an addict starts on cocaine, he stays on cocaine. The gateway drug theory seems to be an illusion that sounds reasonable, but doesn't conform to the reality of female junkies.

A week prior to abducting Stacy and her children, Jenny Lee replaced her mother's Prozac with tablets that resembled the ones she stole. She was unaware that her mother's doctor had switched her mom's Prozac to a different drug (Nefazodone) that kept Jenny Lee awake for days. It is likely that her mother experienced tense moments, too, after taking Jenny Lee's medication. Because of Jenny Lee's deviant and criminal behavior, her continual attempts to instigate trouble between her parents, her demands for privacy and autonomy, her parents either didn't want or couldn't provide the girl with emotional bonds and what can be referred to as social validation. Jenny Lee was uncertain about how to behave, because she had few role models. She lacked a moral compass. She had never known unconditional love. She had few positive models to confirm or recognize who and what she was or should be. I think most of us when we're uncertain about what to do or how to behave, look to others to guide us. We seek the recognition of others. If we want to succeed, we have to depend on other people to say we are not only capable, but the exact person to fulfill a need. The split between Sweet Jenny Lee and her parents moved them all so far apart, it produced an impasse too great to bridge.

Compulsive Pleasure Seeker

While Sweet Jenny Lee served her prison sentence, it was hard for her to hide her thoughts. Although she lacked the bold aggression of Annie and the finances of Underworld Lilith, Jenny Lee acted with the sophistication of a seasoned court attorney in the way she responded to prison custody officers, despite them placing her on suicide watch a few times. Sometimes she was written up for disciplinary reasons, but she was seldom placed in segregation or isolation. Most often, she could pretty well do what she wanted, or so she thought. Because of her age, most prison personnel looked the other way, except when she placed herself in a dangerous situation with other prisoners. Jenny Lee eventually realized, similar to most prisoners, that there are institutional boundaries and limits on her behavior. She usually stopped herself. She understood the structure, mission, and latitude of her keepers. For instance, she had never been in an AA 12-Step program prior to prison. But the first time she attended a meeting, she seemed to know more about it than prisoners who had had experience with it. She acted much older than her age.

Sweet Jenny Lee is a schemer, but she can be described as a person on a roller coaster, because she could just as easily spit on a custody officer as compliment him. Her style is swift and violent. The trigger to commit a crime is found in the explanations of a pleasure seeker.

Typical of the other pleasure seekers, Jenny Lee made little distinction between violent and nonviolent behavior, although she prefers silent or quiet crime to loud crime. She dislikes firearms, favoring knives (or a broken mirror) as a weapon of choice. Similar to other super predators, Sweet Jenny Lee selects victims with care. When she chose Stacy and her children to abduct and terrorize, she knew she could persuade Stacy—who was mentally challenged—to follow her to the abandoned mansion on the beach. She also thought that "the cops would never check to see if I screwed with Stacy or her friggin' kids." After all, Sweet Jenny Lee theorized, "I'm sixteen. So what the hell. I'm not going to do anything as disgusting as screwing a retard and her kids."

The sad fact is that the police never examined Stacy or her children. Furthermore, it wasn't by accident that the officers noticed Sweet Jenny Lee at the McDonalds, and that she attacked them. Imagine a skinny child confronting two police officers and attacking them. She had other choices, but chose a popular spot "to hide." In her journal she wrote, "You should have seen the look on the faces of those cops when I jumped from the john with a weapon."

Keeping her real personality hidden to most everyone she encountered in prison was a drain on Jenny Leer, but that standard among sexual predators. Consider what Sweet Jenny Lee told the intake officer: "I'm no slut. I'm just me." Psychopaths present masks of sanity to hide their real selves.

Sweet Jenny Lee has few personal boundaries. Nothing is sacred—marriage, children, rules, laws, normal behavior. Therefore, the list of crimes in her conviction is small in comparison to all the crimes she committed. She doesn't need someone to tell that "she's an incredible gangster of some kind." Experts fail to understand that pleasure seekers do not require recognition for their crimes, particularly females.

As Sweet Jenny Lee and the others in this book evolve into masters of their craft, expect an escalation in the frequency and intensity of criminally violent behavior in America. Little stands in these people's paths. Similar to most of the crimes predators commit, their crimes will remain unsolved for decades, if not forever. But also expect greater charm and sophistication from super predators, because they have the intellect to charm an Eskimo into buying ice.

The fictitious short story "Dumpling Legs" in chapter 18 is an amazing characterization of Sweet Jenny Lee and how she views the world: simple, uncomplicated, and full of obvious devises and people to be used. In that story she talks about Emily her doll.

CHAPTER 13
Soccer Mom Tammy

Introduction

Tammy is an elegant redhead, but when she disembarked from the white prison van, the thirty-one-year-old wore an expression of disbelief, like many suburban first-timers who arrive in this hellhole. Despite her movements restricted by foot shackles, her cuffed hands attached to a chain belt, and her baggy prison jumpsuit, she still exuded an inner resolve and profound compassion for others. Once I learned Tammy was soccer mom, it all added up. What stealth is to jet fighters, Tammy is to compassion, and both can deliver a lethal blast. Her tall and slim frame spoke of innumerable hours at the gym and eternal diets, yet eluding discovery is the hallmark of the junkie super predator, who succeeds at conforming to whatever crowd she's in. Tammy's skills at deception, similar to Brandeis's, usually allowed her to succeed. In general, as accomplished predators experience more of life, their deception allows them to take center stage in their lives, and to attack targets that thought they safe from the ugly thugs portrayed on popular TV crime dramas.

Many animal species have developed some sort of natural camouflage that helps them either find food or avoid detection by predators. Tammy, Brandeis, Mickey, and Val camouflaged themselves, but they took delight in pretending to be vulnerable. Once attacked, they could justify retaliation. Their retaliations should not be interpreted as equal actions, in the sense of an eye for an eye philosophy. For them, it's a life for an eye. Revengers don't play fair.

Education

Tammy attended college in New England and majored in English. She has a passion for writing. She wrote for the campus newspaper, and for the prison newsletter after her imprisonment. She also had articles published in a few major newspapers while in college. She left college after her junior year, when she learned she was pregnant. Giving up school was a difficult decision, because she was so close to graduating and she was routinely on the dean's list, similar to her high-school achievements. The worst part of leaving early was that she would have to admit to her parents, especially her father, "that he was right and I was wrong about the guy I dated." It was as if "someone in the underworld had a price on my head and tore apart every great chance in my life to get away from my parents. They were nice but when I was growing up, I rarely saw them." Although she'd had no intention of getting pregnant in the first place, Tammy decided to keep the baby. For a time, she didn't dare say anything to anybody about it. Yet, there it was—vomiting in the morning, putting on weight, and dizzy sensations in her blond head. Her folks would figure it out.

Pregnancy

Tammy put her problems behind her once she admitted her pregnancy to her parents. She lived with them at their pleasant suburban home, a bedroom community for a major metropolis, with her three younger brothers. She enrolled at community college, and in seven months earned a paralegal certificate, just before her son Aaron was born. After recovering from Aaron's birth and coping with his death, she accepted a job at a large law firm. In the shortest engagement ever, she married one of their newly hired attorneys, Ted. Over the next eleven years, they had three children (one boy and two girls) as he advanced to a junior partner position. They purchased a comfortable four-bedroom home with cathedral ceilings, granite kitchen counters, and a marvelous back porch with a brick barbeque grill. Tammy stopped working for the law firm, but added to the family income by writing articles for the newspapers. She bought a black SUV and taxied her children to school, soccer, baseball, and the YMCA, until the oldest boy was almost ten. Tammy's in-laws adored her, and both they and Tammy's parents lived nearby. Tammy filled photo albums with pictures of their amazing adventures, and often spread those wonderful memories over the dining room table to share with her husband before retiring for the evening. They sipped wine as they flipped through the photo albums and talked about the future of their children. They were a positive family, always looking on the bright side, but Tammy was cautious not to push their kids toward absolute perfection, as her parents had done to her.

Losing a Baby

Tammy wrote in her prison journal about surviving the death of her baby, which had happened about twelve years earlier. She wrote over fifty-six pages in her prison journal about Aaron. Much of her writing appeared to be random; I have organized her thoughts some. It is easy to feel her agony.

> I want to share my experiences with women who have lost their babies. Aaron was born on a blustery cold winter day in early January, a week after New Year's Day. I was twenty years old. The pregnancy and delivery were trouble free, and the doctor was pleased with Aaron, my son's health, and my health. Aaron is the most gorgeous human being I had ever seen. He had a head of wild dark hair, huge green eyes, and he topped the scale at six pounds, fourteen ounces. My father whisked us from the hospital after two days and brought us home for six happy and glorious days, until I noticed Aaron was breathing with fast shallow breaths and making little grunting noises. He was very sleepy and had lost interest in feeding. I called the doctor about it and he said he would meet us at the hospital that evening. A series of tests were conducted on my poor baby boy that evening and the following day. Aaron was found to have two major heart defects: transposition of the great arteries (TGA, in which the major blood vessels leading between the heart and lungs are switched)

and hypoplastic left heart syndrome (HLHS, in which the left side of the heart does not develop properly). The following day we were transported by helicopter to an intensive care unit at a university hospital, the same university I had attended as a student. Aaron had two six-hour operations in seven days in an attempt to save his life. Both defects are lethal if not treated within a few weeks of birth. He had the arterial switch operation for TGA and the Norwood procedure for HLHS. Both of these procedures are now well-established surgical procedures used to correct congenital heart defects in newborn babies. But then, when it happened to my Aaron, medicine wasn't as advanced as it is today. No one expected at the time that conducting these operations at same time could produce tragic consequences.

Aaron had to go back under the knife because the surgeon was unable to close the hole in Aaron's heart; and he was just too small to cope with a major blood transfusion and two sessions on a heart bypass machine. Two days after the operation, he began to fail rapidly and for the next seven days Aaron was in intensive care.

I was there the entire time sleeping on the chair next to my baby. Those were the most frightening experiences I ever encountered. We lived second to second, and little Aaron's energy went up and down countless times, just like a roller coaster. A few weeks earlier, my life with him was so full of happiness and promise. Now things were strange and hopeless. But my views were optimistic, and I prayed for his safety. Seconds before Aaron died, I wrapped my arms around him, and he seemed to smile at me. It was 10:18 in the morning when he died, and I must have held him for the next hour. Aaron was twenty-six days old. I wept and wept until I had no more tears, only to find that I had more tears.

I realize that other children have gone through much worse than my Aaron. At least I had experienced the joy of Aaron's birth and several happy and wonderful days with him. I couldn't have imagined what this last months would hold for me when I turned in my final exam in my last university course. What I have left are photographs and loving memories that can never be taken away. Yet a parent can never "get over" the death of a child. You just learn to live with your grief day by day, but for me, I drank my grief out of my system. I often wondered about those gods who control destiny and why they brought Aaron into this, world only to take him away."

Tammy continues her discussion about there being no right or wrong way to mourn, "but I never told Aaron's father of my pregnancy or of my son's death. He doesn't deserve to know about Aaron. He called the house several times when the fall semester began and he discovered I'd withdrawn, but I didn't return his calls or his letters. What could he say to me that could make a difference?"

Tammy's father supported her emotionally and financially, and "for that I am grateful, but he never knew the full story of Aaron and he never knew the full story about his devoted daughter, Tammy. The sight of my father and my three brothers at Aaron's funeral was hard to bear. Four males morning for Aaron and his mother, two people none of them really knew.

I'm conscious of the biological clock ticking away. I'll worry every day about my afterlife and maybe pregnancy, if I ever get out of this hellhole. I'm now so aware of all the things that can go wrong that even God would ask my advice. But I can't forget my little Aaron. I used to talk to his brother and sisters [from her later marriage to Ted] and they seemed proud although they never knew him. He'll always be part of my family. But my husband is dead. Worse, his parents say I'm the murderer and they will not bring my children for a visit. I have gone to court to gain custody of my kids and there's little I can do about it—I'm a convict. I lost my family, my home, my clothes, car, jewelry, photos of my children. Even my paralegal certification has been withdrawn. I'm a leper in a leper colony where deplorable demons fear to visit. When I'm released, I can't imagine what my life will be like, who if anyone would ever love me again. I need someone, anyone, to love me."

The Crime that Brought Tammy to Prison

After the law firm's Christmas party, Tammy and her husband drove home, with her husband as the passenger. A snow storm was raging, and patches of black ice covered the interstate. The result was a horrific accident that produced two fatalities—a child in the vehicle Tammy smashed into, and her husband. She said he was yelling at her, and she couldn't avoid a stalled vehicle on the shoulder.

A prosecutor believed that those fatalities were a direct cause of Tammy's negligence, reckless driving, and her intoxication level, which exceeded the state's legal limit of .08. Tammy blood alcohol level was .19. This was Tammy's second driving while intoxicated offense. Officers also discovered an open container of alcohol in the vehicle, though she said it belonged to her husband. She had worn her seat belt; he hadn't. On impact, his head went through the windshield. The accident report said that Tammy must have been traveling at a higher speed than the conditions merited, in order to produce the impact on her passenger and the damage to the stalled vehicle.

Tammy told officers that her husband had telephoned her for a ride home from the party, because he had had a few drinks. She dropped their kids off at her in-laws and attended the Christmas party for less than an hour. She said she might have had three drinks.

However, based on her approximate weight of 130-140 pounds, and given the single hour she'd had to consume alcohol, she would have to have had five drinks to produce a blood alcohol level of .19. Had Tammy not accepted the district attorney's plea bargain offer, the prosecutor could have indicted her on two counts of manslaughter while operating a motor vehicle, which carried an additional sentence of imprisonment for not less than five years and not more than twenty years for each fatality. The weather represented a mitigated circumstance. That is, the storm did not negate her wrongful action, but it showed that the defendant may have had some grounds for acting the way she did.

Sentencing Guidelines

In the jurisdiction where Tammy was tried, the sentencing guidelines mandated that when a judge finds grossly aggravating factors, which can include a prior DWI conviction within seven years of the current offense, and the defendant caused serious injury or death to another person because of the offender's impairment, the minimum sentence is seven years. That is what Tammy got, with an opportunity of early release. The judge added that the loss of her husband, the father of her children, was punishment enough. Thus he accepted the guilty plea offered by the prosecutor.

Also, it is true that Tammy had been previously convicted of a DWI, and her husband was able to reduce the legal sanction to a single line linked to a conviction "with circumstance." Tammy had been stopped many times for DWI, but it is unlikely that anyone knows the count.

When the judge sentenced Tammy, she felt as if someone had hit her—hard. She never thought she would become a convicted felon and sentenced to prison. An officer handcuffed her and led her away. The most hurtful moment for Tammy came when she watched her children wave for her to come over to them, and she couldn't. They cried for their momma. She could not understand why her parents and Ted's parents held back the children. The court seemed to be in chaos as she was pushed down the stairs to a waiting van that transported her to a prison intake center.

Alcohol and Drugs

In tracing Tammy's criminal activity from her teenage years to the time she arrived at the prison,, certain outcomes are consistent with other female prisoners who led predatory lifestyles. For example, Tammy was a heroin addict prior to her arrival to prison, and daily she used a number of prescribed antidepressants drugs. In prison, Tammy similar to the other dual addiction prisoners (Annie, Brandeis, Devin, Dory, Jenny Lee, Lilith, and Margo) learned the signs of anxiety disorders in order to be prescribed antidepressant medication by the prison health services. Also, like Brandeis, Jenny Lee, and Margo, Tammy had been addicted to heroin before imprisonment, and used drugs more while imprisoned than other prisoners who had cocaine addictions. Tammy was also an alcoholic when she arrived at prison.

Tammy's Double Life

Considering Tammy's life prior to prison, while her children were present much of her day except when they were in school, it's a wonder how she engaged in heroin, alcohol, and criminal activities for almost eleven years of her marriage. Not to mention when she was a high school and college student, and through her first pregnancy with Aaron. There are indicators that Tammy got addicted to heroin in college, and had been an alcoholic since high school. Some of those indicators were in her journal. She wrote,

> Attitudes about using or not using alcohol start at home—and parents especially fathers and caregivers play the most significant role in the lives of children. My parents pushed me all the time to be a high achiever because they were Harvard grads. 'The road is paved for you, child' was my father's sorrowful phrase that annoyed me to death. Through my last two years of high school, I got high or drunk whenever I could. That was the only time I couldn't see his lips move and I didn't hear his words because I was out of my friggin' tree house. With all his fancy education, why didn't he learn to love me just as I am?
>
> One of my boyfriends, when I was a senior [in high school] thought he owned me, thought he was my father. I drank hard with him and when he entered me, it was never exciting. I thought of McCrazy's (her BFF from grade school) little eyes staring me down and smiled to myself. When he passed out, which he always did after getting drunk and having what he called the wild thing with me, I got even with him and did it with whoever. A couple times with his little brother who was like thirteen. But I never felt him in me just like his friggin' brother who was like a clump of wet clay. One time, my boyfriend's father came into the party room and looked at his passed-out son on the floor and glanced at my outstretched legs. I invited him with a smile. He shook his head in disgust and walked out, never looking back. He was probably as impotent as both of his vegetable sons.

Tammy's Self-Confidence

Tammy's self-confidence depended on how others behaved toward her. Approval was paramount for Tammy. She took the behavior of others as an indicator of her worth. The less worth or human capital she possessed, the less her self-confidence. When she took inventory of herself, she didn't like what she saw or how others treated her once they learned of her addiction, versus who she was and her potential. In an attempt to compensate for their approval ratings, she became frustrated and feared that she had become a junkie. Consequently, as she guzzled more liquor and devoured more drugs, she felt better about herself and her self-confidence increased. The cycle of addiction for Tammy is similar to many addicts.

When Tammy's dangerous decent due to addiction began, it was centered in guilt and her lack of self-control. She realized she wasn't worth salvation—she didn't care. Still, she wanted to make a difference, wanted to be part of the human race, despite the fact that she believed she was worthless. This need seemed to have started early in her childhood, yet what pushed her, what pointed her in the direction of violent crime—and still does, since she continues to commit crimes of violence—is her sincere desire to make things right, to administer justice or retribution. In this sense, similar to her revenger colleagues, Tammy requires personal gratification, despite her inability to play fair. She cared for her materialistic lifestyle, the one her parents provided, even though there was little love shared; and that translated to her leading the double life of a good girl, a good wife, and a good mother who was also a predator.

Other Crimes

It took seven months of prison in-group sessions for Tammy to reveal the details of three amazing stories, which revealed her compulsion toward sexual predatory behavior. The data were offered in bits and pieces. Piecing together her commentary to make sense of it is similar to making a jigsaw puzzle. Frankly, it was a difficult undertaking, since her stories were filled with dead-ends, inconsistencies, and annoying terminology that might indicate a mental limitation—or an intelligence on the part of Einstein's.

Grade School Crime

One of Tammy's typical predatory crimes can be found in her in group journal. She describes one of her lifelong friends, Melissa. Melissa seemed to have few limitations on her behavior, and Tammy called her McCrazy and Stupid Melissa. Melissa shared her ADHD prescription drugs with Tammy, and Tammy shared her cuteness and logical thoughts with McCrazy. This arrangement apparently fused the girls at the hip for most of their youth. Tammy was the girl supposedly grounded in common sense, and McCrazy was the soldier or crazy person who would do anything for her idol, Tammy.

For example, one day when they girls were in sixth grade, McCrazy and Tammy ditched school together, as was their routine whenever Tammy was bored. They decided to visit the local shopping mall, and rode public transportation there. They had made this trip many times before, and would continue to do so through high school. This time, they were on a mission to steal whatever they could. Tammy made all the decisions about what they would steal. They stole anything their fingers touched, and McCrazy tried her best to look like Tammy when she did it. That is, she tried to look cute. Tammy would watch the clerks, usually smiling at them, while McCrazy helped herself to the loot, which included candy bars, makeup, and facial cleaners. They tossed every item into the trash container in the food court, except for the candy bars, which they gave to some older boys who asked them if they wanted drugs. They declined.

At the food court, the girls danced on the chairs and jumped onto the tables, and ran off after some shoppers shouted at them. Tammy remembers one shopper asking, "Why aren't you in school?" Tammy easily recalled the "excitement of it all and I never wanted it to end."

Tammy spotted a baby toddling out of a retail store. "Hey, McCrazy, let's steal that baby." At first, McCrazy was slow to respond, but Tammy approached the child carefully and looked into the store. She saw a woman who appeared to be the baby's mother talking to a clerk. Turning quickly, she smiled at the child and grabbed his hand. McCrazy grabbed the baby's other hand. They glided down a nearby escalator to the first floor stores. As the awkward threesome continued their baby-slow progress through the crowded mall, hard-faced cosmetic ladies with sparkling fingernails waved for the attention of passersby.

Eventually, Tammy picked up the child and headed for the doorway that led to the parking lot. As they exited the mall, they stood staring at the parking lot, wondering what to do next.

"So what now?" McCrazy asked.

Through the rows of automobiles and SUVs, the baby in her arms and McCrazy close behind, Tammy chose an SUV with unlocked doors. Once they were inside the vehicle, the baby cried because it was hotter inside the SUV than outside.

"I checked the baby's diaper," Tammy said, "and realized baby was a boy." She remembers that the baby's penis was so small, it didn't look real. She yanked on the boy's tiny penis while making cooing sounds, "and it didn't move." She cranked it a few times with her fingers and still nothing. "Then I told Stupid Melissa to put her skinny little lips on the baby's thing to see what would happen. No, she pushed at me. I grabbed her with my free hand. 'I want to see it' I told her. 'Make it pop up.'"

After a minute she pulled McCrazy's head up to check her progress. Nothing. The tiny thing wouldn't stiffen. "Maybe it doesn't get hard," McCrazy said, but Tammy just told her she couldn't give head.

"A woman walked by," Tammy said, "and asked if everything was okay. McCrazy told her we were changing a diaper and I gave the woman a cute smile."

Tammy then carelessly spilled the naked tot onto the vehicle's floor, as though it were a doll. Of interest, Tammy reported a strange sensation yanking deep inside her body. "I can't explain it. It's like I was starving or something. There's this thing pulling at my guts, like a big flash of cold air with teeth. Always felt it when I was doing shit. McCrazy and me ran off and caught a bus to hang with our friends. They'd be out of school soon. I held my stomach the whole time and McCrazy stroked my hands every so often. Poor baby, she crooned, and I sort of felt better."

Kidnapping and sexually assaulting this baby boy was not Tammy's first try. She had tried before, once when she alone at the mall. But she realized that after kidnapping a child, she needed an accomplice as a lookout and a participant. No official action ever came of any of Tammy's crimes. In a review of the local newspapers and other sources when Tammy was in sixth grade, nothing was reported about child kidnapping or abductions. However, there were a several brief reports of an unknown suspect harming children as they sat in their strollers at the mall. Two reports were about someone slapping their children, and others were about soft drinks being poured on children.

Another time, Tammy wrote, "McCrazy loved me so much that when I was on a pity hate trip, I asked her to molest me. I would I cling to the floor in a fetal position. McCrazy would pet me and make me feel good. Sometimes she would shove her little fist inside me. She wasn't powerful enough to do it alone unless I cooperated. But I loved the feeling of being forced into sex and being mistreated by different people, but it was always McCrazy. I didn't trust anybody else. Her little eyes would catch mine, but I had to ask her to look mean, look mad, look pissed. She played her role well. I tried to like sex, but it never was my thing."

High School Crime

Tammy's had five close friends, one of them McCrazy. They all hung together at the school cafeteria, at sporting events, and at the mall. Some kids called Tammy's posse the Femme Fatals. They all lived in Tammy's affluent neighborhood and came from similar socioeconomic backgrounds, except Mc Crazy. In middle school, the girls felt they had to protect themselves from other kids who, Tammy said, were jealous of the material things the girls owned. Many kids were bused from poor neighborhoods and thought "they were entitled to everything, even stuff we had. At first, I was polite with them, but after a few months of their arrogant demands, the Femme Fatals came into being." One of the members of Tammy's posse, Nina, was jailed in eighth grade for using her camera to photograph two drunken "entitled kids" beating their school bus driver close to death. Tammy thought that once they got to high school, the entitled kids would be gone. No luck. So she made plans to destroy them.

Alone in the girl's locker room, Tammy and McCrazy were showering when three entitled girls came in, as Tammy knew they would. The plan was for McCrazy to entice the girls to touch her navel ring, which they had admired earlier in the day. When they took the bait, Tammy put a cord around two of their necks from behind. The third girl ran off. The rest of the posse who had been hiding outside, jumped in. They pounded on the entitled girls, but it was Tammy who administered justice.

"Next time the sentence will be death," she said, and with her heel, pushed hard on the girls' lower stomachs as they lay on the shower floor. One of them was bleeding from the fall and still had the cord around her neck. Tammy urinated on them as she stood over them. Later, it was reported that the bleeding girl died as a result of a shower accident. Tammy said, "I didn't snuff the slut, but I thought about it."

In retaliation, another entitled girl brought a bomb to school. Everyone was evacuated. Students and teachers sat on the grounds and in the bleachers at the sports stadium. Tammy decided to talk to one of the entitled girls, the one she thought had brought the bomb to school. The girl smacked Tammy hard, knocking her into the dirt. Tammy's posse gathered around to hide the altercation. While Tammy lay on the ground, she pulled a small metal object from its hiding place and slid it right into her assailant's stomach. As the police arrived, Tammy and her posse each claimed that the object belonged to the other girl. Of course, Tammy and McCrazy "cried like fools for police and teachers, and I produced short quick breaths and fainted, falling lifeless to the ground. They sent me to the hospital's emergency room. McCrazy came with and prayed on her knees the whole time. I didn't have the heart to open my eyes and laugh at Stupid Melissa. All I wanted to do was to talk the slut into turning herself in to the police, because it was the right thing to do. But I made things right."

Prison Crime

During visitation, while Tammy sat at a table near another prisoner whose children were visiting her, Tammy snatched a photograph snapped by prison personnel of the prisoner and her family. Later, she sold the photograph to the prisoner for $50, and then beat the prisoner close to death because she only had $40. Tammy was placed in long-term isolation for the attack. Three months later, she was released, but seemed to be in a trance of sorts. That was common behavior for prisoners in long-term isolation. Tammy had shallow breaths, dilated but still pupils, and an irregular and faint heartbeat. Custody officers requested a nurse move her to the health care unit.

The nurse pushed the wheelchair with Tammy in it. As she rounded a corner, she entered a blind spot, where correctional personnel in the observation room couldn't see her on the live feed. Tammy climbed out of her chair, yanked the nurse's hair, bit her cheek enough so that surgery would be necessary, and pushed her fingers into the nurse's larynx. As the nurse hit the floor, Tammy kicked her many times in the face, and then collapsed in the wheelchair. As officers appeared, she pointed toward the corridor with a fearful look on her face. One of the custody officers pushed Tammy's wheelchair to the health care unit. Upon entering, Tammy attacked the prison guard, but this time the guard quickly overpowered her and threw her to the ground. Tammy jumped up, spat on the officer, and tried to grab her throat. The guard punched her in the stomach and she went down very fast.

Months later, Tammy explained, "I snapped. I don't know what happened. Those segregation units are designed to make prisoners psycho. I wanted to end my life. There is nothing in those cells. No newspapers, no toilet paper, no phone calls, no visitors, no conversation with anybody. I tell you, doc, segregation is designed to keep the jailers happy. They have no other entertainment than to watch me scream and cry and hurt myself. I know they could see me. All that was in that cell was me and my pussy, and she's so wicked-sore that I still can't pee without pain."

Reviewing Ted's Death

After learning about the above crimes and other crimes committed by Tammy, I reviewed the police reports of Tammy's fatal accident. Although my skills as an investigator come nowhere near those of an experienced investigator, I suspected more went on than was first acknowledged. Chances are Tammy was at the party for a "hello and let's go, Ted." Could she have orchestrated the accident and then drunk the liquor in the vehicle, prior to police arriving at the scene? That is certainly plausible. First, in tracing Tammy's trip from her home at seven in the evening with a stop at her in-laws, then the return trip to the time of the accident, it took less than an hour. That's without adding in parking in a high-rise garage, walking to the party, meeting and greeting, drinking, and leaving. Also, Ted was not wearing a seat beat. Consider: a personal injury attorney, during a winter storm, on the highway at approximately 8:30 at night, his wife driving. He was in no condition to drive, suggesting that he was intoxicated. An entry in Tammy's journal read, "Ted died, and that was tragic, but he had it coming." When asked about the entry, Tammy said that Ted shouldn't have drunk so much and he should have worn his seat belt. "He thought he was above the probabilities of the natural law."

Tammy could have staged the accident; she had opportunity and motive. She saw an opportunity—the stalled vehicle on the side of the road—and could have asked Ted to reach for something in the backseat, whereby he'd have to unbuckle his seat belt. Or she could have reached over and unbuckled it herself. After the accident, she could have retrieved the bottle of liquor she'd brought—the police did find an open bottle in the vehicle—and drunk enough to raise her alcohol level to.19. As for motive, he was mean to her. He was like her father. "He had no right to boss me around. He never hit me but he was emotionally draining. I hate that. He reminds me of my drug supplier. Now he was really mean but he knew better than to hit me. I carry a weapon and have a permit for it. And I know how to shoot."

Question: "Tell me about your children?"
Answer: "My children are very different from each other. The ten-year-old was timid and quiet and the baby, verbal and outgoing, which brought him and Margie closer. She's my second child. They were ill often, but a lot of people helped with medication. I hope they're happy now… with someone who can take care of them. I'm no mommy."
Question: "How'd their dad respond to them?"
Answer: "They have different fathers, and I think my eldest considered the new sibling an intense irritation and wanted a return to peaceful singleton days when the he reigned supreme and unrivalled."
Question: "So Ted isn't the boy's father?"
Answer: "No. And I think he guessed that after a while. I guess I'm a prehistoric mommy. The boy's father left us four days after I learned of my pregnancy. Just as well. He was younger than me and wasn't quite keen on becoming a dad, or maybe he just wasn't interested in becoming a husband. We never set out to become parents, although I thought he was happy. He supplied me drugs, and between his attention and drugs, I thought we were happy."

Question: "So what ever happened to him?"

Answer: "I was driving him to the airport and we had a car accident. He died."

Tammy's hidden obsessions and expectations about her lost child, Aaron, are reflected in the short story entitled "Page One." It can be found in chapter 18. Marrying your own son is not a new perspective, and can be found in Greek mythology, in which Gaia married her own son, Uranus. Tammy mentioned that perspective more than once while involved in prison in-group conversations.

CHAPTER 14
Underworld Lilith

Introduction

This chapter provides a description of Lilith's lifestyle prior to her imprisonment. It describes the four most significant experiences in her life. It talks about her arrival at prison and her in-group contributions. Further, it details Lilith's crimes, including lascivious and lewd conduct, prostitution, and trafficking of human beings. There are sex club raids, T-Boys, and strategies to operate sex clubs. Finally, chapter 18 offers a short story called "Afternoon Delight," depicting how a mother brings her sons into the "art" of prostitution and corruption. There are sins of the father that will take on a new meaning as they relate to Lilith's life.

Lilith's Lifestyle Prior to Prison

Describing the lifestyle of a mob boss and his family would require volumes, so I will keep this brief. Lilith's childhood bedroom windows allowed a view of Cape Cod Bay, an elegant sight at first light. Her twin sisters Angelina and Carmen were twelve years younger and had a bedroom facing inland, with a view of Harwick Center and the Long Pond. Until the twin's arrival, Lilith resided in the Cape Cod estate with servants and occasionally her father. Actually, he was often present, but enjoying a Cuban cigar and a young girl somewhere on the estate where Lilith wasn't allowed to go. All in all, Lilith slept in a wonderful bedroom of an extravagant seaside estate, with its own marbled bathroom and a walk-in closet the size of an 18-wheeler. The thirty-five room estate, along with its many concealed rooms, had six full baths and a lagoon-style pool with a waterfall that fell into Cape Cod Bay below.

Lilith's father, Mario 'Merle' DeStefano, built the 8,500 square foot estate, which resembled an ancient castle, on a bluff overlooking the bay and near a tiny hamlet, after careful research and planning. Part of his research included his desire for privacy, a residence somewhere between New York City and Boston, and a community where his daughter would be protected from destructive city life. He was intrigued with the town because of its history. It was connected to a town in United Kingdom called Budleigh Salterton. The Cape also provided Merle easy access to the powerful American political families that relied on their connections to keep a handle on labor unions, and to keep the remaining family members alive, rather than gunned down by another assassin's bullet.

Merle was an underworld boss who managed the mob's eastern brothels and dealt with various labor union representatives from New York City to Portland, Maine. He also had a reputation to uphold as a man of honor, like a contemporary Robin Hood who provided help to the poor at the expense of the rich. Or at least he thought of himself that way. Merle wrapped his respectability into his personal pleasures, which included smoking Cuban cigars, attending Broadway musicals, and satisfying young girls. Merle could not be bothered with the mundane rituals of a father. He was a labor leader of sorts, a racketeer, and a lover. He carefully hired domestic help that took care of his daughter and his castle overlooking the bay. The twins were a surprise twelve years later.

Lilith's mother was a trendy twenty-first century woman, but stayed pretty much to herself and her career. She was an artist and owned her own art gallery. She lived in her own residence on Park Avenue in Manhattan, except during the winter months. Then she traveled to Naples, Italy, and spent the holidays with her parents, the Sanvis. Lilith's mother and her mother's parents, as well as scores of her cousins, would often visit Lilith and Merle at the Cape Cod estate. Lilith was always excited and pleased during those visits, because her visitors brought her elegant and strange gifts wrapped in silver and gold paper. The gift cards were signed by some amusing aunt or cousin, who would seem familiar to Lilith. But she would never be quite sure who the person was, until he or she pointed at a previous gift given Lilith, displayed in a large glass curio cabinet in the library. Lilith remembers her mother's side of the family as reserved, educated, and generous, "but regrettably, they brought few children for me to play with when I was younger unlike my father's side of the family."

In short, since her birth, Lilith could have anything she wanted, other than her father's or her mother's care and attention.

Early Childhood Experiences

Despite Merle's personal pleasures, he raised Lilith among a sea of loud and boisterous relatives, whose children were also loud and boisterous. They visited the Cape Cod estate, too, but never at the same time the Sanvi family. Merle's family members rarely brought gifts for Lilith, but those were exciting times for her nonetheless. She looked forward to playing with her cousins on the estate grounds. A long winding path led to the estate's private beach. She really thought it odd that many of her aunts and uncles and cousins, on both her mother's and father's sides of the family, spoke Italian, and she set out to learn that language with the aid of private tutors. Much to her disappointment, she learned that she had to master two languages. She discovered that the Sanvi family members spoke a different form of Italian from the DeStefanos, who spoke more Sicilian. She did her best to learn both languages. She learned their cultures, too, and understood why the Sanvis were reserved while the DeStefanos were nosy and uneducated. As you probably guessed already, Lilith was homeschooled at the lower grade levels. That changed when she enrolled herself in the local public high school. She wanted to be around the friends she had met at the country club and church. Merle never realized that his daughter was a typical high school girl attending classes, sporting events, and dances until her junior year, when she had been approached by federal agents at school.

She and Merle decided on a plan. Well, Merle decided on a plan and she agreed because she wanted to continue at high school. She became his driver and understudy during the summer and school holidays. At the time, she was curious about what an understudy was. She was an excellent student and always wanted to learn new things, but being an understudy was also fun. Her understudy efforts included mock interviews with federal and local law enforcement personnel, narratives linked to mediation initiatives with mock city and state officials, and drama skills related to spontaneous improvisation similar to that of a Broadway artist. She learned how to compose answers and remember details about those who approached her at school and elsewhere. *"Dettagii, dettagii, dettagii,"* (Details, details, details) Merle yelled from the backseat of his fancy vehicle as she drove. Despite Merle's concern to educate her, even to the point of providing an experienced coach, she described Merle as a lapsed father who never expressed or showed his love for her. Even her birthdays were spent with servants or at the country club. Their relationship, she said, was always that of "boss versus worker. Driving him around meant I wouldn't be an orphan and I could learn something about the man I called Merle. I wanted to do that at the time, but I also wanted to get out and see Boston and New York City. Maybe I could see my mother when I was in the city too." Many of Lilith's high school classmates thought she was very cool driving her father around, Lilith wrote in her prison journal. She also wrote about the most significant experiences in her life.

Most Significant Experiences

Lilith had four significant experiences:

1. The debutante's ball, where she made her formal debut into society. Months prior to her eighteenth birthday, debate raged about the theme dresses worn by the girls. The committee finally settled on the Katharine Hepburn look, but it was almost the Garbo look, to which Lilith was aggressively opposed. She made her feelings known at one of the debutante committee meetings at the country club.

2. The death of Merle, which appeared to be the result of a mysterious assassination, rather than a massive heart attack. Lilith was driving the vehicle when he died.

3. Her reckoning with Merle's occupation and his entire family:

grandparents, aunts, uncles, cousins, and her godparents, who all thought they were political demigods in their own rights, but were rude, loud, and boisterous.

4. Her conviction on drug charges and her prison life. "No one can imagine the deficiency of prison life until you're here."

Criminal Conviction

Lilith was convicted of unlawful possession of a controlled substance—twenty-five grams of heroin. At least fourteen grams but less than twenty-eight grams requires a mandatory minimum five-year sentence, or a maximum of twenty years. Lilith negotiated a plea bargain during the trial prior to the jury's deliberation, and accepted a seven-year prison sentence with parole potential at the end of four years. After twenty-four months, Lilith was released early from prison for good behavior.

Investigations to Arrest and Indict Lilith

There had been many attempts by federal and state law enforcement agencies to arrest Lilith. First, the federal government attempted a racketeering charge against her. Racketeering is a broad term that encompasses many types of criminal activity. In a range of cases, racketeering charges can be filed under the Racketeer Influenced and Corrupt Organizations Act (RICO), passed in 1961. The legal apparatus of federal and state government was perplexed by their failures to indict Lilith DeStefano. After another failed attempt a few years later, the high court of the Commonwealth of Massachusetts reaffirmed its position through a statement: "Because organized crime carries on its activities through layers of insulation and behind a wall of secrecy, government has been unsuccessful in curtailing and eliminating it. Normal investigative procedures are not effective in the investigation of illegal acts committed by organized crime. Therefore, law enforcement officials must be permitted to use modern methods of electronic surveillance, under strict judicial supervision, when investigating these organized criminal activities."

Because Lilith operated brothels, Massachusetts attempted to indict her on "crimes against chastity, morality, decency and good order," but that charge couldn't even pass a grand jury's indictment. There was also an unsuccessful attempt to indict her locally on buildings used for prostitution, assignation, or just plain lewdness. Finally, the only successful avenue available to prosecutors was a Commonwealth charge of drug possession, which at least placed Lilith in the system. The prosecutor who indicted her and conducted her prosecution, and who accepted her guilty plea, was involved in a sex scandal that eventually cost him his license to practice law. The scandal happened during the small window of time, when the judge was studying presentence investigation report before handing down a criminal sanction against Lilith. The prosecutor attended a legal conference in Springfield, Massachusetts, and his wife and children thought they would surprise him with a visit. They discovered him unconscious and apparently intoxicated, but intimate with a woman, Lilith DeStefano. Photographs were taken by newspaper reporters covering the conference, and those reports and pictures hit the *Boston Globe* within hours of the incident. The judge decided to honor Lilith's guilty plea and sentenced her.

Arrival at Prison

When Lilith arrived at the state penitentiary for women, her incident with the prosecutor was still on the front pages of the *Boston Globe*. It was easy to get the impression that every prisoner and everyone linked to the prison system, from the warden to officers who delivered her there seemed to applaud her. Then, too, her reputation as an entrepreneur and a gangster preceded her. Lilith, thirty-five years old, possessed a physique and an infectious smile that made her seem fifteen years younger. It was evident that this woman never required makeup or a designer's wardrobe to capture anyone's gaze, even in her baggy orange prison jumpsuit. But any observer would never suspect that Lilith was an alcoholic and had a dual addiction. Cocaine before incarceration and heroin after, and antidepressants. In the eyes of the average observer, Lilith was both dazzling to look at and high-functioning, especially when she was using drugs and alcohol. During her prison sentence, Lilith was often placed on suicide watch in a special wing of the prison, although there were rumors that she actually left the prison or had visitors in the isolation unit. She was never written up for disciplinary action and was never restricted in prison. Her health while imprisoned was good, even though she slept between one and three hours a day. Lilith had two sons: fourteen-year-old Sonny and twelve-year-old Michael. She was unmarried when she gave birth to Sonny, and married his father, only to divorce him later. By the time Lilith arrived at prison, she had three ex-husbands that visited her, sometimes in pairs and other times all together. Lilith also had the best quarters in prison, and didn't share her cell with anyone, which was highly unusual in any prison system. While in prison, many of Lilith's prior aliases became known. She was called Belili by some, but Lilly was her favorite nickname. Her PSI reported a host of other aliases, including Belili Accardo, Lilly Accardo, Lilly DeStafano, Lynn Lombardo, Lilith Stefano, Lilith Sanvi, and Lilith Sealy.

Some Observations about Lilith

Some knew that upon the death of Merle DeStefano, twenty-six-year-old Lilith succeeded him on his underworld throne and managed the brothels, the local unions, and the family members who worked in or had financial interests in the organization with professionalism and expertise. Although Lilith had been Merle's understudy since high school, he would be proud of her accomplishments, because Lilith produced greater financial returns with fewer consequences than he ever had. He would be proud, too, that she loved crime for the sake of crime itself. Or maybe he knew that when he was alive and took her under his wing. He often provided her with old Sicilian proverbs to live by. His favorite was *"Cui si marita, sta cuntenti un jornu, Cu' ammazza un porcu, sta cuntenti un annu"* (Who gets married will be happy for a day, who butchers a pig will be happy for a year). In keeping with her namesake, the demon in ancient accounts, Lilith loved crime. She gave the appearance of being compassionate, focused, and pure, and her charade worked. Her ruthless, spontaneous, and violent behavior rarely took center stage, because she never competed with anyone for her throne. But what wind is to cyclones, Lilith is to corruption. She is the both the catalyst and the effect.

In-Group

Lilith dominated conversations during in-group sessions, sometimes to the point of alienating other prisoners and as well as psychologists and group leaders, but it was never in anyone's interest to object. In her journal, she wrote about something that greatly concerned her. It was about the new wars in the Mideast. "It was odd how the American public criticized Muslim women and their dominance by their men when Italian women once were expected to wash their men's shirts whether those men were their husbands or their fathers, but now those women are found to be laundering their money and running their enterprises more efficiently then the men they replaced." Yet the federal government, Lilith wrote, "has little respect for Italian or Muslim women and think they are all connected to the mafia or enablers of terrorists and passive. My little sister Angelina when a grad student at NYU was nabbed for drug dealing because of her family name. I told her to change her last name. No, she said. I am Angelina DeStefano. I am me."

Lilith explained how, when she was in high school, federal agents came to the school to question her. "When I was hanging with friends, same thing. One time I was at the homecoming bonfire before the big football game." The feds raided it, and in front of her classmates explained in vivid detail what Lilith's father did for living. She said that "it got so sickening that I couldn't go anywhere. I grew bitter because of the feds' insults and disrespect. They talked to all my friends and my friends' parents about me. They talked to my teachers and my priest. They talked to my gynecologist about my birth control pills. Talk about racial profiling. Other minorities didn't have it bad when you compare how the government treats Italian and Muslim children."

Following her father's instructions, Lilith wrote down everything about each interaction with each federal and local law enforcement officer including names, eye color and other physical attributes along with her observations included if an officer wore glasses, about the rings on their fingers, the watches on their wrists, and about their gestures and mannerisms. Lilith also arranged to have the agents photographed before, during, and after most of those intrusions, especially when they were conducted later in her life at her offices in New York City and Boston, on the street, and at restaurants and church. When she could have their conversations recorded, they were recorded. The feds had few ideas why Lilith was so cooperative. When she engaged in other crimes, her notes and photographs became assets and her businesses flourished.

Prostitution

Lilith moved the brothel underworld of New York City and Boston in a new direction. "Hypothetically," she said, "I would imagine that for years, the difficulties in recruiting young men and women into the business was an enormous and expensive operation. I'd bet that recruiters searched rehabilitation clinics, jails, schools, and streets for productive candidates to join their brothels." Training lasted for twelve weeks at "stores" near Chicago, Las Vegas, Miami, and New York City. "Hypothetically, I would imagine that professional brothel training is an expensive concern: food, shelter, and medical necessities. Protection from the cops, local politicians, and other gangs trying to make their mark. The gangs causing the most commotion are probably gangs such as Mara Salvatrucha." She went on to say that one way to determine if a trainee "would be productive is if she earned her keep, theoretically, you know. This calculation is based on the equation of income versus expenses." She explained that good girls were known as 5 percenters, because they earn above 95 percent of their individual expenses. Average girls earned 90 percent or below their expenses, and were shipped off to farms where customers lined up for early bird specials, amounting to ten or twenty dollars a pop, regardless if the customer is capable or ready. "Hypothetically," she went on, "5 percenters received advanced training, psychologically and physically, professional protection, fringe benefits, which included weekly medical exams, new identities, and a comfortable lifestyle." Eventually 5 percenters held a high-paying position in exclusive brothels that catered to a wealthy clientele.

"For those clients, I would imagine, money was less a concern than safety and confidentiality. Hypothetically, some of those fashionable brothels are aboard elegant ocean-going vessels, penthouses overlooking Central Park and Boston Commons, and at secluded mansions, such as those at Newport, Rhode Island. If you're not a wealthy, lonely, and immoral soul, this all sounds like a fantasy factory produced by

Hollywood or MTV. But in the real world, wealthy, immoral people pay for intimacy." Lilith added that "It's not sex these clients seek, it's the admiration of a beautiful creation. And who is more admirable than a woman like me?" She laughed and placed her hands on her hips.

"What would a wealthy man give to once again capture that sweet smile of his first lover? And when it comes to accommodating and treating clients like farm animals, no one does it better than a desperate young foreign girl wanting to pay her travel debt and bring her family to America. Boys do it better because they have more body strength and can accomplish things with ease and dignity." With that said, we all waited for Lilith to add her favorite word, and we weren't disappointed. "Hypothetically, that is," she tagged on with a smile.

During one in-group session, when Lilith talked about her father, a participant asked, "When your dad died— I mean, Merle. What did you do?"

Lilith thought for a moment. "Since you want to know what I did, I guess it's okay to tell you. No, I didn't cry, but I had every piece of furniture in his bedroom removed and burned. Then the walls, floors, and ceilings were remodeled. Bought new furniture, and slept there every so often between husbands. My husbands slept in that room and I slept in my own bedroom and in my own bed." She paused. "What? That's not what you want to know?"

The other woman said slowly, "No, no, you're fine. Thanks."

"I want no man smell in my bed. They're good for one thing and when it's over they go to their bed and leave me to my peace."

Trafficking of Human Beings

Lilith said she read a lot, and she saw an interesting article about human trafficking. In the early summer of 2002, two foreign exchange university students, "hypothetically, let's call them Svetlana and Larisa from Taras Shevchenko University in Kiev, Ukraine. The girls looked forward to a summer job placement in New York City. As the girls were processed through US customs after their hypothetical flight, they saw signs bearing their names held by two men, who turned out to be fellow countrymen. They greeted the girls, dealt with their luggage, and took them to dinner. The men must have known they were being video-recorded, but apparently they didn't care. How arrogant! The following day—theoretically that is," she emphasized, "Svetlana and Larisa took a flight to Boston, where they were escorted to their new work assignment."

Their passports and clothes were taken from them, they were drugged, persuaded to submit to sexual contact, taught how to professionally strip down and wrap their long legs around a dance pole. Because they wanted to earn money, they had many sex partners while submerged in what can be described as a mental haze or drug heaven.

Lilith explained that trafficking is the responsibility of the countries the kids come from, because those counties propagate violence against women and children. "Think of the wartime rape houses in those crazy countries. Hooking in the US is humane. Merle always said, Better an egg today than the chicken tomorrow."

Lilith's written work suggests that professionally operated brothels helped foreigners learn a profession, instead of living like the "hordes of humanity," as Lilith referred to society in general. I got the impression that she convinced many of her sexual slaves, through her recruiters, to come to America to work. In fact, she read somewhere that transporting five schoolgirls across the Mexican-US border is less dangerous than transporting half their combined weight in marijuana.

Lascivious Acts

It can be surmised through Lilith's statements and records, as well as a search of newspapers, that her trafficked hookers were deprived of their personal property and identification, including passports. Lilith's organization then obtained credit cards for the hookers, with work verification and addresses. Purchases were made on the credit cards for such things as hotels and airline tickets for future hookers. Lilith's organization committed a credit card "bust-out" by running up charges on those credit cards, inflating their credit limits, and then placing additional charges on those cards. These activities relate to identity theft, grand theft, and credit card fraud. Lilith's knowledge of credit card fraud and bust-outs is so reliable, other prisoners paid her in goods, services, and respect for lessons. Once released, many of those prisoners went to work for Lilith.

Amazingly, the Department of Corrections attempts to teach prisoners how to apply for minimum wage jobs at places like McDonalds, and how to jump off the drug train; while Lilith taught prisoners a profession that daily matched my yearly income. Among Lilith's collection of decadent talents is her natural ability to motivate the "hordes of humanity" to conform to her perspectives. Unlike most of the women I've encountered at women's prisons, Lilith rose to her natural level of stardom or celebrity status and took control, unlike many of the prisoners, who become exaggerated versions of themselves in one way or another. It was as if they lacked different experiences to shape themselves, so they repeated the same old march to the same drum roll, over and over, until only the sound of pounding feet could be heard within the hard penitentiary walls. Lilith was a shooting star, disliked but admired, and to please her meant success and protection now or in the future.

She said that sex is natural and animals did it all the time, so why was it bad. Yet the realization of her conquest would beg the question about her own sons, Sonny and Michael. Lilith believed that young boys made profitable prostitutes. Some of the evidence she offered suggested that she had engaged Sonny, her eldest son, in what she called the art of prostitution. She referred to prostitution as both a profession and an art because "prostitutes must be great actors. The difference between a $5 tip or a $100 tip and a return customer is about fulfilling fantasies. It's about theater! A patron will always get off, one way or another, but it is how the customer got off that counts and how the artist responds to the customer."

Thinking inside the box, so to speak, what had Merle turned his daughter into? The investigation into Lilith's life prior to sentencing never came close to the subject of her children, other than to confirm their existence and their comfortable lifestyle, secured by their twenty-three-year-old aunts. Lilith's sisters and the boys all resided at the Cape Cod estate.

T-Boys

Lilith made comments in-group that suggested young boys, or T-Boys, could earn (ten years ago) $5,000 a night. With the help of a professional manager, they could enter into an arrangement for better than two million dollars for three evenings a month over a ten-month period with several clients. The manager was expected to supply food and beverages, amenities such as a facility for bathing, male enhancement drugs, and clothing. The rendezvous might be on yacht, a private jet, or a secluded mansion. Lilith's son Sonny could be defined as a T-Boy.

One definition of a T-Boy is a boy who behaves like a girl during sexual encounters. A T-Boy, at least among those in the sex industry, continues to have all his male body parts, which turns a higher price tag than others. The best T-Boys in the US are trafficked from Southeast Asia, especially Burma and Thailand. But white, particularly American, T-Boys are in huge demand.

Lilith explained that T-Boys are physically male, but with the aid of surgery and medications possess some female physical features, such as small hands and feet, hairless limbs, and breasts. A T-Boy's sexual behavior during encounters emulates stereotypical female sexual behavior: numerous smiles during the encounter, facial expressions denoting disbelief and surprise, loud sounds when penetrated. Through it all, a T-Boy maintains an erection (thanks to male enhancement drugs), which acts as a handle for some patrons and something to kiss for others.

Lilith described T-Boys as easy to manage compared to "drama queen whores." Professional T-Boys genuinely wanted to please their managers (that is, pimps) all the time, without the emotional mood swings of drama queens. "They have their moments, but their dependence and emotional bond on their handlers is greater than others. The drawbacks are that they require constant protection even during sessions, confidentiality—which means they don't run around town or go to hotel rooms unescorted—and their patrons must be screened to eliminate freaks, especially people who like to beat on T-Boys." It was at this point, Lilith would say or write, "Or so I read in *Time* or *Cosmo*." She'd look around the room at the other prisoners, who were usually eager to hear what she had to say about this or that. The prisoners also enjoyed hearing her Sicilian proverbs, and would stare at the woman they admired most while waiting for the English translation.

T-Boys, Lilith said, "have constant requirements for discretion. Like health aid, particularly in the early stages of their professional career. Boobs, of course, but not too big, hollowing of their back, Brazilian butt lifts, and anus bleaching to be pretty. And they must stay thin, so their food consumption is monitored. But with all the drugs they take to stay pretty, few are tempted to eat. I read somewhere."

One prisoners asked, "Bleaching?"

"No one wants to see a dirty you-know-what."

Children's Visits

When Sonny and Michael visited their mother at prison, they were described as handsome or cute, but one correctional officer said, "They seemed much younger their age. On some of the visits, Sonny and Michael were accompanied by Aunt Carmen and Aunt Angelina. A strip search was not required of the boys, though they were given a pat down. "The boys never made eye contact with anyone and they don't look around. Most kids are always looking around in the visitor waiting room and when they get to see their parent or whatever. These kids mostly looked down. Seemed passive. Never fussed. Never got up and touched the vending machines like the other kids and never went to the john. When I was on watch during the visitation, the mom never tried to sneak a hug. That's unusual for convicts with kids. As soon as they see each other, they're all over each other. Can't keep their hands down. But, hey, who knows, because when their mom is in any room, all eyes are on her. She's one fine chunk of womanhood."

Sex Club Raids

The following information was provided in part by Lilith, but as curious writers write, we research or dig into other people's business.. Sometimes getting information is easy if you know where to look and who to ask. For instance, hypothetically that is, if you were a professor at UMass Boston, and a lot of your students were police officers and employed in the Commonwealth's justice department, information is easy to get. That said, prior to Lilith's conviction, there were a number of raids of Boston and New York City's sex clubs. Some of those clubs were considered famous, and the raids were reported in the newspapers and on television news reports. Most reopened days later at the same location or down the block. It was as if the raids were for the purpose of publicity. For instance, Little John's Club in Manhattan, a strip club that catered to the city's conventioneers, had been an integral part of the city's largest conventions and trade shows, including the National Association of Chain Drug Stores, American Academy of Dermatology, and Home Builders Association. For these conventions, thousands of delegates would arrive in the city, set up exhibits, and attended meetings at the convention centers. They were also customers in hotels, bars, restaurants, and at Lilith's sex clubs. Some of those customers appeared by special invitation, others through the efforts of the grapevine. They went to Lilith's for the exotic pole dancers decorated with body glitter, garters, and Lucite platforms at the end of very long legs. They came for the lap dances. They came for memories of their first kiss.

When the federal agents and the local cops raided Little John's Club, twenty-seven girls and seven boys were taken into custody. Many of them came from former republics of the Soviet Union and from Southeast Asia. Now they were drug addicts, but different girls were on different drugs. Each managers developed his or her own combination of drugs. Two girls died as a result of the inability of the authorities to help them through their withdrawals while in custody. Overburdened drug labs couldn't help, and none of the girls knew what drugs they had consumed—nor did they care.

Lilith the Mentor

Many of those in custody were shown an assortment of photographs of women and asked if they recognized any of them. The photos included Lilith, Princess Diana, and the first lady of the US. Most recognized Princess Diana and the first lady. As for Lilith, one person said, "This one I recognize as a person I saw at the club, I think." A customer reported that she was a bartender, while another thought she was a client." One flatly said, "That one. That's Lilly."

That was the first time authorities realized that Lilith was commonly known as Lilly. Employees at the club reported that Lilly was knowledgeable and caring. She showed them what to do if, for example, a client was unable to perform and wanted his money back. She was reserved with most of the staff, but she engaged in unnatural and lascivious acts with some of the young trainees, in an attempt to improve their "entertainment quality," without identifying herself as that boss.

One girl said that Lilly "helped me build my confidence when I dance." Another said, "She taught me to hook up my neon thong and taught me to be a very exotic girl." And a third: "Lilly taught me how to put on my makeup without looking like a freak." What was learned about Lilly from the interviews with the employees was that she trained most of personnel, from the bartenders, to the doormen, to the dancers. It was also clear that Lilly possessed enormous patience, perseverance, and warm regard for her workers at all levels, and she held their respect and loyalty, regardless of the consequences of what she was teaching them.

For instance, Lilly taught the prostitutes over a long period of time to appreciate themselves, to enjoy their jobs of pleasing patrons. She helped each of them develop a willingness to satisfy a huge range of client requests, which included social and sexual skills. She helped most of them to be less fearful of the odd sadomasochistic requests; aided them to in avoiding police surveillance and entrapment procedures; instructed them how to avoid drunk clients who had no cash; helped them to substitute a business ethic for a hooker ethic; and, compellingly, aided them to identify with themselves as prostitutes and not fallen girls or boys. This occupation was a choice they made, and they should be proud of who and what they had become—a whore. Lilly was their teacher, their mentor, and often their mother, and at the same time, their enslaver. "Chains and slavery are old school," Lilith might say. "Education and enhancement glorifies slavery."

The implications reveal that recruiting and operating an American brothel through human trafficking strategies requires professional expertise and experience, in concert with local and foreign governments and their law enforcement agencies.

Operating Sex Clubs, Payoffs, and Conventioneers

The information that follows was obtained from newspaper articles, official reports, and Lilith herself.

The cover charge at the sex clubs was $20 for new patrons and $15 for conventioneers who showed their badges at the door. All purchases for sexual services in the Champagne Room were paid in advance. Lap dances started at $100 for house dancers for each patron at a table. Boy dancers were $125 for each patron at a table, and all patrons had to purchase a bottle of reasonable quality champagne for $50.00. Glasses were extra but free for conventioneers. Each patron paid $50.00 for a condom, $50.00 for music, and it was expected that at a table of four or less, the tip would be at least $100. Credit cards were accepted. Credit card numbers and security codes were duplicated and used outside the club by Lilith's organization. Paychecks and money orders were cashed for a fee, and most of the money was retained for services (lap dances, oral sex, and "rub and tugs") and liquor. For any patron who parked near the clubs, license plate numbers and vehicle identification numbers were recorded for future reference. Photographs were taken by club photographers and were sold (for $100) to patrons, but they were also stored for future use. It is likely that many of the photos of men in compromising positions were used for extortion long after a conventioneer left the city.

Additionally, arrangements that included payoffs of cash and sex to hotel personnel (the front desk, bellboys, spa attendants, food and beverage waiters and waitresses, doormen) assured crowded shuttle buses of conventioneers from hotels to Lilith's sex clubs, which dotted the city. Restaurant, theater, and taxi personnel also received gratuities—payoffs, sex, and sometimes jobs—from the sex clubs to guide or transport patrons to those destinations of lust and fun. For instance, one hotel bartender and his brother, who worked as a doorman, were successful over a four-month period. They made arrangements for over 500 guests to one strip club. In return for their hard work, the strip club provided a private bachelor party for the bartender and forty of his guests, which included food, drink, and lap dances. Only a generous tip was required, and whatever else the girls (and their handlers) manipulated from the patrons.

Additionally, hotel personnel and taxi and limo drivers who safely returned club patrons to their hotel rooms were equally rewarded. Police officers and emergency medical technicians were always in for a treat when patrons arrived quickly and without incident to their hotel rooms. Above all, the care provided call girls who were visiting patrons in their hotel rooms could be especially rewarding, including job promotions for the cops, family vacations for the medical personnel, and new clients for the limo services. As for other businesses in and near the sex clubs including hotels, bars, and restaurants, each business relied on a city license to be able to operate, and Lilith's organization had more than one city politician indebted to her, either through vote-getting initiatives or extortion, which aided her ability to get liquor licenses. Businesses that served food and liquor relied on the delivery services of local truck drivers, and Lilith's organization controlled the drivers' labor unions, which included taxi and limo services. Piss her off and no deliveries. Lilith's organization also influenced or controlled the trade labor unions, which included the police officers' union, and had influence among the police officer fraternal organizations and associations. But other businesses were also persuaded to aid Lilith's enterprise, such as the hotels chains and popular restaurants. For example, refrigeration breaks down and technicians must be called, who are labor union members.

Lilith's organization dictated to many business which products could be delivered; which waste management company to contract for trash removal; which linen company maintained their personnel's uniforms, tablecloths, and other items; and of course, each of those providers were under Lilith's thumb. They, too, had personnel who visited the strip clubs and sex clubs, but mostly in the afternoons. Nights were reserved for city visitors.

Final Thoughts: Special FBI Agents in Her Jean Pocket

A final thought about Lilith DeStefano. The reluctance of local law enforcement, state troopers, and the FBI to offer substantial evidence for federal and state prosecutors to pursue meaningful indictments against Lilith suggests that the notes she kept paid dividends. There is little doubt that if anyone had a fed in her pocket, it's Lilith. Once she was released from prison, many were shocked that she served so little time. Local newspapers covered the story as a huge event. Lilith married again and continues to operate her family's business.

Just for the record, Lilith points out that according to legend, Lilith was a female demon who searched for newborn children to kidnap or to strangle. Or, in Lilith DeStefano's case, to prostitute. Another legend is that God created Adam and Lilith as twins joined together at the back. Lilith demanded equality with Adam. When she didn't get that, she left Adam, who became very angry. In his anger, Adam called on God to provide him a passive woman—Eve. Lilith explained, "So what's the big deal? All I did was employ Eve to give men what they want. There's an old Sicilian proverb that says *Zoccu è datu da Diu, nun pò mancari.*" (What is given by God, can't be wrong).

CHAPTER 15
Val, an Irish Gypsy

Introduction

Valerie Audrey Carroll, or Val, was from an obscure American subculture that most of us know little about. As a long time educator, I found that when gypsies or Irish Travelers were mentioned in class, students paused, revealing that few were aware of Irish Travelers. For right now what you need to know is that Val was born and reared among affluent and clannish Irish Travelers. She said she lived in a McMansion in Border Village, South Carolina. She was the newest arrival to a Traveler family that already had four boys who resembled one another, down to their short red hair, deep blue eyes, and endless red freckles. Each possessed a wiry, tall frame. Even at twenty-eight years of age, when Val was imprisoned, she resembled her brothers more than a girl. Prison entrance personnel joked that she never shaved anywhere. "Even down there," they said. "It looked like a vineless tomato patch."

Val pled guilty to second degree murder of an elderly couple in Columbus, Ohio. During the trial and prior to jury deliberation, she negotiated a punitive sentence of seven years, which included no option for early release.

When Val entered the penitentiary, she was married with three children. Two boys were fourteen and thirteen, and her daughter was twelve. She was a grandmother; her oldest son had two children. Her daughter was either about to be married or had recently married. Val's occupation was listed as unemployed, and under Remarks, she was referred to as an Irish gypsy. For the record, the intake officer misspelled the word gypsy.

Isolation

Irish Travelers, Val explained, "Take care of their own." For example, similar to all the Traveler children, Val attended the only church and the only school in the village where they lived. The church was supposedly Catholic. Large gold letters on the front wall proclaimed it was St. Patrick's Catholic Church and School. It displayed Christian crosses and had a steeple reaching high toward heaven, but the Pope was never mentioned. This church apparently was a remnant of the Reformation, and somehow existed on its own without interference. The pastor and the principal of the school were both Irish Travelers. Records showed that Val attended a local catholic school for nine years, which was the extent of her formal education.

Border Village has its own police and fire departments staffed by Travelers and supported by the Traveler council. The community members shopped at the small cluster of local retail establishments owned by other community members in the area. Conspicuously absent from the shopping area was any room for parking. The stores were built around a garden, and signs leading to the area proclaimed No Parking, Vehicles Will be Towed. Travelers also purchased online products not available locally, and those items were shipped to local post office boxes or the church. Most Travelers lived in huge homes equipped with amazing amenities, but unlike Val's *Wicked Women* colleagues, her homes did not have servants. Outsiders did not visit, repair, or maintain them. Outsiders were not welcomed. Marriage, childbirth, and death were private matters and conducted in the homes. The isolation and anonymity of each Irish Traveler was complete.

McMansions

Val resided in a huge home. It had an indoor and outdoor swimming pool, a bowling lane, and a unique widow's walk that was never used. That's the winter-spring home. Her family also had a summer McMansion that sat on a lake high in the Appalachian Mountains.

Both homes were ornate, their many rooms soaring to cathedral ceilings and crown molding. Other rooms had hidden staircases that led to concealed rooms, where ceremonies were conducted. They were also used as places of meditation, or places to be protected from southern storms or county deputies.

Val wrote in her prison journal that where she grew up, the McMansion had distinctive architecture. They were huge, two or three stories, with pink stucco and columns. The circular driveways were packed with expensive vehicles, especially SUVs that were usually red or yellow. Outside there was little vegetation and no trees; yet a rock garden was often situated pretentiously on the property, with a water fountain crowded with statues of the Virgin Mary and angels. Inside the houses would be glossy porcelain statues of Jesus and the Madonna. Val described one new house that was decorated in pink: pink leather sofa, pink curtains, pink molding, and pink lamps. Even the cape around the shoulders of the baby Jesus statue was pink.

The windows of the homes were often covered with tinfoil to keep evil spirits from entering the house during family events, such as childbirth, death, or other impure rituals. During those times, family members resided in a double-wide mobile homes stationed permanently in the back of the McMansion. Many generations of family members live in the same house. For instance, in Val's early childhood home, her parents and brothers lived with her paternal grandparents and one great-grandmother; her maternal grandparents and her grandfather's brother. She was never entirely sure who lived there, since every day brought new and unknown family members to the house. With such a large number of people living together, it is easy to get the impression that everyone got in everyone else's way. That might be true, except most of the men often traveled, especially to the New England states; and it might be true except for Val. Her explosive temper earned her private time.

Marriage

Irish Travelers are related to one another, or so the story goes, and they have married cousins, whether first or second. The boy's family always provides a substantial dowry to the girl's family and the

Traveler's organization, Val explained. She was married at fourteen years of age to a fifteen-year-old boy who was her first cousin. Husbands moved to their wives' homes. Also, married girls did not change their surnames to protect their identity, and to shield their families from legal complications concerning consent laws and contributing to the delinquency of minor charges. But as fate had it, Val Audrey Carroll married Shaun Carroll.

Wary of Strangers

Because the Travelers are discriminated against today, as they have been throughout their history, they are usually silent about their ethnicity. That's one point of view. Val explained that because of the discrimination, many verbal codes were developed among the Travelers, such as having two names. One is private and for family use; and other name is public and used for official records, insurance, driver's licenses, property taxes, and conducting business. The public name is often chosen as the most common name in the area where the Travelers settle. For instance, in Border Village, among an estimated 5,000 people, there are but a dozen surnames. Some are Carroll, Costello, Gorman, Murphy, O'Hara, and Sherlock. There are even fewer first names. Coinciding with the few surnames are also social security numbers that do not necessarily match the population. There can be a dozen Val Audrey Carrolls living at the same address with the same social security number.

"I tell you this," Val said, "because I am not the Val Audrey Carroll who committed the crimes I was arrested."

She went on to explain that "State authorities have little clue who lives in my home. There are few street signs [in the town] and those change from block to block." Most often the Travelers "used post office box numbers as street addresses. And most everyone has a private or family name: Black Pete, Bo, Mic Boy, White Man, Z Girl, Teatime, or Lee Gal. Me? I'm called Buama."

Confirmation of Val's thoughts were found in the local sheriff's office of Aiken County, SC. He took several Irish Travelers into custody on March 16, 1997. *The Augusta Chronicle,* the largest newspaper in the area, reported that tax evasion charges had been filed against Pete "Tick"

Carroll, P.O. Box 6592, Butterfly Drive, three counts; Tommy Joe "Big Joe" Riley, P.O. Box 7427, seven counts; and Pete J. Carroll, P.O. Box 6584, two counts. The charge of contributing to the delinquency of a minor had been filed again: Kathie Marie Sherlock, 26 Heatherwood Drive, two counts; Tom Carroll and Ann Carroll, both of 9-A Anthony Street; Tommy Carroll of 78 Foxfire Court; John Joseph Carroll of 78 Foxfire Court; and Mary Catherine Carroll of North Augusta. Several others, all with the last name of Carroll, Sherlock, and Riley and residing at different addresses were mentioned.

Traveler Language

At first there I had some difficulty comprehending Val's prison journal. Her intellectual abilities weren't in question. After several in-group meetings and prison university class meetings, it was clear she possessed a remarkable ability to learn, memorize, and reason. She remembered what she learned, could make sense of it, and could apply it to other situations and social problems. Note: it was mentioned earlier in this work that the intellectual capability of a group of students among high-security prisoners far exceeds the intellectual capability of the students in a typical university classroom. Similar to other subjects inn *Wicked Women,* Val is incredibly bright. That begs the question: why can't they make better decisions about their life?

Nonetheless, Val took on the task of educating her prison instructors and group leaders. The Travelers speak Shelta or Cant, based on an Irish Gaelic lexicon and English-based grammar. Understanding the English influence aided my reading her work, since her spelling and many of the slang terms were so different. But of greater interest, Val said that many Traveler words are disguised through such techniques as back slang, whereby words are spoken or spelled backwards. For example, *yob* for boy (originally used to disguise the word, now used to mean a backward boy or lout); *ecilop* for police, and often modified to *slop*. Also *gop* for kiss, from the Irish *póg*. Sometimes they alter the initial sounds of words, as in *gather* for father, from the Irish *athair*.

Irish Traveler Ancestry

Irish Travelers predate the English legend of King Arthur by several centuries in the United Kingdom. Some claim the Irish Travelers predate the Celtic invasion of Ireland, and were the oldest inhabitants of the island. Val said that Travelers learn their traditions orally from one generation to the next, and that they descended from the pre-Celts. Val said that "Outsiders who think they know about us, link the Travelers with Roma Gypsies, a completely different blood line."

Val explained that there's a lot of confusion between Roma and Irish Travelers. At the time Val was imprisoned she watched a television performance of *Law & Order, Criminal Intent* (Season 2, Episode 21). Detectives Robert Goren (Vincent D'Onofrio) and Alexandra Eames (Kathryn Erbe) enter the closed world of a "thieving Irish Traveler clan," as they investigated the murder of a probation officer. The detectives learn that the probation officer had been involved with one of her clients. According to a synopsis of the show on its website, Goren and Eames investigate an American branch of the Irish Travelers, a stigmatized nomadic subculture often referred to as gypsies.

"That's all duck shit information," Val said.

According to the website, the police investigators found that the Irish Travelers were "petty criminals, grifters, and harlots, [and had] incessant brushes with the law." The murdered probation officer had knowledge of multiple crimes committed by the Irish Travelers, and she was extremely threatening to a group "living so completely outside the law." An arrest is finally made after several references to the Romany legend of gypsies. Other than sharing desegregation and taking protective measures to ensure their privacy, as all groups have done throughout history, there are few similarities between the Roma and Irish Travelers.

Val said that she also saw a Hollywood movie (something Travelers rarely do) entitled *Into the West* (1992). It featured Gabriel Byrne and Ellen Barkin, who misrepresented the Irish Travelers as low-intellect backwater thieves with New Orleans accents.

"Bizarre," is all Val could say, thought she did tag on, "Travelers are not backwater thieves and they're not from Nu' Or'ings."

Street Walkers

Val clarified that because Travelers are rarely visible on the streets in their village or in their yards, it was easy for her to be yonks (wayward). She said that when she was twelve and thirteen and supposed to be in school, it was easy to hop (cut) school and head to the beach or mountain villages, her favorite pastimes. Traveler adults rarely imposed structure or curfew upon their young, because most of them never left the village or surrounding area.

Clothes, Makeup, and Sex

One constant problem Val shared was that when she left the village, whether she was among the workers or on her own, she had to change from the silk-type clothing she normally wore and remove the pounds of makeup on her face. Before returning, she had to change back into her normal clothes and reapply the makeup. As a matter of interest, Val explained that on special occasions, Traveler girls dressed like child beauty queens, with sequined dresses, bouffant hairstyles, and a lot of makeup. Even toddlers had heavy amounts of makeup applied to their faces. Females dress provocatively, revealing as much skin as possible. Even a lacy white wedding gown reveals a young girl's thighs. The job of the female is to provide children and to be sexually attentive with her husband. Goals of most Traveler girls are to remain healthy, to cook, bake, and clean. Outsiders are not part of their lifestyle orientation or sexual tradition. But there are some interesting concerns about unclean things.

Unclean Things

"It was hard on me when I menstruated," Val said. "It is looked upon as being unclean. Better be up-the-pole [pregnant] and hold your husband's respect. When I had my period, my husband and all men had to avoid my shadow or risk contamination. Kissing at that time is forbidden. Childbirth is impure."

When Val was home, her tasks were to satisfy her husband through her appearance and sexual graduation, unless she was menstruating; to prepare food according to custom; and to clean and clean and clean, especially the dishes and utensils. Bad luck could visit a dirty home and cause contamination. Also, male and female clothing, as well as upper and lower body clothing, are washed separately.

Val said that she was fond of cats, although she never had one. Pets are considered dirty animals and are never allowed to live in a house.

To be contaminated in any way can mean isolation from Traveler events, which occur monthly. Weddings and other family events are attended by hundreds of family members. To be isolated or alone is not the Traveler lifestyle. To attend schools or shops outside the community is an easy path to contamination. Travelers are escorted to shops, doctors' and dentists' offices, schools, and church. Val performed extremely well at living a double life. In one life, she was an essential and contributing member of both her family and the community. In her second life, she a predator.

Crimes in General

Val described what appeared to be criminal activities during her youth, which consisted of hunting and violating others as part of her need to cleanse and purge. *Gadjo,* or outsiders, in the thick countryside of South Carolina and Georgia were part of Val's revenge for the sake of justice. At least, that was her justification of her crimes.

She explained it this way. "Somebody would mess with the Travelers, and that person deserved a slam. If I allowed him to do what he wanted, respect for any of us would be nonexistent. America won't stand up for us, they don't know who we are, so I have to do it myself."

The reality is that Val committed crimes against individuals who knew very little about her culture and the Travelers.

Also, many of her victims were children. If asked, "Why hurt a child?" she might respond, "Because the kid is too blinking sweet. They need to be taught that they're defenseless. I'm doing them a service and ask nothing in return. I returned to some of them during other trips as I did some of those *gowl's* [idiots] who were easy targets, and instructed them further."

Youthful Violent Behavior

One time she hitched a ride on the highway, on the way to a city about fifty miles from her home. On the way, the driver of white truck decided to have his way with her. He didn't realize his passenger was a female. He pulled to the side of the road and touched her. Upon discovering he was she, he froze. "But he already had his pecker out. I had my knife ready in my hand and sliced through his blinking fingers. He screamed. Then I cut his blinking pecker. His arms were over the seat and his wounded little thing remained silent. I leaned to pet it so that he would be unguarded, but stuck a pin through it. Popped out my Zippo and torched the pin. The redneck had it coming. I took the gowl's wallet and cigs . Kicked his ass out of the truck and drove back toward home, ditching it on a dirt road."

She was only twelve, but she was tall for her age, so her feet touched the pedals. She already knew how to drive. Men expected their wives to travel with them.

Another typical incident involved two of her brothers, although all of them were victims of her violence. Almost everyone had gone to their Appalachian home, leaving the threesome in South Carolina. One of her brothers held her down while the other pretended to penetrate her. She knew it was a game. She and the two older brothers had played this game before while these younger ones watched. Now it was their turn. This time, it wasn't a game. In the past, they all laughed and none of her brothers had an erection. This time it was different. The younger brother didn't understand the game, Val surmised. She spit in his eyes and kneed him as she climbed up. She pulled the other's penis with such a tug that the "boy screeched like a little girl." She allowed her "temper to shoot to top of the cathedral ceiling, right through the skylight. That's when they knew I was out of control. They tried to hush me. Please Val, just relax. You know we're playing. Come on, Buama. They were trying to calm me when I grabbed my Louisville Slugger and swung it, hitting my little brothers in the head. They should never mess with me – not with something hard to put in me."

In many of Val's accounts, she described her temper. She described how she turned her temper on and off, and how others were fearful of her temper, "That's why they call me Buama. It means bomb in Gaelic," she said. "I like that," she added.

Val manipulates her gender too. When it was useful to be a woman, she was; when it was useful to be a man, she was that.

Traveling

Between March and early June, groups traveled looking for subcontractor work, such as repairing roofs, driveways, and painting homes. Once Val married, she followed the caravans. Once she made some money, she bought an SUV with dark windows, a roof rack, and such a technologically advanced communication system, it would put a state trooper's cruiser to shame.

Val's Specialty

When Val traveled, little was expected of her as a wife, a mother, or a woman, other than working her specialty. For Val, that meant winning the confidence of a mark and collecting the money for the contracted work. Sometimes, she would help the mark in his or her home; other times it meant driving the mark to a relative's home or the bank. She mastered her trade exceedingly well and had an experienced teacher, her mother. "I could be a *slapper* [a female with low morals] when I was on the road. There was so much action. But that was not for me," she claimed, but it is more likely that Val had little time between work and hunting for crime, which she didn't define as immoral.

At seventeen, Val was pretty much autonomous. She had her own vehicle, knew how to pull a score together, and how to collect and dispose of the cash. If she had ever been stopped by slops, they could have confiscated the cash. Thus, Val established networks, safe drops, and codes, as her mother had instructed. Then, too, it worked to Val's advantage to appear to be a harmless boy. Yet she knew how to charm marks, who were largely the elderly and new business owners, their relatives, and their bankers. The end result was that none of the Travelers questioned Val's integrity or her whereabouts. Even her husband had his own vehicle, and he knew better than to demand her company. Taking her independence into consideration, it is easy to understand how Val led two lives.

From the time she was seventeen until the time of her arrest at twenty-eight years of age, Val worked with Traveler workers in northern cities four to five months of every year. Should her activities be believed, then it is a pretty safe estimate that during each road trip, Val engaged in confidence games, extortion, robbery, and sexual assault, or a total of five felony crimes a trip. Three trips a month times four months, or twelve total trips per year, equals sixty felonies a year. When that sum is multiplied by ten years, Val was responsible for or involved in an estimated six hundred criminal acts over her adult life (not counting her youth), which is consistent with what some criminologists accept about chronic offenders.

Clan Jobs

Val revealed that during one of the Traveler jobs, the clan was in Columbus, Ohio. An advanced team had located a mark and informed the other Travelers.

"Like bees to honey, many of us found the home and asked the owners about other repairs to their home. The homeowners agreed. Roof, gutters, drive, and paint on the exterior. We always get cash before the job. I took the sweet old couple to the bank to get the money. But when I saw a lot of zeros behind their bank account, I pursued them to withdraw more. Driving them home, I asked about their children. They directed me past their daughter's home, and I asked questions about Jennifer and her family. After dropping them at their home, I returned to Jennifer's home. Timing is everything when you're on the road. When Jennifer came to the door, I introduced myself and explained my involvement with her parents. Once inside Jennifer's home and after a witty chat, I learned that she was as defenseless as her parents and a single mom, so when I left, I had her young daughter and a hundred dollars of her money in my vehicle. Jennifer thought the money was for her parents and that they wanted to see their grandchild."

Val delivered Jennifer's child to her grandparents, but Val's descriptions suggested that first she parked her yellow SUV at a shopping mall along the way. She climbed into the backseat where the child was strapped into a car seat. Val penetrated the three-year-old child's vagina and rectum with her fingers, which were coated with gel, while she worked herself to an orgasm with her free hand. The entire event occurred in less than fifteen minutes. Val was always prepared, always wanting to be in the right place at the right time. Perfect timing is emphasized with her, and happens to be title of the short story in chapter 18.

In this regards, it is unlikely that little girl, whose name was Beka, or any other child reported their sexual assault. It's equally unlikely that Val was never a suspect for this crime or similar crimes. Her victims were too young, too afraid, too embarrassed, or too guilt-ridden. Val articulated that very young children and senior citizens could not or would not report an assault of any variety. She selected her victims with great care, and returned to earlier victims more than once. Sometimes she used them to victimize others in her presence, or to find others for her to victimize. As Jennifer's daughter grew, Val entered her life in such a way that Jennifer suggested that Beka call her Auntie Val. Val visited around the same time every year for the next few years, and always with presents in hand.

The crime that brought Val to prison was the attempted murder of Beka's elderly grandparents. Val had returned a second time with new plans for their home, which went well. She continued to return for more jobs, until finally they were out of money. They had to say no. "Borrow it," Val demanded. The old couple had borrowed before and remortgaged their home, and Val had taken every penny of it. The wife's social security checks were diverted to one of Val's accounts, yet her husband kept his retirement check each month. Val had wiped out the couple's finances, and they loved her for it up until the day they said no. They cried because they wanted to please her. They were ashamed that they were broke. Val marched out to her SUV and brought back her Louisville Slugger. She started whacking the couple with it. The police arrived when a neighbor called 911 and took Val into custody. She worked out a guilty plea for attempted murder, and all investigations stopped. Little had been learned about Val and her exploitations of others, but that Columbus, Ohio, couple was probably one of two hundred older couples Val exploited, from Providence to Cleveland and down to Charlottesville. Little Beka was one of at least fifty children whom Val sexually assaulted over the years. Val is also responsible for other cases of attempted murder, aggravated assault, aggravated rape of children under twelve, armed robbery, extortion, grand larceny, lewd conduct, kidnapping, murder, rape, sexual assault, and sodomy of children under seven years of age.

Prison

While in prison, Val was never placed on suicide watch, restrictions, or segregation. Her health was excellent, and daily she slept more than eight hours, including naps. She was a social drinker, she reported to prison entry personnel, and enjoyed alcohol during celebrations, like weddings, funerals, and the birth of children. She occasionally smoked marijuana. Her presentence investigation report showed that her worst vice was compulsive gambling, and she was characterized as having a dependence on gambling by the time she was fourteen.

Choice of Weapons

Val dislikes conventional weapons, such as guns or knives. Her weapon of choice was a baseball bat, which could be found in her SUV next to a baseball mitt, softball, and baseball shoes, suggesting that she played a lot of baseball. Yet a better analysis is that she could justify having bats if she had the other baseball paraphernalia. She didn't play baseball, and the shoes were two sizes too small.

One incident occurred while she followed the Traveler men north. She was in North Carolina when a motorist cut in front of her on a small road. She emerged from her SUV, Louisville Slugger in hand, to confront the woman, who had jumped from her own vehicle to yell at Val. Val beat her with her bat. When police arrived, they found the angry motorist with an untraceable handgun in her hand. One shot had been fired, supposedly at Val. There were no witnesses other than Val's husband, who had been in the vehicle behind Val and supported her story of the attack. No charges were brought against Val. While she was in prison, her weapons of choice were chairs, tables, writing utensils, a shiv, and her fingers.

Superwomen Motivators toward Violence

Val looked at the world with Superwoman eyes, as a protector of the realm, who defended justice and public good. Val articulated that individuals became victims of justice, because they produced "the circumstances and the conditions" that merited a response on behalf of the community or the higher power that a Superwoman represented. In a word, payback. Or what I describe as revenge motivators. For instance, when she was in prison and other inmates engaged in illegal behavior, such as drugs, acting disrespectful towards custody officers, robbing or beating inmates, Val stepped in. She might say to the offender, "That isn't right that you said that. Apologize, mother f*****." There would be no further outbursts from the disrespectful prisoner, and I didn't want to ask either one about it. Had I, it would have been a sign of disrespect toward Val and the way she thought, a sign of disrespect toward the Irish Traveler community. Also, I would have lost an ally in the time of need. Implied in Val's comment was a ruthless beating, if an apology wasn't forthcoming. Val was the person most often befriended by in-group leaders, teachers, and custody officers, because she helped keep the peace.

Visitors

Prisoners written up for infraction lost visiting privileges. But Val was never denied visitors. No one seemed to mind the numerous visitors she had, because none of them argued with custody officers, nor would they ignore a directive by a custody officer. Observing Val and her visitors crowded around a picnic table on the prison lawn revealed that they were close and cared for one another. They spoke quietly, their expressions mostly blank, and there was never any laughter. One person spoke at a time, and there were frequent long pauses. A maximum number of visitors were allowed to visit at any one time, and in Val's case she had many family members waiting patiently, including numerous well-behaved children in the visitor's lounge. The notion that Val is a predator can advance the idea that the Irish Travelers were enablers of her criminal career, without realizing the extent of her criminal pathology.

Higher Order

Val holds bold notions about herself. feelings that include her pursuit of criminally violent behavior. As a schemer, she accepts both the informal social values and the formal rules of the Irish Travelers, as well as the

Department of Corrects, in order to further her vocation of violence. In return, her personal community and the prison system seemingly protect her interests. Recall the activities of the others in *Wicked Women* who have led double lives in an effort to further their predatory ambitions. Living a double life is relatively easy when protected by others. Surely many responsible people were aware of Annie's drug-trafficking activities and her reckless lifestyle. Brother Pious was protected by the Catholic Church, similar to today's protection of priests who abused minors; and Janelle, Mary, and Mickey were protected by individuals who enhanced their personal agenda, and were insulated from legal scrutiny because of their occupations.

Significant Behavioral Patterns

Revengers tend to step further into the cesspool of violating others while believing they are akin to the Knights Templar or the morality police. It is Val's duty, even her responsibility, to administer justice to wrongdoers. Yet justice cannot be fulfilled by a single act. Val feels she is responsible for providing multiple offenses against the same violator. Once a person is on Val's "deserving justice" list, it is hard to escape her wrath. Her idea of punitive sanctions isn't measured in a single event, or even a life for a life. Killing a person is too simple and too quick a solution. Repeatedly harming a violator over a period of time and then killing the violator is more in line with Val's philosophy. The child in Columbus, Ohio, whom Val sexually violated was more than a victim of Val's attacks. She was being punished. Had Val not been stopped by the police when she attacked the child's grandparents, she would have killed them and then killed the child and her mother, just to be sure. How many children or others Val had killed remains unknown. By the by, Val was released from prison in 2008 and lives with the Irish Travelers in South Carolina, approximately a two hour drive from where I currently reside.

CHAPTER 16
Wilma the Dominican Princess

Introduction

This chapter offers a look into the private and professional life of Mariasela Rebecca Guzman, born in the Dominican Republic, but she is better known as Wilma. Early experiences in Wilma's life include her older sisters and a description of their ancestry, cultural heritage, and the occupations of their parents. Wilma's early experiences are highlighted, along with a Dominican Republic presidential grandfather, the meeting of US officials, and descriptions of Wilma's youthful activities. The chapter describes Wilma's favorite foods, her alcoholism, and her compulsive gambler activities. We follow her move from the Dominican Republic to New York City, into a marriage and a career with the Department of Corrections. We see her rise to a powerful position within the New York prison system, and her cruel behavior toward prisoners and personnel. The chapter offers an overview of Wilma's trial, conviction, and prisoner experiences. Finally, in chapter 18, a short story called "The Train" about this extraordinary woman centers on her paranoia perspectives.

Early Life

Parque Central, an affluent area in Santo Domingo, Dominican Republic, is where Mariasela Rebecca Guzman grew up. Her older sisters called her Wilma, because she preferred to wear her long, silky hair stacked on her head like Wilma Flintstone. The nickname stuck for life. Wilma never referred to her sisters by name, but they were about three and five years older than she, and looked different from her. Some have suggested Wilma had a different father from her sisters, yet no one would say that out loud. Wilma is a serious, humorless woman. Her eyes always look like she's caught up in some distant thought, and she appears to be ready to make a point, but doesn't. The Guzman bloodline includes West African, French, and Spanish, and the Guzman girls possess light golden-brown skin and light hair. Wilma is lighter skinned than her sisters, and unlike her drop-dead gorgeous sisters, Wilma is ugly. Their religion is Roman Catholic Dominican, which dominated the entire early lives of the girls.

Wilma's Parents

At the time of Wilma's criminal conviction, her mother, Amelia Milagos, was an administrative assistant at the Center of Marine Biology at The Universidad Autónoma de Santo Domingo. Her father, Rafael Morla Guzman, was a full professor and dean of humanities at the same university. Her powerful grandfather had taken his own life years before Wilma was incarcerated.

Wilma's Early Experiences

By Santo Domingo standards, Wilma's family led the life of the privileged few. Wilma followed her big sisters through the prestigious and private Carol Morgan School. Yet life wasn't always so joyful, although it was difficult for Wilma to recall those days when her country was engaged in a bloody civil war. For the first years of Wilma's life, prior to her family moving to Parque Central, both her immediate and extended family lived together in an unpretentious residence in central Dominican Republic, on the Camu River in the historic village of La Vega. La Vega has three claims to fame: it's the oldest city in the New World, dating back to 1498; it has bad sanitation; and it's the birthplace of Silvestre Antonio Guzman, the former president of Dominican Republic, representing the Reformist Party, and Wilma's paternal grandfather. In comparing photographs of her grandfather and Mariasela, it is easy to recognize her ancestry.

At Guzman's inauguration in 1978, on the 113th anniversary of the Restoration of the Republic from Spanish rule, the Guzman family attended one of the many jubilant dinner parties. The party was also attended by the US delegation, headed by Secretary of State Cyrus Vance, the United Nations Ambassador Andrew Young, and a host of others. Wilma only remembered Young. While this long-legged child sat on Young's lap, their picture was taken. Several photos sparked innuendoes that were hardly worth notice, until the *Boston Globe* featured a bizarre story linked to the photographs, which included bizarre descriptions of a birthright fantasy to a lunar landing on a distant moon. Wilma wrote that when she jumped into Ambassador Young's lap, she felt her job was to welcome the ambassador to her grandfather's domain in a polite and dignified manner, in keeping with her role as *"el favorite uno"* (the favored one). As she slipped onto his lap, she squeezed his thigh, enough for Young to grimace. She wrote that he recognized that she was, indeed, a female, but it is more likely that his expression was in response to her repulsive features. Yet it was also the eve of destruction for many Dominicans.

The Eve of Destruction

The eve of destruction for Wilma wasn't the difficult civil war during her early childhood, but rather Hurricane David. In 1979, the hurricane took a thousand Dominican lives at a cost of over a billion dollars. In prison, Wilma continued to hear the hollowing winds and shivered from their presence. However, she felt better talking about family vacations to Madrid, London, and New York City when she was a youngster. Sometimes the family trips ended in Miami, Caracas, or Rio de Janeiro, so her father could attend academic conferences. When Wilma spoke about Hurricane David, I did not fully understand her desperate words: "Mother Nature humbled every living thing, including God." A few years later I was buried in Hurricane Katrina, and I finally understood. Humbling, indeed!

Descriptions of Youthful Activities

Wilma's stories about her youth generally characterized self-defense tactics, rather than the actions of an aggressor. According to her descriptions, she was the picture of innocence. For instance, she described one experience when she was preschool age. Her grandparents gave the three girls gifts, as was their custom on Epiphany, the day commemorating the visit of the three Magi to the baby Jesus on January 6. Wilma's gift—a doll resembling a little Taíno girl (indigenous to the Dominican Republic)—was different from the other dolls, and her sisters snapped it up. They put it into their dollhouse, telling Wilma that little Taíno could not live alone and had to be with the other dolls. Wilma would not be able to take Little Taíno out to play, they said. "I asked which doll could go out and play with me, and once I knew, I adopted that doll and gave Little Taíno to my sisters," Wilma wrote. "That was the right thing to do, I suspect. But my oldest sister was mean to me and said no. At first, I cried and then I jumped on her, biting her face until she gave up."

Another memory from Wilma's childhood occurred during *Semana Santa* (Holy Week, the week before Easter). The family went on holiday to the beach. Wilma mentioned that holiday more than once in her journals, because her sisters were "extra nasty toward me, especially the older one." By "nasty," Wilma meant that her sisters made fun of her "because I was lighter than they are, and when they were really nasty, they would call me Anglo girl, referring to a person with English blood, a very disrespectful label to every Dominican girl." After being called Anglo girl several times, Wilma poked her sister's eye so hard, her parents had to take her sister to the hospital. She wore an eye-patch for several weeks. "She had it coming. She didn't play by the rules," Wilma wrote. It is just as likely that Wilma poked her sister's eye without provocation.

Wilma and her sisters loved music. They often visited the square in town and danced as little girls could to the merengue. Most often, it was a three-piece group of musicians consisting of a melodeon (an accordion-like instrument), a *güira* (and instrument that looks like a cheese grater), and Wilma's favorite, and a *tambora* (a double-headed drum). Maybe it was the heavy-set boy who played that instrument that struck her fancy? On one occasion, Wilma wrote that her sisters and she got into a physical fight over music. The sisters liked *Bachata* and wanted to listen to the musicians who played melancholy music. When little Wilma said no, her older sister reminded Wilma that she was the baby and half the size of her big sister, and you "must listen to me." But even then Wilma was a big girl and taller than most kids her age; and eventually she would grow to just under six feet tall. Her lips were thick, and seemed puffed all the time. She refused to leave the square and her beloved merengue. Instantly she attacked both sisters with a scream that attracted onlookers. When several men tried to break the fight up, Wilma dug her fingers dig into one man's face. This incident occurred when Wilma was seven years of age.

"They didn't keep the rules," she said, "and I did."

Whose Rules?

It is easy to ask Wilma, whose rules? Getting an answer was a complicated matter, and in a final analysis, her responses rarely addressed any questions. Wilma made up rules as she went through life, and those rules were often modified and altered to fit the occasion, yet she always got her payback. For instance, she mentioned that one of her teachers singled her out in class and embarrassed her in some way that she couldn't recall thirty years later. But Wilma remembers being called out by this teacher, who was an American lady and pretty. Wilma wrote that the other kids made fun of her for a week or more after the incident. Four years later, when she was in eighth grade, the pretty teacher who had singled her was involved in a dispute with parents about her professional conduct. Wilma asked to tell her story to the parent group, and when she entered the room, she broke down in tears and compellingly presented her story. She said the American teacher had inappropriately touched her private parts. "I begged her to stop," she told the parents, and fell to the ground in utter despair.

"It was all a lie," Wilma wrote in her journal, "but it served the American bitch right. She was in the room when I told my story, and she said absolutely nothing because she knew she was wrong for messing with me when I was a kid." The pretty teacher never taught at the school again.

"Vengeance is always mine," stated Wilma, as though she has the responsibility of administering justice to every transgressor on the planet. Yet it also seemed that Wilma decided which individuals fit her definition of a transgressor.

Food and Carnival

Dominican Republic cuisine is predominantly influences by Taino, Spanish, and African cultures over the last few centuries. When Wilma lived in the Dominican Republic, she ate her main meal at midday, and it often lasted over an hour. Families ate this meal at home, and Wilma continued to go home for lunch when employed at the prison in the US. Of course, things changed once she was imprisoned. She missed dishes made with *sofrito* (a mix of sautéed herbs and spices) and family events, which occurred all the time in the Dominican Republic. When Wilma thought about it, she wrote that she missed "carnival, the pre-Lenten festival, parades, costumes, and the throwing of pig bladders at spectators that lasted for weeks." Her favorite costume was that of Wonder Woman, but she preferred to wear a mask to hide her face. She never thought she was pretty, which was an astute observation on her part. In fact, she was so ugly, many would unknowingly present a look of disgust when first they saw her.

Wilma loved her rice, but only white rice served with beans and cassava or fritters. She liked fruit, particularly plantains, bananas, and avocados. Wilma ate only the things she liked, she insisted on specific foods, refused to eat little else when in the Dominican Republic. She experienced a food awakening when she moved to New York City, but still managed to get food from her homeland (perhaps because of her marriage to a weapons dealer, she continued to get what she wanted), but another awakening occurred once she was imprisoned.

Nonetheless, when in Santo Domingo, she would accept *sancocho*, a rich stew made with vegetables and meats during special occasions. She never drank coffee as an adult or a youngster, but enjoyed rum and drank buckets of sweetened fruit juices.

Guzman Grandchildren's Trust Fund

Like her sisters, when Wilma turned twenty-one she had access to a moderate trust fund left to each of the Guzman girls by their grandfather, who committed suicide in 1982. There were rumors that their "trust funds were remnants of the Dominican old money population, which our grandfather pieced together and deposited in a New York City bank," Wilma wrote in her journal. Other rumors were that he was a countryside rebel who arose after anguish and despair to legitimate power. He then allegedly traded his freedom to the US and became president with CIA influence. Often when he spent time with his favorite granddaughter, Wilma, he told her again and again about the "Imperialist Empire" (referring to the CIA) and how they came to his rescue. After his death, the veil of safety covering the Guzman girls was a clear and ever present declaration to every Dominican and Haitian alike: No harm shall come to any of my children on this planet, ever! Or I will rise from my grave and devour your eyeballs and swallow your breath. I will take my revenge on you and your children's children.

Wilma learned long before her grandfather's rise to power that she was "untouchable," because she was the favorite and resembled her mother and her grandmother more than the others. She tested her favor at school, especially among American classmates. When Americans were her teachers, not only would her sisters stand up for her, but so would her classmates because she was the favorite one.

Wilma's Reasoning

Wilma thought that she had to fight for survival among her headstrong sisters, because she was the youngest of three girls, but realized that she was happiest when she "did the right thing," she wrote. She emphasized that her sisters were control freaks and that she considered their behavior ridiculous. Of equal interest, Wilma usually reacted quickly and aggressively with individuals, but with a frame as bulky as hers, her motions were never graceful. All through her life, she was in constant motion. For instance, her fingers were somehow connected to her lips, because when she spoke, twelve things would move at the same time. When she slept, jarring sounds penetrated the area so much, prisoners in her wing complained all the time. It was reported that Wilma slept facedown, with her arms outstretched and her legs spread-eagled, and rarely moved from the second she lay down to the moment she awoke. It must have been uncomfortable, because she covered every square inch of that prison bunk.

According to Wilma, her reflexes were swift, and she developed a rationale for that supposed swift response. "When I react quickly to people, they become insecure about their defenses." Apparently, her sisters and other targets either didn't learn, didn't care, or weren't aware that Wilma would attack quickly and violently. Yet her sisters loved her and showed her in many ways that they wanted to protect her. For instance, when Wilma was five years old, soldiers came for Guzman's granddaughters. Her sisters, out of concern that the soldiers were a threat, told them that Wilma was the housekeeper's child. "Look at her, she looks nothing like a Guzman." The soldiers said they were sent to protect the girls from a threat, and if they would hide somewhere, the soldiers would stand guard until the all clear was given. Wilma wrote similar accounts emphasizing her sisters' protection in her journal.

Despite her perception that her responses were swift, in her journal Wilma described her reactions when she was young as "delayed and slow." Further, I observed her in a prison in-group program for two hours a day, twice a week, for the better part of a year. Her movements were slow and clumsy movements. My observations of her reaction time during that time suggested to me that there wasn't any speed in anything she did, contradicting both her own accounts and the official reports about her seemingly spontaneous and almost instant attacks on others including her sisters. However, regardless of how quickly she responded to aggressors, one thing was certain. Whether incarcerated or free, she was lethal.

It should be clarified that Wilma possessed the capacity to kill another human being. It is not clear from her journal or from her comments when she first committed homicide, but her early experiences with killing can be linked to the family pets when she was child in the Dominican Republic. It took her family some time to comprehend that their youngest child bore more than just a physical resemblance to her grandfather. She could kill without provocation.

Her father, however, was not a violent man and had, by all accounts, never raised his hand to strike any family member. Not even Wilma when she displayed bizarre, unacceptable behavior. For instance, when she was six years old, she explained that she masturbated one of the family dogs and tried unsuccessfully to strangle the dog to death. Her father arrived on the scene unexpectedly, but, Wilma wrote, he had no clue what really happened. She cried and said that the dog attacked her. Her father hugged her and assured her that everything would be okay. He watched over her as she pretended to nap. The following day, when again alone with the dog, she tried again, but failed to kill the dog. Wilma recalled practicing with one hand on the dog's neck and the other hand moving its penis back and forth. Finally, she lured the dog into the bushes, and this time her efforts paid off. She left the dog in the brush and ran home to explain to her father that the dog had attacked her again and that she "had no idea what happened next. My little dead dog was lying next to me. It was terrible." Wilma described a sense of accomplishment in fulfilling her plan of killing one of the family's pets. "I remember pulling open the dog's eye so I could see inside it once it was over. There was nothing. I really thought I could shake the little puppy and it would come to life before my eyes. My poor *perrito*."

Two weeks later, she killed the puppy's mother, and knew it wouldn't come to life if she shook it. "That's just it. I thought I would feel something, but I stared at the dead dog and I did not feel sad. I didn't feel anything except that I succeeded. Is that wrong?" (Note: Wilma didn't feel sad the dog was dead, nor did she feel sad that she killed it. This is a consistent characteristic expressed by each of the participants in this study).

Wilma's capacity toward lethal aggression against another human being can be typified in this statement: "When my grandfather told me about arrogant American CIA people, he would always say that they were dogs and that dogs should be controlled or they defecate wherever they want. My grandfather should have taken those arrogant dogs into the field and marched them into an ambush."

Alcoholic

Wilma was an alcoholic when she arrived at prison, and her descriptions suggested that she had been an alcoholic since she was fourteen or fifteen. She liked Brugal rum so much that when time permitted, she was a regular visitor at the bottling factory in Puerto Plata along the north coast of the Dominican Republic. Her favorite was Brugal Blanco rum, produced in the Dominican Republic. Some of her descriptions revealed that initially she consumed a bottle of rum every few weeks. When she moved to New York City, she began drinking a bottle a week; and eventually was consuming two to three bottles a week. As expected, Wilma had other vices too.

Compulsive Gambler

Wilma is a compulsive gambler, and had early practice in the Dominican Republic as a teenager. She bet on cockfights, popular daily events in the Dominican Republic, and she bet on dominoes, which were largely played by men in front of most of the homes where she lived. She drank with them, too, but it isn't clear if she had sexual relationships with any of the men. As Guzman's granddaughter, her presence anywhere in the country was never questioned, and through her accounts it appears that she could have committed murder without being arrested. Betting, winning, or losing had little impact on her behavior, because this young woman was never challenged by anyone.

In the United States, Wilma made wagers all of the time: football, baseball, inmate recidivism, how long a correctional officer would stay employed, love affairs between inmates, love feuds between inmates, and success or failure of politicians. Wilma wrote that she often spent two hours or more a day engaged in waging, and she would usually drink rum while betting. She says that on a single event she lost as much as in the low double digits (I read that to mean $20,000 to $30,000) and won as much as in the low six digits (I read that to mean $100,000 to $200,000).

Move to New York City

Although Wilma's sisters graduated from the university where their parents were employed, Wilma eventually persuaded her parents to allow her to move with her cousin to New York City and work in Manhattan after graduating from Morgan. Still, it isn't clear if she had their permission to leave the Dominican Republic, or if she packed and moved without the support of her parents. Her notes about the next three years of her life were sketchy. She partied, drank, gambled, traveled to Las Vegas and Atlantic City, moved twice while living in New York (the second time with the man she would eventually marry), and shopped. "Sometimes, the weeks were a blur," she wrote. Nonetheless, before long she was recruited by the state as a social service provider for the Department of Corrections, because she was fluent at English and Spanish. She was twenty-one years of age at the time of her employment, and she was engaged to be married. "I was ready to settle down. I was exhausted."

Marriage

Somewhere during Wilma's "blur," she sobered up long enough to realize that she was engaged to a man forty years older than she. He was Dominican, and a friend of Wilma's cousin. He also had a fantastic condominium high above Central Park in Manhattan. It was furnished with expensive wood furniture, imported marble from Spain and Italy, and fine Spanish leather. Valuable French paintings covered the walls, and elaborate crystal and stained glass chandeliers hung from the ceilings. Her new husband was the CEO of a weapons supplier to the American and Israeli military. He had four ex-wives, three of which lived in the city. The threesome saw Wilma as an intruder and treated her with disgust at local restaurants, society dinners, and at the small Dominican Catholic church where the newlyweds went each Sunday. Eventually, Wilma and her husband stopped attending mass because of the women's treatment of Wilma. They criticized her for not taking his last name, even though that was common practice in the Dominican Republic. They also said that Wilma was a prize her husband received for supplying her grandfather with weapons during the civil wars in the Dominican Republic.

On one occasion, Wilma ran into one of the ex-wives in the restroom of a prominent restaurant and slapped her hard several times. When the police arrived, the woman said her injuries were the result of an accident. She had slipped and fallen, hurting her face on the restroom sink. There were no other police reports linked to Wilma, other than one concerning her husband after her arrest.

Early in Wilma's Career: The Death of a Drug Trafficker

Early in Wilma's correctional career, she was assigned a visitation detail at the state women's facility. She held the rank of sergeant at the time and was in charge of visitor screening. During her screening detail one afternoon, she observed an individual whom she thought resembled a Santo Domingo drug dealer. The drug dealer's picture had been flashed on news reports for weeks when she was in the twelfth grade at Carol Morgan School. What was striking about the drug dealer was that few drug dealers in Santo Domingo were female or Haitian. (Haitians are not welcome in the Dominicans Republic, even though both nations share the Hispaniola Island.) Yet more striking was that the news reports said that the dealer had denounced the Catholic church and practiced voodoo. It was alleged that the dealer, Cathorey D'Albigen, had consumed the sperm of her sons during voodoo rituals. At the time of those reports, Wilma wrote, she prayed to Saint Dominic, the patron saint of the Dominican Republic, to grant her the opportunity to cross paths with D'Albigen so that she could bring her to justice.

Not surprisingly, Wilma confronted D'Albigen. An altercation ensued. D'Albigen was beaten to the ground, restrained with handcuffs, and carried off to a cell to await transportation to a county jail. During D'Albigen's confinement, Wilma entered the cell to interrogate this former high-profile drug dealer. The interrogation went well, despite the fact that officially Wilma was not authorized to interrogate D'Albigen.

It was learned that heroin was coming into the correctional facility with D'Albigen's support and the assistance of her colleagues, which included two correctional officers. Once the deputies arrived to transport her to jail, Wilma notified the warden's superior about the D'Albigen altercation, because she feared the warden was part of the problem. In the end, Wilma was promoted to deputy superintendent and authorized to pursue the drug connection inside the facility.

D'Albigen was eventually convicted and incarcerated at the facility where Wilma was second in command. The commissioner of corrections supported Wilma, and she was rarely if ever contradicted by the warden, her official supervisor. Strange events that occurred at the prison included D'Albigen admitting that the warden was her contact. The warden was eventually arrested by state troopers. In the melee that followed, D'Albigen was shot and killed as she attempted to escape the prison. State troopers said they had little knowledge that D'Albigen was attempting any escape, but correctional officers under Wilma's command fired their weapons from the gun tower to prevent an inmate's escape. Later, that inmate was identified as D'Albigen. An investigation by the criminal justice director of the state led to the conclusion that D'Albigen's killing was justified and in keeping with DOC policy. Protestors, some of whom were connected to the warden, said that Wilma had staged the escape for the purpose of having D'Albigen killed, rather than allowing D'Albigen to testify at the warden's trial. Some said that D'Albigen was not linked to the warden, but acted independently in a drug trafficking enterprise at the prison. Others said that D'Albigen was not trafficking drugs at all, but Wilma used the victim's background to bring down the warden, a job she wanted because she was trading drugs, sex, and weapons at the prison. Eventually, Wilma was promoted to warden after prison personnel were cleared of any wrongdoing linked to D'Albigen's death. Those reports regarding the shooting were buried in administrative files, but they eventually arrived at the penitentiary where Mariasela was serving time.

Cruel Behavior

Superintendent Mariasela Guzman operated the women's penitentiary with an iron hand. Rules were specific and violators, personnel and inmates alike, did not have a second chance to redeem themselves. Personnel were terminated, and unless the prison union fought for the rights of the employee, there was no turning back. The prison union's business manager and other local leaders answered to Superintendent Guzman. Getting on her wrong side had consequences. For instance, assignments for custody personnel could and would change, such as assignments to the graveyard shift, or to the isolation unit, the HIV wing, or the sexually transmitted disease wing, with a few hundred inmates suffering from syphilis, gonorrhea, Chlamydia, trichomoniasis, and human papillomavirus.

Personnel Cruelty. Wilma would transfer employees to at-risk environments. For instance, one custody officer was assigned the isolation unit, which had twenty-four violent inmates on lock-down. No other custody officers were assigned that unit during his work schedule. Eventually, the inmates, taking their clue from the absence of other custody officers, cornered the correctional officer and attacked him. He was in a coma for months. He had also been sexually attacked. His spinal column was damaged and his anus destroyed, so that tubes were used to remove waste from his body.

Inmate Cruelty. For inmates, getting on her wrong side could mean being transferred to a distant prison in another state, far from family or friends, or losing visitation privileges. There are other reports confirming Wilma's vicious, cruel, and calculating behavior. For instance, a year or so after the D'Albigen case, another inmate, Beatrice Delano, a convict who had assaulted her six-month-old child, rebelled against the custody officers during count (a process of counting the inmates, which occurs four or five times in a twenty-four-hour period). There were 35 inmates lined up in the corridor. The custody officers called their supervisor, Mariasela Guzman for help, and followed her policy that in an area where correctional officers are physically threatened by inmates, the video equipment is shut down.. When Wilma arrived, she confronted the tiny and unobtrusive Delano. There was some back and forth, until Delano pushed Wilma, who responded with a quick slap, followed by several blows to Delano's head.

Wilma ordered that Delano be taken to isolation, but added that she would not be housed alone, which was the usual policy. Wilma told the custody officers to lock her down with Juanita "Animal" Bronstein. Two days later, Delano's tiny body was found lifeless, hanging by a bed blanket. Her skull was crushed, eyeballs were ripped from their sockets and found in Delano's mouth, along with her own feces. "Someone had dirty hands," Wilma wrote. An investigation determined that Delano's death was a suicide, and that an inmate found the body and violated the corpse. However, an investigator wrote in the DOC report (not shared in the prison files) that placing "pretty Delano in a cage with Bronstein was similar to putting a sheep in a cage with a wolf. The cruelty suffered by Delano at the hands of Bronstein must have been so devastating over a two-day period, she must have thought she died and went to hell. It's odd that none of the duty officers reported hearing her screams, but then her tongue was missing. Surely someone saw something during the four daily counts?"

Public Documents Justifiable Homicide

In other episodes, sketchy reports emerged after Mariasela Guzman's conviction. A website now available on the Internet shows Mortisea Santos v Mariasela Rebecca Guzman, with the state Department of Corrections as a joint defendant. Santos was an inmate at one of the prisons that employed Wilma. At the time of the alleged incident, Wilma was a correctional officer and held the rank of sergeant. Santos testified that while playing basketball with other inmates in the gymnasium, Wilma violently beat her without provocation or cause, and refused to stop beating her even after two custody officers intervened on Santos's behalf. Many inmates and personnel observed the beating. Wilma and the state contended that Santos was distributing drugs, disobeyed a directive from a custody supervisor, and attacked Wilma with a prison-made shank. They further claimed that during the altercation, Santos passed the shank to another inmate. The medical examiner reported later that there were lacerations on Santos's right hand consistent with someone "wielding a shank." However, Santos sustained injuries that rendered her immediately helpless. Santos alleged that Wilma used gloves that were lined with a hardened substance, acting as brass knuckles. The plaintive further alleged she was not distributing drugs, and had been involved in a prison-sanctioned sporting event. The courts ruled in Wilma's favor. Santos's lawyers unsuccessfully appealed. Santos received an additional prison sentence of twenty years for attacking a correctional supervisor. Santos had been scheduled to be released from prison four months prior to the altercation with Wilma.

Another public document is now available about Wilma's days as a prison warden. She felt that capital punishment had a higher purpose, and that "many offensive criminals would be better off dead than alive, and I would be happy to hit the switch. Some of these convicted bitches think they're better than everybody else, but prison has its humbling ways. When they're offenders of children, I cared little how my custody officers treated them, but no witnesses, I told them." She had trainers come in to teach her personnel how to deal with convicts without losing their jobs. "When you want things done, you do it yourself. I worked several training details." All of the above is a little surprising, because on a wall in Superintendent Guzman's office was a sign that most Dominicans recite time and time again: *Aji Aya Bombe!* (Better dead than a slave). These words were spoken by the great War Chief Guarionex of Otuao (Puerto Rico), November, 1511.

State Police Sting Operation to Bring Down Guzman

It took some time for the federal government to arrest Mariasela Rebecca Guzman, because most investigations of state personnel are the responsibility of state police agencies, unless a federal crime had been committed. None of the alleged offenses against Wilma were within federal jurisdiction. In her case, state police agencies had failed on several occasions to produce any evidence that implicated Wilma in criminal behavior. On two occasions, state police attempted a police sting. The plan was to infiltrate prison procedure, get evidence linked to Wilma, and then contact one of two correctional officers who were also working with the state police, so they could get the undercover agents to safety. The correctional officers would alert the police, and the state police would conduct an arrest.

The first sting employed a new state highway patrol officer, Sarah Rivers. Rivers was convicted of aggravated assault and sentenced to the state facility where Wilma was the warden. Her position as a law enforcement officer was never disclosed. However, it is believed that a correctional officer who attended a refresher course at the state justice academy recognized Rivers. While incarcerated, Rivers was apparently overwhelmed by prison life, because prison records show that she visited the mental health clinic at the prison and was prescribed antidepressants. She died of an overdose; it was three weeks before state authorities knew of Rivers's death.

A second sting was developed. It was fronted by Jane Parker, a young correctional officer fresh out of the justice academy of an adjoining state. With state police assistance, she applied for a job with Wilma's prison. Parker was eventually hired, trained, and on duty, when an inmate slashed her throat with a prison-made shank. Parker remains hospitalized at the writing of this book. The inmate was tried for the crime, but died before the case was adjudicated. The inmate testified that she had good cause to attack the correctional officer, because Parker had humiliated her mother when her mother visited her in prison the day before the attack. On an earlier occasion, Parker had denied the inmate her medication during count. The inmate was HIV positive and knew she was on death's short list prior to attacking Parker. Wilma was never implicated in the case. Both cases have Guzman's touch all over them. Parker had never met the mother of the inmate who attacked her, and Rivers was a stable, resilient young woman who wasn't likely to be bothered by anything short of an magnitude seven earthquake, her state police training officer explained.

Trial, Conviction, and Inmate Experiences

Wilma was forty-one years of age with twenty years of prison work experience, which included her last job as a warden of a women's state prison, when she entered the prison system as a convicted felon.

She plea-bargained with the federal prosecutor for a twenty-year sentence, with the stimulation that she would serve her time in state facility, in another state than the one that employed her. Questions arose from time to time about her deal with a federal prosecutor. However, one perspective was that the state that employed her put pressure on the federal prosecutor to sentence her to their state facility, because she was "one of their own"; and once the prosecutor agreed, Wilma persuaded the prosecutor to make arrangements with another state. It was a good decision for the prosecutor. He didn't have to prepare and wage a lengthy court battle, and the state could show by example through her conviction that correctional executives were not above the law. It was a good decision for Wilma, because she would be incarcerated out of state, so that she would not have to deal with correctional personnel and inmates whom she mistreated. Then, too, the US state department had an incentive to close this case as quickly as possible.

Wilma became a "renter," serving a sentence in another jurisdiction than where she was convicted. She was an alcoholic and a compulsive gambler when she entered the prison system, and was forced through detox upon entry. A few months after her arrival, Wilma was placed on suicide watch, but she was seldom written up by custody officers for disciplinary purposes or restrictions, and was never in segregation or isolation (other than suicide watch). Her health was good, and she slept an average of eight hours or more every day. Her salient behavior is described as an aggressive authoritarian Her primary motivator toward criminal behavior was strongly associated with controller. Wilma had serious premenstrual reactions every month, which in her case was referred to as a health issue.

Police Report about Wilma's Husband

After Wilma accepted a guilty plea and before she was sentenced, investigators spoke to her son, who was graduating from Columbia University and lived on campus. His concerns were that he hadn't heard from his father since Christmas, and this was May. The young man told police that his father was confined to a wheelchair, but had nurses to attend his needs twenty-four hours a day. When police investigators went to his New York City condominium, they found a very old man strapped to a wheelchair who had apparently died of starvation. He had been dead for several weeks, and he and his wheelchair were locked in a closet of the apartment.

Wilma suspected one of the attendants as the perpetrator of the crime, but there wasn't enough evidence to charge anyone with it. Many looked at Wilma as a suspect in her husband's death, but she was jailed awaiting the outcome of her case. Further, she had her own apartment near the prison where she worked, some two hundred miles from New York City. She said she knew nothing of the incident or her husband's condition, because they had been estranged, and she had not been in the condominium for two years. Surprisingly, Wilma had total control over her husband's finances, a responsibility that bewildered her, she explained. She expressed her bewilderment in her journals three times. Finally, she had not seen her son since he entered college, four years prior to her husband's death.

What follows (last story in chapter 18) is a short story characterizing the woman known as Mariasela Rebecca Guzman, or Wilma. We talked often about what she intended to do after her release, and I was under impression that she would not return to the Dominican Republic. She conveyed rather specifically that she would seek a comfortable townhouse in a condominium community somewhere in the suburbs, and would develop a service business of some type. She envisioned taking the train to work. (Wilma does not have a driver's license and does not know how to drive.) Her thoughts suggest that she wants to fit in with the "maze"—as she called the general public—and go about whatever enterprising and private life she could muster. In today's terms, that might mean she wants to be just a random or an anonymous person on the street. However, with her background, her ugliness, and her list of enemies, how is that possible? No doubt ugly people who have histories of criminally violent behavior have a huge challenge with the maze and with being random. "It might be hard to be a convicted felon and live a regular life," Wilma wrote, "but I can try."

Yes, this woman known as Wilma could be your next door neighbor. But that should be okay, if you don't ride the train to work or mess with her at the YMCA's swimming pool.

CHAPTER 17
Tentative Conclusions

A common denominator among the super predators in *Wicked Women* is that they are wired-wrong. To explain that another way, they a strong biological predisposition toward sexual assault, sexual homicide, and brutality. Super predators characterize the intention of destructive behavior early in their childhood. One day, when the opportunity presents itself through circumstance or manipulation, sexual homicide—among other foul acts—follow as a natural progression, consistent with the means (physical strength and skill) of the violator. For instance, at fourteen years of age, Devin sneaked into the home of the child he babysat during the day. Because he lacked the physical power and sexual tools to rape the child's mother, he used props. Brandies's mom told her best friend that her daughter "was a difficult child. Demanding. Crying. Screaming. Never a moment of peace. Always even before she was born, fighting and demanding her own. I would give her anything but my soul. I stayed out of her way. Now that's she such a lovely young lady, maybe things can change between us."

Had any of the super predators in *Wicked Women* possessed the expertise, physical size, and opportunity to commit violent crimes earlier in their lives than they described, a strong likelihood exists that they would have committed those crimes. The intention to engage in violent crimes, especially sexual crimes and murder, was always present. On the other hand, had these super predators been guided by positive parental or care-provider supervision and been provided a moral compass, the likelihood of these potential predators to control their personal urges and refrain from acting is highly probable. More specifically, the urge, motivation, or intention to engage in a heinous crime is always present for super predators from birth through death.[1] An analogy might be similar to a recovering alcoholic—the urge to drink is always present, demanding fulfillment.

Moral Compass. Before moving on, a moral compass based on information provided by the participants in *Wicked Women* can include positive and reinforced social values and norms. Yet unconditional love, respect, and admiration, along with structure, parental affection, attention, and approval or validation were absent from all of their descriptions of their lives. The participants described the opposite experiences, especially a huge lack of concern for their personal welfare and safety. For instance, Annie wrote that her sister whined about her behavior in first grade, and since Angela was bigger, Annie had to try a number of ways to stop her from whinning. She finally prevailed when she discovered fire. "What worked was fire, and she never messed with me after that. I waited till she was asleep and lit up her blankets. My parents knew it wasn't an accident, but they ignored my attacks on Angie"

Because the participants also shared a predisposition toward violent behavior, evolving into a true super predator is not as complicated as some might think. Physiological predispositions are the seeds that when nourished, evolve and demand gratification. When the seeds are nurtured, it is plausible to advocate that the predisposition component (and there can be more than one predisposition, such as alcoholism) can mature to fruition, especially because these individuals lacked a moral compass. When the addiction stage occurs, it may be at different biological times for different people. Nonetheless, the addiction will become a way of life.

The predisposition is also nurtured through a thinking process that is flawed and convoluted in a design of its own making. Similar to all addictions, a provocative remedy is death, revealing that if the individual cannot control his urges, it is up to the state (through capital punishment) to do so. Similar to all predispositions, wired-wrong does not automatically translate to an individual acting on the predisposed behavior, but it does mean that predators have the intent to commit violent crimes. Some experts say, and maybe they're right, that those characteristics are salient at age five.[25]

Personal Accountability

For many individuals who possess a physiologically predisposition of some variety, many take action to prevent their own undesirable conduct through personal accountability, perseverance, and high levels of resolve. Taking charge of one's own behavior requires acceptance of one's own flawed or criminal thinking processes. Obliviously, criminal thinking processes can well be the distraction that sidetracks recovery. Many must hit bottom before they can realize that they must change. Hopefully hitting bottom doesn't include an egregious act. Next, centered in the perspective that for every action (or every stimuli), there's a reaction, a predisposed offender can construct an invisible wall around at-risk individuals, places, and circumstance thereby defusing action or the stimuli that triggers the criminal thinking process. Self-imposed isolation and a strong resolve are key components in altering one's opportunity which tends to trigger criminal thinking processes. Most smart and responsible individuals understand that it is dangerous to tempt fate. If you're a drunk, you don't work in a bar or put a bottle of rum in your cabinet next to the pina colada mix. If you're a pedophile, you don't cruise schoolyards or allow a child to be alone with you. If you enjoy violence, you don't play football, or join law enforcement or the military.

Because criminal intention always impacts criminal thinking, they seek occupations such as ministers and priests, counselors, and law enforcement where they can engage at-risk individuals whom they perceive as easy prey. Inexperienced pedophiles talk about accidents. Individuals with a predisposition toward anything, including sexual assault, know accidents don't happen. Priests don't become pedophiles after becoming priests; they are pedophiles when they choose the priesthood.

Maybe this is why it is so hard to stop super predators. They have to stop themselves. History tells us that it is unlikely they will be identified, apprehended, or even stopped. Control through an open mind is the best we can expect.

Compulsive Sexual Homicide

Compulsive sexual homicide, as discussed in chapter 1, stems from a longstanding and developing urge to kill, when the killing itself is eroticized.[26] Schlesinger's first stage relates to a thinking disorder, which I suggested above in the form of a flawed thinking process. For instance, Margo explained that while she was bring transported to prison, the driver of the vehicle warned her about prison life but in a way that made her "feel better. He made me feel like a girl. I liked that. I kept saying to him, okay, yeah, that makes sense. Then I'd cry a little bit and catch myself. But I couldn't help but think that this was all a mistake. A dream that turned bad ... I'd be out of prison in a few weeks." Margo's flawed thinking is also typified by her idea that she never belonged in prison despise all of her acts of violence.

Another example of flawed thinking is mentioned by sixteen-year-old Sweet Jenny Lee, who explained that a few days after she ran away from home and to avoid a felony prosecution, police arrived at a McDonalds on another matter. When one of the officers recognized Jenny Lee, she ran to the ladies room. The officers pursued her. She attacked them with a piece of broken mirror.

The second stage is when a plan is created to commit a violent criminal act, which can show that the offender has the intent to commit a predatory crime. This stage is pervasively described in every vignette in this work. For instance, similar to other super predators, Sweet Jenny Lee selected victims with care. When she chose Stacy and her children to abduct and terrorize, she knew she could persuade Stacy to the abandoned mansion on the beach. She also thought that the cops would never check to see if she had sexually assaulted either Stacy or her children. And, in fact, they didn't.

Keeping her real personality hidden to most everyone she encountered in prison was a drain on Jenny Lee, but it's standard operating procedure for most sexual predators. Consider what Jenny Lee told the intake officer: "I'm no slut. I'm just me." Psychopaths present masks of sanity to hide their real occupation as a predator.

Schlesinger's third stage relating to internal emotional tension is reported through every vignette in this book except when required as a disguise. For instance, similar to her revenger colleagues, Soccer Mom Tammy requires personal gratification, despite her inability to play fair. She cared for her materialistic lifestyle, and that meant she had to lead a double life—a good wife and a good mother, but also a stone cold predator.

As part of the fourth stage, compulsive sexual homicide offenders know that satisfactory execution of their crime requires their attention, calmness, and calculation, as Schlesinger postulates. For instance, when Dory caught Britt sexually molesting the girl he claimed was his daughter as well as Dory's son, she sliced his throat without hesitation and then immediately killed the girl. After cleaning up, she pulled a blanket up over herself and her son and fell asleep.

The fifth stage suggests that the mind adjusts itself. It understands that the thinking process that caused the commission of the criminal act was flawed, and the mind makes adjustments in order to prevent further criminal activity. This seems to be the case of the predators in *Wicked Women*. They never stop, but continue to operate in a cycle between stages two and four.

An understanding of the five stages helps to locate super predators within a sea of offenders, yet there are other patterns of their behavior that set them apart from garden-variety offenders. In general, human beings can be characterized as rationalizing social animals who behave for all kinds of crazy and not-so-crazy reasons. Unlike other creatures on this planet, human beings justify those behaviors. Relying upon the work postulated in justification, excuses, and denial of prominent colleagues can help better clarify the differences between garden-variety violators and super predators.

Justification and Excuses

Stanford M. Lyman and Marvin B. Scott suggested that justifications and excuses are more often invoked when an offender is accused of a criminal act or wrongdoing.[27] Lyman and Scott explained that justifications are accounts in which one accepts responsibility for a criminal act, but denies the pejorative quality associated with it. For instance, a police officer returning fire in a gunfight admits to justifiable homicide, but denies that the act was immoral. The act was necessary under the circumstances. The police officer, for instance, who had used excessive force to control a defenseless suspect, during an altercation that lacked imminent danger can redefine his action and state that "training and orders dictated my action. My use of force was reasonable."

Super predators in *Wicked Women* justified their criminal behavior, and they never saw their behavior as immoral. Sexual homicide, for instance, was accepted as part of their mission on this planet. People who crossed paths with Annie, Dory, Joey, Margo, Sweet Jenny Lee, and Underworld Lilith should be responsible for the outcome of those encounters. These super predators were merely doing what God intended them to do—seeking pleasure. Brother Pious, Devin, Janelle, Mary, and Wilma felt their behavior was the result of their necessity to control others. Their victims knew what they wanted, they just weren't sure how to get it. Before their victims could make these control freaks feel even more insecure and vulnerable than they already felt, methods of control brought them closer to their mission. Quick sex with a child, and the child would never learn about the weaknesses of the super predator.

Finally, Brandeis, Mickey, Tammy, and Val all felt that each of them represented an instrument of justice. Val looked at the world with Superwoman eyes, as a protector of the realm who defended justice and public good. Mickey implied that individuals, including her sister and former husband, deserved to die. She added that, "I'm sort of a god, you know. I champion the weak and smash the wicked."

Revengers justified violence and a lethal response by believing they represented a higher order of morality and justice.

Why Super Predators Are Dangerous

What makes a super predator dangerous regardless of his or her trigger (pleasure seekers, control freaks, or revengers), and distinguishes their decision-making process from garden-variety violators, is that once super predators validate or justify their actions against an individual, they utilize manipulation toward circumstance, time, and place. That permits a swift and lethal response without the threat of identification or apprehension. For instance, Val always possessed the intention to commit any crime, including murder, but only when she could justify it to herself. Her lethal actions were reasoned behavior, and her strong conviction that her behavior was morally appropriate provided her with the courage to continue. The only limits on her behavior were her physical strength, her experience, and her skill.

As predators physically grow and improve their skills through trial and error, their personal and physical limitations are reduced; and the frequency and intensity of their violent behavior rises. Their criminal acts are therefore only a matter of time, and while they are advancing, they also learn how to deal with their victims' defenses and other intervening circumstances, which might include an erotic relationship with the victim. In Annie's mind, when her best friend and her husband were no longer sexually active with her, they died. In Val's mind, the use of deadly force was unsuitable when she was sexually involved with a victim, such as the little girl in Columbus.

When a super predators attacks, there are no discussions, no threats, no conversations back and forth, such as seen in television dramas. Furthermore, I feel it important to explain that many violent offenders tend to justify their behavior after committing the crime.

Excuses are accounts in which an individual admits that the behavior is bad or immoral, but denies responsibility for his or her action. That is, "Excuses are socially approved vocabularies for mitigating or relieving responsibility," advise Stanford and Scott. The concern of garden-variety violators is to neutralize or reduce any civil, moral, or criminal penalties associated with crimes of violence. In this regards, the super predators in *Wicked Women* failed to identify their behavior as bad or immoral. What makes super predators dangerous is that they believe it is both their destiny and their moral obligation to violate others. Thus, their behavior is moral. Then, too, violators of all descriptions like to provide excuses as an *appeal to accidents, appeal to defeasibility, appeal to biological drives*, and *scapegoating*, despite their acceptance or lack of acceptance about their corrupt behavior. These thoughts widen the earlier perspectives associated with denial.

Appeal to accidents can include an excuse that includes the source of conduct or its consequences, in order to relieve their responsibility of their behavior by pointing to the hazards in the environment. For instance, Tammy explained that the heavy snow on the interstate caused her to lose control of her vehicle, which caused her husband's death. Then there is the "inefficiency of the body" appeal. As Annie explained, since she was physically smaller than her victims, she used devises like drugs, intelligence, and sex to victimize others. The human incapacity to control all physical motor responses is another appeal. We see Brother Pious victimizing others with the help of religion, and his excuse suggested that he did so to make children strong to survive a tragic world—the tragic world he helped build.

Appeal to defeasibility is linked to knowledge and free will. This excuse can include perspectives relative to an individual lacking available information. For instance, Underworld Lilith advanced the idea that she helped foreigners (and her sons) learn a profession, despite that fact that she engaged in human trafficking, kidnapping, and sexual assault. Her perspective was that since she didn't know that human trafficking and sexual exploitation was against the law, she shouldn't be prosecuted. An excuse based on free will can include a link to duress. Anne maintained that while the people around her, including her husband, were killed, children were sexually exploited, college kids were strung out on drugs, and retail establishments lost merchandise, she shouldn't be imprisoned because she never held the criminal intention or motive to commit any of those crimes.

An important point is that all of the predators in *Wicked Women* demonstrated the intent or motive to commit all of the crimes they talked about, from the time they were very young. This finding is not consistent among garden-variety or first-time offenders. Garden-variety violators require time to develop intent, while predators absolutely know what they want to do. They might have to practice and wait until they are skilled and physically capable of carrying out their mission. Mary, for instance, practiced while in grade school and among her caregivers. At fifteen, she was implicated in the murder of a fisherman. It could be suggested that means, opportunity, and motive (MOM) can simplify the components linked to chronic offenders. Means can translate to actually that—a suspect requires the means or capability to commit the act. Mary held the intent to kill, but required physical training and experience to commit the act. The means refers to her training as a shark killer. Opportunity is linked to the chance to kill. Devin demonstrated a similar pattern of behavior, as did all of the predators in this study. Through manipulation of time, place, and people, such as cruising seaside resorts, he sought potential victims who were vulnerable to his suggestions. And as a child, Tammy roamed shopping malls with McCrazy, a girlfriend who would do anything for Tammy, including aid in the victimization of little children.

Appeal to biological drives is part of a larger category of "fatalistic" forces which, argued Lyman and Scott, "in various cultures are deemed in greater or lesser degree to be controlling of some or all events (p. 115)." For instance, some individuals in American society, such as those in poverty, might believe that they are less likely to succeed than those in middle-class families. Biological acknowledgements can be credited with influencing or causing some of the behavior, for which individuals wish to relieve themselves of full responsibility. This thought can include homosexuals, Lyman and Scott offered. Frequently, homosexuals account for their violent behavior by invoking the principle of basic biological nature. One incarcerated priest explained his sexual attacks on children by saying, "It's part of nature. There's nothing I can do to alter Mother Nature's driving force over me. I was born with this infliction."

Scapegoating is derived from another form of fatalistic reasoning, and usually involves other people. To place the blame of a super predator upon someone else is a sure way to appear innocent. For instance, one of two males who were responsible for the sexual assault of a young girl explained that he had intercourse with the victim because his partner told him to do it. "If I didn't do it," Lou said, "he [the other man] would the beat crap out of me. What was I to do?" Lyman and Scott used the example of a young man who tried unsuccessfully to meet a girl by showing off on a bicycle. "She got me into trouble with my father by lying about me. She said I tried to run her down with my bike and that all I did was hang around spying on her" (p. 117).

I interpret scapegoating as blaming the victim. It might be helpful to consider Benjamin Mendelsohn's delineation of a typology of criminal victims. Scholars in the twenty-first century (finally) avoid his discussion, because it blames the victim. The typology consists of six categories:[28] (1) completely innocent victims, (2) victims with minor guilt, (3) voluntary victims, (4) victims more guilty than the offender, (5) victims who alone are guilty, and (6) the imaginary victims. It is noted by Mendelsohn that two of the above are concerned with victims whose guilt is less than the guilt of the perpetrator, and he presents an argument that the strong orientation toward the culpability of the victim lies in the preponderance of rape studies in victimology literature. This is a pretty good story, and the predators in this case study would confirm that Mendelsohn was correct. That would enhance their own validity and their own attack strategies. In a similar situation, I wrote about rapists some time ago. The popular literature at the time argued that some chronic rapists commit rapes because they want to relieve anger, and sex becomes a hostile act. Others can be categorized as power rapists, in which sexuality becomes an expression of conquest. Still others are referred to as sadistic rapists, in which anger and power become eroticized.[29] The impression is that these rapists hold a monopoly on violence, and that to resist would simply provoke additional violence. The literature said that violence is the real mission of most rapists, and that when a victim fights back, she enhances his violence levels, and the event could end in her demise. My findings strongly included sex or lust as motive for most chronic offenders. For example, a guy has a drink or two and wants sex. But the literature is more complicated than that. As usual, some experts made it impossible for females to really understand that some men are dogs, and similar to dogs, they would chew anything in front of them. Nonetheless, what I learned about chronic sexual offenders is that they enjoy the myths about anger, power, and sadistic rape, because typically: "If babes keep thinking that we're violent freaks, half our job is done for us," said a convicted felon who had raped twenty-four females that he could remember. Then, too, imprisoned sex offenders are typically separated from other prisoners, because they're usually passive and cowardly, and are frequently attacked by general prison populations. So where's all the violence they allegedly harness?

Back on point, when all else fails, blame the devil. For instance, Annie explained that when she became severely depressed in prison, she tried to talk to God, "but the only one listening was the evil one." The devil made her do it. Yet when I asked her why she didn't pray before being imprisoned, she said, "I didn't need to pray then."

By this time, you're getting the idea that offenders—and most of us, for that matter—often resort to an excuse (better known as a lie) to make ourselves look innocent. In part, excuses similar to justifications are socially approved vocabularies that attempt to reduce or neutralize an act or its consequences when one or both are called into question. However, to justify an act is to assert its positive value when all the evidence says the act is anything but positive. For instance, underage drinking is looked upon as something many young adults must do in order to be accepted by their peers. Individuals who are responsible for taking the life of another human being can cite self-defense, defense of other people's lives or property, or an action against a declared enemy of the state, such as a terrorist. The best defense against an indictment is to deny, deny, deny. The one problem I see here is that most super predators don't deny their actions. They may deny the morality linked to their crime but not the crime itself. For instance, before Pee Wee Gaskins (Donald Gaskins) was executed in South Carolina for the murder of a huge number of individuals over his lifetime, his last words typified what the participants in *Wicked Women* would reveal: "I have walked the same path as God. By taking lives and making others afraid, I became God's equal. Through killing others, I became my own master. Through my own power I come to my own redemption."

Earlier Studies

Consistent with earlier studies, what has been learned in *Wicked Women* is that wicked violators are rarely indicted or convicted of unspeakable acts. It is easy to think that the criminal justice community embraces witch-hunt strategies among targeted populations, such as Mexicans who cross America's border, the homeless, junkies, and those in poverty.[30] Clearly the US prison populations are consistent with these thoughts, because they largely represent targeted populations and the individuals who are the most likely to be arrested and convicted. There are few official methods of control over wicked predators, in part because of misguided experts and bleeding-heart liberals who contribute to the scholarly literature, the popular press, and popular media performances. Because of their influence and moral panic (such as the promotion and overselling of safety through such strategies as sex offender registries), the rule of law, public policy, and official practices are geared to accommodate an entitled population. This weakens the justice system and signals evolution of super predator status. Super predators develop astounding abilities to disguise their true selves, and an enormous body count is buried in mounds of political rhetoric and misinformation. What has also emerged from this case study is that the criminal justice system lacks both the financial and professional leadership it needs to resolve one of America's worst problems—super predators. That said, it is equally evident that federal intrusion into local matters enhances super-predatory advancement, through the feds tinkering with local capital punishment processes, local immigration matters, and the justice system's ability to identify, apprehend, and convict violators. Someone needs to remind the federal government that the backbone of the rule of law is to control a centralized government's arbitrary intervention in local matters. Let's be mindful that the feds could have prevented 9/11, the economic downturn in the US, and ridiculous combat around the globe to protect what—the victims of the fifteen predators in *Wicked Women*? What about all the victims of other predators yet unidentified?

But what about children like Sweet Jenny Lee and Devin? There are numerous magical moments-of-change stories that can be addressed by many mental health providers of many varieties. Some of those stories can be found in Lenore Terr's *Magical Moments of Change: How Psychotherapy Turns Kids Around* (Norton, 2007), among many other books. In the real world, the time it takes to charm a child who makes destructive choices is more time than it takes for a villain to violently destroy another human being. Some wonder why we send our kids to therapists when they misbehave. "What about personal accountability?" asked Eric Leberg, a parole officer with a lot of experience. "It's the choices we make that decide whether we sleep at home or in a cell." This idea is consistent with positive change, which begins with individuals changing themselves. For example, if Jenny Lee and Devin made conscious decisions to commit crimes, it is equally possible for them to have made righteous decisions to aid others.

Also, it is plausible that criminals like Val can posses feelings that prompt sexually violent behavior. Yet because she is a schemer or manipulator, she accepts the informal directives and formal practices of the Irish Travelers to further her vocation, while that community protects her interests. Yes, a manipulator works people, but a manipulator also adapts to the standards of others for the purpose of exploiting others. Recall Annie, Brother Pious, and the others who have led double lives to further their ambitions to abduct, assault, murder, and so on. They made conscious decisions to stay under the justice radar while feeding their lustful addictions.

If America wants to control criminally violent offenders, the myths of crime control that glorify corruption among criminal justice agencies—such as overly aggressive enforcement and vigilante police officers—and liberal expectations of predator rehabilitation must be separated from the realities. The dumbing down of the American population must cease, the entitled few must pay their own way, and the federal government should keep its legal nose where it doesn't belong. The consequences of weakening America's rule of law (by using it to the advantage of America's enemies or those who feel entitled) confirms the thought that in every previous civilization, when the well-being of criminals, enemies, and politicians held precedence over common good and morality, the citizens were restricted, swindled, and murdered; and the civilization eventually perished. Freedom has a price, and part of that price is keeping society safe from thugs, terrorists, and anyone else who wants to mess with our children.

CHAPTER 18
Short Stories

Annie: The Pilgrimage

Annie's Imagined Meeting with Lenz

"Cab, ma'am?" the hotel doorman asked, a slight smile on his a heavily lined face.

"No, thanks," Annie replied, and swallowed a little of spring's sweetness. "There's an outdoor café, Pastel's. Is it still there?" She wanted to say that she's looking for some magic, magic that can stir a dull heart that drowned somewhere in a dark place before prison.

"Ahh." The doorman sighed and rubbed his chin in thought. "Yep," he said, and pointed the way.

Annie glided down several busy sidewalks. She felt the crowding breeze grabbing her white pleated skirt as stately men glanced at her as they passed. Many of whom, she decided, would give their morning for a single peek at her smooth brown thighs, and many more would buy her wonderful gifts from these exquisite shops, whose windows looked out at her as they had many years ago when she, Mrs. Annie Johns-Rothman, was simply Sweet Annie. Was it wonderful to be alive—again?

Passing many amusing canopies and boisterous signs, the colors of a playful Sunday fair, Annie fantasized. *I'm pleased, more than pleased. I'm delighted I made the decision to see him, even though there are two sides to me. The practical side is for living! But I'm pleased with my braided hair too. Will he recognize me?* she asked no one, but everyone. Then answered her own question. *Naturally.*

Surely, he wouldn't miss a chance! Her eyes were frosted with excitement. Can everyone see the frost? she wondered.

In another hour there would be a long line at Pastel's, each customer insisting on a table near the street so they could see the little people of the world moving on. That waiter had seen them all. *Will he remember me?*

"Where would you like to sit?" he asked.

Mrs. Annie Johns-Rothman decided he was so polite, as he waved a square hand toward tables nestling with wonderful roses. Other tables seemed so barren and weak without nature's prize.

"That table, there," she said, pointing. "Nearest the street with the single pink rose"

He seated her, and she added, "I'd like some coffee and a lightly toasted bagel with apricot jam." She smiled, a soft smile that many used to see. Maybe this waiter would nod approvingly too.

There it is again, she scolded. *Why do I have an insatiable appetite for men to notice me? Or do gardens cry for water? Men always think with their eyes and forget with their hearts. They're like a mortician among mourners!* Since she was a little girl, Annie recalled, she had been taught to please the morticians first, then herself. It wasn't easy to undo all that education.

The waiter snapped his dark bow tie and said, "Right away, madam."

She pressed her lips and briefly closed her blue eyes. Wasn't that snap-of-the-tie reserved for older women wearing thick glasses? He never did it when she was with Lenz. But maybe doing that isn't for older women or girls like Sweet Annie. It's for a sophisticated woman like Mrs. Annie Johns-Rothman, she decided, and squared herself on the thin corner of the cold chair.

Who was staring at her? She tightened her lips and shot a look at the intruder. Is that him? No He was far too old. Too well dressed!

I really love Lenz. Love him with that other side of me, my idealistic side that I keep especially for loving! An awareness pulled at her, and a childhood wish like a sweet morning kiss.

"Annie, Sweet Annie," he cried as he stood. "Oops." His tone changed. "I'm sorry, you look like someone ..." He stopped in the middle of his thought and stood over her, pouting.

Annie raised her chin, "Lenz." Her own expression thoughtful, she appraised his pout and sad eyes. "Sit down, Lenz. You haven't forgotten me, have you?" she asked, an eyebrow arched coyly, the arch of a sophisticated lady!

Lenz's face became animated, and with bravado in his voice, he said, "Annie, I was sure it was you!"

Look at those rich mocha eyes, teddy-bear eyes, sliding over my crocheted white sweater. I love soft scented sweaters. Has he changed? Next he'll ... Yes! He loves this brown leg peeking through my little skirt, and a quick bounce will get attention.

"You look fantastic, absolutely fantastic," he said.

And now, he should take in every part of me that he neglected during that first inspection. He did. She smiled. *Will he add "sweetie" to his statements like he always did?. I hope I'm not going to be disappointed.*

He tagged on, "Sweetie," as if an afterthought, and grinned.

"Actually, I'm still upset with you, Lenz," she teased with a thin look. "You left me holding the bag for a lot of your sins."

"Me?"

He waved both hands, spiteful, warm hands, soft with patience, as only the hands of an artist could be. Hands that patiently turned a proud girl into a beggar, she remembered. "What's a few sins between friends, sweetie?" he asked. "I left because you paid more attention to your"—he paused—"poems." He looked down for a moment, as if in thought. "But that was three years ago." He laughed. "But we were great together. We made a lot of money together."

She needed to correct him, but then she always did. "Not three years ago, Lenz, but four." She relaxed her lips, full yet thin lips that he could never ignore. She hoped he didn't see the creases under her eyes.

"But, of course," he said with one sharp nod, and added, "sweetie."

"I never thought you would grow a mustache," she said, and leaned back. "It looks quite ... attractive." Quickly, she added, "I see you have a new tailor too." Then with an approving smile but a voice full of certain resignation, she asked, "Have you a new little friend?"

"Yes," he immediately replied. He scratched his head. "I have a new tailor. I'm glad you approve, sweetie." His mouth opened, as if he were going to say more, but he stopped.

Had he changed? What was next? He always repeated everything, and always saw the truth like a big city mayor or a French impressionist.

"Yes, I am glad you approve, sweetie. I was fortunate with some of my ah ... paintings. I can now afford a few of the world's luxuries, like a tailor. I, uh, paint," he stammered. "I paint diligently every morning and enjoy my afternoons browsing at galleries and such." Lenz glanced at his long fingers as they tapped the rim of his coffee cup.

"How interesting," she said.

He widened his eyes in anticipation.

"It is morning, my sweet. This isn't little Annie you're talking to." She took in a shallow breath and focused on his striped tie, which seemed like it belonged to someone older. What boring colors! "You obviously finished some great masterpiece earlier this morning. What's her name?"

Lenz cleared his throat like a Wal-Mart welcome. "I can see, sweetie, that you haven't lost your sting." His gaze trailed a girl in shorts walking across the street. He returned his attention to Annie as she started to speak.

"Lest we forget, Lenz," she said in a lofty tone, "we worked together for a long time, and you always claimed you only worked with me, but ... I was so dumb."

She paused, patted his hand, and added, "Why did I ever give you so much control over me, over my life?"

I'm going to hold this smile. I've wanted to tell him this for years, and now that I am being so completely honest with my feelings, I feel so much better. But this won't do. I have a different mission today! But if I were Prometheus, my liver would be reborn to be consumed. But my torn heart would have to be delicately woven from patches of warmth from a summer moon and pieces from a virgin sea of truth. My truths have always been like the stories children hear about cemeteries as told by deaf morticians!

Can he see the chills rushing over me? If I could flow through every nook and cranny in his body, and merge with every secret in his life, I would fill myself with his fragrance, his energy, his every hard lie, and still come out his lover. A thin needle pierces my heart. Can he see the piety in my smile or the wet greed in my spreading thighs? God, I hate him!

"I loved you because I didn't have control over your life," he said and looked at a distant nothing. "I loved your independence, woman," he claimed while he still stared at some void.

"What is it, Lenz?" she urgently asked. "Why do you look away? What do you see?"

"Nothing, Sweet Annie. I see nothing. But I know you're trying too hard to understand everything. Feelings and visions tell reality when it's real," he replied, and cracked his knuckles.

"Ow! Why do you do that? You know I can't stand that sound. For heaven's sake." She took a hollow breath, on the verge of a sharp remark, but caught herself. "I'm sorry, Lenz." She touched his cheek. "I've forgotten what a sensitive man is like."

She felt moist beads forming on her forehead. Would they fall? Would they mar her makeup and reveal the lines under her eyes? He was so relaxed, and she was a wreck. How could she flatter him when she felt like this? "Excuse me," she said. "I need to powder my nose."

Minutes later she returned, back in control. She slipped easily into her chair. *I'll reveal the portion of my legs he adores. Will he ignore them? He's taking in one leg. Yes, he's treating it tenderly, caressing it, giving it new life with his eyes, those eyes that can sap my confidence and turn me into Sweet Annie. He's a dangerous man!*

"Annie, do you know how many nights I have thought about you? About your fantastic body?" His eyes brightened, and he slowly added, as if counting cadence, "About tasting you and lying in thick delicious sweat with you as a grateful look slid across your face." For a moment, he turned his attention to the bright sky as if in calculation, and when he looked at her again, he answered his own question. "Every night. I have thought about you every night. I have imagined your sweet body—"

"Lenz." She cut him off and feathered his lips with her finger. "Don't ..." She filled her voice with spirit. "You left me, remember? I wrote to you. I even mailed my letters to your parents."

"Oh, Annie, I couldn't read them. I cared too much," he murmured as his voice fell to a whisper.

He's entangling me in his look. If he stood inside my body with those eyes, he could see every switch, every button. He'll speak again, but this time in a soothing voice. It will be measured and offer me the quality that hints that I, Annie. am the only person in his life. His eyes still absorb me.

"If I had read any of your letters or saw you on the street, I would have cried! I surely would have cried. But remember, Sweet Annie, you gave me up to the prosecutor."

Annie easily crossed her legs, tugged at her hem, and clasped her hands. This boyish-faced man was always active. Never slept, but knew how to look at her dreams.

"Everything was fine back there, Lenz dear, until you decided to run my life, remember?" Is that sweet little Annie look building in my eyes? Is that flesh under his eyes? It folded and creased as he squinted back long years.

"Yes, I remember. You had a schedule for everything. Schedule, schedule," he repeated with several short nods. "Everything has its time and place. Put everything on a list. Nothing by chance with you, right?"

"I haven't mentioned your 'as it comes' world," she sniped back.

He lit a cigarette and watched the smoke ascend, flowing in the still air. "I wondered what I would say to you if we met. Did you ever—"

Sharply, she broke in ."I imagined your life like a midnight rain. I felt that the rest of your life passed by, and I never knew anything about it. Sometimes, a shadow would run through my mind and it had an offensive smell, like a bus."

"You turned me in," he crooned.

"I didn't want to, I had no choice." She paused. "Remember, Lenz."

She watched his face, his fresh face smothered now with an ugly mustache. *When we worked the streets the world, was a dark flood to me, and I was a haystack somewhere on a dark shore in our room.* "Don't be silly, Lenz," she said, smiling to show the dimple in her cheek. "If I didn't, the state would have asked for the death penalty." *Does my face glow the way it used too when I talked about life and death? He is my inspiration. He stimulated my thoughts. No man has ever stimulated them and left me thoughtless and barren! It's almost as though the only time my mind puts the world together is when I catch his scent. But, the scent of a bus?* She snickered. The couple sitting next to them quickly looked away.

"No, no, Annie," he said softly. "I understand. I really do. It saddens me. It saddens me that I wasn't strong enough to understand you. I wasn't fully a man." He laughed. "At least, well ..." He shrugged. "I didn't know what time it was. My clock is set on num. Those days were great. I seemed centered with the world when you were around. Tell me?" He tilted his head. He didn't have to finish his question; his eyes did it for him.

"Yes, I miss you," she answered, and added, "A lot." *I didn't mean to say that. God, I hate to lie, but he deserves his own medicine!*

His eyes are crowding me, but will they follow my hand as I slide it across my body and smooth it across my tummy and finally tuck it between my legs? As she moved her hand, she noted that his eyes attentively followed, offering nothing of shame. *This is no fun,* she concluded. *Not even a challenge.*

Centuries ago, I had something to offer him, nothing special except money. Centuries ago, I left my childhood for him, all in a moment of time. All of my life led to that moment, and the rest of my life mirrored back to that time. There is the child who wanted to stay with him now, right now, especially since I know him for what he is. A self-righteous drug peddler who adores young girls. Maybe I didn't know him then. But there is the woman who demands something more, at least today.

"Do you remember, Lenz, when we had coffee and bagels here? It was great."

He chuckled. "Every Sunday morning. Yes, how could I forget? We spared heaven and hell at many of these tables." He paused and added, "Annie, we never were seen in public, if you remember."

"Lenz." *Is there a bare, subtle note of encouragement in my voice? Is that the same tone I heard in his police car long ago? What a magic man. Was it all fantasy? I need that magic today.*

"I miss you too," he said, emphasizing each word.

"Do you miss a woman," she asked, "who felt like a girl years ago, or the woman who thinks she's a girl today?" Looking across the street at the familiar shops with their colorful displays, she wondered if she was like those old shops. As she glanced at Lenz, he was busy studying two girls who were staring back at him from the next table.

"Forgive, me," he said softly. "There is only one woman I wish to admire. Would you like to spend the afternoon making love?" His eyes, those teddy-bear eyes, reflected a kind of empty glitter, and there was something about his expression that was distant, even though his eyes are gentle, mingling, and consenting. Suddenly his fingers snapped wildly for the waiter. "Check please."

She stared at him. *Annie Johns-Rothman will have her day in court. I'll win.* She looked hard at the girls and back at his expectant grin. Her tongue flitted between her teeth, and she moistened her lips. "Lenz," she said smoothly, "I have plans, thank you." *Why does he think I'd accept? I need to get away now or I'll linger in his magic forever.* She stood.

"My, my. You're sure anxious, Sweet Annie! I'll be gentle."

"Take off the god-suit, Lenz. I am anxious—anxious to leave you forever."

"Are ya sure?"

"Yes, I'm sure! I can resist you, you know. And I'm here because I was curious to see if I could walk away from you."

"Sweetie, you love me and you know it. There's fire between us. Besides I was your best supplier ... of love. I always delivered."

"Good-bye, Lenz. And pay the waiter this time ... sweetie."

As she reached the corner, she glanced back over her shoulder. The young girls were leaving. Lenz searched his pockets as the waiter stood over him. Annie Johns-Rothman wore the warm smile of a child. *I did it! I'll kick off these heels and skip down the street singing, "Mecca, hearts, four bits a dollar, the higher he jumps, the louder he hollers."*

Brandeis: Voices

What wonderful times those were in my small Pettet family. I was a happy child and didn't know it. All I had to do was to swing open a huge kitchen door and walk a few steps through the narrow hallway. I'd pass the water closet with its too-tall-for-me seats and enter a room full of love—the kitchen. Pots were usually full with browned bubbling onion butter, sometimes blanketed with layers of green peppers and herbs. There was love and voices in the kitchen that still push through my mind, and I can actually see the faces of those I love.

I can see me, a pathetic little child aimlessly wandering in the kitchen, wrapped in an itchy plaid flannel nightgown. But I remember thinking better to be itchy than deal with those unrelenting city winters. I'd climb to the table to find two steaming circles—a mug brimming with hot cocoa and a bowl full of hot cereal. Right in the center on my cereal was a melting glow of butter. Because I was a spoiled child, I was allowed to sweeten my bowl with dark brown sugar, until *Mémère* Pettet interrupted, pouring warm half and half from her tiny enamel pot. She hummed my favorite tune, a tune her grandmother had hummed for her when she was my age outside of Paris.

As hard as I tried to bring to mind a picture of two grandmothers in the same household, in a distant city far away on the other side of the ocean, I couldn't. I guess my imagination whirled into a bowl of hot cereal, running butter, and those wonderful voices.

With my tummy full, we would play, sing, and straighten up until nap time. Mémère would sprinkle the corners of my bed with holy water, keeping the devil away until I awoke to the handsome eyes of *Grand-père* Pettet. Always he said, "Come, *mon enfant.*"

I remember him holding and shaking me just a bit, as he said, "Mémère, mémère, come home from work and take this child from me. Give me peace." I didn't mind that sometimes both Mémère and

Grand-père were away, as long their voices and laughter cluttered everywhere.

Mémère and maman cleaned the medical offices and rooms at night in a giant hospital with big windows that looked over Boulevard Diderot near the Bastille, a flocking place for tourists to Paris. *Père* called their jobs "midnight superintendents." And because everyone worked, there was little time to make some of my favorites, such as vegetable soup, but I closed my eyes and thought about the midnight jobs of my favorite people.

Daytime was just as happy. Mémère and maman took Grand-père's place as chef and entertainer. He loaded the great black trains at the train line; while my papa butchered veal at the exciting Montmartre Market during the day, and often into the clutches of the cold night. Every grand-père, mémère, maman, and papa worked hard in those days and helped each other. It was the same story, so I never felt strange with strangers.

Saturday mornings, it was my job to set the huge wooden table that had a secret ledge, short drawers, and curvy pillars. I was the only one who ever saw things from under the oil cloth, so I had special secret about the world. I did share my secrets with Yanta, my red-haired doll. You see, I was the only one who ever lifted the oil cloth and chose the spoons and forks from the short drawer, while my fingers slid down the curvy pillar. Then Grand-père raised me high enough to reach the dishes and glassware in the cabinet over the counter.

Once everything was in place and the glasses were filled and the plates steamed with goodness, Mémère breezed through the door from work with a knowing smile and a shopping bag stuffed with work clothes. "Oh," she exclaimed, "how helpful of you two to prepare breakfast." I braced my chin like a soldier, and Grand-père did the same. Mémère gave us a special kiss and sat, sniffing the air. "Nannie, you must be proud." she would always say to me.

In the afternoon, Mémère, Maman, and I baked apple pies and listened to the serials on the radio. My favorite was *Our Gal, Sunday*, probably named after the day we went to mass, I'm sure! But I listened most attentively to *Cinnamon Bear* just before I'd march across the hall in time to watch Mémère wrap a scarf around her silly hair. Busy hard hands tucked it tightly under the bun at the nape of her neck. We would wash the kitchen floor.

My job was to crouch on the cold linoleum floor and stir the smoking water in the bucket with a bar of soap, and I imagined how my favorite people in the world, Mémère and Maman cleaned the floors at the hospital. Even now, I could easily hear Mémère singing a wonderful little French tune; I envisioned her on the Bir Hakeim bridge over the Seine River, staring at the one of the statues made by Injalbert while she snacked on a *formule gouter*. And there that sweet dear remained, not at the bridge but on the floor in the hospital with Maman at her side, both hunched over buckets and singing folklore about kittens and dolls, filling in my name in places, until the floor sparkled because of their powerful hands. As always, she covered the floor with newspapers and dried her hands inside her apron. "Clean, yes? Now we cook."

I watched so eagerly as she turned a heavy round caraway loaf over and scratched a quick cross on it. Then she flipped it over, braced the loaf with her left arm, and carved a perfect slice as if by magic. The large blade passed her right shoulder with the same margin with every slice thereafter. I could hardly wait to learn how to do that, but my arm was too short to hold the bread.

Saturday evening was also spent in the kitchen, where the pots were boiling and the galvanized tub had been placed next to the oil burner, making it easier for Papa to pour the hot water for my Saturday ritual—a bath. With a shining face and squeaky hair, I performed my interpretation of a ballerina across the hall for my Saturday night fun.

Grand-père turned on the music hour and Mémère mumbled under her breath as the sparkling linoleum was again in sight. She raced to gather the flying newspaper, which Grand-père and I let skip away from our dancing feet. Soon the hour was over, and I was tucked under a chest-crushing quilt, dreaming of angels as the corners of my bed were sprinkled with holy water and my forehead gently blessed by Maman's lips.

One Saturday night in July, Grand-père did not turn on the radio. There would be no music hour. He was in bed and he didn't move. Aunts and uncles and neighbors came, not to dance or sing, but to whisper and weep. I asked if we could dance, and when I climbed on Grand-père, my father carried me away. Grand-père wouldn't speak to me either. Days later we were in church and then at a graveyard. As the casket was lowered in silence to its final resting place, it stole glitters from the summer sun and dried my wet eyes. Those voices never returned to my kitchen, but they do return into my mind. I hear them now, even though I'm centuries away. So many years away from those voices I once heard. I suppose home is really the place we all go to hear those voices, voices of dead generations that I'll never hear again.

Brother Pious: Unknown Flavor

Professor Pious Christian used to be an active man, but now he only directs his housekeeper, who prepares meals and tends to every household chore. His enjoyments were the hearty maple scent of tobacco and eager students like young Dr. Karsa Mitchell, known as Mitty. Before supper, the professor strolled into his study while Mitty napped on the professor's favorite leather sofa. Through ferretlike eyes, the old educator glanced at the dust-laden books lining the wall, and then at the fat letter Mitty had delivered earlier that day. He dry-washed his withering hands and slid a once-sturdy frame into a teetering chair that would cry out with the slightest lean. He grinned and clutched an alabaster pipe between his teeth.

Drawing a kitchen match from a sagging vest pocket, he sparked it with a brittle thumbnail, sniffing the air after starting his pipe. Sure, the professor thought with a frown, all these young graduate students ignored him since his forced retirement three years ago. Although for their own gain, they had helped themselves to his research. He sneered. At least the results of his last research would never reach the medical press.

Earlier that day, when Mitty gave the letter to Christian, she said, "After supper, I must begin my field trip. Do *not* read my letter, Professor, unless I fail to return in three days. I told my colleagues that I've gone fishing, but I wanted someone to know my whereabouts."

Humph, the professor thought. Why didn't she ask advice? But he knew that few listened to an old man True, Mitty had used his files when she started her career; and now, like the others, she considered Christian obsolete. Mitty's greatest sins were pointed out quietly by the professor's new housekeeper. The young doctor worked herself to the bone and ignored her teacher. Why wait three days to read her letter? Christian decided, and opened it.

Dear Professor Christian:

I can be found sixty miles north of your summer home. I am in the Allagash Wilderness of northern Maine, near the unmarked community of Norris.

Perhaps you will remember, although it was a long time ago. You provided the Emmett Thornton file for me to review. When I arrived at Bellevue Hospital in New York City three years ago, I examined Thornton. Your memory might be vague, but he was the man who was in a somnambulistic condition, wandering through the subways tunnels of the city, and subsequently arrested. The police said that the "wino" was incoherent and, of all things, coated with excessively fat maggots.

They brought him to Bellevue for treatment. When the interns examined him, they reported several gouges in his pasty flesh. They nearly lost the pathetic man when they bathed him. His heart stopped twice, and after further treatment they wheeled him to the psychiatric unit. That's when they called you for your evaluation, but you had retired weeks before.

When I arrived at Bellevue as a staff member, after I graduated from med school, I elected to conclude your evaluation on this strange fellow, Emmett Thornton. His voice was impaired, and he pushed deep growls through a parched throat. He sneered even as he slept. Weeks later, he responded to therapy, and painstakingly, he agreed to write about his experiences.

After reading Emmett Thornton's journal, I committed him to maximum security at Kencone Mental Hospital. His parents were deceased, and, as a matter of course, I contacted Dartmouth College, his alleged alma mater.

Their answer and photograph forced my review of Thornton's absurd tale. You see Professor Christian ... I was fooled by his appearance. Thornton's eyes possessed wild hatred, and his ruddy complexion seemed riveted with corruption, suggesting that he was an old man who had neglected his way—decades ago. The timid face in his college photograph and the new knowledge that Thornton had graduated from college last year told me I had done him an injustice. Hence, my visit to Norris. I didn't want to be wrong twice!

"Indeed," the Professor bellowed. He put Mitty's letter down, deciding he would read the rest of Thornton's account after checking on the housekeeper's progress in the kitchen. Returning minutes later, he whispered, "These young interns think I'm a decayed fossil." A tiny tear meandered down a cold cheek.

Thornton's account:

Bruce Winters, my college roommate, and I had planned to go camping in northern Maine. We decided to both drive, since Bruce would depart afterward for his Nova Scotia home and I would be off to Long Island, my home.

I had presented Bruce a token of fellowship: a blue and white paisley shirt with tapered ends and his initials, BMW, over the chest pocket. Bruce wore it for the trip. We left after lunch, but I stopped at a bookstore, browsed pleasingly, and made four purchases. I would need entertainment while Bruce hunted.

Hours later, I arrived near our campsite. We agreed to meet at the ranger's station, shown on the map, twenty miles from the main highway. I had driven twenty-five miles. Although the area was desolate, I found a roadside tavern. I cautiously entered the establishment and ordered a drink before asking directions. My uneasiness in the past with fellow students had provided me with the nickname Hermit. I pledged to leave Dartmouth and Hermit behind.

After I finished my second cold drink, provided free of charge by the bartender, Charley, I stood next to my small car. I was dizzy but proud. Proud that I, Emmett the Hermit, had spoken so confidently with my new friend, Charley. I had acquired a new voice too! A voice I would use forever.

After driving a few miles, I remembered Charley's warning, "Be careful, these roads are foolers at night." He was right. The once smooth road narrowed and was now an unpleasant graveled path. I must have traveled in the wrong direction! Emmett the Hermit screwed up again.

I stopped in the veiled darkness of the wilderness. The trees bordered the path tightly, and their twisted branches scraped against each other, tossed by a scurrying breeze. I snickered with my illusion that the branches were communicating with one another. I looked for the quarter moon that had been guiding me, but the tree limbs seemed to have shunted its glow. I heard an owl's hoot and the clucking of ducks. I must be near a lake, I thought.

"What's that?" I said aloud as a figure swished through my headlights. I immediately accelerated and was now barreling through thin, chilly air. I reached under my seat for a hunting knife that I couldn't use to save my life, and held it tight. The fellows were right. I was a hermit and a coward!

Suddenly there, off the road, I saw a wavering light. I squinted to read the faded letters of the sign—Happiness Inn. I made a sharp left turn onto the dirt road leading to the inn. The absence of automobiles should have warned me, yet the welcoming lights, which glowed like the eyes of a neglected pet, hastened my entry.

The inn's business was conducted in a dim taproom. The food, liquor, and room rates were posted on the wall over the head of a bright-eyed girl. "Evening, sir." She slurred the two words into one and swept her long, dark hair over her shoulder. "Can I help you?"

I dropped onto the wooden bar stool. It teetered from unevenness, and I firmed my balance with both hands on the bar. I wanted to look worldly, but failed. "Hi," I said almost loud enough to be heard in the quiet of that room. In my new voice, I added, "I'll have a beer, please," and smacked my lips the way Charley had done.

"Certainly," she sang, almost as if she'd expected my request. "My name is Melody. Would you like anything else?"

"Just some directions. I'm lost. I'm looking for the ranger's station that was supposed to be twenty miles from the highway."

"It looks like you'll have to spend the night. It's thirty miles away, but it might as well be a hundred. The bridge is out and you would have to circle around the highway," she said matter-of-factly. "We have a lovely upstairs room that overlooks the lake," she added.

"Oh," I replied. "Do you have a phone I can use? My cell is dead."

I entered the telephone booth near the doorway, and after a ridiculous conversation with the information operator, spoke with the ranger. At first, the tiny voice sounded like Charley's. Then I decided that everyone in the area spoke in a slow, even drawl. The ranger said that no one had been by that day, and suggested that my friend might have checked into an inn for the evening. Another heavy rain was expected.

I returned to Melody's inviting smile. I sipped my beer slowly; it was appallingly warm. I paid for a room, got my overnight case, and said good night to Melody as I climbed rickety but polished stairs. I turned when I reached the top and smiled. She was busy with some ritual at the cash register. Sensing my stare, she paused and looked up with a mischievous half smile. I was enticed, but my experience with girls had never ventured beyond my dreams.

As I lay under crisp linen sheets, I hoped Bruce had found a cozy inn too. If he found Happiness Inn, Melody would be his by this time! I tossed and turned restlessly the rest of the time, and welcomed morning's light, which rushed into the rustic room. I felt like a child in a strange bed. Pushing my uncertainty away, I washed and dressed. I only shave once a week, and this wasn't the day. I always told myself that when I get older, maybe I'd trade my baby face for a man's face.

Walking down the stairs, I slid one hand along the wooden rail. The other held my case. "Good morning," I said in a cracking voice to Melody.

"You can't leave yet," she said urgently. "Mother has set breakfast for you in the garden, and you need your breakfast."

I scratched behind my ear, shrugged, and walked into the garden. Breakfast was quite delicious and filling, and the coffee was hot and strong. I was glad I stayed. I studied the log inn while I drank more coffee.

The inn had been expertly built, and the grounds were well tended, well fenced, and well watered, having in this latter respect a trickling stream that branched in exactly the right angle past a garden of bright flowers before feeding a picturesque lake. The forest creatures busily went about their daily routine, unaware of my presence. The sun sanctified the area, crowning the grounds as if it were the birthplace of some religious leader.

As I looked across the lake, something glistening caught my eye. It was a peculiar shine that seemed to run the lake's width and at a height of four or five feet. My quizzical expression must have attracted the attention of my hostess, Melody's mother.

"Don't ya look over there," the old lady said.

"I beg your pardon?" I asked, as my fancy remained fixed on the distant gleam. "I'll be darned," I added and glanced into her hard steel-gray eyes. "It's a fence. A wire fence!"

"That's a quarantine area, no trespassing." Her raised eyebrows suggested she had more to say.

"It seems like an odd place for a fence!" I remarked.

"That acreage belonged to Mr. Cosgrove, and the folks in the area had it fenced up," she said..

"Mother," Melody shouted, walking toward us. "You're talking about Cosgrove's, aren't you?" She glanced at me, "Mr. Thornton, pay no attention to Mother. She loves her tales.".

"Off with ya, child," the mother said dismissively. Then she changed her voice to just above a whisper. "My daughter thinks she runs the place. But I'll tell you about Cosgrove's if'n I want." Her small chin jutted out.

"I don't want to cause any trouble, ma'am."

"Such a fine lad. If I were Melody's age, I'd marry ya by noon."

I didn't know what to say, and rubbed the back of my neck. "Tell me about Cosgrove's," I finally said. "I've got a little time." There! I had said something commanding and felt better already. I looked sharply into the old lady's eyes.

"That's what I like," she said. "A man who knows what he wants. Well, sir. One afternoon this fella, his mute wife, and daughter arrived. He claimed that he had purchased that piece of swamp land. Said his name was Cosgrove and wanted to know how to get out there. Being neighborly, I told him to walk along the shore to the boathouse." She pointed a stubby finger that ended in a discolored nail. "You can't see it from here," she explained, "but it's near the road.

"There's a boat there and they could use it to cross the lake. So I told Cosgrove that they should take the boat to the pier. Then a hundred yards or so away from the pier, they would find a path that winds around and would lead them to a small cottage."

"Mother," Melody complained, "that's enough."

"Oh, hush, child, and tend your chores. Well, Mr. Thornton," she said in a confidential tone, "several months later Cosgrove stopped in for the first time since they went to that godforsaken place and had a warm beer—"

"Mother," Melody protested, "our beer isn't warm."

"It is, child, and that's because you keep the refrigerators off to save electricity," her mother replied. "So, Cosgrove told us that he was very pleased that his wife was with child. Now, his daughter would have a playmate." She added in a low voice, "They rarely left that place. God only knows what they ate!" Her fingers danced on the table as she continued her yarn. "A few months later, he returned. This time he told us that his child had died during delivery.

"And It's no wonder. Living in all that filth, what did he expect?" She caught her breath. "A few days later, when I saw the sheriff, I told him about Cosgrove's baby. The sheriff said that he would stop out, although I could tell he didn't want to go. Then what do you think happened?" she asked me.

I reclined in the my chair. "I have no idea," I said, half-amused, half-annoyed.

"The sheriff returned with Cosgrove's wife. He said that he couldn't find Cosgrove, his daughter, or the dead baby anywhere, and that the lady needed urgent medical attention."

"I see." I traded a covert glance with Melody. I knew the old lady wasn't done with me.

"When they took the lady to the hospital, the doctor said she needed mental treatment." The old lady nodded. "'Course, I knew all along that she was nuts, being mute and all. But then, her eyes were filled with Satan's own fire too." She threw up her arms. "But who'd listen to an old lady? Well, sir, the weeks passed, and we learned that Mrs. Cosgrove escaped from the institution and was seen in this area. The sheriff and some ole geezer, who spoke words no one understood, searched everywhere."

"Finally ..." She exhaled and blinked rapidly. "They found her. And when they did, her bones were clean."

She sat back in the chair and her eyes widened. "Whatever happened out there, only Cosgrove knows—if'n he's still alive. No one has seen him, his daughter, or the remains of the unborn baby. The ole geezer, who said he was studyin' Cosgrove, said that he had seen two empty graves." The proprietor covered her lips. "I tell ya, it's the devil's work. Ain't no man big enough to go over there anymore," she finished, and folded her arms.

I stared at the sky, that now looked threatening. The sun had been hidden by several dark cloud tufts. "Might rain," I offered. I smoothed my hair and fought the chill off my back with a confident expression. I thanked them both for their hospitality and jumped into my car. I was anxious to find Bruce and tell him about my adventure. A half-mile down the dirt road, I stopped.

"Darn it," I muttered. "What would I tell Bruce? That I was still a hermit and scared of my own shadow? Heck, I only briefly glanced at Melody's sweet body." I slammed the dashboard and glanced out the window. I spotted a ramshackle roof in the distance. "It's the old boathouse!" I exclaimed. I decided to answer the challenge and strapped the knife to my ankle. I hurried down the ravine and ran over the soft earth to the boathouse.

The battered boat was still curiously afloat. An inch of stagnated water covered the bottom, and I scooped it out. After I had got rid of most of it, I realized that I could have turned the boat over. But the uncertainty of making a wrong decision put me in a strange state of mind. Rowing toward the pier, I noticed the lake became murky and shallow. The pier was damaged, so I walked carefully along the side rails and fought my way through the towering foliage on the shore. At last, I found the path. I looked at the darkening sky and took a deep breath before continuing. Bruce would be proud of me, and Melody would know I was a man.

The odd density of the wild stirred my senses. It reminded me of a primitive scene that I had once viewed in a magazine. I shivered. I should have worn my jacket. It was getting cold. My tennis shoes were covered with the sludgelike substance that passed for dirt. I wiggled my toes and felt the dampness. Sniffing the air, I grimaced at the foul and harsh odor, worse than a gym locker. And the stillness was disturbing, an almost stoic stillness that might be felt by a person awaking in a buried coffin.

"Why am I here?" I asked out loud. "Gosh, I wish I was at the library."

Something else was wrong too. I searched for a logical answer, and then snapped my fingers. I didn't see any animals, not one. I didn't hear any birds. "What kind of a godforsaken place is this?" When I realized that I had used the old lady's words, I grinned. Now, the stillness was laughable and in keeping with her morbid tale.

"Even the trees are dead in this twilight grove of disaster," I said, and laughed at my description.

Finally I saw the cottage, Cosgrove's cottage. It was as lifeless as the area I had just walked through. It stood on a slight mound in a clearing. Its windows, although crusted with dirt and neglect, seemed to return my curious stare. Jovially, I tapped on the door. "Anyone home?" I called. It felt good to be brave!

Entering, I left the door open and cautiously walked a few paces. It was a dark and dismal chamber of abominable filth, just as the old lady had said. More than abominable! The cottage seemed plagued by an antediluvian condition. I realized that the foul odor I'd smelled earlier originated from this place, this place that once had been a home.

I grabbed my hunting knife and held it at the ready as I moved about in the darkness. Even God's light rejected this place. Now, another nauseating odor was collapsing my lungs with a malevolent smack, as if someone had hit me. I covered my mouth and turned. Nothing could keep me there now. I envisioned running all the way to the lake.

A sound. I heard a sound, or was that my mind shouting at me to get the hell out of there. *Worry not, I'm going.* I gagged. I felt ill and wanted relief, but turned when I heard that groveling sound again.

"What's that?" I cried as a thin chill penetrated my wet skin. Something small was crawling on the ground. "Sure," I said, staring into the void, "my brains. Don't be silly, Emmett,"

Another sound … and then I saw it. Lethargic, vacant eyes in a hairless moon face that protruded from a small grotesque body.

I froze with fright. It wasn't large enough to harm me … but its skin was crowded by pustules and its form was hideous. It wailed an insidious snarl as its jagged, tiny teeth snapped repeatedly.

Never had I seen such malignant expression, nor would I ever forget it! That putrid, convulsing expression seemed from Satan's own imagination.

My mind teetered on insanity as I stared at that mutation … that child that had poured out of a woman's womb, and had now been mutated for survival!

"Oh, God!" I ran through the door, only to stumble and fall as the sky broke loose in its fury, and rain hammered the sludge. I felt a sharpness slice my leg and realized I had fallen on my knife. Desperately, I squeezed the bleeding wound. From inside the cottage, I heard that mindless wail insidiously as the hideous corruption crawled closer to the door … and me. When the clouds cracked, I looked up, but saw more than I wanted. I was looking into the primitive, opaque eyes of a young girl. She snarled like the thing in the cottage and swung a club at my head.

I awoke, maybe hours, maybe years later, bound and in a pit. Staring at me were those primitive eyes of that girl. I struggled for freedom, but was too weak. I glanced at her shirt, tied under her small breasts, and I saw... Oh, God, what I saw! I saw the initials BMW. I swallowed and breathlessly demanded, "Where's Bruce?"

She stared back at me. She didn't speak. A sick feeling jammed my soul. I screamed again. She seemed unmoved by my action, and offered me several pieces of foul-smelling meat.

I cried ...

When I slept, my dreams were so aggravating, so inhuman, that I dare not recall them. When I was awake, that small form of corruption would stare down at me and wail. And she—or better still, it—looked at me with steady eyes, the way a girl had done when I was in eighth grade. She liked me too. At least, I think she liked me, because she fed me constantly. Sometimes even when I slept. The food tasted vapid and unpalatable and had an aged rank odor. After several days or weeks, or even months for that matter, I actually became fond of that unknown flavor, but I hated it when I would wake with a mouth full of food. If it wanted to get me fat, it did a good job. My leg healed, which was a surprise. I thought I'd die of infection. I regained my strength. Finally, I escaped from that place and ran as fast as my sore feet would move.

Mitty had added at the bottom of the page, "Now, Professor Christian, that you have read Thornton's account, you may be able to understand my journey."

The professor placed the letter on the desk and lit his pipe. He telephoned Kencone Hospital, and his eyes closed when he heard the answer to his query concerning Emmett Thornton. He had escaped. His doctor suspected he was heading back to the Allagash Wilderness.

The professor stood and smiled. "Now the whole story fits into place," he said. Calmly he went into the dining room and made himself comfortable at the table. Mitty was already there.

A thin smile crossed the professor's face. "Eat, Mitty," he said.

Mitty spat out the meat in her mouth. "I can't. My hands are tied!" she screamed.

"Oh," the professor remarked casually. "My housekeeper will help you."

The kitchen door flung open and the housekeeper entered the room. Her primitive, opaque eyes rested on Mitty, and she wailed her insidious snarl, summoning her baby brother.

"Yes," the professor said. "You're much too slender for our purposes, Mitty. And I think you'll discover that the meat possesses a delightful and unknown flavor."

The End

Dory: Mandarin Collar

Dory stopped on the second to the last step and rubbed her chin, wishing away the weak odor of the subway. Hordes of sweaty people pushed into her like a dark flood, but she couldn't decide which it would be: a sheer white dress with scads of lace and a lapis blue ribbon to match her eyes, or an elegant ivory satin outfit with a mandarin collar and a pin, adding a Victorian flavor. Either outfit would make her irresistible at Manny's Garden Café once more.

Had the world been unfair? No. She shrugged inside her shapeless brown sweater and sniffled. A few more dollars, and that mandarin collar outfit would be hers. It was logical that she sought out Doc. He was the only one she could turn to, the only one who would provide the necessary funds to buy it.

Dory frowned. What was this angry face about on such a cheerful day? Surely, the doc couldn't forget the girl he'd bought a solid gold bracelet for last year. Mmm, the incompetent have terrific obsessions for logic and order, as have artists and hookers down on their luck. Would not one new outfit paint her world perfect? She smiled at her thoughts.

The rudeness of the commuters reached her, and Dory was pleased. She blended in with something, rather than staying impervious in the unlabeled jar of nothing that had encircled her. But who had laughed? There ... that man who stood to the side and slid into the corner of her eye. He had laughed! He was the kind of man who had to do with the odor in the subway. She thrust her hands into the pockets of her worn jeans and clutched the wad of money that made the difference between that man with the weak eyes and her.

What did that broken man know? She certainly wouldn't have looked at him at Manny's, late Sunday afternoon or not. Ah, Manny's. That's the ticket. The absolute charm of it held the crowd on the street as they watched, pointing fingers and sighing at this one or that. *But they watched me most. Me, Dory, with a wide-eyed look that sprinkled magic as well-dressed men approached my table with scented words and money clips in their efforts to possess me, until they fell madly in love.*

Sweet doc. She couldn't recall him completely. They had wine that made her feel giggly, girlish, even grateful. She wore an enchanting gown that flowed pleasingly, and those repulsive heels that were a smidge too small. They pinched, yet they looked so terribly elegant. He was a good dancer, and spun her away from him and then brought her back at the precise moment that her gown was at its fullest. He had no idea that she was bothered by her heels. She removed them and his tie, tied them together and pitched them into the crowd.

Now, she glanced at her running shoes as she walked toward his office. She feathered the dark hair that had always been managed into tight French braids. She stopped to look at the fat pigeons that grouped everywhere. Were they laughing at her, too?

It was obvious that the pigeons had no idea that she used to scatter peanuts at them. Perhaps, when she was draped in that sheer white dress with scads of lace below a ribbon that matched her eyes, they would remember her. Now, they approached like underpaid policemen, and she ran.

The doc's office was on the next block, and thank goodness her charade was at an end. She sniffled and wished she had a handkerchief. What color would it have to be? If only she could find one that matched her eyes. But he would be so delighted that she came to him. She pushed out her lower lip, which she knew was enough to do away with any appearance of indecision. *No, I simply mustn't promise the doc more than the others. Will he ask about that gold bracelet? I'll tell him that a blind lady has it.*

The brass plate read Dr. Edwin Jensen, and before she went up the stairs, she recalled the lines from a silly nursery rhyme: "I stuck in my thumb, pulled out a plum, and said what a good boy am I." It was the glow of her heart and her Cheshire grin that made her bright. Dory felt all the better for it!

Had she not learned her lesson about finances? Now it would come to an end. Imagine! Trashing about on pigeon-ridden streets, as if she were a child. Alas—not for her!

As she opened the door, she sprang back and squinted at that skinny man she had first seen at the subway. Such gall! And why the smirk? He's surely mad or a fool. Had she known him? She let out of breath and climbed the stairs, unconcerned about the desperate swish from her shoes.

A hard-nosed nurse stopped chewing something long enough to ask, "Yes?" She did not wait for Dory's reply and returned to her ledger and her chewing.

"Quite," Dory said, out of breath. "Dr. Jensen please."

"I'll try to fit you in," she said. "Can I tell the doctor your problem?" she asked almost as an afterthought.

"Tell him Dory is here. He'll know."

When Dory sat on the tweed sofa, a woman of immense size moved away. Her piglike eyes, small yet effective, peered at Dory from across the room until the nurse interrupted. "The doctor will see you now, Mrs. Oppenheimer," she said.

Dory noticed that the nurse had smiled away her hard-nosed expression and stopped chewing when she spoke. She scooted back on the tweed sofa, crossed her legs, and listened as the woman snorted through the doctor's inspection.

At long last, Mrs. Oppenheimer appeared at the doorway with a settled look. "Go right in, sweetie," she said to Dory, and walked as though she were stepping on cherries.

Dory glanced at her. Oh my! From what cupboard had the doc found that flush color for his patient? She smiled and entered the examination room. Dory heard the voice of the nurse behind her. "Sit, I'll check your pulse."

Dory sniffled and turned. "But I—"

She wasn't able to complete her sentence as the nurse shot a finger at a chair and said, with a stepmother's glare, "Sit or leave." She chewed wildly on whatever it was in her mouth.

When the doctor came into the room, Dory stared hard at him. He wasn't Jensen. This man was heavy limbed with slumping shoulders and a repulsive wriggle under wobbling eyes. "Where's Dr. Jensen?"

He didn't look at her. He had found something of interest in a cupboard and was engrossed with his discovery. "I am Jensen," he said in a slow voice, while the nurse pulled up Dory's sleeve without missing a beat in hr chewing.

"Heard your sniffle," he said, needle in hand as he approached.

"Wait!" she said urgently, and pulled her arm away, although not far enough. She felt the tingle than the sting.

"Two, three days," he said as he turned leave, "and you'll feel much better."

"You've made a mistake. Don't you understand," she pleaded.

"No mistake," the nurse replied. "The doctor knows exactly what he's doing," she added with raised brow.

A noodle reeked with sudden hostility found its mark. "Ow!," she cried. "That hurts more than the shot."

"It should," said the nurse. "My word!" she exclaimed, pressing the pad harder. "The doctor was kind to treat you for free and you tell me that he made a mistake."

"Free ..." She pulled away her arm. "I didn't want treatment, and I don't want your charity." She locked her stare on the nurse and pushed out her lower lip. "Where did you ever get that idea?"

The nurse scratched the back of her neck, gave her the she had given Mrs. Oppenheimer, and said, "Forgive me, miss. From the way you were dressed, I assumed--"

"Don't you know that you can't judge anyone by the way they're dressed?" Dory said, emphasizing each word. "How much do I owe, please?" Her voice made it clear that she always got what she wanted.

The amount towered a lonely Sunday afternoon, and Dory did not have to count. It equaled the wad in her worn jeans.

"I shall like to speak with the doctor," she said.

"He went to the hospital," the nurse replied cordially. "Please take his card and call him in the morning. Or shall I have him call you?"

Dory stood on the pigeon-ridden street. Her hands were tucked inside empty jean pockets. She felt the sting in her arm and closed her eyes for a moment. Had she been dreaming? When she snapped open her eyes, what would she see? Somehow she knew that that weak-eyed man from the subway would be near, and she wasn't disappointed. *Ask not what you can do for your country, but what it can do for me ... right?* Dory asked herself as she stared at that weak-eyed man.

Janelle: Raindrops

The rain reeked with cold and the carelessness of a stepmother, Janelle recalled. Had there been days when she didn't mind the rain? She scratched behind her ear. There were times when rain had sparkled away a shaded routine and scooted a fresh promise in the eyes of her daughter. Janelle nodded with the look of woman who saw something that wasn't there. But something changes when you're a cop directing traffic in the rain, and the only thing between you and a cold car bumper is a yellow raincoat.

Remember when rain caressed courageous linen that swayed like parade flags? "Ah," the wet traffic cop said to no one, but who would listen? They don't make rain the way they used to.

A patrol vehicle stopped in the middle of the street and a face popped out. "Hey, officer, where's your new rain gear? You gotta look sharp today 'cause you're breaking in a new guy. Take a break and I'll direct the traffic for a while." The sergeant spoke around the cigar in the corner of his mouth.

"Sure thing, Sarge." Janelle walked from the center of the street without pause. A fast-moving vehicle spattered her shoes, but Janelle continued. They don't make shoes the way they used to either, she thought. Those shoes used to be shined all the time, but truth is, she hasn't taken a shine to her shoes in months.

Ready to enter a little diner, Janelle glanced at the sky and wiped away the rain as it bounced on her weathered face. October had its way. It ransacked the quiet street, and its aggressive wind might as well be a ruthless slap on the face. "Rain," she whispered, shrugged and went inside. "Hey, 'morning, Harry," said she to the busy grill man, and sat on a stool that had changed colors once, ten years ago. So someone said.

"'Mornin', officer," the grill man replied with a huff. He rubbed an eye, and plump fingers tilted a once white hat. "Evelyn, get the officer a cup of java." He flipped a stack of brown pancakes on the grill and man raised his voice again, this time to the dishwasher. "Sanchez, get that table over there cleaned up, please." And then turning to Janelle, he asked, "Where's your new rain gear?"

"Hmm? Who told you? I'm in no mood for orange juice today," she added.

Janelle rubbed her hat with two fingers that merely touched the brim and nothing more. She mopped her forehead with a wad of napkins, and lifted her hair when no one was looking. She knew that her thinning hair made her look ten years older than she was. "This ain't no job for a lady," she mumbled to herself. "What the hell was I thinking? I wanted to be Rambo without the dick."

As soon as Evelyn slid a cup of coffee in front of Janelle, she thanked her and looked at the grill man. "How long have I been coming in here?" she asked.

The grill man's chin pierced the thick air as he stepped away from the oily grill. "So you finally want breakfast. No problem, officer, it'll be our honor."

"You got it all wrong. I don't eat breakfast. I want to talk, that's all."

The grill man looked across the diner and caught the inquisitive stares from the regulars. Janelle knew he was avoiding looking at her He cleared his throat. "I know what you wanna talk about, and believe me, nothing will change the day."

Janelle tightened her lips. "Go back to work, Harry."

Moments later, Harry stood next to her. "You told me to give these to you, remember?" he asked in a low voice. "Parking tickets."

"Yeah, sure, no problem." Janelle folded them into her pocket. "Gotta go, Harry." The officer throw a dollar on the counter and departed.

Janelle headed toward "Janelle's Crossings," That's what the *Daily Mirror* newspaper called the intersection where Janelle directed morning traffic. It had been a year or so since she'd removed the newspaper clipping from the door of her refrigerator, although she liked that vigorous smile she'd flashed at the photographer that day.

"You could get killed out there. Why a traffic cop?" the reporter had asked.

"Why not?" she'd said, grinning at the photographer. "I could be sergeant. But then I'd have no time for my family, would I?"

The rain felt even colder. She had never felt so cold. She wanted to shiver as she walked into the middle of Janelle's Crossings. Watching the signals of the recently installed traffic lights, she knew how to make them respond to her direction. She waved off her sergeant and took her position. It didn't look like ten in the morning at all.

Bang, clank! The sounds made Janelle move quickly past the rows of cars to the accident. She tapped on the window. "Move to the side," she told the driver of the small car that had been tapped from behind.

A young woman leaped from the vehicle, voice first. "Look here," she said to Janelle. "I have to go. Send the accident report to my office. The sergeant knows me."

Janelle smiled easily. It was little Ginny Warner from Second Street. She used to pick her nose when she thought no one was looking. Fancy clothes and all, she looked like a child, and what a way to talk to police officer. "Driver's license and registration, please," she said.

"Come on, I'm going to be late for an appointment." She jerked her thumb at the car behind hers. "You blind? Can't you see that that old lady behind me hit me?"

"Hmm. That's interesting, Ms. Warner. You didn't call me blind when I pulled your butt out of the McShane's pool. You would have drowned, girl." Janelle tilted his hat while changing his stance. "You remember my Molly? You two used to be friends. I buried her last week."

"Sure, sure," Warner said impatiently. "I didn't recognize you, with the rain and all." She handed Janelle her driver's license and registration for the car.

Janelle returned to the center of Janelle's Crossings. The rain had softened as the morning breezed by. An hour later, she halted the traffic as soon as she saw a cruiser's flashing lights. Several motorists shouted at her, "Hey what the heck is happening?"

The cruiser stopped in the intersection. Benny's big face came out of an opened window. "Hey Jacy, where the hell's your rain gear, girl?"

"Not today, Benny."

"You want mine?"

"Nope. Hey, ain't you on a call?"

"I'll get there. Same stuff. The Martins are tearing each other up this morning. I'll law one of them up and go back next week to arrest the other one. It never stops. And by the by, the mayor wants to talk to you about an accident concerning one of his aides. You know the Warner kid? Well, she works for the mayor. Stop at his office before checking in, okay?"

While Benny spoke, Janelle kept time with the windshield blades that sliced across his window. Titta tatta. She glanced at the patrol car's brave white puffs of smoke that challenged the October weather, only to disappear in seconds. "Want to eat lunch at Harry's after you book one of the Martins?"

"I'll be west today. And, sorry to hear about your daughter. It was so sudden. Brr, it's cold." The large faced man gripped his chin the way Janelle always had. "My wife planned something last week and we were out of town. Sorry."

"I understand. Listen, I'd like to talk to you later."

The siren stained the air as Benny left without answering. Janelle stared after him. Never had she heard Benny's wife called anything other than Jenny. Today it was "my wife." Janelle caught from the corner of her eye a motorist breaking the line and moving through the roadway's parking area. Another impatient motorist followed. "Why don't you watch what you're doing she screamed," at him as she passed.

The very idea of it made Janelle shake. This was Janelle's Crossings, and the rest of the world may have whirlpooled into a sea of indifference, but not here. Even the governor of the state stopped at Janelle's command, and the *Daily Mirror* wrote about it too. She held her hands up. *I should have worn my rain gear.* Focusing on the backs of her hands, she thought they looked like they belonged to an old man. Were those spots sign of some plague or something? *Mothers shouldn't bury their children. This world is nuts.*

The rain stopped, yet the shiny dots were everywhere. Janelle walked to Harry's for coffee, and was about to enter when she saw Harry scurry out the back door.

No one really wants to talk to me and I don't blame them. I'm a broken-down cop who buried her kid. Janelle turned on heel and as she walked, she paid little attention to the boarded-up old stores and the staggering men, whose smell would stay in her nostrils till dark. She recalled that on that very block a few months ago, a young mother, child in hand, had stopped Janelle and said to her child, "If you don't behave, the police officer is going to take you away." Janelle smiled at her memory, and then reminded herself she had to go to the mayor's office.

She stopped and stared at a building across the street. Its glass and steel swirled splinters of sunlight to the wet street. She pursed her lips and snapped her fingers; they sold the business to a foreign company that bankrupt it.

A different thought struck Janelle about her daughter that misty morning. Perhaps it was better this way. She wouldn't find out about her now. She wasn't a high-paid executive. She was a traffic cop. When she had planned her retirement, her pension had seemed enormous, but now that she's a few years away and alone ... it seems like nothing.

Janelle watched a police officer exit a police cruiser and approach her. "Officer Gregg?" she said. "I'm Officer Silverman and I was on my way to Main and Vine."

Janelle stared for an unmeasured moment, and noticed that the younger woman's eyes reflected a kind of cold glitter. "You're a volunteer crossing guard?"

"No. I'm sworn just like you," said the young woman with razor-sharp eyes. "And I'm working Janelle's Cross."

"You mean Janelle's Crossings. Hey, how old are you?"

"That kind of question is against regulation," she said, and patted her revolver. She had a similar tone in her voice as that Warner girl.

"Let's have some coffee and discuss Janelle's Crossings," Janelle said.

"For the record, Gregg, we call it Janelle's Cross because I just want to get this assignment behind me and move on to real police work. I'm taking the sergeant's exam in a few weeks.

Janelle Gregg stood still. She felt clumsy and out of place. She shook her head. "Okay, Officer Silver..., whatever. Lead the way."

When the officers headed toward the police cruiser, they heard the sound of a child crying and stopped. A young woman spoke crossly to Janelle "Your harsh voice made my baby cry. Do you know how many problems I'll have this afternoon because of you?" That was really not a question.

It was then and there that Officer Gregg realized she was no longer Officer Gregg. That was little excuse for the crimes she committed after that day.

Joey: The Shower

One afternoon over the backyard fence, Jeanie Cole learned about one of those old scary movies from her neighbor, who vividly described what happened to a traveling woman who stayed at the wrong motel. The movie was playing at a run-down theater uptown. How silly, she thought. Who would want to see a woman sliced and diced in the shower? Not her.

When she told Joey, her husband about it, she wasn't prepared for his reply.

"Sounds great! Let's see it for ourselves.""

"No, Joey," Jeanie begged. "It's sick."

He would get his way. He always did!

Joey sat snugly at her side as they watched the showering woman hum to herself. Jeanie resented his stares. How long has it been since he'd looked at her that way?

Suddenly, like a monsoon, the horror came. Jeanie's clammy hands enveloped her moon-shaped face. She gasped. Peeking between her fingers, she witnessed the savage attack.

"My God!" she cried. *Could that be me?* she thought.

The woman's slashed flesh bled hideously on the movie screen.

Jeanie's terror-filled eyes caught the sneering expression on the attacker's face. His beady eyes glowed in sunken sockets as he raised his instrument of death, festooned with dancing blood.

Oh, God, how he loves plunging it again and again into her body.

Jeanie felt helpless. Worse than helpless—devastated.

"Nooo," she screamed, and jammed her eyes shut, painfully folding her toes.

Joey's nudge intensified her fear. He snickered as he pulled her hands from her face. "Come on, open your eyes," he said playfully.

She looked at the shower walls that resembled an artist's collage, splattered with blood. She watched as it rolled into spaces between titles, looping downward and washing into the tub. The chrome drain swallowed crimson water as if it were a vacuum, indifferent to everything it was consuming.

Cries of horror and disgust from the audience filled the theater as the final scene flashed across the screen. Someone's life had ended, her flesh pelted by the water from the shower.

Her executioner admired his deed through glaring eyes and a primitive grin.

Yes, it was only a movie! Yet the experience that would remain alive in the minds of the viewers for years—hinting at its terror, as meaningless as a piece of twine, until the twine twists into a noose and slowly, placidly, squeezes out life.

During the drive home, Joey gave his favorable critique of the movie while Jeanie stared steadily at the stars.

Her prim voice, thin with strain, finally interrupted his folly. "It was horrible, Joey," she challenged. "It was vulgar and evil."

He glanced at her from the corner of his eye as he adjusted his glasses. "Come on, honey," he crooned. "It was only a movie."

He drove onto their driveway and turned off the ignition. Hoping out of the car, he waited for her on the sidewalk.

"Ugly things should be forgotten," she said to herself. She stared at her favorite star and closed her eyes, wondering if life would be easier there. Pulling herself from their car, she shivered from the cruel winter weather and the scenes in the movie.

Joey used to put his arm around her and escort her to the door. That was three children ago. In the darkness, he was unable to see her whitened fists, the terror in her eyes.

She remained motionless as he opened the front door and hung his coat in the closet.

"Joey," she said in a pleasing voice as he walked toward the kitchen.

"Stop whining, woman," he yelled over his shoulder. "Put your friggin' coat away. I just took you to a movie. You should be grateful."

"It's the first time we've been out in eight months." Changing her tone, she added, "But it's not that, Joey.". As she faced the open closet door, she knew she would be talking to herself. "That movie brought back memories. I could feel that woman's desperation, her helplessness."

A tear rolled down one cheek. "My God, how I felt her helplessness! Something terrible happened to me too, Joey. Something I have never told you about." She shrugged. "Who wants to hear from me anyways?" she asked no one.

Long ago, when he had felt her tension, he embraced her. He would hold on tight and whisper words of assurance. When their meager pocketbook afforded a shared hot dog, life was simple and fun. They were content with hours of conversation about their dream home, and laughed during long walks. They talked about sharing. They laughed when they discussed children that would dress in oversized yellow raincoats.

Now, his success had washed away those dreams of sharing, and their laughter.

Jeanie defined their relationship as a stale sandwich, as she waited for Joey to arrive from work. Jeanie's stale sandwich was jammed with chilled emotion, topped by melted promise and shredded feelings, and scornfully salted. Devoured cowboy style, quickly saddled, and left to roam lonely pastures. *Why doesn't he understand that I have feelings and needs?*

As Joey became more successful, he flaunted his medals of success as though he were an Olympic champion, while she prepared peanut butter sandwiches in the silence of her kitchen.

His achievements boosted him into the country club, his private locker enhanced by a silver name plate awarded to the Man of the Year. A photograph of his locker hung in his mahogany-filled office, and was occasionally dusted by a deep-voiced secretary. She had stimulated Jeanie's imagination: "Wonder if she polishes Joey's Gucci shoes with one breath or two?"

She heard the refrigerator door open as her fortitude choked from disappointment, disappointment in Joey.

She wanted to tell him about her attacker that had plunged her into guilt. Guilt that she could have done something to prevent that corruption woven into her mind and her body—deep in her body. Jeanie never knew the intention of her abductor. For that, she was appreciative. Now, when she would approached a supermarket's parking lot, it was with extreme caution.

The shower scene ignited her buried fuse, and she knew she would think of that movie and her parking lot experience every moment in the months to come. A sleepless night ended as she dressed the children for school and tried to kiss Joey. "I'm late for work, damn it, woman!" he shouted.

She removed her powder blue robe, allowing it to drift to the floor. She stared at her figure in their full-length mirror, raising her hands to sleek down her already perfectly smooth brown hair. "If that ... despicable was interested in my body, why isn't Joey?" She tilted her head and thought, *Maybe he knows. Maybe Joey knows and that's why he doesn't touch me.*

She examined her breasts with their faint stretch-marked breasts and noticed their slight droop. "I always feel like Santa Claus, but when's my Christmas?" She nodded, deciding to join a health club.

It was time and she knew it, but she did not want to take a shower. She apprehensively peeked at the tub, at the showerhead, and then darted a glance back to her mirrored reflection.

She tried to smile. "Don't be a silly girl," the brave Jeanie said, while the fearful Jeanie thought, *Could that happen to me?*

Hesitantly, she stepped into the tub and looked at the drain.

Small uncertain hands adjusted the water temperature, and the downpour met her small body. "See, nothing to be afraid of."

A sudden thought, as if someone or something was behind her, forced her to leap from the shower. She covered her breasts with her arms and held on tight.

In the following weeks, Jeanie forced her children to play in the bathroom as she bathed. She nagged Joey, when he was home, to read an important article to her while she washed. She queried him on trivial points. She also pestered him until he installed another lock on the bathroom door. But alas, it fell apart. Jeanie called the hardware store, who sent a handyman.

She marveled at the number of defenses she had created. Should anyone take refuge in the tub before her entrance, they would be drenched by scalding water. Her hands could find the faucets without opening the curtain. From inside the shower, she practiced turning the nozzle on any assailant, flooding the floor yet serving her purpose. A wet towel, waiting to be thrown, lay over the faucet. A fat knife rested alongside the tub, and a chair wedged under the doorknob added strength to the locks.

"Don't be so damn foolish, Jeanie. You've carried this ridiculous nagging too far," Joey thundered. Months had passed, and his casual mood had changed to aggression as he taunted her about her fear. He made joked about her to their friends, neighbors, and business associates, immensely embarrassing her.

At the beauty shop, the ladies whispered to one another when she entered. The teachers at school refused to discuss her children's progress with her. Joey had gotten to everyone and iced her out of her own life. *Next they will be committing me to the funny farm, and he will take everything from me—my kids, my house, my clothes, me.*

Coffee klatches were no more, as she was never invited. One afternoon, she called her friends, indicating she had coffee perking and a carrot cake cooling. To her humiliation, no one arrived.

She received a few phone calls from "Jack the Ripper" and received nasty letters. Joey's indifference isolated her as her friends dropped her. Even the kids working the drive-up window at McDonalds pushed her through without a thought.

She lost weight and her eyes resembled bottomless pools, as if a midnight rain hammered them into a silent river. Joey arranged for a doctor to treat her at home.

"How do you feel?" the gray-haired physician asked.

"Like an empty jar in a dirty cupboard," Jeanie answered.

Tranquilizers and sleeping pills were prescribed in heavy doses. Jeanie knew she was being placated—neutralized—but she had a cavern in her mind in which to retreat. Maybe the doctor, she thought, would deliver her message to Joey. Someone had to tell Joey about her agony, her distress, her fear.

Someone had to tell him before it was too late!

Two days later, while Joey sat on the porch, she moved into his arms easily. She had forgotten what a man smelled like.

"It's been terrible for you, Joey," she said serenely. Her terror was briefly subdued by little white pills; pills that she imagined as tufts of clouds in capsule form.

"Look, over there!" Joey said.

For a few moments they watched the last of the sunset fade with dying traces of sharp reds and yellows. A warm breeze scurried through the air, suggesting memories of their first date. Had love returned to their marriage? she wondered. His anger and distance had been her fault. A tear fell, unseen, untouched.

The children were astonished as Joey carried her to the bedroom and closed the door. A chime rang out in her heart as he laid her on the bed. Anxiously, she watched him undress, but to her deep regret, he was still a cowboy.

It was sex, not love! It was rough, not gentle!

Ugly things should be forgotten. She stared at the darkened ceiling overcast by faint shadows. Her eyes searched his sleeping body and gazed at his pillowed head. By morning, she knew she would not be able to bridge the painful gap of unexpressed emotions. Joey had proved his insincerity. He could have treated her like a lady. The lady she wanted to be instead of the thing he wanted her to be.

"Wishes," she said to the wall, as in a reverie. "If wishes were real, the pigs would walk." She swallowed several cloud tufts and closed her eyes.

At the supermarket, she casually and instinctively grabbed jars and bottles. She studied her coupons, and then froze.

Something had seized her.

She jerked her gaze up, meeting penetrating eyes that pierced her. Beady eyes were locked on hers. They shrewdly tore into her tattered defenses. What did he want? She had seen those eyes before.

It's him.

He'll be the one! Look at him gaping. Looking at me, wanting to hurt me. Have me.

Once home, Jeanie downed several magic pills. The battle would be hers and hers alone. Her husband belonged to his job. Her friends were unsympathetic and uncaring, and her children, her very own children whom she had fed, were disdainful. More than disdainful—scornful.

She awoke, rattled. Had she dreamed that she had been at the supermarket, or had she really been there? She didn't know, but the grin of that man lingered in her memory.

Oddly, one afternoon, Joey introduced Jeanie to someone he called an associate "Listen," he said, "you two talk. I'll pick up the kids."

Tactfully, the associate quizzed her, and after a few more visits, apparently gave Joey the news.

"Involutional melancholia, I believe," the psychiatrist stated, drawing his white eyebrows together.

Joey watched the ascending smoke from his cigarette. "Oh," he said with easy acceptance. "I understand. She's crazy, right? And you've got to put her away."

"Let me put it another way, Joey," he said carefully. "Your wife is a fearful woman. Fear," he emphasized, "is an unpredictable emotion ignited by aggravated expectation."

Joey's gaze danced around the room. "Sounds like she should be put away," he said, nodding firmly.

"Off the record, Joey, a fearful woman needs love and understanding." His voice ushered in a lighter tone. "Why don't you take her on a vacation? Get her out of that house and off those pills. Try it my way first. If that doesn't work, we'll consider other alternatives."

Joey decided to follow the doctor's suggestion, yet knew it would fail.

"How about you and me, darling, having dinner for two tomorrow evening? And then, we can spend a week out of town? Maybe go somewhere."

They planned their festivities cheerfully. They arranged for the children to stay with their neighbor. Leaving for the office that morning, he kissed her meagerly and said he'd be back at two.

He called at lunch. "Look, something's come up. I'll be home by three. Do me a favor. Stop at the supermarket and pick up some cherries. I won't have time. I'm looking forward to our trip."

"Sure, sure. Okay, Joey," she said in a sing-song voice.

Cradling the phone's receiver, Jeanie paused. "The supermarket," she murmured. "Not the supermarket today," she begged, but knew she would have to go. He asked.

Joey arrived home late at night. Late again, nothing new. A big-time executive never says no. The house was dark as he entered, wilted flowers in hand.

"Jeanie, darling, I'm home."

No response.

He called out again and turned on the lights. "I'm home."

Nothing. Except for a noise. Like water running. He quickly went to the bathroom and tapped on the door. "Honey, it's your Joey boy. I'm sorry I'm late."

He glanced at the floor and saw a puddle of water. Another quick rap on the door,. "Shut the water off. It's flooding everywhere."

That little bitch can't hear me, he thought.

"Honey, you bitch," he yelled. "I'm home."

Nothing, except the sound of battering water.

He tried the doorknob. It wouldn't turn. "Damn locks. Open the friggin' door, Jeanie!". He pounded and shouted, "Damn it, bitch, open the door!"

He pushed and shoved. "Shit, she has a chair under the knob." Finally, the door gave way. He was angry. He was ready to slap her back into reality. He wanted to hurt her. He bolted into the room, fists clenched.

A body lay floating facedown in crimson water. It was lifeless, pounding water hitting its slashed and torn flesh. Blood everywhere. Joey turned the water off and closed his eyes, slumping down on the stool.

"Who the hell did this?" he cried in a sickened voice. He covered his face with his clammy hands and groaned. His stomach heaved. "My God," he moaned desperately.

He flung open the toilet seat, because he was going to vomit, but Joey Cole was about to discover true fear. He would discover the wrathful torment of a thousand twisted crosses.

He didn't see the deadly blade dripping blood rise over his back. It pierced his flesh and sank deep into his body. The sound etched the air like the sudden screeching of train brakes. Again, the steel knife rose and fell, sizzling its horror into Joey's flesh as he was pushed deeper into the bowl.

His executioner sneered at him.

How could this be happening? he asked silently, tattered thoughts rambling. If wishes were real, pigs could fly!

"I've been waiting, darling," Joey's wife said. "Why don't you try to fly away now, you pig."

Margo: À la Carte

Fantasizing About Pregnancy

Margo Clinton tossed and turned endlessly. No matter what she did, nothing seemed to help her sleep. She snuggled her narrow face into the crisp linen of the pillow, and its fresh scent soothed her. Disturb Anthony, certainly not, she thought. Margo rose slowly and glided into the living room, only to spill over the sofa like a child. It was uncomfortable. Now she nestled into a puffy chair, folded her legs, flicked on a light, and paged through a magazine She was bothered by the glare on the glossy pages.

One bite into a Hershey bar reminded her of the "diet of the decade." *But this time I'll get rid of some fat.* And she deserved a reward; she had lost three pounds. Margo played with a cigarette for a moment and put the candy bar back into its package. She couldn't live with herself if she ate that chocolate bar right now. She cranked the top back on her Zippo, marveled at the flame for a moment, and then drew on the cigarette.

There was chill in the room that flowed in an awkward pattern. *Wonder why,* she mused. *Oh, gee, my mind is on a roll and I might as well forget sleep. What should I do? Have this child or what? Forget this life?* Her delicate brows furrowed at her thought that having a baby. *Will that make Anthony proud of me? Will Anthony accept the news joyfully, or will he shut me down as fast as I revealed my secret?*

She tilted her head and crushed the cigarette in a soiled ashtray. The previous night she had searched the 'net until after eleven for information about babies. She had accomplished little, and hadn't even emptied the ashtray. Margo exhaled a deep breath. Well, she thought, whatever. It's done. But she felt secretly pleased with herself for her condition. After all the abuse she swallowed from Anthony, she wondered how much more she could handle. That would take time to know. *I need sleep.*

Margo went to the kitchen instead and spooned a little sugar and extra cream into her favorite cup, the one with lilacs and a tiny handle, and filled it with coffee. "Let's see," she whispered, a small blush on her cheeks. *When did I decide to have this child?* She counted on her fingers. Yes, it must have happened the night the two of them celebrated ... something. Whatever it was, it had been fun. Anthony had been so thoughtful when he came home from work and surprised her with a wonderful gift—a pleated floral print dress that was exactly her size. How had he known?

Of course, she wore it, and a delicate gold necklace and a crimson ribbon. Later she freed that ribbon and whisked it away with an eager breath. Yes, it was easy to remember."

Oh yes, I prepared an evening of candlelight, sweet music, and his favorite meal. But that call to my sweet sister to get the recipe cost more than the ingredients.

She sipped her coffee. It was perfect. Her tongue fluttered between her lips, and she decided that the stale taste came from lingering chocolate. Cup in hand, she pranced to the washroom and pushed a worn toothbrush with freckled toothpaste into her mouth and brushed her teeth. That was better, she thought as she slid her tongue past each tooth. If she smiled, she imagined her teeth would glitter.

Yesterday, as soon as she'd known for sure that she was pregnant, she had wanted to tell Anthony.

Last night, before he'd closed his eyes, they planned to take a drive to a fancy little resort up the shore for lunch. She would tell him then. She was very excited at the plan.– Lunch at the resort and she would tell him about the baby. Maybe she should have told him last night, but she had been much too nervous to discuss anything.

Would Anthony suggest an abortion? No, not Anthony. When they visited Anthony's brother, Anthony's little nephews gathered around him and listened round-eyed to his fables. He had borrowed a little from Mother Goose and some from his favorite television programs and laced them together, suggesting he was in the wrong business.

Anthony's boss, Miss Rosen, humorously agreed when Margo told her about Anthony's story-telling ability. Miss Rosen had dropped off some files for Anthony one Sunday afternoon. Margo had noticed that Ruth Rosen looked exactly the way he had described her. Except that he had neglected to tell her that Miss Rosen was a very striking, but older, woman.

Margo leaned over the sink to study her reflection in the mirror. "Why do you look so clunky?" she whispered. When she smoothed her hair, she heard Anthony turn. He would wake soon.

Anthony ... Her brilliant smile came before her thought, and Margo's attentive eyes remained fixed on the mirror. Anthony insulated her from the coldness of deadlines, currency exchanges, and Wednesdays' sales. She loved his comfortable, soft laughter. He made her feel like morning sun caressing soft rain.

She bounced on her toes. Now she knew why she felt different. She had not been regular for two months, but thought it had to do with her new step class at the gym or her new method. If she had continued on the pill rather than relying on a bedroom door chart, would things be different? It was that handsome man, Anthony, who suggested she find another method. He had discovered that she had been on the pill for five years, and made his views known—"Varicose veins and heart attacks," he said. Then he snickered, as he always had.

Margo turned to the full-length mirror and dropped her robe to the cold floor. Her hands cupped her small breasts and she wondered how large they would grow. Anthony admired women with spacious assets. Assets like Miss Rosen's. Hmm.

Her tiny fingers slipped to her tummy and she gently squeezed it. She had decided sometime in her brief slumber that if she kept the baby, Anthony would have to make a definite commitment. Of course, he might try to talk her out of marriage. They had agreed that they would live together for a year, no strings. They had also agreed that either one of them could end the relationship at the end of any month.

Pregnancy? Well, they had agreed that should that ever happen, they would discuss it then. As for marriage ... They both had the same view on that. None of their friends stayed married very long.

Margo filled her cheeks with a gasp of air and held it in while her gaze fixed on her torso. She nodded approvingly at the thought that she would join the university's fitness program and quit smoking. She exhaled, pushed her bangs off her forehead and set her hands on her hips. Turning, she studied her profile and tried to remember Shelley's poem on motherhood. When her gaze fell to her knee, she remembered Dannon.

Margo had turned down three offers for the movies, but kept her date with Dannon Franco. They had known each other for several months, and yes, they had arranged their date before Anthony and Margo had come to terms six months ago.

Margo was pleased that she had not allowed Dannon to become intimate, although she could envision it. But there was that time in the car when he had pinned her to the seat and held her head, forcing his shaft into her mouth. It could have happened the night; it could have happened very easily. Accidentally. Well, almost accidentally, but she had supplied the relief he required and that had been that. Margo gaze had lingered on him a little too long, but she pulled her stare away and looked at the other vehicles parked alongside the street near the club she often frequented. It would be closing soon, and people would be staggering out to get into their cars. Many would be holding on to each other, looking for a good-night kiss or anything else they could get in the moonlight. Dannon said something like, "You're not very good at this," to which Margo answered, "I haven't done it before, sorry."

Dannon was much too serious about everything. Much too serious! After that night, he had stayed out of the club for weeks. When he did return, he wouldn't have a cigarette or a beer with Margo. He simply ignored her. But things were better for Margo by then. She had met Anthony. He wasn't a local, but he owed a nice beach house. He worked at home, and one day a week or so he drove to the city.

Margo, pregnant Margo, sashayed into the front room, dragging her robe behind her. She picked up the unwrapped candy bar, hesitated briefly, and slipped it into her mouth. She delighted with its taste. She looked out through the half-draped window. At first, her stare was vacant, then she realized that ole Jenkins was staring back from across the courtyard. She felt his steady gaze and froze. *What a pervert. Why doesn't he gape at those repulsive magazines other old men buy?* With a defiant expression, Margo slipped the robe on and neatly tied the sash. She flinched when the alarm clock piped out its demanding whine.

"It's time," she said, and lifted her chin. How would her words sound? Should she be serious or cheerful? Should she imitate Anthony's precious sister when she presented her news?

Margo was worried. More than worried, frightened. Anthony had an easy manner, but would he be easy with her?

She could hear the sheets rustling as he turned off the clock. She darted into the bedroom, "'Morning, bright eyes," she said. He sniffed the air, smiling with pleasure. "Stay where you are, darling. I'll get a cup of coffee." Her voice was weak at first, but she finished in complete control. She lightly touched his lips with one finger. She knew that when his eyes were bright, he would laugh. Right now, they were flashing.

"Anthony," she said urgently. although she wanted to sound subtle. "While I'm getting your coffee, I want you to think about something." She kissed his neck, and Margo Clinton felt that weakening chill bubbling over her, and praised the Lord for his kindness.

Mary: If She Only Had a Heart

The long-haired girl slid along an icy sidewalk as an automobile glided beside her, keeping pace with her stride. When Mary heard the car accelerate, she glanced casually over her shoulder and watched it slip down the street. Her careful step and distant stare were often challenged by men, who jingled their pockets as they uttered sleazy words of endearment. Sharp remarks that once had been alarming now amused her. The longer she lived in the city, the less she feared it. What she feared more was the black ice and white snow. "Good god almighty, will it ever end," she said to the snowy dark skies, wondering why she had moved from the wetlands of Louisiana.

Mary knew every crevice in the sidewalks, which were now clogged with uncaring January ice. She wouldn't read the drooping signs plastered on the neglected store windows of the endless shops. They announced the same special, month after month. Mary Bayuga had read them all on many barefooted nights two summers when she first arrived.

She knew the faces of the burly men who stood motionless in the dark doorways. Their massive arms were folded and they held a look of resolved indifference, as she watched them watching others. Yet their rank odor of yesterday's beer was rivaled by their obvious lack of hygiene, and could make a girl gag. Or anybody for that matter. She covered her mouth as she passed and smiled at the short, fat man, whose toothless face quickened her stride. Sometimes he would ask, "How you doin', Dolly?"

As she neared the door of a nightclub she frequented, the bouncer opened it wide for her as he always did. A collage of voices clattered above a buzzing sound chopped up by untalented musicians, yet the warmth of the small room pleased her. She heard one man's question creak through the lacquered air. "You old enough to drink?" he asked,

365

and laughed. There was a dull rhythm in the large man's tone, because he said the same thing to Mary every time she was there.

A young fellow about Mary's age turned abruptly when she passed him on her way to the bar. "Hey," he called, and jingled his pockets. "Want some company, honey?" Before he had gotten all the words out of his mouth, the enormous hand of one of her many protectors was on the man's shoulder.

"She ain't sellin' nothin'," he growled in the young man's ear. "She does nothin' but walks and makes the neighborhood, like, respectable. That's Dolly." Of course, while the large man was talking, he was shaking the other man too. "Don't even look at her if ya wanna stay alive, got it?"

Mary always felt twenty years older in that place. *I'm not that desperate for attention?* she asked herself.

"Dolly" had her one free drink and left for her apartment down the street. As she walked a city bus, decorated with winter's filth, rattled to a halt. Mary watched the passengers carefully exit, stepping with wet boots into the snow mound that had been accumulated by a thoughtless shopkeeper. Earlier that day after school, Mary had exited from a similar bus and plunged into the mound, backpack and all, almost falling. If this had been Louisiana, she would have playfully fallen, delighted with the snow's fresh wetness on her knees, and then would have been helped up by neighbors. But here, if she had fallen her backpack would have been stolen and her body would have subjected to several careless touches. Men were dangerous creatures who throw around their meaty weapon as though it were invincible and could never be injured, she had decided long ago.

Her cautious gaze slid from the bus to the all-hour restaurant across the street. Yes, she'd treat herself to some lemon tea. The streets were so cold tonight. At the counter she gave her order to a silent waitress. The waitress knew Mary always sat alone and always ordered lemon tea.

"Pass the salt, please?" a man asked in a fresh voice.

Such a voice. It was a fascinating voice with a friendly tone. A voice she could have heard in her little hometown near the wetlands. She smiled as she handed over the salt. They spoke about the snow and the crowded, noisy restaurant. Every so often she watched glistening snowflakes through the restaurant's huge windows, and at one point remarked, "I don't think the snow will ever stop." She glanced at his hands too. Any rings?

Mary decided his hands were strong and sturdy and, yes, small-town hands. But was that tension or loneliness creasing his forehead? she wondered. Spencer—he had told her his name—wasn't like other men. Maybe he didn't even have a penis. He wasn't looking at her as though he was buying a used farm tractor.

"I—I just wanted to talk to somebody nice," he said.

If he had asked her, she would have said, "I understand lonely." She probably would have added, "I feel like a damaged mannequin in an abandoned shop."

Spencer looked more like a country veterinarian than a downtown clerk. Mary surprised herself when she said, "I live down the street. Walk me home?"

Spencer's thick eyebrows rose. "You live here?" he asked in a different voice.

"Yes," she replied, her tone revealing embarrassment. "I attend the university," she said at length. In a slow voice, she added, "After my parents divorced. things changed. So ..." She shrugged. There wasn't any need to finish her thought. She busied her hands with the silverware. "I live close to the modeling agency where I work parttime. That's how I get through school and pay my rent."

"Oh!" he exclaimed. "That's exciting. A lot of parties?" he asked with a new sound in his voice. It was a voice that suddenly took on the city's tone.

"I'm not that kind of model. I model clothes for a retailer's catalog." She added in a different tone, "I don't know many people. They move in and out so fast." A tight smile crossed her face. "I see the same faces working on the street, but other than that, most people come and go as quickly as fashion." With a coy look, she added, "The new people's ideas are the same as the old ones. They just move the buttons around. Does that make sense?"

Was this really her, she asked herself, looking for the approval of a male. One photographer had told, "Mary, you have a hungry child's chin. It makes you look capable of holding your own in any situation. Insistent, I'd say. Chin up."

Mary didn't want Spencer to think her assertive; she didn't want to appear aggressive.

"Come on," she said. "Which way do you live? But this ain't no invite to anything else," she added. Mary was proud of her statement, and nodded.

They crossed the slippery street, hand in hand, and walked halfway down the block of neglected brownstones. It was then that Mary saw a brightly-colored figure pop from a doorway. It was the girl Mary privately called Big Bertha, who belonged on the street behind them.

Big Bertha cried out banteringly, "So, Dolly has gone into business on her own."

"Dolly?" Spencer asked in a voice just above a whisper, but still in that new tone.

"Whenever I pass them, they call me Dolly for some reason," she informed him, and released his hand.

As they reached Mary's apartment, Spencer jumped in front of her and peered steadily into her eyes. He held her shoulders firmly and pulled her against him. Mary almost heard Spencer's pockets jingle. She pushed him away and dashed to the door as he asked, "What's the matter? I thought you wanted some company."

Over her shoulder, she said, "Nothing. Just leave me alone." As she hurried inside, she said under her breath, "Is that all they want? Men are dogs. Slip them a smile and they think you're on the menu."

Safe behind the security door, she leaned against the wall. She sighed, unbuttoned her coat, and folded her arms tight. When she closed her eyes, she wished she was in grade school running from her first kiss.

In her disappointment, many memories unfolded. When she had hopped off the bus earlier that day, should she have fallen? Would she have found a friend? Rather, she had hurriedly walked home and anxiously tried to open her mailbox. It was cold, and she'd had to tap it a few times before it opened. A letter ... "Oh please, Dad, a letter." Nothing except "Occupant."

Now, she climbed the rickety stairs and paused, as she always did, on the second landing. She heard the guy who had moved in last month tapping down the hallway. *Here comes Rover,* she thought. It had to be him, because everyone else lost that bounce years ago. When he turned the corner, he hopped down the steps and stopped in front of her.

"Hey," he said in a friendly way. "'Have you seen the landlord?"

he asked, and flashed the grin of indecision that most young men possessed. He added impatiently, "You need help?"

"No, no," she answered. *Dogs always want to help, but they really want to lick.*

He called, "See you later," as he skipped down the rest of the stairs.

There was no avoiding that simmering, thick ravioli smell. She sneezed. After struggling with clunky boots, she slid her key into the apartment's lock. Open slowly. Powerful Isis would be guarding the other side. He would be very hungry too. The sun had shone most of the day, offering Isis millions of shadows to chase. Silly kitten!

Mary bent over and smoothed Isis's short fur. "*Cher*, you missed Mama?" she fussed. "Yes, yes." She stroked her kitten all over with tender hands.

She licked her lip and squared her shoulders with her newfound understanding; "So, that's how I rid myself of all my stored love. I fuss over Queen Isis, who can take or leave my attention."

Isis shot to the window when she heard a knock on the door. "*Cher*, you be good," Mary said, pointing at the kitten. "Yes, who is it?"

"It's me, David, your neighbor," he said as if they were old friend.

She put a hand over her heart. "Uh … you can't come in. I'm not dressed." Did he hear the crackle in her voice when she lied?

"I made too much dinner for one person. Would you like—"

She cut him off before he finished his offer. "I have a dinner date," she said firmly. Her brow furrowed, and she bit her bottom lip.

"Your voice sounds strange," he said. "You coming down with a cold? Maybe you should stay home. You've had a date every night."

"My date will be here soon. Please go." If only he knew.

Mary heard David close his door. It made a lonely sound a sound that was absolute. She puffed her lips like a little girl and returned to her effortless ritual with her kitten. With Isis at her heel, she walked into the bathroom and glanced at the border paint around the mirror. She had removed some of it with a razor blade. Where the paint was jagged and notched, she somehow related to her own feelings.

Mary felt that when she finally smoothed all the borders, her life would be smooth too. This was the real Mary, a Mary who had feelings.

The instant she touched the brown ribbon in her jet black hair, it came undone. She looked at her reflection and tossed her hair forward, crowding it around her face. How easy to hide from the world. She shook her head and fingered an opening. "Poor li'l orphan girl," she whispered. "What shall you do tonight? Write poetry or listen to music? How about a nice chignon?"

An hour later, she sat in a comfy chair, mirror in hand, admiring her new hairstyle. Her helper coiled gracefully on her lap, purring with approval.

She dialed the information operator in Atlanta and asked for the new listing of Peter Bayuga. "But I know he's there," she repeated. After she cradled the receiver, she whispered, "Oh, Father, where are you? Mother said you were in Atlanta." Mary wiped her cheeks dry and moved to the window.

Her attention was drawn by a silhouetted couple walking arm and arm. "Lucky ... How lucky they are." *They have someone to dream with at night. All I have are these radiators that laugh at me but keep me warm.*

She slouched forward under the unfolding memories. She saw her friend's face from the catalogue agency. As Mary had that afternoon, she decided she hated men. Kittens were safer. "Are you a kitty?" she asked herself.

Another night, she had roamed into a church. She marched solemnly into the confining, dark confessional and reported her sins as though they were colossal tragedies of passion and lust.

"Anything else, my child?"

"Yes, Father," she said, and bowed her. "I—I ... feel like a pair of desperate oars."

There. She had said it, and waited his magic wand to pass over her head, calming her.

His answer was the same as the Lutheran minister's. "Go, my child, and find yourself. Look in your heart."

Mary left the church with the same feeling she had when she entered. Then, she knew why Isis was her friend. Like Isis, she chased shadows, but a kitty never asked her to look into her heart.

Mary Bayuga stopped her reverie and stood perfectly straight. She didn't care how long she had been there. An hour, a day. She pouted and knew she would cry all night. Maybe someone had been by and fixed the hissing radiators.

A knock on her door and a voice that sounded like her neighbor's. "Look, miss," he said. She opened the door and stared at him while he said, "I guess a pretty girl like you wouldn't understand what it's like not to know anyone." He paused for a moment, and then stammered over his next sentence. "I—I would just like to talk to someone. I mean ... could we?"

"You got any change in your pocket?" she asked, and felt like Big Bertha and Shirley Temple at the same time.

His face went blank and he started to walk away. "Wait," she said. "Let's have tea together. I've got some spring water that will help."

They smiled at each other. Mary had a heart.

Mickey: Free Again

Mickey couldn't remember the limousine ride to Emma Tower's brownstone in the Georgetown section of Washington DC. There was so much on her mind. Stepping up the stairway, once packed with snow and now crowded with rock salt, Mickey hunted for the switch plate containing the doorbell. Where was the bell? Ah, there it was, so little and brassy. Uneasy, she combed her fingers through her dark red hair, and then squared her shoulders, freeing loose snowflakes. A recently manicured finger pushed the little white dot.

The buzzer arrogantly interrupted Emma's evening, like a big-bellied sheriff. *No matter who's out there,* Emma decided, *I'll shoo them away.* She firmed her jaw as she looked through the tiny peep hole at the figure shivering in the night. "Mickey Stone?" She must watch over her, protect her. More than protect—save her endlessly from herself and all the humanity of this planet.

"Oh my God, she's free again," she whispered.

Emma nervously pushed the button that would let Mickey open the heavy glass door. She wondered if Mickey was tilting back and forth because of the wicked ice that had ripped through the city, or had she been at Mickey's World.

"Hello, sweetie. What are you doing here?" Emma asked with welcoming arms and a quick smile. She wanted to ask about prison, wanted to ask about Mickey's World. There was so much to ask, but she wouldn't ask how Mickey knew her address. This woman was forty years old, and looked like the schoolgirl Emma had met twenty years ago in Paris. Mickey hadn't aged a year or added a pound, but she still didn't know how much blush to use on her freckled face.

"Can we talk?" Mickey asked softly. When she saw Emma's friend, she added, "Alone. Can we talk alone?"

Emma saw Mickey examine her friend, an obvious military man with a military haircut, military eyes, and US Marine Corp ring.

"Semper fi." Mickey pushed the words out of her cold mouth.

After A moment of hesitation, spent studying Mickey, he returned, "Semper fi."

"Nathaniel, would you mind?" Emma nodded to the door.

Nathaniel grabbed his big winter coat, flipped up the hood, kissed Emma's forehead, and left without a word.

There was an ambiguity about the man, Mickey mused, though it didn't necessarily mean anything wrong. It wouldn't work in his favor at a country club or a casino, she decided, and dismissed him as a plaything or college professor. People who weren't really in the world of others. They were just a devise to amuse and amaze with skilled tongues and thin realities.

Emma opened a bottle of Russian vodka and filled a crystal wine goblet. "Don't look surprised," she said as she handed Mickey the goblet. "I know what you like."

Mickey knocked the vodka down like a mad Russian or French artist and slid into a large leather club chair. "Pottery Barn?" she asked.

"You know your styles."

"And where's this chair from?"

"Oh, the guy … A fellow jarhead. He's one of the president's color guard and a full colonel. He works in the office of the US Defense Security. We graduated West Point together."

Mickey ignored her comments and went right into her thoughts. "I was released from prison yesterday and took my jet here to see you. I would have called, but—"

Emma cut her off with two fingers against Mickey's lips. "You're fine, sweetie. But it sounded like you were about to show some compassion. Not the Mickey I know."

"I saw my lover yesterday, and he confessed to me that I reminded him of a marble fawn. Now that I'm free, I need to take care of business." Mickey paused, as she always had when she had more to say. "There's something else too. Something small that needs your … attention." As she talked, she pushed the empty goblet to her host. Emma refilled it, smiling.

"Enjoy. But what did he mean by 'marble fawn'?"

"Guess I'm cold as frozen art. He used to see me as a beautiful woman, immortally young, but now he sees me as corroded and discolored stone. I tried, but when we had sex, I was thinking of you. I wasn't about to get on my knees. If the bastards like it so much, let 'em do it to each other."

There was resentment in Mickey's comment, no doubt, Emma decided. Resentment filled her mind about so many things. Emma easily remembered all the times she observed Mickey Stone pleasing herself. Now she wondered if she should have helped. Was that a mistake? This forty-year-old woman had lived fifty lifetimes and still looked innocent, but Emma also knew about her wiring. She knew that Mickey Stone was absolutely wired-wrong, and she was not a person to challenge, despite Emma's training and physical attributes.

Mickey always possessed a gentle look in her eyes that signaled concession. Thoughtfulness laced her every word, offering approval. In fact, her every motion hinted at a naturalness, suggesting that even prison life hadn't transformed her. But maybe prison had disconnected the wrong wiring and made her whole.

Emma's father had never called Emma perfect. She hated her father for his authority, but authority and rules were one way to characterize Emma Tower. Yes, Mickey Stone was the lifeblood that filled her heart, but Emma always followed the rules. Yet she saw in Mickey pieces of male domination. She saw parts of her father in her. Perhaps, her dad had been right. Emma wasn't perfect.

Dark and cold entered the room as the front door opened. Emma," Nathaniel said as he walked back into the apartment. "Emma, this isn't right. We're a couple. We're supposed to share everything."

The chill swept through the apartment, even though he had shut the door.

"What's going on, Nathanial?" Emma asked. "This woman is Mickey Stone, an old client. Am I to share her with you?"

He froze. "No. I'm sorry. I just knew who this woman is." He turned his attention toward Mickey. "I've seen her picture in the newspaper and heard about some of her crazy behavior on television. Anything you can discuss with her, you can do in front of me."

"You rotten son of a bitch," Emma said. "I'm not a child or your slave. I won't live like this."

Mickey stood slowly. "I'll go. I didn't know I'd be a home wrecker."

He smoothed his hair. "Uh ...,Maybe I made a mistake here."

"Look, Emma," Mickey said in a crisp voice. "I came to discuss business with you, and maybe we can meet at another time when you're not so ... occupied."

"No, Mickey," the older woman said urgently, and squinted at Nathaniel. "Nat, all the time I was helping you, you were helping yourself." She grabbed the lamp off the end table and flung it at him. He ducked. The lamp smashed the wall.

"That's it," he said., "She's all yours, honey." He bolted out of the cold apartment, slamming the door.

Tears streamed down Emma's face. She squeezed her eyes closed and wished she were elsewhere.

"It was not your fault," Mickey said compassionately, and since it was totally out of character for Mickey, Emma stared at her.

Mickey arched her eyebrows coyly, as a timid lover might. She wanted to tell Emma that her tears were filled with reflexive emotion. Emma defined everything as being centered in a man's world, which was always wrapped in the pretense of needing to be, at all times, what he wanted and how he wanted it. In truth, reflexive emotion was a total betrayal of what and who Emma was.

"What are you talking about?" Emma asked after Mickey had explained that.

"Honey," Mickey answered, "you define the world from a man's perspective. They can't understand a woman in love with another woman without adding their own sexual dimension to the equation."

Mickey drank another vodka and said, "I hate sex with men, but sometimes it's great. Men are bigger and awkward, so their mere size controls the way your body moves. You're helpless and forced, even when you consent. A woman gets pressed into whatever she's lying on. Men are so self-indulgent and impatient too. A woman doesn't crowd her lover. She has patience so they both can enjoy all of it. Put a dick on a woman and you've got god. But most lesbians are under the impression that the holy grail of loving another woman is sex. Poor kitties! They erotize the relationship between two women in love. Never the compassion, never the sense of belonging. But, Emma Tower, I love you for who you are."

Silence stood between the two of them, and it lasted for a long while. Emma was hesitate to believe that those words came from Mickey Stone. She knew she was not as bold as father had wished. She wanted to tell this woman about her dad, about all her past lovers. But when you talk about feelings, you talk about men-things and the things men do. Women don't cry about women.

Mickey stared out the window at the softly falling snow. She wanted to run to the street and dust angels under the streetlights; but instead thought about Emma and wondered how she would have acted, had she been Emma.

She turned to Emma, and somehow knew that she would never be pleased with yesterday's purchases ever again. Was this what she had been waiting for? She felt like a huge house full of ornate fixtures, nestled in a crack in the sidewalk. How quaint, she thought, because in a moment, she relived her youth by taking in Emma Tower's eyes. Could Emma be the secret design to help her be the woman of the times?

Hand in hand, the saint and the sinner shared each other for the rest of the night.

During the quiet of breakfast, Emma wondered uneasily what had happened. Had last night been Mickey's night of charity and mercy pussy? Her eyes narrowed in her quest to understand the moment. She had broken down fast when Nat confronted her last night. Would Mickey see her as weak?

Mickey wondered if her new lover thought of her as a marble fawn. She wanted a person, a lover, to be more than a partner or a possession. She wanted a partner to be happy, not ritually carried baggage—locked but empty. She wished they had known a friendship long ago that would have allowed pleasures to unfold easily. Many pleasures. She wished they had tried bizarre kitchen recipes, adding odd canned goods to yesterday's leftovers. Sharing preciously touching conversation, meaningless to others, while exploring calm secrets left somewhere in their pasts seemed interesting. And hands clasped in an easy rain that sparkled with vital promise seemed necessary. She wanted a partner to be more than a person. She wanted her partner to be indulged, instead of styled traditionally as a breadwinner or homemaker. She wished they had shared fantasies. She wanted to be with a daring lover who would allow those fantasies to unfold as naturally as their night unfolded.

She felt fulfilled for now, and smiled as she sucked in the smells of the kitchen.

Finally, Emma broke the silence. "What do you want of me?"

From her pocketbook, Mickey withdrew some papers and handed them to her lover. There were three photographs—her aunt, her uncle, and their son. "Study these. Here's their addresses and assorted information. Memorize everything, then destroy these pages and photos. Eliminate them for me and you will have everything you want and more."

"How do you expect to waltz into my apartment after all these years, have sex with me, and ask me to do something like that?"

"What's so different about my request than any tribal or political leader directing her second in command and her jarhead boyfriend to cancel our competition? That's a natural step toward ultimate control, particularly if those eliminated deserve to die."

"Because they're bad?"

"No, because they're alive, silly girl. They stand between us and the Stone Corporation. It's the only way we will be free. Screw the rules. Men made the rules."

"What about dying and meeting your maker?"

"Screw him too. He's my father's god and they're both men."

Sweet Jenny Lee: Her Mom and Dumpling Legs

"Mommy, Mommy, are there ghosts here?"

"Only beautiful ones from my childhood," replied Alice.

"Then why'd we stop?" Jenny Lee asked.

"Oh, I was just thinking about ..."

"About what, Mommy?"

Alice clung to her daughter's hand as the two of them moved closer to Alice's childhood toy chest in the dusty attic. Would Jenny Lee laugh with amusement or glow with excitement? she wondered. Alice had thought about this moment many times. She had spoken to Jenny Lee about it too. She knew the chance she would take. A small smirk on her daughter's face could tarnish lifetime memories, but and a widening grin could turn those lifetime treasures into golden moments.

"Suppose Jenny Lee doesn't care for Emily," she had asked her husband weeks ago. "Children can easily bring so much hurt to their parents."

His response had seemed practical. "Introduce them and find out." Glenda, Alice's older sister, had offered similar advice in one of their long conversations on the phone.

A few steps more, Alice thought, her gaze fixed on the dust-covered chest that contained so many memories. Especially memories about Emily and a gigantic green moving van parked in the driveway.

That day, Alice's childhood home, usually filled with a familiar lazy hum of insects and echoes of birds, echoed with the sounds of busy workmen. Father said everyone would love their new home, but Alice knew she would leave behind her fondest friend, Janice. Tearfully, the two little moppets had watched furniture disappear into the big belly of the green truck. They held hands when the workmen carried the brown box filled with Alice's toys onto the truck. Their apologetic tones did little to make the girls smile.

As soon as their furniture was delivered to their new home, Alice sought the one box she and Janice had so carefully packed. Taking inventory, she realized that her most treasured doll was missing—Emily. "Mommy, Daddy, where is it? It's gone," the little girl cried. When her daddy came to her room, she explained her loss. In disbelief, Alice hid in a strange closest as huge tears rolled down her cheeks. When daddy opened the door, she flew into his arms. She sobbed as grief burned in her tummy. "I'll never see Emily again."

Gently, he wiped her cheeks, his dark eyes expressing warmth and love. She drew in a deep breath when a mysterious smile crossed his narrow face. "This is for you," he said joyfully, and handed her a new doll. "I was saving it for an important event. This is pretty important, isn't it?"

Alice nodded. "I hate it," she said flatly. "I absolutely hate it." She throw it at the wall. "I want my old doll back. I want Emily back. Please, Daddy," she begged.

"There now, sweetie." He stroked her hair. "I want you to take care of this homeless little doll until I find yours Can you do that for me, honey? This little doll's owner was a little girl just like you, but she lost her way and asked me if I knew of anybody who wanted to take care of her."

Her hands encircled his neck and she kissed his cheek. She drew back slowly, her lips stinging from his stubbled face, and smiled. "I'll always love you, Daddy."

Curiosity promoted her examination of the gift. This intruder! Who did this new doll think it is? She stared into the faded denim eyes of her homeless charge, while her fingers absently played with the bonnet's dangling ribbon. Gliding little fingers slipped to the doll's lace pinafore, her daring touch discovering a surprising softness. She drew it to her heart with a small hum, and hummed her to sleep.

"What have named your new doll, Alice?" her mother asked as she entered the room with a glass of juice.

"I haven't yet," Alice answered.

Alice tried many names, yet none seemed suited as she tried them out on her quiet companion. It took forever to name Emily. Finally, as the name formed on her lips and popped out, she felt the doll smiled. "Emily, that's you. Emily, do you like your name?"

Before Emily was named, she was only a thoughtful gift from

daddy. Now that she had a name, she came alive. "Emily," Alice said several times in different tones, and nodded. Alice and Emily eventually became friends. They went everywhere together. She did miss Janice, but explained everything to Emily, who seemed to understand. Alice's older sister felt neglected. She had not received a present as nice from their father.

She pointed at Emily and said, "She doesn't look like other dolls. Her green bonnet doesn't match her lavender pinafore. Ha ha."

With new devotion, Alice said, "Emily isn't like other dolls. She's Emily, so there." She stuck out her tongue. Alice squeezed Emily's dumpling legs. Emily didn't seem to mind about the color difference, Alice learned, when she asked her daddy. Daddy said when he found Emily, she did not have her own bonnet. The nice man at the shop where Emily was waiting for a new little girl to adopt her had taken one from another doll. Alice explained that to Emily in the privacy of her room, imitating as best she could daddy's deep voice.

"Emily?" Glenda said another time. "Emily is an awful name. She's stupid."

Alice ran to her room, clutching Emily under her arm. She didn't want her friend to hear her sister's comment. They fell asleep on the floor next to her bed as the afternoon sun warmed the room.

"Glenda, be more considerate of your sister," Daddy said during dinner. "After all, you haven't lost your doll like Alice has."

Alice smiled at her doll, on her lap, and then sneered at Glenda across the table. Glenda's spiteful expression should have warned Alice her taunting would continue.

"If only you and Glenda were friends," Alice whispered to Emily. Emily's brave smile seemed to agree.

Her sister returned from school one afternoon and found Alice and Emily napping. She quietly whisked Emily to a hiding place and departed for a friend's home. When Alice awoke, she searched everywhere as best she could with tear-filled eyes.

When she returned home, Glenda's mischievous smile told Alice of her deed. She met Glenda's challenge with aggressive little fists and high-pitched yells. Their mother put an end to their fight with salty words and a smack to their bottoms.

"To your rooms, young ladies. I will inform your daddy when he gets home," she promised.

Upon his arrival, court was immediately held. He locked his firm eyes onto Glenda's. "Where's Emily?"

Her lips trembling, Glenda answered, "I'm sorry."

"Glenda, you know they love each other," he said.

That new word buzzed through Alice's head—love. What could it mean? she wondered. It was then that she realized she loved Emily. Her lips pursed, and a small tear rolled down her cheek.

"Glenda," Daddy said. He paused for a moment to make his point. "Taking something that belongs to others without their permission is a serious matter."

Alice held her hands behind her back and swayed, awaiting his conclusion.

"Your mother and I are disappointed in you. Is that the way you would want us to feel?"

Emily was returned. Alice closed her eyes, cupped her hands around her mouth, and whispered into Emily's ear, "Daddy says I love you." She repeated the word in a deep voice, unaware she was talking loudly. She looked steadily at daddy and wondered how he knew that she loved Emily. After all, she only gave Emily a new home.

Glenda's sorrowful masquerade lasted a few weeks, and then she started in again "Emily is ugly. Emily is ugly," she sang. "And she hasn't got any friends. Na na na nana."

"She's is too pretty," Alice said, and covered Emily's ears. She carried Emily to the kitchen. "Mommy, mommy," she pouted.

"Mommy isn't home," Glenda sneered, close on Alice's heels. "Besides, Emily is stupid, she doesn't do anything. She's dumb."

Alice was furious. "She's beautiful and does a lot." Holding Emily close, she added, "She talks to me all the time. She told me you're not nice. So how do you think I found that out?"

"Who needs dolls anyway? I've got a boyfriend." Her hands immediately covered her mouth. Their father had it clear that boyfriends were forbidden until Glenda was older.

"I'm going to tell," Alice yelled, pleased with this new knowledge. Glenda gasped. "No, please don't. I'll get into trouble."

A truce was declared that lasted for a few weeks, until Alice made a remark at the dinner table. "Glenda and her boyfriend went to the park." Confiding in Emily, she nodded her head and added, "Didn't she, Emily?"

Daddy's heavy eyebrows drew together, revealing his displeasure. Turning his attention to Glenda, he asked, "Is that true?"

She shot a *you'll pay* look at Alice, and then in a quivering voice made an effort to answer. Alice delighted in Glenda's awkward moment. But once the whole truth was uncovered, her victory brought an unbearable punishment. Alice had to accept life without Emily. She was missing. Glenda must have done it, again. She had stolen Emily. But nothing happened to Glenda. Mommy only spoke with her for a long time in her bedroom. Finally and at long last, Daddy said Emily would be returned. But when he went to collect Emily, she was missing.

"Oh, no," cried Alice, and glared at her sister.

Daddy took charge. Satisfied with Glenda's innocence, he searched the house and yard. Buried at the base of a sweet-smelling lilac bush, Emily lay in ruins. Her pretty lavender dress had been ripped, her bonnet was missing, and one of her eyes bobbed by a single thread. Her once dumpling legs had been ripped open, prompting her father's sad suggestion, "Perhaps a squirrel." She cried and cried, finally falling asleep in the arms of her daddy. She awoke alone, in her own bed, and glanced out the window at the overcast sky, in search of an answer. The night sky was suddenly illuminated by a bold strike of lighting. As the sound of thunder crashed through the rain, she hid her face under her bedcovers and remained as still as she could. She tried to sleep, but an active imagination leaped to strange creatures and poor Emily. She recited a poem they had composed to recall their happy moments.

"'Friendship and love is like a steeple. The higher they claim, the more happy the people.'"

Finally, it was morning, and Glenda was standing next to Alice's bed. "It's going to be all right, little sister of mine."

Their parents walked in, nodding approvingly and smiling.

"Good can come from bad," Mother whispered, and the family hug continued for a while.

Life was empty without Emily. Her dad wanted to buy her a new doll, but she always said, "I love Emily." Alice decided she was sick, hoping she would get a lot of attention. Glenda came into her room and handed Alice a big brown bag. "Alice, you can have whatever is inside," she said, and rolled her eyes. "But you have to promise that you will feel better if you take it."

Alice peeked inside the bag. "It looks like Emily," she cried. "It is Emily."

"I sewed her together and made her a new bonnet, just like the old one. Mommy helped me."

"Oh, Emily! Glenda, you're the absolute greatest sister any girl ever had."

Alice opened the old toy chest as the word love filled her. She stared affectionately at Emily, and almost heard the lazy hum of insects and bird calls. As she rested Emily in her own daughter's cradled arms, the small attic light shadowed little dumpling legs.

"What is it, Mommy?" Sweet Jenny Lee asked. "Don't cry, Mommy."

"It's nothing, sweetie. Do you like my doll? Her name is Emily."

Tammy: Page One

"Give it to me straight, Doctor!'" she demanded with little hesitation in her voice, while her gaze took charge of everybody in the room.

The doctor stared at her prim, narrow face, speechless. He had delivered other stressful messages to the wives of patients, but this time it was different.

Though her eyes were compelling, a single tear rolled from one, smoothing quietly toward her chin. Not knowing what to do with her arms, she crossed them and shifted her weight onto one leg.

The doctor rested his hand on her shoulder as they stood together in the hospital's emergency room. He wanted to comfort her, he wanted to hold her the way he had before her marriage to Aaron, his best friend. He even drifted in thought about a hospital TV drama would, at moments like these, fade to black and a commercial would appear. But this wasn't television.

Aaron lay but ten feet away in critical condition from injuries suffered from an automobile accident, and the doctor knew he would have to operate. "Tammy," he said, "I'll do the best I can. But the outcome is uncertain."

She trembled, and then wept and murmured, "Please help him, Tommy. I love him so." She bit her bottom lip while her hand cupped her neck in an attempt to hide it from the man who had once declared his love to her. She remembered the day he had asked the meaning of her name. She told him that it meant a woolen cap of Scottish origin, and had lifted her chin. *Am I the only one with memories?*

"I will, Tammy," he replied in a tone just above a whisper.

Tammy and her three kids sat restlessly near the operating room, waiting. Waiting for fate and Tommy's experience to determine their future. *It's so terrible!* Tammy thought, and glanced at her small children, seemingly unaware in their play of the seriousness of their vigil.

The aggressively clean odor of the hospital coupled with her feelings of inadequacy at that moment stirred her imagination. If only she had let Aaron drive the car, this might never have happened. She thought of Aaron's crumpled body as it was placed inside the ambulance. She had never seen him helpless, nor had she imagined the possibility.

The first time she had seen Aaron was at a sorority party. She had worn her new ruffled white blouse and beige slacks, a birthday present from her parents. Aaron, covered from head to toe in snow, had entered the room, prompting laughter from several of the girls. "Oh, look at the snowman."

She had offered him a towel, waving it several times before he noticed. When he wiped the snow off his face, he glanced into her eyes and froze. She would never forget that moment, that fraught split second while they measured each other. Quickened warmth careened through her body, like drinking hot apple cider the first time. He could be someone very special! Later he would tell her, "You looked more exciting than your Christmas tree."

They dated the rest of her junior, their love blossoming with the lilacs in spring, hinting at a promising summer. To Tammy's dismay, he accepted a position with an engineering firm in New York City, nine hundred miles from her Midwest home. His last letter suggested she quit college and join him. They could live together until he was comfortably established with his employer. His short letter was lying on her nightstand next to the telephone, when he called and said, "I'm being selfish, Tammy. Finish your last year of college as I did."

Tammy packed a suitcase and, his letter in her hand, announced her decision to her parents. Her father wished her happiness, saying, "I know times have changed." He glanced at her mother and added, "But people haven't. Marriage is for families, not roommates." His challenging smile dared her to comment, yet words were unnecessary.

She dropped her suitcase to the floor. The throb in her heart cried for relief, and her knees grew weak at the memory of Aaron's touch. But being a wife, not a roommate, was her goal.

Unannounced, Aaron arrived a few days before her birthday. Tammy was pleased with his visit and anticipated, perhaps, a marriage proposal. Assuming his intentions, she could feel her body quiver

"I thought I'd see you sooner than this," he said. She frowned, puzzled. "I've quit my job and will be working on my uncle's charter boat in Florida for several months." Hurriedly he added, "It's something I planned long ago and now is the best time to do it."

His words sank into her mind, crushing her aspiration. She feared that she might never see him again, that he'd die in some bizarre mishap at sea. Why hadn't she been consulted about this trip? Had there been a change in his life? She studied his face for some sign of that change and asked, "What would you like this girl to do while you're tanning yourself on a Florida beach?"

It was then she knew her deep love for him, and she realized she should have said something profound or understanding. "For whither thou goest, I will go, and where thou die, I will die," would have been acceptable, she realized later, but too late. Aaron had left for Florida, suggesting his love by warm comments, although neglecting to say "I love you."

The brother of a friend, Tommy, a medical student, helped her pass the time the remainder of her senior year. He was reassuring and definite in his future plans. Tammy felt comfortable in Tommy's company. He tenderly flirted with her mind but never placed demands on her virtues.

To her astonishment, one bright afternoon as they strolled hand in hand, peering into shop windows Tommy said, "You know I love you." She stood still as her blithe smile vanished from her face. His inviting eyes locked into hers as he held her hand, and then proposed marriage.

Tammy had thought it natural that Tommy and she sought in each other some desperate solace that disguised itself as love. Yet Aaron's distant memory somehow invited itself into her thoughts. She remembered the multitude of letters she had sent him. Page after page, day after day, she had written to him in Florida; and each on page one, she wrote, "I want to share my life with only you." She had written about the colorful flowers she had carefully picked. She had written about her graduation and her teaching assignment.

Whenever she traveled the thirteen blocks to meet Tommy at the hospital several times a week, she thought about her next letter to Aaron. She hoped that each step she took was another step away from Aaron, though his memory persisted.

Aaron had occasionally responded to her letters, but was vague with his plans. Rather, he asked her about her past letters and always complimented her prolific writing style.

Finally, reluctantly, without any note of aggression in his tone, Tommy's voice gained her attention. "You still love him?"

Tammy reflected for a moment of wishful thinking, and then sighed.

"I'll always be here, Tammy," he said sincerely, as his eyes softened with understanding.

"Tammy, Tammy," The doctor's voice was insistent.

"Oh, I'm sorry, Tommy," she said. "Guess I was daydreaming." She stared up at him as he slid onto the chair beside her.

"There is no easy way to tell you this," he said. "Aaron is …" he paused. "He's in the recovery room. But I must warn you he is on the critical list." Tammy's arms hugged his neck and she kissed him, thankfully.

"He'll need all the patience you can muster."

As the weeks passed, Aaron's condition improved. His speech was slightly impaired, while his blindness was diagnosed as permanent.

Tammy's parents were supportive. While Tammy spent her afternoons at the hospital, they entertained the children with exciting visits to the zoo and museums. Grandma's "privilege" produced secret tummy aches and drooping eyes.

The children's laughter always interrupted Tommy's interpretations of children's fables. Only a bachelor could have Little Red Riding Hood climbing a beanstalk, while Jack and Jill unlaced an old lady's shoe. His stop-bys at the house were "just checking," though his visits became routine and expected. He did suggest Tammy write anecdotes about the children for Aaron. "It will lift his spirits when the nurse reads them to him," he explained. Tammy agreed.

Aaron seemed to accept his situation at first, but there was no mistaking the hard ambition that was showing beneath his incapacities. Her warm kiss was always followed by her latest written story about the children. In his slow way of speaking, he would express his pride in his tiny accomplishments, yet Tammy felt a shadow of future uncertainty in his remarks.

One time he said to her, "Tommy's out at the house a lot, I understand."

She struggled to answer calmly. "He's been wonderful to the children.'"

"I'm glad," he answered serenely. "Tommy said he would look in occasionally." Aaron's eyebrows rose, and his blind eyes searched the room almost purposefully.

His hand reached for hers. "Tammy," he said tenderly, "remember when I went to Florida?" Without waiting for her answer, he continued. "It took a long time to convince myself that I could provide for you forever. Let alone keep up with you. You see, when I got your letters filled with sensitivity and compassion, they confirmed my thoughts. You're too good for me."

His hand, guided by devotion, found her unseen tear and tenderly whisked it away.

"When you came to Florida," he went on, "you made a believer of me. With you at my side, I could do anything." His fingers smoothed her hair. "But now ..." His voice faded.

"Aaron, is there something I should know?"

"If anything happens to me, consider Tommy. You'll need someone to take care of you and the children. Loving you has made my life timeless without regret. My only sorrow is not comforting you in my absence."

No! Tammy screamed to herself. *It isn't over. I'll find a way for you to live forever.*

Aaron's hold on her was too strong to be dismissed. If anything, it was growing stronger. She had worked too hard and too long to lose him.

Fired by her nature, she poured her thoughts through the keys of her computer, and presented Aaron with stories of their love and their children. She knew a few of her stories hinted at private matters, perhaps embarrassing his nurse if she happened to be the one to read them. But Aaron's reaction was all that mattered.

Bleak and vacant through his funeral, she survived. This was happening to someone else, she imagined. Her probe for an answer as to why him, smashed all logical answers. She thought about souls that come and go as easily and endlessly as fashion. She thought about remembrances of things past and her children's future and the greatness of his once being part of their lives.

Weeks later, Tommy's knock on the door was anticipated, but

his explanation certainly was not. Seating himself, he requested the children be excused and pulled from his briefcase several magazines.

His smile was hard to ignore. "Aaron had the idea, and I guess I was in on it. We both knew his condition was hopeless, and he elected to keep that from you. He said"—Tommy's eyes narrowed in a questioning manner—"you need more time. Perhaps you understand what he meant?"

He handed her the magazines. "Aaron sent in your stories and letters."

Bewildered by his comments, she paged through the magazines. She stopped when she saw an article with her name on it author. It was entitled, "Page One."

"There are more articles in the other magazines," Tommy said. "Aaron had everyone in the hospital licking stamps and addressing envelopes to publications. I understand why he'll always be your man. He'll live forever."

Underworld Lilith: Afternoon Delight

"Hey, man, you from the city?" the limo driver asked in a cheerful way.

"Yes," Arthur said, and an easy smile spread across his face. "But the more I make this trip from Providence, the more I want to stay."

Arthur Machen read again the letter in his suit pocket. "Do come, darling! It will be absolutely marvelous. I have some new friends for you. Lilith, your eternal servant." He took a short breath and glanced at the countryside. Cape Cod Bay was coming into view.

The mansion stood on the peak of a hill, and before Arthur rushed into Lilith's welcoming arms, he gazed at the water stretching to the horizon. Its lapis blue sheen seemed to fill the air with the fresh scent of immediate promise. *A new day—at last*, he thought.

"I'm so glad you've come, darling," she whispered provocatively in his ear. She pulled back, but kept her suntanned face close to his. "Do stay forever, darling of mine. You know I adore you." She looked at the driver. "Darling, do take his baggage inside for the houseman."

"You've been swimming," Arthur said softly. "Are the others at the beach house?" He drew in a deep breath and exhaled. "Mmm." He closed his dark eyes in remembrance. "This air ... I feel like a schoolboy."

Her hand smoothed under his white coat and found the small of his back. He was well-moneyed in his touch but bitterly poor in his pocket.

"Come now," she whispered, and they walked along the path as if they were children. "Everyone, everyone, come out, come out," Lilith sang as they neared the two-story beach house.

"You remember Howard, darling?" she said as a man approached. "He paints those simply divine water scenes and sells them in Paris for breathless fortunes."

The men traded casual smiles. Arthur extended his hand to the man he had met twice before, and still had no opinion of. But Lilith pushed their hands aside. "Then, of course, there's Cahill, remarkable man of words from the womb of a desert on the other side of antiquity or ..." She tapped her lips with a finger. "Or," she repeated gaily, "was that Antigua, darling?" She grasped Cahill's shoulder. "Oh, well! What does it matter?" She lit a cigarette, and the smoke poured from her mouth when she spoke. "Where's that girl?"

Lilith turned abruptly on her heel, and Arthur almost felt the frown that lined her face. "Victoria, Victoria!" she called insistently. Her screeching tone winged through the crisp air and found a batch of sluggish birds. They ascended in a chattering rage above the water, only to return moments later, reckoning that Lilith was not rebuking them.

"At least there's, mmm, Dominique. Come here, darling, and meet Arthur." She smiled as he watched Dominique approach with a happy stride. "Too young for you, my love," she exclaimed. "And she'd look far better gift-wrapped under someone else's tree!" Lilith caught her breath and added in a rare soft voice as Dominique stood still, "Besides, Arthur, this child is a—"

"A dancer," he said.

"How did you know that, sir?" Dominique asked in a pleasant voice .

Arthur and Cahill exchanged a glance before Cahill said, "In her naïveté, all the experience of the world is stored." He spoke with a gentleness that bordered on affection, and his prominent jowls tightened.

"Ooo, how silly of me, Mr. Arthur," Dominique said, much like Lilith, yet in a girlish tone. She slung a lemon-yellow towel around her golden frame. "Lilith must have told you, no doubt," she said, as if offering some revelation. "You must be warm with all those clothes, sir."

"You can see why we aren't in love with her," said Cahill, and his round belly jiggled. His fluffy side whiskers were uniquely tufted. He added in a monotonous voice as though he had said it a thousand times, "We just love her."

Arthur felt that the arrogant body lines of Dominique could stir the stillness with quiet envy, while bowing to her generosity. Was there a feeling in the air much like the day before a Sunday parade? He bowed to the woman. "Arthur's my first name, Dominique," he said, and lifted her chin with of his finger. "Writers like Cahill narrate through silent phrases that make little sense, like *The Great God Pan*, but dancers move for everyone to see."

"Oh, bravo." Lilith beamed. "Such genteel frankness. Really! Darling, you have not wasted any time with your crafty remarks. You know, Arthur, how those innuendoes affect poor Cahill!" She laughed. "But let's have tea, and where oh where is that fretting Victoria?"

"Lilith." Dominique spoke apprehensively. "I must return to practice."

"Run along, child," she said in a half-annoyed, half-pleased way.

Dominique assessed Arthur as Lilith turned away. He wasn't staring at her casually nor merely by chance, and how brave of him to defy Lilith's lead!

Dominique sensed that his soothing meant he spoke easily with small children, yet cursed hard with his peers. She half-closed her eyes and whirled her towel, her active thighs moving with intention. He looked like the kind of man that could teach a young woman all the very special things everyone merely hinted about. Had Arthur more strength or more magic than her physician? How absurd! she scolded herself. Arthur was simply another man.

Arthur held her gaze with a steady look as the air ripened with urgency. He felt as though he could assist nature with things wondrous and new. Yes, he decided, Dominique had a womanly, yet girlish, way of speaking; of understanding and of not understanding; of lifting her blue eyes to ask a question; and the warmth from her eyes seemed as delicious as an afternoon kiss.

The sky shimmered as if an incandescent sherbet, yet they scarcely took note,, being lost in a different delight, until—

"For heaven's sake, Arthur," Lilith said heatedly over her shoulder. "Dominique must practice and you need your tea."

"Dominique is as graceful as Margot Fonteyn," Howard said as Arthur sat next to him. "Dancing is her only lover!"

"My, my," someone caroled at Arthur, and right behind that voice stood a plump, rosy blonde. "Our little one has tempted your soul."

"You must be Victoria," he stated, and noticed the faint scent of decadence about her.

"But of course," she sang, fingered her over-managed hair. She took a deep, deep breath that Howard attentively observed with a spreading grin.

"You know," Lilith said, "girls"—she glanced in the direction of Dominique—"and women"—she peeked at Victoria in a way that hinted her swimwear belonged on a smaller woman—"are absolutely wonderful at these little love tricks, Arthur darling. Simply wonderful!" She flitted her lashes, one hand on her hip. "Don't you agree darling?"

"*Cherchez la femme*," Arthur said, whirling a finger. "Seek the motivated woman!"

Cahill could hardly resist. One hand over his heart, he fixed his ferretlike eyes on Victoria. "I'm touched and conquered too! I'll commit a thousand follies of heroism for but a breath or her bosom."

"Isn't he sweet?" Victoria said. "No wonder Dominique said n-o." She spelled out the word.

"Do tell," said Lilith. "Has Cahill been fascinated by our dove?"

"Who would have interest in a man who could hardly out-Herod Herod?" Victoria said impatiently. "Except this magical man from Oz."

"What notions are these?" Cahill asked.

Howard laughed. "Victoria loves her meaningless dramas, like all good actresses. She's a wonderful drama queen, don't you agree?"

An expression crossed Cahill's face, the expression of a man caught in a moment that he could not define. He wrinkled his nose and opened his hands.

"You seem confused," Victoria said. "I'll riddle you this, you desert gypsy, about our sweet dove. When is a woman less than a woman?"

Cahill looked up and whispered, "When is a woman less ..." He snapped his fingers. "Ha, ha," he said, and then frowned. "Dominique?"

"Really, loves," Lilith said. "Our dove is not for sport, and is more of a woman than most. She has more equipment than most, and that is why Victoria has such hostility toward her. Besides, she needs no other mother than the theater."

Arthur rubbed his chin. "What is said?" he asked them all. "Only mothers can love children? A monopoly of sorts! Isn't just loving the special part?"

Supper was served at eight on the veranda. Everyone was famished, but Dominique merely enjoyed salad and tea. The evening was fragranced by a southern breeze and a moon brimming with thought.

Howard and Victoria aggressively danced. She laughed a great deal, but her laughter was stiff, a device, no doubt, rather than a sign of enjoyment. She threw her head back in time with the music while her voluptuous body shimmered.

"The Dutch should study her stitches," Cahill suggested, then laughed hard but alone, and wiped his eyes with a purple handkerchief.

"The champagne," she would say later, had made her feel "easy, girlish, and giggly."

Every time Arthur and Dominique engaged in quiet conversation, Lilith asked Arthur a question. She accepted his answers, nodding approvingly while she chain smoked cigarettes.. Finally, she said, "Arthur, darling, I wish to speak to you … alone."

Morning swept impatiently into the room where Arthur slept. The tide had returned, and now announced its presence with prideful sweeps, while the birds ranted with complaint. Yet the complaints were never his. He'd had the night of his life with Victoria, and he was so totally in love with her. What a difference a day makes.

He groaned and stretched, and then buried his head under the pillow for a moment, absorbing its comforting silence. Leisurely, he dressed, ran past the breakfast being served at the gazebo, and trotted to the beach house. "'Morning, love," he murmured to Lilith.

"'Morning, darling," she answered back. "Tell me, darling, when you return home, which one of my darlings will be the subject of your short story?"

"Aren't you at the age when you know all the answers?" asked he. "But I am in love after last night. I heard about it, was curious about it. But now, I am in love and my soul belongs to Victoria. Can I see—"

Lilith cut him off. "You know these things are booked way in advance. But Victoria told me she can hardly wait for your next visit and I can hardly wait for your next short story. Do be careful this time!" she cautioned. "Remember the time we both lost a friend because you were too honest in your work? Oh, well! What does it matter? They all want the same from us until—"

Arthur kissed her cheek. "Excuse me," he said, and walked briskly to Dominique, who was practicing nearby.

Her tanned face was fresh and soft with a schoolgirl look, and her alert eyes shone like glass. She studied him carefully and said, "You're leaving soon."

He scratched his temple. "I thought I knew everything about you. I didn't know you read minds too."

"There are many things you don't know about me," she replied urgently. "Sometime I might discuss one thing with you. If you knew everything, you would think I was a freak or …" Her voice faltered, and she looked across the sand. She crossed her arms over her chest, her hands holding onto her shoulders.

"I'll be at the Pearl Theater in three weeks. Will you come?" she asked, and her smile revealed rarely seen dimples.

He nodded. "Perhaps afterwards we can dine near the theater. I know this magnificent club …" The cheerfulness in his tone faded as he went along, for surely, he would now discover if she had a handsome younger man as an intimate. "Oops, I forgot," he said. "Dancers rarely dine. Tea then, but I'll call. You may be too weary after your performance."

Dominique smiled again, but not enough to display her dimples. "Yes," she said. "That would be nice. But I'm sorry you haven't enjoyed your stay here."

She looked like she would say more and she moved one step back. When she looked at him, she might as well have kissed him.

Arthur touched her arm. "You seem to have a worry the size of a Buick about catching a friend," he said. He bit hard on his lip. Would her response reveal more that he wished to know? He feathered her lips with his finger. "My stay," he said, "concerned my métier. You know, my profession, like you and the others."

Two weeks later, when the postman made his regular stop at Lilith's, he left a fat envelope. Cahill demanded that she open it at once, while Howard smiled. Dominique and Victoria watched with amusement. Lilith briefly studied each of her guests while her fingers danced aimlessly across the envelope. She slowly removed the many typed pages and cleared her throat before she read the title. "*Lilith's Children,*" she said. "A short story by Arthur Machen." She glanced at Victoria and Dominique. "So he wrote another one of those short stories to amaze his godless readers. Excellent."

"Naturally, it's about me," Victoria said.

"Naturally," replied Lilith, and patted his shoulder. "The world can't help but to fall in love you. You are such a beautiful young man." She looked at Dominique. "Your turn is coming, little one."

Val: Perfect Timing of an Irish Gypsy

"Joy," she shouted through the doorway at her dedicated assistant. "Here! In here."

"Yes, ma'am," Joy replied quickly, and drew in a deep breath.

As Joy entered Val's office, Val bellowed, "You told my contacts that Vanessa left the convent in Naples to holiday in Bucharest?"

"Yes, ma'am," she said quickly and proud, and then added, "Her Mother Superior said that they wanted no inter—" She struggled with the word, knowing that Val would stop her. Whenever she told Val what Mother Superior said about her mother's sister, Vanessa, she would cut her off.

"Enough," Val said as her hand sliced the air. She rounded the desk, her cold blue eyes fixed on Joy. "I'll call at five. Don't leave early like yesterday." Her words sounded more like a warning than a request.

Joy darted a forbidden glance at herself in Val's office mirror. Her head had once been full of pretty sweet hair. "I'm sorry," she said, and looked down at yellow carpet. She managed a frail smile. "Anything else, ma'am?"

"I know I'm on the road most of the time, and I pay you to stay here during business hours. If you try to fool me, payback can be hard." She strode down the hall like a sailor on liberty, tossing over her shoulder, "Payback can be hell."

Ten minutes later, Val Audrey Carroll flopped onto a cold leather bar stool and yelled at Barney, "The usual, here." The slow-eyed bartender flashed a knowing grin and nodded. His fat hands busied themselves in a secretive ceremony until—"Violà." He set a stemmed glass in front of her.

Val had a look that told everyone she loved sweet-eyed boys dressed in white who made a point of this or that, yet sighed easily in the shadows of her bedroom. Perhaps her look had to do with a tarnished patience that stained the air, as she spent the blood money she made through the confidence games she played all over the country. But there was something else that marked her appearance, a confident grin at the women who passed her.

At five, Val told Barney to call her office. "And if Joy isn't there, I'll kill the little slut."

Barney returned, an interested expression on his face. "Your daughter said she must speak with you, ma'am."

With an impatient chuckle, Val waved Barney away. She turned her attention to the lady sliding onto the stool next to her. "You're an intriguing thing." Val took in the woman's hard green eyes and waist-length mahogany hair. She grinned. "We've met," she said. "But where?"

"Humph! You Americans," the long haired lady said with some difficulty. "You all tell this woman the same foolishness." She pressed her lips together. "We never met."

"Don't be rude," Val said. "And we have met. I have an exceptional memory."

She woman laughed from somewhere deep. "You see this woman in your dreams, no?" Her words were musically accented, and she motioned her hand in a half circle, as if performing a magic act. "You like what you see, yes?"

Val's eyes stared hard through her cat eye glasses. "Do you know who you're talking to?" she asked in perfect Irish. Oh, how Val Audrey Carroll detested insolence, especially from Gadjos. Didn't she know she was talking to Superwoman?

She would reject her, leave her to the insolent stares and offers from local patrons, who lavished in imperfection and things that shouted with genuine vulgarity. No, not a generous nod nor a courteous comment, she decided. This Gadjo will recall this incident forever. Val turned to her martini, plucked out the large green olive, and flicked it to the floor. "There," she said to no one, and narrowed her eyes as if she were a cat.

The Gadjo settled against the back of her stool. Her hands rested quietly on her lap, and her legs, encased in glistening dark hose, were crossed at the ankles. She listened as many patrons offered to buy the Gadjo a drink. When one asked her name, she replied, "Vastavikta."

My home is Bucharest." Then she asked in a suspicious tone, "You have heard of it, yes?"

Val turned to the woman, met her eyes, and knew that in the woman's threatening glare was a sparkle possessed only by people of the streets or a gypsy. Val decreed that an imperfection. The only thing perfect about this Vastavikta was that her eyes—and now her smile—brought back memories of Vanessa. Yes, that was it. Sweet Vanessa, the sister she hadn't seen for many years, since her accident. Odd that Vanessa was holidaying in Bucharest. Val stole a look at her watch, something she would do to test the vulnerability of a mark or someone she was about to seduce. Vastavikta didn't take the bait. She didn't follow her glance to her watch. Instead, an impish grin stretched across her face. *She's a Romany,* Val decided. *What's a gypsy doing here?*

"Val, Val," Barney sang out. "It's Joy. Your daughter. She says it's urgent." He waved the telephone receiver. "She says you're not answering your cell."

Val shot a look at Vastavikta, and in so doing, caught the stare of many grinning patrons. "Tell her no," Val said, catching Barney offguard. As an afterthought, she added, "No, tell her I'm busy tonight." Her chin lifted higher in the air as she stared at Vastavikta. For a moment, Val Audrey Carroll was a babbling tower of memory. Why look like Vanessa? "Look here," she said, and slouched her shoulders. But before she got the next word out, Vastavikta's fingers feathered her shoulder and rested on Val's knee while Vastavikta held her gaze tight in hers.

"Mult'umesc," Val whispered, and squared her shoulders. "But I didn't say no."

She would not be taken in by this strange lady from Bucharest. Vastavikta was turning the tables on her and playing gypsy games with her head.

"Why are you here?" she asked nonchalantly. They talked. The more they talked, the more Val felt a sweet motion taunting her tower of memory. Memories about Vanessa; the girl who had grown with her; the girl who had felt her touch until she went away.

"To repent," Vanessa had said when she went away. "To forgive," she vowed. At first, her few letters were etched with regret. Over the years, they progressed to the sorrow of a martyr, and then advanced to the brimstone prophecies of a pavement minister. Finally, they settled on an unstated resolution. In Vanessa's last letter, she asked Val, "Do you believe in justice? Do you believe in payback?"

"You live alone, Val?" Vastavikta asked. When Val slipped from the stool, she followed her into a taxi.

"You find me exciting, don't you?" Val asked as they sat close in the vehicle close, so close that their knees almost touched.

"I like excitement. Older gals pay more."

"What?" Val asked seemingly annoyed.

"Bolder gals say more," Vastavikta replied.

Val gave the cab driver instructions to her brownstone. When he dropped them off, the two women approached the front steps.

"Careful," Val said. "That top step has always been weak. I can't find anyone to repair it."

She opened the door and waltzed to the bedroom. Now, she was close to Vastavikta, this woman from Budapest. She hesitated for only a moment, and suddenly, Val felt her Vastavikta's warmth and snapped opened both eyes. *Wait? Is this my sister Vanessa?* Like Vanessa, this Vastavikta hesitated with their first kiss. And like Vanessa, this Vastavikta responded to her every move. Vastavikta was a bundle of promise, and her lengthy breaths stifled other sounds in the room, and probably the entire planet. Until—

"Stop," Vastavikta said. "Stop it. We can't … I mean." She didn't have to finish her statement. The rest was obvious as she stood. Tears filled her eyes. "You're a devil," Vastavikta whispered from the door. "You're a red-eyed devil."

Val was enraged with passion. She punched the air. "You gypsy witch! You calling me a devil? I am. I know your desire."

Vastavikta howled at the moon, and the look in her eyes blinded Val.. "It isn't you I want. And you're not bad enough to be a devil. Val, honey, do you believe in justice? What about payback?"

Those were Vanessa's words. Pain shot down her chest to a hole in her stomach. "What's going on?" Val felt as if she were losing control—and that never happened.

"What's going on here?" Vastavikta mimicked Val. As if a serpent had infected her with venom, she said, "Don't ask hell, ask me, you filthy whore. I've been waiting for the perfect time to get debts paid. You know, justice." She paused. "Payback."

Vastavikta was using Val's own sister's words. How could this happen? Vastavikta was using Vanessa's purity and returning it wrapped in filth. She was impure. Val never cared each time she consumed her sister for her pleasure. Once Vanessa's senses were burned away in a fire of arousal, her "Don'ts" poured out as "ohs." But when it was over, her melancholy sister promised, "You'll pay, dear sister. Someday, you'll pay."

Val's ultimate control over Vanessa had been their filthy secret all these years. Val wanted "our" child, had quick sex with a stranger, saved his fluids, and floated them into her pure baby sister. Joy's birth was a happy time, yet Val sent Vanessa to a distant convent and kept Vanessa's child as her own. Questions gouged Val, but answers never surfaced. She slipped into insanity as her hands found a different woman's body. When it was over, she studied the body, Vastavikta's body, that she had hurled to the floor as if it were a rag doll.

"There," Val said. "You'll never forget this night. I'm glad she's dead." Then in a different voice she asked. "What have I done?" Her murderous hands tightened around her own head. She looked down at Vastavikta. "She had no business looking like Vanessa,'" she screamed. "Vanny, I've always been true."

"Open up, open up!" someone yelled from the front door. "Police. Police." They banged again on the door.

It's the slop, Val thought.. *How did they know?*

Val searched for her eyeglasses that had fallen during the struggle. She was unable to find them, and walked down the hall from the back bedroom where Vastavikta's body lay. She called through the door, "What do you want?"

"The police," a voice said.

Val opened the door and stared into the darkness. Finally, she saw two police officers staring back.

"You're Val Audrey Carroll?" the older officer asked.

"Yes, yes." Val darted a glance behind her.

"Well, Ms. Carroll, we're here to notify you that—"

"Notify me?" she questioned with a new alertness.

The officer wiped his forehead. He glanced down at his report, and using the light from his flashlight, read it. "At around four o'clock our time, your sister ... I'm sorry, is it Vanessa?"

"Yes, yes, Vanessa, what about her?"

"Well, ma'am, she was aboard an aircraft that crash-landed in

Budapest." The sergeant paused. "I'm really sorry. There were no survivors."

Suddenly, in the bedroom where Vastavikta had been murdered, a blot of flames erupted through the open doorway. The other officer ran down the hall. Reaching the room, he yelled over his shoulder, "Hey, Sarge, you need to see this." And he covered his mouth.

As the smell of an oily thickness reached Val's nostrils, she felt imminent doom take her in a flash. She galloped for freedom through the front door. Her foot slammed down on that weak step, hurling her into the air, and her head slammed into the sidewalk. Blood splattered everywhere.

The officers quickly ran down the steps. The older one checked Val's neck for a pulse. Finding none, he shook his head.

The younger officer also shook his head. "She lost her footing on that weak step, too bad. Where was she going?"

''Beats the hell out of me," the sergeant responded. "She has no next to kin, I understand, other than a single employee." He turned his flashlight to the report. "Someone named Joy Carroll. Must be her daughter or a niece."

"Too bad," the younger officer said, and looked back at the house.

"What you see in that back room?" the sergeant asked.

"Smoldering clothes in a ball of fire. Looked like something a nun would wear. Nobody was in the room, just the clothes burning. I'll call the fire department."

Even as he spoke, they heard a fire engine approaching. It stopped in front of Val's brownstone.

"What timing," the sergeant said.

"Yeah. If you were a mental case or something, you'd say it was perfect timing. But too bad the lady couldn't fly like Superman. She'd still be alive."

Wilma: The Train

When she awoke that morning, nothing told her anything would change. She used to say, "'Mornin', Sam," to the conductor, but of course that was when someone else owned the train. Once the 8:05 became "My train," a nod replaced her polite murmur whenever Sam glanced at her monthly ticket tucked into her ID neck pouch. Easy to tell the commuters from the peasants by their ticket, but there she was in her martyr's march to her "last row window seat." That was her seat on this train, as it had been forever. Mariasela's bulky body spread out as she sat. She crossed her legs easily. No need to tug at her hem. She would sit alone as usual.

She unfolded the newspaper. What would it be today? she wondered. Humiliated companies, arguing countries, or presidential resolutions? She glanced down the aisle, wondering who else would be going to work after the lazy weekend?

There was the person Mariasela had named Sneaky Lloyd. He covertly glanced over his newspaper and half-glasses whenever a woman walked down the aisle. Weeping Wanda was taking her seat. She always seemed like she wanted to cry, but she never did. Buxom Betty was already seated, and her insistent fingers were already inside her large lunch bag, breaking and tearing. Mariasela watched Ear Boy, slumped in his seat. He adjusted his earplugs with a tap, and somewhere under his baggy clothing was a tiny iPod or whatever, although no one has ever seen it. She knew that once the train's clickity-clack rattled through the car, Ear Boy would rhythmically bob his head back and forth. At least, it wouldn't be to the sounds of a big boom box that boys used to carry many years ago.

"Excuse me, miss, are you saving that seat for anyone?"

What was this? Had he not seen her annoyed glare at the others? Hadn't she made it clear that she wished no violation of her privacy?

"Sorry," she said in her best English, and moved her briefcase to the floor. An approximation of a smile crept onto her face. She hoped that she hadn't looked like a miser counting gold!

He moistened his lips and moved forward with squared shoulders. "Sure thing!"

Sharply tracing her sarcasm. How very clever. He did have the same kind of soothing voice that the luncheon lecturer had on Friday. She had five hundred calories instead of four. That she recalled immediately, but ... "I don't think so," she declared without looking up from the story about an insolvent company.

"Certainly," he said, and snapped his fingers. "You're Mariasela Guzman," he said, pronouncing her name correctly, with the appropriate Dominican slur, "Of course you don't remember me."

Of course not. That was because he was a client's little employee, Right? But work ... Well, her job and that size nine dress stuffed in her closest had something in common. Nice to say it fits, but only to a new acquaintance. "Where do you work?"

He ignored her question. "My name is Jim Carlson." He paused, but she knew there would more. "We went to school together."

"We did?" she asked as her gaze leaped from the paper to him. She didn't see that coming. Now, as she noted the pouches under his eyes, she could tell he was much older than she had thought. "How nice," she said, and busied her hands on her lap. *Liar*, Wilma screamed to herself.

"High school was a long time ago," he said.

She borrowed a smile from her youth. "High school? Yes, of course," Mariasela spoke half to herself. "I'm honestly afraid I don't recognize you," she said.

Sure, it was always the woman's choice, that she knew, no matter what happened. She could encourage him or make him feel indifferent. He wouldn't follow her to work the way that tall red-haired man had. This Jim Carlson was civilized..But then why was he still staring? Men didn't usually stare at her, and women always looked at her in pity.

He could visit her at Potter's Field if he wished and stare for weeks. That was where she would be buried. Everyone without someone would always be buried at Potter's Field ... wherever it was. Maybe she should have been a man. Men weren't bothered when someone stared. They were so uncomplicated. Why should she lower her standards or break her vow just because he was staring? This was her train! She hadn't lowered her standards when she was in school, why should she start now? Obviously, he was not moneyed. His coin was in his aggressive spirit. He wanted something, and she didn't know what it was. Experience told her it wasn't her body. She raised her chin and put on her reading glasses. She gave him a small look. "Was there something else you wanted to say?" She hated sensitive, haunting eyes. No man would make her feel like an unwanted gift. "Look," she said firmly. "Stare at someone else."

"I—I …" he stammered. "I'm sorry. Please forgive me. Can we—"

"What is it that you want of me, Carlson?"

"Lunch?"

"Don't be foolish. You can't afford the restaurants I frequent."

"Bed?" he asked, and grinned.

Should she say yes, she thought. "Cute," she said.

She buried her eyes in the morning's news. She glanced at Ear Boy, whose head had stopped bouncing. Looking out the window, she realized the train was at the final commuter station. She stood. "I'm sorry to have been short with you, but I know we've never met …"

With a wave of his hand, he said quickly, "I understand, I understand. I was trying to get your attention." There was a hint of defeat in his tone that told her he wouldn't bother her again. "Have a nice day," he said automatically. He blended with the other commuters in the aisle and walked away. Mariasela had defeated another man! After all, this was her train.

As he reached the doors of the train, she yelled out, "Jim!" When he didn't turn, she yelled again. It was as if he couldn't hear at all! Who did this Jim think he is? Didn't he know who she was?

Ear Boy sang the chorus from the Beatles' "Eleanor Rigby" as he passed her. Mariasela stepped off the train and instantly froze. Jim was waiting for her. His weapon was small, dark, and hardly noticeable, but the pain painted her insides white, and she fell to the concrete. Jim stood over her and whispered words she had been expecting. "That's for Mom, "whose life you wasted, you pig liar." Wilma was drifting into an eternal sleep. She never heard which woman he was talking about. There were so many. Guess that would be her end—thinking through every single soul she had ever harmed.

ABOUT THE AUTHOR

Dennis J. Stevens received a PhD from Loyola University of Chicago in 1991. Currently, he is an adjunct at the University of North Carolina–Charlotte and Belmont Abbey College; and has worked for the University of Southern Mississippi as director of the criminal justice PhD program. Stevens was a professor at the University of Massachusetts–Boston, and chair of the criminal justice/sociology department at a North Carolina regional college. In addition to teaching traditional students, he has taught and counseled law enforcement and correctional personnel at law academies, such as the North Carolina Justice Academy and Boston Police Districts; and provided crisis intervention sessions after Hurricane Katrina for officers of the New Orleans Police Department and deputies of Jefferson Parish. Stevens has taught and counseled felons at maximum-security penitentiaries, such as Attica in New York; Eastern and NC Women's Institute North Carolina; Stateville and Joliet near Chicago; CCI in Columbia, South Carolina; and MCI Framingham (women), Norfolk, and Bay State in Massachusetts.

Stevens has published fourteen books and ninety-two scholarly and popular articles on policing, corrections, and criminally violent sexual predators. Stevens has been retained by private agencies, such as Wachenhut, to develop their "use of force" protocols; by state legislators to examine the flow of drugs into prisons, and recidivism rates among student-incarcerated inmates; by US federal agencies to study corruption among narcotic officers; and by foreign governments (e.g., the Provincial Government of Canada) to aid in prisoner research.

As a volunteer, Stevens has guided many sexually abused children and their families through church-affiliated programs in New York, North Carolina, and South Carolina. Finally, Stevens is currently the managing director of Justice Writers of America, an organization that guides criminal justice professionals in their personal pursuits of constructing journal articles, documents, and books. Should you have questions or comments, feel free to contact the author at dennisstevens@carolina.rr.com or dsteven7@uncc.edu.

Dr. Dennis J. Stevens
Justice Writers of America
PO Box 11543
Charlotte, NC 28222

REFERENCES

1. Dennis J. Stevens, "Education programming for offenders," in *Compendium 2000: On Effective Correctional Programming* (Provincial Government of Canada. Correctional Service of Canada, 2001), 57-64. "The impact of time-served and regime on prisoners' anticipation of crime: Female prisonisation effects," *The Howard Journal of Criminal Justice*, 37(2), 188-205.
2. Dennis J. Stevens, "Pedophiles: A case study," *Journal of Police and Criminal Psychology* (2002); 18(1), 36-51.
3. Dennis J. Stevens, "Origins of police officers' stress before and after 9/11," *The Police Journal* (2004); 77(2), 145-184. Jeffery T. Walker, "Civil liabilities and arrest decisions," in *Policing and the Law*, (Upper Saddle River, NJ: Prentice Hall, 2002).
4. Dennis J. Stevens, "Violence begets violence: Study shows that strict enforcement of custody rules causes more disciplinary problems than it resolves, *Corrections Compendium: The National Journal for Corrections*, (1997); 22(12), 1-3.
5. Laurence L. Motiuk, "Contributing to safe reintegration: Outcome measurement," *Compendium 2000 on Effective Correctional Programming* (Ottawa, Ontario, Canada: Correctional Service Canada, 2001);190-98.
6. John Dilulio, "The coming of super-predators," *Montgomery Citizens*, 1995, http://www.mcsm.org/predator.html
7. Stanton E. Samenow, *Inside the Criminal Mind.* (NY: Crown Publishers, 2004); 192.
8. Clive R. Hollin, "Preface XIV," "Classical theory in criminology has its roots in the theories of the 18th century Italian nobleman and economist, Cesare Beccaria and the English philosopher, Jeremy

Bentham," *The Essential Handbook of Offender Assessment and Treatment.* (Chichester: Wiley, 2004); 2, 181.

9. Edwin Sutherland and Donald Cressey, *Principles of Criminology, 10*th *ed.* Philadelphia: Lippincott, (1978).

10. American Psychological Association, *The Diagnostic and Statistical Manual of the American Psychiatric Association (DSM-IV-TR).* (Washington, DC: AMA, 2009).

11. Dennis J. Stevens, *Media and Criminal Justice: CSI Effect.* (Sudbury, MA: Jones and Bartlett, 2011).

12. Dennis J. Stevens, "Forensic Science, Prosecutors, and Wrongful Convictions," *Howard Journal of Criminal Justice* (2009) 31-51.

13. Nicholas P. Lovrich, Travis C. Pratt, Michael J. Gaffney, Charles L. Johnson, Christopher H. Asplen, Lisa H. Hurst, and Timothy M. Schellberg. *National Forensic DNA Study Report, Final Report.* NCJ 203970 (2003), http://www.ncjrs.gov/app/publications/abstract. aspx?ID=203970

14. George F. Bishop, *The Illusion of Public Opinion: Fact and Artifact in American Public Opinion Polls.* (New York: Roman and Littlefield, 2006), P. XV. Also see, David Weisburd, "Hot spots policing experiments and criminal justice research: Lessons from the field," (Paper presented for the Campbell Collaboration/Rockefeller Foundation's meeting at Bellagio, Italy, November 10–11, 2002).

15. Bureau of Justice Statistics, *Suicide and homicide in state prisons and local jails.* (Washington, DC: U.S. Department Of Justice, 2005), http://bjs.ojp.usdoj.gov/index.cfm?ty=pbdetail&iid=1126

16. Human Rights Watch, "No escape: Summary and recommendations (2006), http://www.hrw.org/reports/2001/prison/report.html#_1_3

17. Randall G. Shelden, *Controlling the Dangerous Classes: The History of Criminal Justice, 2nd.* (Boston: Allyn Bacon, 2007).

18. Office of Justice Programs, (Washington, DC: US Department of Justice). Retrieved online July 10, 2010 at ojp.usdoj.gov.

19. Uniform of Crime Reports. Retrieved online July 10, 2010 at http://www.fbi.gov/ucr/ucr.htm#cius.

20. Louis B. Schlesinger, *Sexual Murder: Catathymic and Compulsive Murders.* (NY: CRC Press, 2003).

21. Louis B. Schlesinger, "Sexual homicide: Differentiating Catathymic and Compulsive murders," *Aggression and Violent Behavior,* 12(2) (2007); 242-256.

22. Michael R. Gottfredson and Travis Hirschi, *A General Theory of Crime,* (Stanford, CA: Stanford University Press, 1990); 89, 111.

23. Emile Durkheim (1958), *The Rules of Sociological Method,* trans. S.A. Solovay and J. H. Mueller Glencoe, (IL: The Free Press, 1958); 67.

24. Clearance Rates, (FBI). Retrieved online July 10, 2010 at http://www.fbi.gov/ucr/cius2007/offenses/clearances/index.html

25. 27 Stanton E. Samenow, *Before It's Too Late*, (NY: Times Books, 1998); 2-6. Myriam S. Denov, *Perspectives on Female Sex Offending: A Culture of Denial (Welfare and Society)*, (Burlington, VT: Ashgate Publishing, 2004).

26. Louis B. Schlesinger, "Sexual homicide: Differentiating Catathymic and Compulsive Murders," *Aggression and Violent Behavior*, 12(2) (2007); 242-256.

27. Stanford M. Lyman and Marvin B. Scott, *A Sociology of the Absurd*, 2nd ed. (NY: Dix Hills, 1989); 113-114.

28. Mary C. Sengrstock, "The Culpable Victim in Mendelsohn's Theory," *Education Resources Information Center*, 1997, http://www.eric.ed.gov/PDFS/ED140138.pdf.

29. A. Nicholas Groth, *Men Who Rape: The Psychology of the Offender.* (NY: Plenum Press, 1979);. 13.

30. Dennis J. Stevens, *Media and Criminal Justice: CSI Effect.*

CPSIA information can be obtained at www.ICGtesting.com
Printed in the USA
235918LV00005B/37/P